MW01110158

"An enga[...] never quits its pace. [...] and turns, it is also a battle for the heart of the Christian religion. Similar to The Da Vinci Code by Dan Brown, it unravels the puzzle of the 'Q' document, a find that threatens to discredit the Bible. The author's Biblical knowledge and a great deal of research have created a novel of depth and complexity with distinct cultural flavors from Arizona to the Middle East. Through fully dimensional characters, this story is wrought with a battle between faith and ambition, brimming with action, political conflict, and even a bit of romance."

--Barbara Gow

"A fast paced thriller with more twists and turns than a Dan Brown novel. Schleimer has the reader zipping from one locale to another in a dizzying race to the finish. This book will leave you breathless!"

--Kathleen Y'Barbo, best-selling author of
The Inconvenient Marriage of Charlotte Beck (Waterbrook Press)
and Flora's Wish (Harvest House)

"I love the story!!! Alan Schleimer in The Q Manifesto wrote a fast paced story of suspense and intrigue. It keeps you turning the pages and wondering what will happen next."
--Margaret Daley, author of Shattered Silence, The Men of the Texas
Rangers Series

"During my search for God, I have encountered both fact-based and fiction-based books. As an investigative writer, Alan Schleimer exhausted all avenues of information to make this an exciting thriller that ultimately will stimulate your imagination to the maximum."

--Ulises Baltazar, MD, FACS

"I found The Q Manifesto to be a masterfully crafted, full-immersion thriller written with intelligence, heart and virtue. A brave story, brilliantly plotted and played out at machine gun pace. A magnificent debut whose stunning depths, pivotal settings and tangible descriptions manifested themselves in imagery akin to an HDTV movie."

---*Cheryl Wyatt, multi-award-winning Christian fiction author*

THE
Q MANIFESTO

Alan Schleimer

StoneHouse Ink 2012
Boise ID 83713
http://www.stonehouseink.net

First eBook Edition: 2012
ISBN: 978-1-62482-010-6

First Paperback Edition: 2012
ISBN: 978-1-62482-030-4

Cover art: Fuji Aamabreorn
Layout design: Ross Burck

Published in the United States of America
StoneHouse Ink

Acknowledgements

WHERE TO START? EVERY member of the ACFW who gives their time and talent to help aspiring writers develop, but especially to DiAnn Mills. Much thanks to Robert Crenshaw for reviewing an early draft. The wonderful people at MacGregor Literary and StoneHouse Ink who cut a rookie a break, but mostly to Vicki, the most wonderful wife in the universe.

To Vicki, the wife of my youth.

THE
Q MANIFESTO

CHAPTER 1

OF ALL THE WAYS to die, Jay Hunt decided dehydration wouldn't make anyone's top ten.

He slowed his feverish hiking pace and paused in the meager shade of a Joshua tree. The setting sun's hazy corona appeared to scorch the scrubby pinyon pines dotting the canyon rim four hundred feet overhead. With sundown looming, he calculated an hour of decent light remained. The challenge would be reaching the canyon's end in that time, and with luck, finding Mike. It was Wednesday, Mike's fifth day overdue. If he had not found drinkable water by now, he would be incoherent by nightfall. By morning his organs would begin irreversibly shutting down. If they hadn't already.

"Mike," he shouted into the tunnel-like abyss of the box canyon. "Are you in here?"

The ninety-degree heat felt more like September than early November. Jay grabbed a water bottle from a mesh pocket on his backpack. He swallowed a squirt. At forty-two, after seeing his fair share of deserts, he considered Arizona's Mohave to be as beautiful and dangerous as any desert he had lived in. He removed his Aussie bush hat and tousled his matted hair.

"I have an extra bottle just for you, Mike. Can you hear me?"

A raven answered with a solitary shriek.

With no other response, Jay continued his upstream march along the bone-dry arroyo that had drawn him into the canyon earlier—about the time he should have returned to the mobile Search and Rescue base camp. The twenty-foot-wide dusty creek bed trickled more hope than water now, but dark stains in a deeply eroded bank at the entrance to the canyon suggested it had been wet a few days ago. If so, Mike may have followed it hoping to find water at its source.

The thought quickened Jay's pace. The dead radio on his belt swayed against his leg. He was bugged that the batteries had died. It wasn't the end of the world, but it felt amateurish, and he wished he could tell Doc his status. She'd be worried and was probably kicking herself for letting him search alone.

Something metallic clicked in the distance. Jay stopped.

A slight breeze bristled through a stand of spiny ocotillo cactus on his left. A dank smell momentarily swirled around him. He squinted, rousing every sense. A hawk cruised overhead in an ever-widening circle until it sailed over the jagged south wall and out of sight. Jay pictured Mike eyeing the hawk and dreaming of flying to safety.

Jay started walking again, listening and watching for clues to pinpoint Mike's position. He assumed this lost hiker wanted to be found, and his disappearance wasn't related to the Q document. The ancient papyrus was baffling scientists as well as theologians. After a high-profile Bible translator swallowed a pound of pills, his Q-linked suicide note begat other suicides. This could be just one more, albeit more scenic.

Fifteen minutes ticked by in what seemed like seconds, and

no sounds intruded except the crunch of Jay's boots on the sand-covered slickrock. Worse, the sun had all but disappeared. Fiery reds and maroons blossomed across the canyon's mineral-streaked north face. The hike back to base camp would not be as postcard perfect. Unless he found Mike.

The canyon made a sharp left turn, halving its width to a couple hundred yards. The sun shone on the mesa above, but only evening twilight reached the canyon floor. Doc had probably radioed repeatedly by now. Maybe it was just as well they couldn't talk. He could just imagine her sweet little honked off voice. Before he could say a word, she would revisit her agreement this morning to split up the team to cover more ground. "I never should have let you go alone. You should have turned around hours ago. Search and Rescue has protocols for a reason. Blah, blah, blah."

Technically, she was right. But with only three volunteers, they hadn't made enough progress as a single team. Doc had blamed the pitiful turnout on the Q document's revelations. Whatever the reason, one of the three had to search alone, and they couldn't have sent Tina out alone. After the shapely rookie's undisguised overtures toward Jay, Doc had insisted the two women stick together. Besides, Doc would know his exact location thanks to his GPS tracking beacon.

A westward bend brought Jay into an area littered with dozens of huge rocks and car-sized boulders. As the bend straightened, he could see that the canyon walls merged into a u-shaped prison a quarter mile ahead. There was nowhere to go but straight up, or back the way he had entered.

"Anyone in here? Mike? Yell if you can hear me."

A baby lizard scooted across a rocky outcropping on Jay's left and into a clump of fluff grass. A putrid odor enveloped the area. Taller scrub fifty yards ahead to the right hinted at water. Jay advanced to it and found a thin puddle of stagnant water and a coyote's bony carcass. Jay yelled, "I've got clean water and energy bars. Shout, if you can."

A rock clattered off the canyon wall ahead on the right.

Jay ran toward the sound, zigzagging through the field of boulders. "I'm coming, Mike."

The stench intensified as he entered a clearing. A person lay on the ground twenty yards ahead. "Mike?" The khaki hiking shorts and tan long sleeve shirt matched the tourist from Ohio's description. Still running, Jay shouted, "Are you okay?"

There was no response or movement.

Ten yards from Mike—if it was Mike—Jay slowed to a trot. The man lay on his side, facing away with his arms behind him. The wrists were tied. Jay charged to the man's front.

Half of a maggot and fly-infested face gaped back at him.

AFTER FORCING HIMSELF TO scan the decaying body, Jay backpedalled to the boulders and sank against a waist-high rock. The man had been executed. A bullet to the back of the head had seen to that. Why? And the maggots . . . Jay shuddered as the unwanted image lingered, reinforced by the smell of death that victimized the tranquil canyon. Shaking his head, he failed to dislodge the sight. Like his mother's accident scene that never—

Stone fragments exploded into the air. Jay jumped behind the rock he had been leaning on. Falling into a crouch behind it, the delayed sound of a gunshot cracked like lightning. His heart raced as he struggled to get his breath.

A second bullet whizzed by, high overhead. It, too, had come from the canyon's box end. Another bullet thudded into the sand short of his position. What was happening? Why was someone shooting? Only questions popped into his stalled-out brain. *Think. Think.* He had been shot at before, but that was during a military prep school exercise, and he doubted those bullets were real. *Don't panic. Turn negatives into positives.* He shifted into a seated position.

Two rounds shattered the false calm.

Moving was imperative, but the safety of a larger boulder might backfire and force the shooter to enter the canyon. Or to seal off the exit. Running from one huge rock to another had merit, but at the end of the boulder field, the canyon lay wide open. He'd be an easy target. The best that could be said for that option was that the shooter could wait until morning to check his kill.

Turn negatives into positives!

Jay moved again and watched for a muzzle flash. *One one-thousand, two one-thousand.* He spotted the flash. North side, high on the ridge. The shooter was no pro, taking a full two seconds to react, and missing by a mile. Jay looked back toward the canyon's entrance. *Good.* A wide egg-shaped boulder stood about fifteen yards away on a diagonal to the south. Satisfied with his strategy, Jay took a long drink and secured his water bottle. He loosened his backpack's straps, and then gathered them taut in his hand to keep the pack snug against his back for his next move. He drew a deep breath and exhaled forcefully.

Darting toward the massive stone shield, he counted, *one one-thousand.* A yard or so short of the giant rock, he planted his right foot. *Two one-thousand.* He flung himself against it, as if propelled by a bullet. In the same instant, the real bullet pierced the sand a few yards away. Jay slid down and around the boulder. Hidden behind it, he released his grip on the backpack's loose straps and shifted it onto his chest. He landed on his back out of sight, except for his left hand. He extended it into the shooter's view.

Jay slowed his rapid breathing and focused on keeping his arm motionless. It would be essential once target practice began. Dead arms don't flinch, and he expected to be tested. It was a less than enthralling prospect, but a hand was an awfully small target to a lousy shot two football fields away. The trouble was, if the shooter got lucky, dead arms don't bleed. Distance and the diminishing light would hide minimal bleeding, but just in case, Jay removed a tourniquet from his pack's first aid kit. Wrapping it slack around his upper arm took some doing one-handed, but there wasn't much else to do except wait for pitch-black.

Why kill a lost hiker, leave the corpse to rot in the open, and then shoot whoever found it? And whoever killed Mike didn't use a rifle from the rim. What was there to protect in this lonely canyon?

Jay wished he could warn Doc. He recalled inserting fresh batteries in all three radios this morning, checking them, and setting his down when Tina asked him to—

A bullet pinged off of stone nearby. His body jerked. Did his hand twitch? Another shot ricocheted among the rocks. *Here we go!* Rifle shots erupted one after another at three to four second intervals. High and long shots alternated with short ones. The shooter was narrowing his range, finding the right height to aim his scope above the target—his hand—to adjust for distance and elevation. *Don't move. Don't move.* Would it work? No, the body follows the mind. Speak positive actions.

Stay still. Bullets pummeled the area. Stay still.

Shots and their echoes pierced his eardrums like hot pokers. The reek of decay suffocated him. How many shots would this maniac fire?

Something struck his hand. A burning sensation screamed up his arm. *Am I hit?* It should hurt more, but the boulder blocked a view of his hand. Maybe it's a rock fragment.

Ignore it. Skip the tourniquet for now.

After a few more rounds, the shots stopped. Jay's heart was racing. How long before the merciless shooting started again? His hand throbbed. "Let it bleed," he whispered. Wasn't *Let it Bleed* a song by the Stones? The thought struck him as funny, and he began laughing, shaking. He gasped for oxygen. What was happening? The walls closed in. *Don't panic! Fight it.*

He repeated his mantra, "Stay still."

Sweat soaked his clothes, and he shivered in the desert's cool night air. Minutes had passed. How many times had he told himself to stay still? His breathing mellowed as he plotted his escape, systematically recalling his steps into the canyon and the safest route out.

Night in all its darkness enveloped the canyon. Shapes appeared as hazy outlines. The canyon walls would have been imperceptible except for the star-crammed sky that spilled around them. The moon had been full on Monday night, and would be up before long. It was time to go. The hike back to camp might take four or five hours. Add a two-hour drive to town, and he could be treating Doc to a breakfast burrito at Lupe's before the shooter took his morning leak.

Jay moved his left arm an inch. His pulse escalated, waiting for a shower of bullets. None came. He withdrew his arm a bit more. Finally, he yanked it back to safety and held his hand inches from his face. It might as well have been invisible. He rubbed his aching shoulder and wiggled his fingers. Inspecting the wound would have to wait. He unclipped the GPS from his belt.

Ready to move, he cinched his backpack tight on his back, wondering if it could deflect a bullet. He hoped it didn't need to.

FOOTFALLS, RHYTHMIC AND DETERMINED, advanced

toward the priest's cell-like office. The Vatican's top scrolls specialist squeezed several last papers into the accordion-style file folder already bursting at its seams. Like other windowless rooms in this section of the Société des Antiquités Archéologiques's Paris headquarters, Antonio couldn't see who approached. The unbroken cadence drew nearer. He hurriedly pushed the folder away, hopeful that the small scrap of papyrus was well camouflaged inside it. The footsteps halted. Was it a guard? A single rap on his door sank his stomach. Most colleagues, even the security brutes, knocked multiple times and waited for a response. Not Duvert. The Directeur Général entered without a pause.

"Doctor Duvert, you startled me," Antonio admitted.

"Sorry, monsignor." The Director, an aging French scientist, had sharp features and the cagy wariness of an ex-boxer. "I heard that you and your team will be leaving this morning to present your findings to the Holy Father. I trust you possess all of the information he requires for the inquisition."

"Stop! I won't listen to any more of your mockery." Since work began in March, he had endured the Frenchman's constant jabs at Catholicism. "Do you consider anything sacred?"

The director feigned twisting a knife in his heart, then moved closer, and extended his hand with a smile. "Let us part in peace."

The monsignor silently confessed his sin for judging the man evil, and stood to shake hands. In truth, Duvert was overseeing the examination of the Q document in a fair and competent manner.

Duvert gripped his hand with surprising strength. "There are many things I consider sacred," he said, finally releasing his grasp. "Like me, they are private. You have no such luxury representing Rome. What is your conclusion?"

"I only take observations. His Holiness will draw the conclusion."

"I think you take more than observations, no?" An unsettling twinkle lit Duvert's eyes. "You're the scientist, he will value your input. Expert after expert has triple-checked every detail—from first century grammar, dialectic consistency, and sentence structure to handwriting style and page layout. Who would imagine such an esteemed international team could be assembled for so many months? Tell me this Q is not reality."

"Paleography is critical, of course, but it is—"

"Not an exact science? Shush," Duvert whispered with a conspiratorial grin. "Don't let them hear you. They come very close though, no?" Duvert's eyes opened wide. "Then what of the ink and above all—*le papier*—stringently investigated. Dated here, then at great expense in Cambridge, and finally in America for the ultimate carbon dating. Do you really believe another test will have a different outcome?"

Did Duvert know of his theft? The guilt-ridden monsignor's knees threatened to collapse. Of course, another test was foolish. As crazy as stealing a fragment, but what else was there?

"I only collect the evidence."

"*Oui*, evidence." Duvert clenched his teeth. "For you, the final security inspection will be most thorough. My guards know all the tricks of . . . smugglers."

The priest from Rome froze.

Duvert placed his arm around his shoulders, squeezing one with force. "Don't worry, *mon ami*. You may leave with the fragment. The guards will not harm you, if that is your sole infraction." He released his grip and smiled. "Run your independent test. I want you to be convinced when you speak with your boss. That is all. The embarrassing video of you snatching *mon petit* piece will remain unseen." Duvert back-stepped to the doorway. "Let's forget popes and politics. Man to man, what do you really think?"

Antonio summoned his courage. "I'm suspicious."

"*C'est bon.* That is good, very good." The director nodded with a knowing grin. "It means you cannot sleep with your conclusion."

CHAPTER 2

TWENTY YARDS AHEAD, THE cliff-side trail dipped under
an eight-foot overhang of eroded rock. Its familiar form, sculpted
over eons by scouring winds and mighty floods, vanquished Jay's
growing fatigue. He knew that just past the chiseled landmark,
the trail turned north and descended into a flat where the team had
established base camp. He checked the time. It was 4:16 a.m. He
had made great time. Once the moon rose, the trail became visible,
but so had he. Mindful of that, he had taken the long way around
Old Lady Butte, a southeastward track that pointed away from Doc.
Then after the long detour, he doubled back through a draw that
didn't show on any map he had ever seen.

Now, before turning the final corner, he quickly sidestepped
into a fissure and watched for movement. Visibility at his feet was
near zero, but further out, where the harsh contours of the earth met
the soft night sky, features and movement leapt into hi-def. Nothing
moved, and nothing looked out of place.

Jay readjusted the makeshift glove on his left hand. Cut from
his backpack's top flap, it had kept his wound closed and protected
it. He used a mesquite branch like a blind man's cane to sweep the

dark trail for ankle-twisting hazards and critters that liked to bite or sting. He rejoined the path for its final few yards, but halted under the outcropping, alerted by an eerie glow outlining the corner. He peeked beyond it.

Two oil drums belched fire, and a fully stoked campfire lit base camp like an Aggie bonfire. Two additional vehicles flanked the twin pop-up SAR trailers with tent-like tops. A sheriff's department pickup truck with an ATV in its bed paralleled his Jeep. A monster pickup that had to be Dale's F-150 closed ranks behind them. The tires were taller than their owner.

Either Doc or Tina paced within the girls' pop-up, her silhouette projected onto the nylon and canvas side. Jay drew closer and recognized it was Doc. Her long hair, freed from its ponytail, danced back and forth with every fluid step. Her raised elbow and hand to her head suggested she was on the satellite phone.

"That's far enough," a deep voice said. "Stop where you're at and show me your hands." The voice sounded forced, the fake, low kind a skinny young deputy might use.

Jay spoke calmly to ease the man's jitters. "Glad you're here, deputy. My name's Jay Hunt, and there's a bunk in that trailer on your right with my name on it. It's been a long night."

"We were going to look for you in the morning, sir." A lanky officer with a military haircut stepped out from behind the shadow of the sheriff's department truck. Like Jay, he stood about six feet tall. Flames trying to escape the nearest barrel of fire showered him in flickering light and shadow. He looked late twenties. "I'm Deputy Randalls. Everybody calls me Randy. How'd you know my rank?"

"A lucky guess. What are you doing out here Deputy Randy?"

"Doc got worried. You were late, alone, and she couldn't raise you on the radio. Your GPS thing wasn't sending, so she called us." He nodded and shifted his weight. "Doc said your team carries

GPS units that automatically relay your position and can send an emergency beacon on demand. Yours went dark, and she never got a distress call. It worried her you might be unconscious."

"I never sent a distress signal. If I had, she might have come looking for me." Jay crossed to the campfire for warmth. The temperature had fallen to around forty degrees. "I don't understand why the tracking signal quit though."

"Well, it sounds like slick technology. Maybe the sheriff will get us some. Is it new?"

"No, it's not that new, just special. Your department won't be able to buy any. Let's just say, I've got friends in low places."

Randy meandered closer to the fire and laughed. "Just like the song, huh?"

"Probably lower."

"Mind if I look at it?"

"It's on Mike, our lost hiker." Jay stared into the flames. A log fell, ejecting sparks into the night.

"You found him?" The deputy eyeballed the perimeter. "Where is he?"

"He's dead. Executed at short range. He's in a nameless box canyon with his arms tied behind his back. I think it was Mike. Let's call him that. If the GPS is turned off, he didn't do it." Mike's image returned. "I'd like to know when he died. His corpse smelled, and he was flexible again, but his body was mostly intact."

"So you think that rigor had already played out, yet the animals left him alone. Are you sure it wasn't a fresh kill?"

The deputy displayed some smarts. Jay appreciated that the sheriff had sent a good man to look after Doc. "All I know is, in today's heat, he would have been stiff in an hour. If that's the timeline, I would have been almost on top of him when it happened. I attached the GPS to Mike forty-five minutes after I found him."

The technical conversation activated knowledge long dormant. "There were already large maggots in the exit wound. That takes a couple days."

"Are you an ex-cop?"

"No. And, somebody was babysitting Mike. They emptied a barrelful of cartridges in my direction from the canyon rim. I'll fill you in more, but first I need to say hello to Doc and Tina." Jay motioned to the girls' trailer with his head. "Any idea who Doc's talking to?"

"Yup. She's reaming out my boss for not sending the whole department." Fingers of light crisscrossed the deputy's smirking face. "Only Doc's in there. That other lady bugged out around three this afternoon. Somebody came and got her. Drove way out here. Can you believe that?"

Warning bells rang that could wake the dead. "Randy, I need to get Doc back in town pronto. And you should call for backup sooner rather than later. Wake Dale—I assume he's asleep in the men's trailer—and I'll get Doc packing."

The sheriff's deputy stood erect. "Yes, sir. What's the rush all of a sudden?"

"Tina is the one who suggested I search the area near the canyon where I found Mike. And a waiting sniper."

UNLIKE AMMAN'S RESTRAINED DOWNTOWN souk, the city's west-end marketplace was a noisy jumble of fruit and vegetable stands mixed with endless racks of clothing, stacks of pirated DVDs, and torrents of bargain hunters. Professor David Hunt worked his way to the souk's perimeter and strode past a dozen or more of the hard-walled shops that encircled the hodgepodge market. A tall woman in a dark blue burqa approached, her full face veil unusual in this liberal part of the capital. Behind her eye screen, the whites of her eyes betrayed a stare that followed him as she shuffled by. Something about her seemed familiar. Was it her walk?

Still puzzling over her, he stepped into a small antiques shop one-tenth the size of most stores back home in Texas, happily leaving the pandemonium of early afternoon shoppers and peddlers outside. He lowered his sunglasses and allowed them to hang by a cord from his neck. Remnants of ancient stone columns lined the shop's left side and faded mosaics were arrayed on the right; their age measured in millennia. What was called an antique in America would have been considered like new here.

The shop's owner moved in quick birdlike struts behind a glass case in the middle of the shop. He wore western-style trousers and an Egyptian cotton shirt with rolled up sleeves. Born to trade, and wirier than the professor remembered, Hassan Tariq al Rhaheem blinked as he caught sight of David. Hassan neared seventy years old, a milestone David felt fast approaching.

"*Marhaba.* The years have been kind to you, Doctor Hunt. I wondered when I would see you." Hassan placed his right hand on his heart. His large, black eyes gazed up and down David. "You must have British blood, for I am told all Americans are fifty kilos overweight."

"Hassan, you always were the consummate diplomat. Why aren't you in the Jordanian State Department? You could be Ambassador to any country you choose."

"Ah, the government men, now *they* know how to make money. A poor shopkeeper like me would be a blight on the diplomatic corps. Only important men such as yourself are allowed in the service of our king. May Allah grant him and you peace and blessings." Hassan raised his hands in praise, then allowed them to flow back to his sides.

David approached the counter. "See what I mean? You're a diplomat to the bone, but you know what they say about loose lips. I trust we're alone?"

"But of course. Excuse an old fool's poor English. Far be it from me to reference past services best left unspoken. I only meant to place you in the company of important men. I would forfeit my tongue before I uttered one word that might damage you." Hassan bowed his head in slow motion, then raised it looking both repentant and ecstatic—sorry that he had mentioned sensitive information and pleased his subtlety had been noticed. Few men still alive knew of David's government connection. The Jordanian was always negotiating.

"I was a young contractor of no real value. You can take that to the bank." David pointed at the glass case, its surface miraculously dust-free. "You have enough Roman coins in there to start your own bank."

"Yes, but it's the lamps next to them that I am most proud of. First century, most definitely. May I interest you in one? Or . . . perhaps I should inquire what it is you are after?"

David looked Hassan square in the eye. "You know what I'm here for. Did you move it?"

Hassan's faced dropped as though it would fall to the floor. "Sometimes a man such as myself is favored. Alas, for quite a while I have been out of favor with, what is your expression, the man upstairs." Hassan shrugged. "I have been party to scraps of papyrus here and there over the years, but nothing of consequence in decades. And never anything like the Q document."

"So who did? Who sold it? You must know."

"I have heard rumors. Only rumors." Hassan looked off into space.

"That's what's wrong about this whole thing. The Q document is a colossal incongruity. Ten dealers should be claiming they handled it, yet none do." David slammed both palms on the counter top. "Virtually nothing of value has been found in the caves for decades, and suddenly the most explosive Dead Sea Scroll ever discovered turns up nearly intact. And who found it? No one takes credit for unearthing it or for selling it. Only an unaccomplished, blundering historian claims he bought it on a street corner at midnight." David could tell his blood pressure was spiking, and he decided against discussing more of the Q's absurdity.

"Who can say differently?" Hassan shrugged. "I don't know your Bible, but I have heard that German scholars theorized years ago that its Gospels were written from a common source document, the *Quelle*. Aside from its unexpected content, I don't understand your surprise that it was found."

David erupted, "Because the Q was hypothesis, nothing more. It was a device to explain certain commonalities and omissions among three of the Gospels. But rather than containing sayings of Jesus, this Q document turns out to be an instruction manual to create him." David started pacing as though he was in front of a class. "We're supposed to believe that the Q's author uncovered hundreds of obscure messianic prophecies and fit them together like so many pieces to a puzzle. Then he exhorted colleagues to write them into a fictional life story of an executed teacher." He stood still. "How could such an explosive plan—the invention of the messiah—have been kept secret for two minutes, let alone two millennia? Look at the astonishing speed with which it has spread today based solely on anonymous leaks in only the past month."

"I'm sorry this has upset you. Until now I didn't care that Christianity was on its deathbed." Hassan eyed the floor. "You know the leaks won't be anonymous much longer. The official sanctioning is in two weeks."

"A preposterous timetable that the Société claims is to erase the doubt engulfing the world. Never mind that it's their news leaks stirring the pot. They've been evaluating it for months, then suddenly they go high-profile. Only the Vatican's members on the team have kept quiet, and as top-notch as they are, their silence only serves to confirm the worst." David caught his breath. "Still, once it is sanctioned, the Société has pledged to make it available to everyone. We'll see if it can stand that kind of scrutiny. And, if it is legitimate, then it rested somewhere for two thousand years. That cave must be evaluated as rigorously as the document. So tell me please, what rumors have you heard?"

"Some say it was sold in Bethlehem. Aha, the town of David." Hassan chuckled. The leathery skin surrounding his eyes formed deep creases. "That is where you'll find the answers you chase."

Chase? David's chest tightened. For weeks, he'd sensed his every move being analyzed and catalogued. Did Hassan somehow know of his traipsing around Europe and the Middle East probing for information about the Q document? It had to be a forgery, but how was it defying rigorous scientific tests? There was only one explanation, impossible as it seemed. It was why he had relayed the most significant details to Ezra yesterday. Ezra would know what to do, and he could be trusted above all others. David's muscles relaxed. He studied Hassan.

The Arab trader's jovial countenance faded. "An American can visit Bethlehem easy. I have heard no names, but there is only one man there that a wise seller would contact."

"I just came from Bethlehem. Imaad died last month. His widow blamed bad medicine. She was so near despair, I felt horrible leaving her alone. Two sons are in Egypt, and a daughter disappeared right after the funeral. The widow prays she didn't join a Freedom Brigade." Bethlehem's sad state filled David's mind. Between the terrorists' consuming hatred and the Israeli wall, the years had not been kind to the town. "The daughter might have done just that. Who would blame her? Live bodies and honest answers are getting awfully hard to come by."

Hassan stared blankly.

David drew imaginary circles on the counter's top, then looked up. "But, I did find Faarooq, a lesser known dealer. He directed me here."

Hassan flinched.

The trader's reaction eased David's conscience. There was no Faarooq, but Hassan didn't call the bluff and worse, he had reacted—he was lying.

A man in a tailored jacket and a starched shirt with no tie entered the shop. He surveyed David from behind dark sunglasses before turning aside to twiddle with a three-foot-high remnant of a Corinthian column. His short black hair looked plastered in place, and his jacket accentuated a strong upper body. If he wasn't Jordanian Intelligence, he believed in overdressing.

Hassan ignored the man and removed several coins from the case. "Then these coins should please you," he said to David. "I assure you they date back to your first century. You can see how the palm tree has been over-stamped across Nero's likeness. The coins were re-minted by the Jews on religious grounds. After Jerusalem fell in 70 AD, nothing remained. Only these coins." Hassan extended his hand. "Here, you may hold them."

David attempted to study one of the coins with a magnifying glass lying nearby. His sunglasses annoyed him, swinging back and forth, so he unslung them and placed them on the counter. He tried again. "Yes, I see the image underneath. That is exactly what I was looking for."

Hassan began his odd walk toward the man in the suit.
"*Marhaba.* May I help you?"

"No, I was looking for rugs." The man turned and left.

Hassan returned to the counter and stood next to David. His
quizzical smile revealed dark tobacco-stained teeth. "Why bother
with finding the dealer, whoever it was? Surely your friends
evaluating the Q document in Paris at the Société will throw open
the gates to receive you. They will want your professional eyes."

David choked back a laugh. "Yeah, and my hide too. Claude
Duvert, the Society's Director, was never a friend." Paris had been a
bust, but there was no point in sharing all the gory details. Duvert's
caustic dismissal of assistance had communicated more than
professional jealousy. Precisely what, though, was hard to peg.

Hassan paced back and forth. David peered out at the market
through the shop's front windows. The man in the suit and two
others loitered at nearby stalls. Hassan coughed. "Usually, the man
credited with purchasing the scroll sells for others. I was never
impressed by him."

"Veillon?" David clucked his tongue. "He couldn't find a flea
at a flea market. I tried to talk with him, but I was told he's cruising
the Caribbean. He's the only reason Duvert's Society obtained
exclusive rights to the Q document. I imagine the Dead Sea Scrolls
team was livid."

The aging dealer's face contorted.

David handed back the coins. "Sorry. Livid means angry, only
more so. Kind of like me right now. I don't think you're telling
me—"

Hassan brought his right index finger to his lips and turned
on a small radio on a shelf behind him. He whispered, "I know
the word. Convenient, these deaths and disappearances. There is
danger for me and for you. Do not look outside, but there are more

men like the one looking for a rug earlier. They circle like vultures, awaiting an order, I think. You must leave. Not out the front. Do you remember?"

"Yes, but . . ."

"I'll call you."

Leaving seemed a bad idea with Hassan on the verge of talking, but he wasn't going to speak freely in his shop. "Okay, let me give you my number."

"There's no time. Take this." Hassan thrust a cell phone into David's hand. "Now give me yours so I can call. Go my friend. Quickly."

David dug his phone out of his back pocket, but held it firmly. "Come with me."

Hassan looked at his watch. "Impossible. In ten minutes, I close for two hours. I'll call you. We'll meet and re-exchange phones. Go."

David quashed the protest shouting in his head, and handed over his phone. He scurried to the back, and ran up steps to an outdoor walkway that led to Hassan's apartment and an external stairwell. David hustled past the apartment and back down to ground level. He emerged into a narrow passageway of stone and crumbling mortar that ran behind the row of shops. Sweat poured down his face.

It wasn't like Hassan to panic. But what did those men want? Maybe Hassan had become paranoid. Age did things to you.

The passageway ended at a stone arch and exited into an alley that connected to a main road. David squinted in the full sun. He reached for his sunglasses. "Drat." He'd left them lying on Hassan's counter. He debated going back to get them, turning in a full circle twice.

A woman in a black burqa hustled past and into the alley.

Finally, the professor retraced his steps to Hassan's apartment and listened from the top of the stairs. A song blared from the radio. David tiptoed down the steps and listened again. Hearing only music, he peeked around the corner.

The glass counter had been smashed. A large bloody shard jutted into the air. Broken glass littered the floor. David rushed around the demolished counter. Hassan lay on the floor in the middle of toppled columns. A crimson line encircled his neck, blood soaked his severed throat.

"No!" David gasped for air. "What have I done?"

He ran out the shop's front, screaming for the police and a doctor. How could it have happened so fast? A small crowd gathered near him, then parted as he continued running and yelling. No one seemed to care. A huge explosion deafened him. Flying glass and debris knocked him to the ground.

CHAPTER 3

JAY TURNED HIS '94 Jeep Cherokee into The Springs subdivision just before eleven a.m. Bright sunshine and mid-eighty degree temperatures poured in through the open windows of the metallic gray 4x4. The air-conditioner made the warm morning air comfortable, but Doc's perfume made it worth breathing. She had Chaneled-up earlier at the sheriff's office. Jay took a right onto Cactus Lane. Doc's modest brick ranch sat on a half-acre lot in the nice part of the city of Evergreen. The front porch looked out on a desert garden of agave, yucca, and other native plants. He pulled into her driveway and parked in the shade of a Palo Verde tree.

A glance at the rear view mirror confirmed that the street remained quiet. No one had followed them, or tried to. The last thing he wanted was to bring trouble to Doc's doorstep. It was one thing to have someone shooting at him, but he would leave no stone unturned if someone took a potshot at her. Jay relaxed his grip on the steering wheel and turned off the ignition. He looked at Doc.

She smiled. "It's nice to be home." Her long auburn hair was twisted and clipped behind her head so that only a short ponytail dangled out the back of her Astros baseball cap. A few loose strands of hair blew across her face. Vivid green eyes and a sprinkling of freckles highlighted her fair skin.

Doc's warm smile revived him more than any jolt of caffeine. A pot of coffee at the sheriff's office had produced no direct effect, although countless trips to the restroom had kept him awake. Sheriff Henson had promised to investigate the mystery shooter and Mike's killing, but it was clear he was overwhelmed by a recent surge in home invasions. The sheriff blamed the Q document for the county's problems. Who didn't?

Doc opened the passenger door. It squeaked, and Jay made a mental note to actually do something about it this weekend. He got out when she did, and shuffled to the vehicle's rear.

"I'll get your stuff."

He opened the rear hatch and muscled her backpack and duffel bag clear of the SAR gear jammed around it. She walked to the Jeep's rear. A former tri-athlete, she was five-foot-eight, well sculpted, and ran or swam nearly every day. She looked twenty-eight, not thirty-eight, her true age that she once let slip. Jay pulled her equipment to the edge of the cargo compartment, lacking any desire to lift it out and searching for a reason to stay.

Doc came along side him. The scent of her perfume was torture. How could he leave?

She spun him around and hugged him like she would never let go.

Every aching muscle responded to her tight grip. "I'll give you half an hour to cut that out," he whispered. Apparently it wasn't his imagination that she had looked at him differently ever since he had returned to base camp.

Doc relaxed the bear hug, but kept her arms locked around his waist. She studied his face. Her cheeks flushed.

"I've needed to do that the whole way here." Her silky voice showed no sign of embarrassment at her confession. "At the sheriff's office, I almost jumped across the table."

"You mean you didn't? Oh, that's right. That was in my wildest dream."

She drew him close again and pressed her lips to his. The kiss was over before it started, but the effect lingered. He regretted every night he had spent platonically gazing at the stars with her during the last few search missions, unsure how she felt about him. "Wow," he said, wishing he had managed a more romantic comment. "Maybe I should come in and look around for, um, security purposes."

A cat-like grin crossed Doc's face.

Jay swallowed hard. "Seriously, as tired as I am, I couldn't sleep without knowing that you're safe. You know what Sheriff Henson said about the Q document and break-ins and all."

Her grin morphed into a full-court smile. "I'd like that." The smile faded as she pressed her lips together. "The sheriff is never going to find out who shot at you, is he?"

"Even a blind lizard finds some bugs. But all I know is, if you ever need help, I wouldn't count on Henson. He's a politician, not a law enforcement pro." Jay dug a piece of paper out of his back pocket. "Here, save this in your phone. It's Officer Randalls's cell number. It turns out he's a former army ranger. If you're ever in a jam, use it."

"I'd rather call you." She tucked a few wisps of her hair behind an ear.

"That's nice, but I might not be around, and he wears a gun."

"I hate this talk about guns and crime. And I don't believe that Q document for a second. All the tension between Muslims and Christians since 9/11 has caused some people to treat religion like a disease. Then this Q document comes along, and it's like a match lighting a fuse."

"Match? More like a blowtorch."

"The experts verifying the Q must have overlooked something. Jesus was not just some first century con trying to dupe the Romans."

Jay turned and faced the Cherokee's cargo area. "You sound like my father."

He gave Doc her nearly empty backpack, and she slung it over one shoulder. He grabbed her duffel, closed the hatch, and took hold of her hand. They walked to her shaded porch, which was ringed with hanging baskets overflowing with tiny pink and yellow portulaca blooms.

Doc crossed to the porch's center and sat on a green-cushioned glider. She pulled Jay down beside her. "I think I'd like your father. Tell me about him. Is he a believer?"

"Yeah, only worse. He's a retired Dead Sea Scrolls expert. Dad worked with the Rockefeller Museum in Jerusalem, and I hope he keeps his nose out of this Q business."

Her eyes narrowed. "Why? When medical experts declare a case is terminal, that's when I get interested. Maybe your dad is like that. I've seen it in you. Anyway, someone has to prove the Q document is phony. Why not him?"

"Because for the last half-century, the Scrolls have been more about politics than religion. Dad was probably *the* leading expert, and when he retired, the political Scroll gods rejoiced. He refused to play their games and wound up with a heart condition." Jay's pulse thundered. He took a deep breath and smiled. "Sorry. He's been through a lot, and he never received the recognition he earned. The Scrolls team didn't deserve him."

Doc started the glider gently moving back and forth. "I'm sorry it was so tough on him. He did important work. It's nice that you're protective of him."

"I never thought of it that way," he said, nodding. "So tell me, what makes you certain the Q is a hoax?"

"People think with their brains, but they know with their hearts. The Q document can only plant doubts in the brain. There are some things you just know, Jay." She squeezed his hand. "I know when someone lives in my heart." The brilliant green of her eyes shimmered.

Hearts can be deceived, he thought. Glad that she hadn't experienced otherwise, he kept silent. Maybe her heart was smarter than his.

Doc stood and tugged him to his feet. Inches apart, he wanted to kiss her again.

She wiggled her hand into her jeans pocket and drew out her keys. "Come on in, but remember this is official business, strictly a look around for . . . security purposes. Remember, if the Gospels were faked, it just means that the Old Testament is the Only Testament. You wouldn't want me being stoned for immorality would you?" She pushed herself a foot away and plucked at the front of her ASU tee shirt. "Besides, I need to shower, and trust me, so do you."

"A shower sounds great. When I stood by the sheriff's dispatcher, I was waiting for her to clothespin her nose." They both laughed. He inched nearer and summoned his best Sean Connery imitation. "Your shower or mine?"

A foxy smile lit her face. "That was pretty good. I didn't know you could imitate Humphrey Bogart." Doc laughed and touched his arm. "I'm so glad you're okay. I was really worried about you yesterday."

"Keeping you out of harm's way was all I thought about." He locked his eyes on hers. "You kept me going."

She exhaled a sharp breath. "All of a sudden, being stoned doesn't sound so bad. But you're still leaving, mister." She put her hands on his chest, as if to push away, but she moved closer. "The hospital hates it when I'm gone this long. After nabbing some sleep, I'll be spending the evening catching up on cases with the locum tenens, a surgeon on loan. Then I'll be rounding all night." She twisted her lips in thought. "You know, Lupe's stopped serving breakfast before we left the sheriff's office. You promised to buy me a breakfast burrito. How about tomorrow instead? I should be done by six."

"Six is when they open, but if they opened at five, I'd be there just in case you finished early."

"Jay Hunt, where has the real you been? And what else are you hiding?"

PASTOR BOB SENT HIS last email and gazed out his office window at the group of five diehard saints, milling around a giant coffee dispenser in the church's parking lot. Five-gallon paint buckets, ladders, and several cardboard boxes surrounded them. He wondered if they were disappointed with the small turnout. Not a single Henderson or Foster had shown, and his associate pastor, Ellie, was unaccounted for.

Two hundred and thirty families call this church home, Lord. Where are they?

A twinge of guilt struck him.

More than once during this dark week, he had thought about shutting the doors and finding a job. Sunday attendance had dwindled from abysmal to near empty. On Monday, vandals destroyed the gorgeous stained glass window with Jesus kneeling in Gethsemane. Then came the spray paint attack two nights ago.

It was a wonder anyone had showed today. *Thank you, Lord, for providing these tireless folks.*

He grabbed his sweatshirt from the floor. Its decades-old stains and caked on dirt had prevented him from putting it anywhere else this morning. He pulled it on over his good sweatshirt, and feeling like the Pillsbury doughboy, he went outside.

All eyes found him. Steam curled from the tops of their paper coffee cups. An overcast sky had settled in for the season. Today's calm air was heaven sent. Novembers in eastern Indiana could be windy and cold. Without wind, they should be able to use the sprayer on the large sections. The plan to get the job done during lunchtime just might work.

He shook hands with all but Lester Hartnett, who gave him a hug. "Thanks for showing up, guys and lady. I know it's a little chilly, and I have to tell you I'm praying that the paint will stick in this weather. Let's thank God that it's not raining or worse. Does anyone know the temperature?"

"It was thirty-seven when I opened the store at eight. It's about forty-two now." Johnny Bingham could always be depended on for repair projects, and fortunately, he owned the local hardware store. "I'm a little worried about the temperature, but it's close to the day's projected high, and it's not supposed to get any warmer for a week. We sure can't leave the front of the church covered with swastikas and orange spray paint."

Lester grabbed a paintbrush from a cardboard box. "And the words, my land. I still can't believe someone would write that—on a church. If they want to accept this Q thing over the Bible, let 'em. But why'd they have to do this? Let's get started."

"Good idea, but first things first." Pastor Bob decided to keep things positive, but real. "I've struggled lately with all that has happened. I prayed for strength and received it. God is good and his son is authentic. Amen?"

Each answered with a hearty, "Amen."

"Remember, Jesus was written off once before. He was crucified, died, and buried. That wasn't the end. He rose from that grave. His death was the basis of our forgiveness, but his resurrection is the basis for our faith. I am confident that he'll rise again. Not physically, like he did then, but in people's hearts. Jesus said we must be born again. Maybe it's true of his church too, because I tell you this—on a glorious day to come, a larger, more vibrant church will be reborn in this country. Let's start the ball rolling right here, right now. Grab a bucket!"

THE ROUTE HOME FROM Doc's went through the city's heart. It wasn't beating very hard at the moment. It never did, which was one of the city's main attractions. Jay tapped on the steering wheel to a song without words or music. Evergreen, Arizona. A misnomer if ever there was one. Bronze dust encrusted the town like a Remington sculpture.

He decided to check on Marge at his office before going home. It was one of a couple dozen businesses in false two-story Old West buildings that ringed Evergreen's town square and historic county courthouse. He parked in an angled spot on Franklin Street, facing the courthouse. After waiting on a couple pickups to rumble past, he jogged across Franklin, eyeing Martin's Drugs. One of Martin's large front windows and the glass door were broken. Two doors down, he strutted into Pink Hummer Tours.

Marge, his only employee, eyed him from behind one of three gray metal desks. "You look terrible and then some."

"That's a weird expression." Poster size desert photos covered the walls. Several action shots showed him driving a roofless pink Hummer, rock crawling in impossible situations with white-knuckled tourists yelping for more. "Think about it."

"Maybe I'm just too much of a lady to say what you really look like. Think about that." Marge was sixty-two with short gray hair and built like the pink hummer parked out back. She winced as he drew near. "You need a shower."

Jay laughed and raked his hair with his fingers. "So I've been told. I offered to take one with Doc, but she didn't go for it."

"It's about time you did something about her. And that's how you finally make your move? With your sandy hair and movie-star looks, all you gotta do is be yourself." She gave a motherly scowl. "You've been drooling over her ever since midsummer when she moved to town—"

"I have not been drooling—"

"Yes, you have. Most single women in this town have more kids than teeth, and that's how you talk to the classiest lady in Evergreen? Maybe you can claim post *dramatic* stress disorder. I heard you got shot at yesterday."

"Yeah, wrong place, wrong time. Does anything happen in this town that you don't know about?"

Her glare told him his attempt to change the subject had failed. "It wasn't as bad as it sounds, and it probably wasn't as clever as it seemed. I get it. She's a lady, and I should treat her like one. Now, can we get off the Doc subject?"

"Done. I thought you were in an awfully good mood. But don't worry, I have some news to spoil it."

"Give it your best shot, but you better hurry. I could fall asleep standing up."

"Okay, just remember you wanted it quick. Business stinks." Marge fanned a stack of Pink Hummer Tour brochures. "The hotels stock your brochures just to be nice, but they don't actively promote you because you're never here. The whole town knows that if someone is in trouble, you'll go look for them. They respect you for that, and so do I, but you need to stick around the office. No more chasing after every fool hiker that gets lost."

"He had a wife who depended on him, and he had a name. It was Mike."

Her reality-scarred face softened. "Sorry, I heard about that too. It must have been awful. But the truth is you're broke. The checking account doesn't have enough money in it to cover my next paycheck, which is tomorrow. I can skip a payday or two if you need it, but you haven't taken a draw in months."

"Are you being nice to me?"

"You're going to starve if business doesn't improve." Her eyes glazed over. "Most days, I don't hardly eat. While you've been out in the desert, things have gotten worse. Martin's got broken into. Ebert's Deli too. That kind of thing never happens here. More and more crime, it makes me sick. I heard this morning the pope is going to make a big announcement next week. All because of this dreadful Q document." She rested her forehead on her palms. Her shoulders sagged and began to shake. "I'm so confused."

"Marge?" His stomach knotted. "I've been where you're at. All I know is everything will be okay."

She lifted her head and yanked a tissue from the box on her desk. The box fell over empty. "Maybe for you," she said, wiping her nose. "It was good you were gone. I haven't felt like working or doing much of anything lately," she sighed. "I just don't know what to believe anymore." She opened her top desk drawer, looking like she would cry again, and retrieved a new box of tissues. "When my son died, the Lord kept me going. I felt him, it wasn't just my imagination. That's why this whole thing makes no sense."

Jay couldn't bring himself to say maybe it was her imagination.

She shook her head, no, as though she heard his thoughts. "Jesus couldn't have been invented way back then by a bunch of Jewish monks just to keep Rome from destroying the Jewish temple."

"Whether it was way back then or not, science can decide. The so-called monks were probably Essenes. But I doubt more than one man created the fiction. No group, no matter how zealous, could have kept this plan secret. Either way, it wasn't just the temple he was worried about."

"What do you mean?"

Jay pictured the ruins of Qumran, near Jerusalem. He saw the partial walls outlining the room where the many Dead Sea Scrolls were likely hand copied—Princess's favorite place. They were only kids, but Princess and he had shared a lifetime of adventures in that desert. "The Essenes feared the zealots would spark a war with Rome, which would destroy the entire Jewish nation. I imagine it was a common fear."

"So what does that have to do with inventing Jesus?"

"Have you read what has leaked of the Q's preamble?"

Marge looked away, scratching her wrist. She looked back. "I haven't ever actually read the Bible, so I figured I had no business reading the Q document."

Jay nodded. "Well, the preamble refers to Jesus as a popular teacher. When Rome executed him, the Q's author rewrote Jesus' life to fit Scripture's messianic profile. Except rather than re-create a military hero like people expected, he framed Jesus more traditionally as the One destined to unite Jews and Gentiles under a common god. The rest of the Q document is the detailed instructions to write three different versions."

"I know, 'non-identical narratives with meaningless contradictions that agree in substance.' I'm tired of hearing it."

Marge scowled. "So where did John's Gospel come from?"

"Same place as a dozen other gospels, except the others never made it into the Bible."

Marge's eyes had dried. "I don't like all this logic. It bothers me that you might be right."

"I'm neutral. I don't believe one way or the other."

"Something tells me different. You know too much."

Jay stepped back. "I've read reports and speculation, that's all. I didn't mean to get into all this. Do you need anything else? I'm fading fast."

"Give me something to do or I'll go crazy feeling sorry for myself. Not to mention we need the business. I can't have you starving."

"No one is going to starve." Jay patted his stomach, still flat, but softer than a few years ago. "I can't give up searching for lost hikers, but when I *am* here, I'll dedicate myself to pursuing business. Well, and pursuing Doc." The memory of Doc's hug and kiss quashed his growing fatigue. "I'll take care of the checking account."

"Okay." Marge tilted her head. "Just make sure you do it before you leave town."

"I'm not going anywhere."

"That's the other news." Marge grabbed a spiral notepad off her desk. "Your dad called yesterday afternoon and left a message. He's traveling; so call his cell phone to confirm receiving it. Boy, is he traveling."

"Oh yeah? What's the message?"

"It's pretty strange. He was in a hurry and kind of rude, but I got every word. You're lucky I take shorthand." She flipped the notepad open, revealing a page of hieroglyphics. "I'm a little rusty, but here goes. He said, 'I'm looking forward to the vacation with you. Mine is going well, but I'm taking an unexpected little side trip. Remember our arrangement? Well, ignore my letter, and don't meet me at home in Houston.'"

The hairs on Jay's neck bristled. It was like finding Mike and being shot at all over again. How could he forget the arrangement? Dad had said this day might come. "Were those his exact words?"

"He made me read it back to him." She shrugged. "Then he continued, 'Meet me in Detroit. I want to go to the U-P to fish and get away from crowds. I plan to get in late, so don't wait dinner. I'm not confirmed, but I dislike the hot dog connections out of Amman, so I'll be driving to Damascus.'"

"His little side trip is to Jordan?" Jay collapsed into a guest chair. The stilted language, the misdirection. *How much trouble are you in?* He drummed the chair's arms. "I knew he couldn't leave it alone. But, what is he doing back there?"

"I didn't ask. I take it he's been there before. There's more. He said, 'I can't get in Friday, the picture's not clear, but I'll see you on Saturday. You should know I'm trying to avoid Heathrow, shooting at JFK first, National next. You can bet on one of them to get the right picture.' See what I mean about it being strange?" She set the pad down and began rummaging through neat stacks of files on her desk.

Jay rubbed his temples. "His message said something about a letter. Has it shown up?"

"Not here, maybe it's at your trailer, but he said ignore it."

"True." Jay considered his options. If he explained that Dad's message to ignore the letter really meant to be sure to read it, then he might have to explain everything else. He wasn't sure he should do that. Or could. "Would you please type the message word for word?"

She retrieved a thin manila folder from a foot-high stack

and pulled two pages from it. The aging assistant handed them over, grinning like a college fullback who just scored the winning touchdown. "I already typed it. The other sheet has your Saturday flight and car rental info for Detroit. Your dad asked me to book them right away. You leave from Phoenix. He gave me a credit card number to charge, which was fortunate, all things considered."

"Very fortunate," he said, starring at a wall poster of Diamondback Mountain, his mind half a world away. A credit card that someone was meant to track. But who? One thing was as clear as the desert air—time was short. "I'm going to need tomorrow for personal business, so I need you to hold down the fort a little longer. If you want, forward the phones to your house until I get back. When did my dad have you book my return flight?"

"He recommended an open ticket."

IF THERE WAS ANY way to get out of meeting with Dad, Jay decided to find it fast. A short hallway led from the large customer area at the building's front to his cramped office in back. Lining the hallway were cardboard boxes stacked shoulder high and swollen with files that smelled like watered-down vanilla. The desert was his real office, but this stuffy cave in back served its purpose.

He hadn't flown anywhere in a while, but the office's scuffed black and white linoleum floor reminded him of the checkerboard bath tiles in New York's Waldorf-Astoria. Wall Street was a lot like a desert; a harsh landscape devoid of compassion and full of palms—most of which were always open. He smiled at his change of careers. Now his stock-in-trade was the desert, where only a Hummer-full of tourists depended on him, and then only for a few hours at a time.

Except now. Dad needed him. Or at least, Dad thought so. For a second, Jay wondered if being shot at in the canyon was connected with Dad's problem. With no idea what Dad was up against, he let it pass.

Jay fished around his center desk drawer for his cell phone, which was useless in the desert. The signal was bad enough in town. Jay dialed his father's cell and immediately got a recording. Dad's voice quivered with age, but his intelligence had never wavered. "Dad, it's me. Marge thinks you're rude, but she doesn't understand you like I do." He thought hard for a moment, then committed. "If I don't hear otherwise, I'll meet you as arranged, but I wouldn't mind you confirming that it's necessary. Call me when you can."

Too tired to fool with his computer, he dialed Houston First National's bank-by-phone to beef up his local checking account. The bank's welcome message correctly warned that its ridiculous menu had changed. It now offered every option except press nine to shine your shoes. Finally, he got to the money transfer option. It declined his request. After a deep breath, he booted his laptop and accessed his account online. A withdrawal of $78,550.37 three weeks ago left an account balance of exactly one dollar. And absolutely no sense.

CHAPTER 4

THE CHORUS TO "A Horse with No Name" played on Jay's phone, jolting him awake. A semi-truck blowing past the rest area assaulted his eardrums. He stretched his cramped back. It was nearly 4:30. What a difference 24 hours made. The sun was hidden behind a distant ridge, but at least nobody was shooting. The ringtone continued, displaying an unrecognizable number. Leave a message.

The phone stopped. Grit from the unpaved lot coated his teeth.

He reached for a nearly empty Caffeine Express. Lot of good it had done. He had pulled over forty minutes ago when his eyes kept fluttering shut, interrupting his drive north on Highway 93 to McCarran International Airport in Las Vegas. The rest area was little more than a parking lot with a dumpster, but it had its share of traffic. At the moment, a young family was piling into a minivan across from him. A clunky old Buick Riviera, a dozen spaces away at the end of the small lot, slammed its car door.

His phone rang again. Same odd number. "Hello."

"Did you get my message?"

The voice popped Jay's eyes wide-open. "Dad? Didn't you get

my message?"

"I asked you first, Ezra."

Jay shook the final cobwebs from his brain. "You know I don't use that name."

"Why not? It's Biblical."

"So are Peter, James, and John. And David, come to think of it. I might have used one of those."

"Just be glad we didn't name you Habakkuk."

"It's not funny, Dad."

"My favorite was Artaxerxes, but your mother vetoed it. She always was the sensible one."

"No comment." Sweat glued Jay's shirt to his chest where his arms had been folded in sleep. Even with the windows open and the sun down, the Arizona heat refused to dissipate inside the Jeep. "Yeah, I got your message. That's why I'm in Michigan's Upper Peninsula, freezing. The snow's as deep as a Pharaoh's Tomb. Since when do you like ice fishing?"

The Riviera at the end of the lot turned over its engine with a powerful growl. So much for the Riv's clunky appearance.

"You *understood* my message, didn't you son?"

"Enough to get started. I got the arrangements." If he remembered the decades-old coding right, everything in Dad's message after the word "arrangement" was reversed. Dad expected to meet in Houston tomorrow afternoon, not in Detroit late on Saturday. To avoid blowing the cover off the bogus flight to Detroit, Jay headed to Vegas where he assumed paying cash for a plane ticket would raise little suspicion. How necessary these secretive games were, he couldn't guess. "You can explain the rest when I see you. Are you okay? I mean—"

"Fine, but I need your help to track money on a few folks. Get a pen and write their names down. Ready?"

"Just a second." Jay cradled the phone with his shoulder and retrieved a small spiral pad and pen from the center console. The Riv left a cloud of dust in its wake as it entered the two-lane highway south toward Evergreen. "I'm ready."

"Start with Hassan Tariq al Rhaheem who is, well, was a Jordanian. Next is a Parisian Dr. Jean Veillon and a Palestinian in Bethlehem named Imaad Khalid al Wahiri. He's dead, but see if you can find anything on him and a daughter named Faatina. Check the wife too." Forever the professor, he rattled off the wife's name and several others until Jay insisted he spell them. Finally, Dad added, "Oh and speaking of money, I borrowed some from our account."

"That was you? *Some* money? You emptied it. And it wasn't *our* account. You were an additional signatory is all." Jay wanted to ask him what he could possibly want with that much money, but there was no way he'd get a straight answer over an unsecured phone. Legitimate or not, he had to respect Dad's concerns that someone might be listening. "Fortunately, I keep emergency cash at home. My other funds are a little less handy."

"Well, I don't have the kind of cash lying around like you do."

"Yeah, well, now neither do I. Thanks to you. This Q document has cratered the market. You forced me to sell some stock in a lousy market, and the trades won't settle for a few days. Who knows, though, usually a little pruning turns out to be beneficial in the long run."

"I thought you sold off a bunch of your holdings when the Q was first broached. You told me to."

Jay smiled. "I did, but I plowed the proceeds into some short-term Asian paper. It's tied up for another week."

"Why not use a little margin money? You taught me that trick."

"Not in this market, Dad. What am I looking for on those people? Anything specific?"

"Large transactions. Or maybe a series of small ones that adds up to big dollars. That is, big to them, not you. Pruning to you is probably a lifetime of scrimping and saving to them. Are you on schedule?"

"More or less, but keep talking, I should get driving again. And, tell me that getting together is really important. This isn't the most convenient time for me to take a vacation."

"Convenient? People are dying. If anything, the last 24 hours have proved it's more important than ever. I have a job for you."

"If you're talking about what I think you're talking about, forget it. I already have a job."

"Do you call hiding behind the steering wheel of a *pink* Hummer a job? With your education and expertise . . . I just don't understand—"

"Dad, we've been through this before. Can we just—" It sounded like Dad dropped the phone.

Jay started the Jeep.

"Drat. Jay, can you still hear me? This thing just slammed onto the concrete pretty hard."

"It's still working," he said, backing out of his spot.

"Good. Unfortunately, I just noticed this phone is low on juice, and I don't have a charger for it. I'll talk fast. If we're interrupted, I'll call again from a pay phone at the, um, from where I'm going. Remind me to tell you about Duvert. Ooh, I neglected to put him on your list. Dr. Claude Duvert. Maybe you remember him? He's in Paris now. What a lazy fool. One sentence, one lousy sentence where the Q's writer says that he'll travel the world to convince the Gentiles of his story, and Duvert's concluded the author is Saul of Tarsus. It answers so many questions so easily that the bird can't resist jumping into the net. Never mind why it's unthinkable. Thankfully, Duvert hasn't gone public with it yet. The media will love that one."

So you are working on the Q document. Where are you anyway?
A day ago, Dad told Marge he was heading to Amman, and then
driving to Damascus. He'd never drive anywhere in the Middle
East, let alone Syria. He'd take a bus. But where? In Dad's crazy
message, pointing north should mean south. But the only thing
south of Amman was sand, so he had probably headed to Jerusalem.

Jay accelerated and merged onto the two-lane highway, beating
a large motor home with a parade of cars jammed behind it. "Okay,
talk."

"Are you driving? It would be better if you pulled over."

"I know, but my schedule's tight." Dad's timing might be even
tighter. In Israel, it was 1:40 Friday morning. He was probably
headed to Ben Gurion near Tel Aviv for an early morning flight and
would probably need triple the time required to clear US security.
"I'll drive safe."

"It's 'safely,' and I really think you should pull over, son. I have
a confession to make."

"Geez, Dad. I just got going, and I'll be stuck behind—"

"I stole something."

"What?"

"Years ago, close to thirty. I can't believe it's been that long.
But here's the thing, even our mistakes can produce something
good. God can do that. It was small, insignificant . . . I don't even
know why I did it. But now after all these years, it might save
mankind's soul. Imagine that. You should know that your mother
took the secret to her grave, God rest her—"

"Dad? Hello? I can't hear you. Are you there?"

CHAPTER 5

FAATINA HUMMED A FEW more bars, having forgotten the rest
of the lyrics about bombs and jukeboxes. She crimped the last pair
of wires together; confident the fate of countless infidels had just
been sealed. She wondered why an out-of-the-way North Carolina
roadhouse had been targeted for today's lunchtime surprise.
Scrunched into the room's corner, and kneeling behind the coin-
operated source of death, she prayed for a large crowd. And she
prayed that the stench of beer and cigarettes would wash from her
hair. "I love bombs and rock-n-roll—"

"You sing nice, and you look good, too, but I don't think you
have the words quite right." The honky-tonk's manager surprised
her. He had been busy in a back room, which had been perfect. But
now, here he was; bushy mustache, bad breath, and a cowboy shirt,
moving closer. "Besides, we don't play no rock songs. We got one
hundred percent country in that machine."

"I noticed. That's one of the reasons I am installing this." She
pushed her hair back and looked up at him. She poured on the smile,
hoping to dissuade him from getting a better look at the device.
"I'm done. I just need to screw the back on."

"So what kind of improvement is that, anyway?"

"Just like the song said, it's a bomb."

"No really, what is it? Let me see." He leaned around and peaked inside. His hand brushed across her shoulder. "Is it that black box? Why's it got a little antenna?"

"So I can detonate it remotely."

His eyes narrowed.

She had played him a little too much and regretted it.

"I confess," she said, forming her hands prayerfully. "It's a wireless link so we can see what songs are most popular. And the company can process the playtime royalties faster, all by computer." She needed to change the subject. "My back is killing me."

She stood and waggled her shoulders and chest in slow motion. The moves released her back muscles and garnered his stare. To seal the deal, she bent over at the waist to put the back on the jukebox and pointed her bottom toward him, her tight jeans straining at their limits. "This should just about do it." She wiggled a little more, then stood and faced him. She tightened her grip on the screwdriver.

"You want me to plug it in? It won't be no trouble." He smiled a cute country-boy smile.

She returned the smile, and wondered if she'd have the pleasure of killing him now, or if he would die at lunch with the others. "That depends. What time do you get off work?"

"I'm stuck here 'til midnight."

"How about a break or something? Isn't anyone else working with you?"

"A couple waitresses should show up soon enough, and my cook's already gettin' after it, but I'm the only one behind the bar today. Without me, this place would be closed up tighter than a drum."

"That's a bigger disappointment than you know."

"You're kinda anxious aren't you, darlin'? There's an office in back. It's real private. The noon crowd won't show for another couple hours."

"I have two more repair calls to make this morning. I'll be back later. So you be sure not to leave early."

"No problem. What did you say your name was again? I'm usually pretty good with names, but I have trouble with foreign-sounding ones like yours."

"It's Faatina. Now you stay here while I'm gone, and I promise you'll remember it the rest of your life."

JAY COULDN'T DECIDE WHAT shocked him more; that Dad had stolen something, that he admitted it decades later, or his claim that what he took might save mankind's soul.

Whatever that meant.

Calling Dad back last night for an explanation had failed, and Dad didn't call back as promised from the airport, if that's where he had really been headed. *Guesses piled on clues added to mysteries.* It had to stop. With any luck, he'd get some straight answers this afternoon at 2:35 when a Tel Aviv to Houston Lufthansa flight landed. Even that was a guess, but the timing matched all of Dad's clues about landing on Friday before dinner, and it had connected in Frankfurt, which Jay supposed was the "hot dog" connection. Five and a half hours and no more riddles.

His own flight to Houston from Vegas had been bumpy, hot, and sleepless. As if driving from Mountain Time in Arizona to catch a Pacific Time Zone flight from Vegas to Houston's Central Time Zone hadn't confused his biological clock enough, the flight had touched down forty minutes late, at one a.m. Scaring up a cab at that hour willing to drive to White Oaks, a suburb sixty-five miles to the southwest, had been a chore. When he finally collapsed at Dad's, it was almost three a.m.

Refreshed for the first time since Wednesday morning, he was two minutes from the nearest supermarket. Dad's pantry was empty. The traffic light a half block ahead showed green. Jay sped up and turned right onto the suburb's main thoroughfare. He passed a church and thought about the Q document. It had been a strange month since its rumors began dominating the news and spawning TV specials about its emergence from a cave near Qumran.

His caves.

Jay wondered which cave had coughed it up. The caves that surrounded the one-time desert refuge of Qumran had served as a dusty, crumbling playground growing up. Some caves were little more than dark holes in rocky hillsides. Others were large enough to hide in. He pictured Princess, and wondered what she looked like today. Beautiful no doubt. His stomach felt hollow, and he checked his watch. Ten minutes to nine. He couldn't recall if it was set to Texas, Nevada, or Arizona time.

Arizona! "Doc, oh, Doc." He'd completely forgotten his breakfast with her.

Dad's dashboard clock read 8:50. That was 7:50 in Evergreen. He jerked Dad's SUV into a drugstore's empty lot and parked crossways over two spots. He rubbed his unshaven face, and then dialed Doc's landline.

"Hello?" Her voice sent shivers down his spine.

"Doc it's—"

He should have anticipated her hanging up. He redialed, unsure how he could convince her to answer and listen.

Her machine answered.

"Doc, I'm so sorry. Really sorry. More than I can say. I had two hours of sleep in forty-eight hours. My brain was mush. I had to leave town to meet my dad. Now that I've finally gotten some sleep . . . Doc, are you listening? Pick up if you are. Please forgive me. I don't know what else to say."

Was that a click at her end? "Doc?"

"Where are you?"

Relief washed over him. "Doc! I'm so glad you picked up."

"Wherever you are, you could have called." Doc's voice was cold and ten times more distant than the thirteen hundred miles separating them.

"I know, I know. I could have left a message. I *should* have left a message. I wasn't thinking, just reacting. My dad left a message with Marge. An urgent message. I had to clean up, pack, and leave. I never got to sleep until late last night. The next thing I knew, it was after six on Friday."

"Way after six. I waited until, well, I waited a *long* time." She exhaled hard into the phone. "Where are you?"

The relief that flooded his mind seconds ago changed to dread. If he gave it to her straight, it might endanger Dad. Even saying that he couldn't speak about it might alert listening ears. The fact he doubted there were any didn't change things.

"It's not a trick question." Her cold voice had turned icy.

He stared into the parking lot, tapping the steering wheel. Dad wasn't the paranoid type. He would have called from pay phones and spoken openly unless he suspected both of their phones were tapped. Jay swallowed hard.

"Like I said, I'm meeting my Dad. All I really want to do is come home and make things right."

"I can't believe you're lying to me. I called your office when you didn't show. Marge told me you're meeting your dad in Detroit, but not until tomorrow. Tomorrow, Jay!" Her voice increased an octave. "You told her you had personal business today. I guess I'm not it." Her tone had lost its edge and given way to despair. "I'm going to hang up."

"Wait. You're right. You're not my personal *business*. You're not any kind of business. You're more than that. And, no matter how it looks, I'm not lying to you."

"So why didn't you call? In case you can't tell, I'm very upset."

"You have every right to be. I was sleep deprived, beyond tired, and anxious about meeting Dad. I fell asleep without setting an alarm. But the bottom line is I forgot." The admission made him feel a little less like a heel. "All I can ask is that you forgive me."

"It's not about forgiveness. I thought you were different. Don't call me for a while. I need time to think. I'm tired too." The chill in Doc's voice returned.

"Thanks for picking up the phone and letting me explain. I feel awful. I hope you'll give me another chance. I still owe you a burrito."

"I can make my own."

Jay closed his phone and rested his forehead on his fingertips. A lawn crew had parked, and began firing up their mowers and weed whackers. He started the car and left.

He turned on the radio and caught a male announcer in mid-sentence.

> *"... as Congress debates the most ambitious gun control law ever proposed resulting from the Q document revelations and aftermath. The bill's co-sponsor Illinois House member Bill Stallings met with the press today on the Capital's steps. Here's what he told the gathering."*
>
> *"This temporary collection, and let me emphasize the word temporary here, this temporary, ah, measure is absolutely necessary in the wake of recent increases*

*in crime. Guns kill. We know that. This bill will remove
the criminals' ability to visit their crimes on society by
leveling the playing field during these highly uncertain
times. Thank you."*

*"Later, XBC's correspondent Jenifer Jones caught
up with Texas Representative Floyd Pattson from
Waxahachie. Representative Pattson is leading the fight
to defeat this bill. Jones asked for his reaction."*

*"Miss, times are uncertain, but confiscating every
gun in America is impractical, and it'll be about as
temporary as the income tax. This law will not level the
playing field, it'll tip it in favor of all the horse thieves
out there. It is precisely times like these that honest
American citizens are entitled to protect their lives, loved
ones, and property."*

"A vote on the bill is expected late next week."

Jay pulled into a Kroger's grocery store parking lot, which
was a third full. A gray Chevy pickup sped the wrong way up the
parking aisle that Jay was about to pull down. He squeezed right
and waited for an old, blue-haired lady driving the truck to pass.
He turned as she swept by, curious to see if her truck's tailgate bore
a red decal—the latest Q-inspired mania. Sure enough. A red Q,
similar to a circle with a line through it, was pasted over a Christian
fish symbol.

Ahead, a BMW's alarm system bleated. Its driver's side
window had been bashed in. Jay scanned the area, but whoever did
it was gone. A woman in the next row walked along unperturbed.
Up ahead, an SUV backed out of its parking spot near the store's
entrance, and he grabbed it.

Once inside, he added fruit, soymilk, and English muffins to his cart in quick order. He was in the cereal aisle when an attractive Lebanese or Palestinian woman skittered up it in jeans and a tight black long sleeve shirt. Her cart contained bread and a huge leopard-skin purse. As she drew closer, she stared through large dark eyes, open excessively wide. A thin scar ran across her right cheek. The woman was fetching, but unsettling—like her purse. With her last steps, she averted her stare.

Steaks were next. Dad loved a good strip streak, which meant bone-in and exactly an inch and a half thick. Jay walked to the meat counter in the store's back corner. Tony the meat guy was nowhere in sight. Jay dinged a little bell.

After nobody showed, Jay walked twenty feet to an aisle that led to the front of the store and looked for a clerk. The Arab lady's cart with the leopard skin purse stood unattended, parked in the aisle halfway to the store's front. A trusting lady, he thought. Jay heard a bang behind the meat counter. He waltzed around the counter and into the walk-in freezer.

"Tony? You goofin' off in here?"

The door slammed shut as the sound of an explosion rocked his eardrums. The side of the freezer collapsed, raining meats and shelves down on him.

THE SELF-APPOINTED JUDGE WATCHED the prisoner, a woman named Brustler. She shook her head free of the crimson head scarves as they were removed from her eyes.

Brustler lurched forward, screaming, "What judge wears a hood? Unless . . . you're that sheikh. Why else would you be wearing black hoods? This is Jerusalem. There's no Sharia law here. You're not a judge!" She ran two steps before the two female guards pummeled her back and arms with their batons. Brustler buckled

THE Q MANIFESTO | 61

onto her knees, moaning and weeping. Ammar, the night's honorary witness, helped the guards pull her upright.

The judge spoke in an unhurried monotone, weary of impersonating a Muslim judge, but hopeful the deception might yet prove fruitful. "I am the Black Sheik, and I am *your* judge. I will allow you to speak your defense, but you must remain orderly. If not, your judgment will be twice as harsh. Do you understand?"

The prisoner nodded. Glad that Brustler had finally held her tongue, the thought presented an intriguing idea. Isis, mother of the new faith, desired front-page notoriety. Pleasing her was a top priority. Tonight the Black Sheikh would deliver as promised.

"The Prevention of Vice and Promotion of Virtue officials caught you running scantily dressed through a Muslim park this morning. It is against our law. Do you admit this?"

"But I'm not a Muslim. I'm a runner—a Christian runner. I didn't know you had parks here. I'm sorry. I'm just a tourist."

"Ignorance is no excuse, and Christianity is no defense. Your Christ was a fake, a figment of a sick Jew's imagination. The Q document has proven he was not a Christ. What we do, we do for you."

"You're right, absolutely right. He was faked. I'll convert, repent, whatever you want."

"That is a worthy choice, but it has no bearing on your crime. A crime for which you must be punished."

"You have no right—" A swift blow from each guard silenced her.

"You shall not shout again." The judge nodded to Ammar, who gagged the criminal with a scarf. "Your ten lashes shall be doubled. As to your outbursts, be filled with the joy from above that you have already proclaimed your decision to travel the righteous path. You will soon *hold* your tongue."

Brustler wailed unintelligibly into the deserted night.

"Silence. Take your medicine like a man!" The judge shouted the words, unable to stop them. The impossible command the judge had sworn as a child never to repeat, the identical cadence, emphasis, and derision. The room spun out of control.

CHAPTER 6

A WARM HAND PRESSED on Jay's neck. He couldn't tell if he was awake or dreaming.

"This side of beef has a pulse. I need some help."

The voice and the warm hand belonged to a woman. She spoke from behind a surgical mask, and knelt beside him in mustard yellow clothes. They looked like rubber. A bar with half a dozen tiny LEDs strapped to her helmet splayed light wherever her head pointed. Why was she wearing a helmet? Snowflakes floated in the air. Wrecked shelves surrounded them. *No, not snow. Ashes.* Was she a firefighter? Had he been in a fire?

He tried to sit up.

Pain rocketed through his body, coming from his left thigh. He collapsed back to the cold floor. His legs refused to cooperate. Her light moved down his body. Shelves and raw meat covered his legs, pinning them in place. Blood covered his left pant leg. He looked back at her.

"You're waking up. That's good. Let me get a better look at that." She was on his right and leaned across him. "Ooh."

"My leg hurts."

"Yeah, I see why. I need you to lay still." Her light swung back to his face, blinding him.

He brought a hand up to shield his eyes. "What did you see?"

She lifted her chin, redirecting the beams. "Sorry about the lights" She twisted her head toward a two-way radio mounted on her coveralls just below her shoulder. "Come on, guys. I need you both in the store's meat locker. Bring a stretcher and those new wire cutters. Southwest corner. That's back left, Rodney. And bring the oxygen."

The radio crackled. "We're on our way, Lieutenant."

She refocused on Jay. Her face was round with deep-set brown eyes. Short dark hair peeked from under her helmet. "I don't know how you got in here, but you're going to be fine. Besides your leg, how do you feel?"

"My head. It hurts." He coughed. The pain in his leg exploded again. A deep breath produced a wheezing sound. Why was everything so hazy? "What happened?"

"Try not to move. There was an explosion. We're trying to figure out why. Do you know where you are?"

He coughed again. His leg felt like a torch lit it up. The base of his skull hurt like mad. He remembered driving, talking to Doc. Steaks. "Yeah, I remember. Food shopping."

"Do you know where you are?"

"Kroger. In the freezer. I was looking for Tony. Is he okay?"

"I don't know. You're the only one in here. I'm Lieutenant Garcia. What's your name?"

"Jay. Hunt." The room started spinning. It twisted his stomach. Focusing on the nearest shelf slowed the motion. It stopped. His head pounded and his pulse throbbed in his leg. "Why can't I move?"

Two more firefighters arrived, carrying a stretcher with an

oxygen tank on it. Debris forced them to park it just outside the freezer. Something looked odd. What was it? The small room danced with three sets of LEDs bobbing and weaving as they cleared a path to him. The answer dawned. The freezer's ceiling and side wall were missing. A pile of twisted metal lay past the opening. An air duct hung diagonally from overhead to the floor.

The lieutenant looked at the man carrying the oxygen tank and a mask. "Set that up on his left and give him some air." She turned her head. "Mr. Hunt, I'd like you to breathe through the mask for a minute or two, okay? A couple good breaths, then nice and easy."

Jay did as she asked. The air was warm. He watched as she motioned to the other man. He carried a pair of wire cutters over a foot long. They looked like hedge shears.

He stood above Lieutenant Garcia. "What should I cut?"

The lieutenant looked at Jay. "Mr. Hunt, you still with us?"

Jay nodded. He took a deep breath.

"Okay, I need you to relax. Before we lift these racks off your legs, we have to cut you free. That hunk of cow near your left leg came down with a big old meat hook in it. It's like a double-pronged fish hook. One hook is in the cow. One hook is in you. I'm going to let a doctor remove it 'cause the end's barbed. We're just going to snip it off so we can get you home."

Somehow he didn't think she really meant home.

"There's not much blood, so I don't think it perfed any major blood vessels. It might sting a little, though, so Rodney and I are going to hold you to the floor while Pete does the honors. Try not to move."

She leaned on his right side and nodded at her cohorts to start.

THE TWO POLICEMEN POSTED outside Jay's private hospital

room checked the doctor's badge before granting him entry. He looked to be mid-thirties and drifted into the room, shaking his head and flipping through the pages of a brown folder. The doctor had disheveled black hair and an oblong face that accentuated his perpetual smile.

"Mr. Hunt, before all this Q business started a few weeks ago, I'd have said it's a miracle you're alive." He continued reading, clucking on occasion.

Jay squirmed in the hard-backed chair, which he had repositioned to expand his sightlines down the corridor. If he was ever going see Doc again or assist Dad, it dictated minimizing risks, even though the threat level was hard to assess. Two other bombs had detonated around the country. That muted his personal alert system, but it didn't fully silence it.

The doctor closed the folder. "Yes sir, you're one lucky son of a gun."

"Oh?" Jay fumbled with strapping on his watch. "I don't feel all that lucky. Even my fingers hurt." It was half past one. The feds had peppered him with questions all morning.

"For the next few days you'll feel sore in muscles you didn't know you had. How's the head? Any vision problems?"

"Depends, which one of you is asking?"

The doctor harrumphed. "You may have suffered a slight concussion, but your cranial CT scan shows absolutely nothing." The doctor paused. His smirk ruined his deadpan delivery.

"Are you waiting for the bot-a-boom drum sound?"

"Most people don't get my jokes. It shows you're doing fine."

"Maybe it shows my sense of humor was injured along with everything else."

"That wouldn't show up on a scan. Neither would a stiff neck, but yours will probably be sore for a while. With head trauma, the body unconsciously restricts head movement to protect the meninges, which strains the neck muscles. So expect it. Let's look at the big stuff." He flipped through several charts. "Somehow, it missed everything that would concern me. Ultrasound shows good circulation above and below the wound. There's no nerve damage and x-rays show the bone is fine. I've prescribed hydrocodone for the pain and ampicillin, an antibiotic. My assistant will fill you in on dosing and keeping the wound clean. That'll be important."

"Fine. How about some Advil too?" Jay planned to stockpile the hydrocodone. The meds would just louse up his thinking and reaction time, which he'd need to meet Dad at the airport by 2:35.

"I'll have a nurse get you some, but the local anesthesia in your thigh hasn't completely worn off. When it does, you'll want more than ibuprofen. The best thing for now is to stay off the leg for twenty-four hours, then take it easy getting around. In three to four days, run a marathon if it feels okay."

"Yeah, sure."

"I'd like to see you again in a week. Will you still be in town?"

Jay shook his head. "I doubt it."

"Do you have a surgeon or doctor back home to check on you?"

"Yeah, the best. But I'm not sure I want her near me with a scalpel at the moment."

The doctor scrunched his face. "Well, if you want your records transferred, let me know. Assuming the FBI doesn't take them." He tapped the folder. "One more thing. When you celebrate tonight, whether you take the IBs or especially the prescrips, skip the alcohol."

"I usually do, but celebrating isn't part of my plan. Not when so many others died today."

The doctor's face drooped. "They're saying eighteen died here. The toll for all three bombings is up to sixty-four. Of course, there won't be a final tally for a while. There's a lot of gruesome work to be done, matching pieces parts."

"That puts things in perspective, doesn't it?" Jay stood to test his leg. It wasn't too bad leaning on the cane.

"Thank God the bombings have stopped."

"What do you mean? I was in tests and interrogations all morning. I only heard about two additional bombs. What did I miss?"

"The bombs didn't all go off at once. There was a pattern. Ours went off at 9:10, then the bomb in California detonated exactly one hour later. The one in North Carolina was one hour after that." The doctor spaced out for a few seconds. "My little girl is four. The bomb in LA was at a daycare. How sick is that? People around here, me included, don't know if we should pray or not. Or to whom. You know what I mean?"

Jay scratched his stubbly cheeks. The doctor summed it up well. There was too much confusion. On too many fronts. "Has anything been reported on the hourly pattern?"

"No. They think it was just to make people crazy with fear."

Jay checked his watch. "It's 1:20. If they had kept the hourly pace, there would have been two additional bombings by now."

"So far, you're the only survivor. I think that's why the FBI and everyone else with initials on their backs were so interested in what you could remember. They quizzed me about your head injury. How reliable your memories were, whether you'd remember more later, that kind of thing."

The ATF, ATTF, CT-goons, and FBI had all asked their questions individually. Jay wondered if they shared his answers or hoarded them to gain a departmental edge. Whichever it was, Jay had relayed everything he recalled, including the leopard-skin-purse lady.

"I didn't have much to tell them."

The doctor arched his eyebrows. "They said you're a hero."

"Holing up in a freezer by accident isn't very heroic."

"You must have told them something good. The FBI team was pretty excited after talking to you. The news reported a solid lead in the Texas bombing, and they keep showing you getting rolled out of the grocery store. The press has mobbed the hospital. We can hardly get an ambulance in or out. It's ridiculous."

"Have they identified me yet?"

"No, and the FBI wants to keep it that way. We're all under orders. Notice your chart? You're John Doe. In fact, the FBI wants to get you out of here as soon as we're finished." The doctor closed the folder. "I'm done. Do you have any questions?"

"Plenty, but I don't think you're the guy to answer them."

THREE OFFICIAL-LOOKING FBI TYPES and two uniformed cops ushered Jay, dressed in doctor's greens, out a back service entrance and into a black Chevrolet Suburban. Jay had resisted wearing the pitiful disguise, suggesting most doctors don't receive a five-man escort home, but he lost the argument. The two White Oaks cops jumped into a police cruiser parked in front of the big Chevy and drove interference. The need for a lead blocker became clear after rounding the hospital's corner. Box trucks with roof-mounted satellite dishes crowded every available patch of cement. News crews roamed the parking area in packs.

"I need to go back to the Kroger to get my dad's car."

The head agent named Greene swung around in the passenger seat and faced Jay. His forehead had permanent worry lines that formed dark furrows across his light black skin. He was a tall man with short, wiry hair and the businesslike manner of an FBI veteran.

"Nothing anywhere near the Kroger is moving. It's all evidence until the onsite team clears it. Besides, based on where you said you parked, it's probably totaled. Where do you need to go? We can take you."

Jay considered whether he should tell them. As their best and maybe only witness, they'd probably follow him. "The airport. My dad's coming back today. I need to pick him up."

"You never mentioned that."

"I told you he was out of town. I guess I didn't think to mention when he was returning. Did you ask?"

"We'll have someone meet your dad."

"Great." *That'll impress Dad. He goes out of his way to keep a low profile, and I have the FBI give him a lift home.*

Greene grabbed a notepad from the dash and turned back, grinning. "There's something I guess I didn't think to tell you. We're going to be good friends the next few days. We'll be staying at a hotel for a while. The press will figure out your name soon enough, and when they do, your dad's street will look worse than the hospital's parking lot. So what's your dad's name and his flight info?"

This could be tricky. If Dad was flying incognito, he might not be using his legal name or his US passport. The FBI might not appreciate that he had a few spares. The Advil he had taken for his headache was failing fast. "He's David Hunt. Professor David Hunt. I'm pretty sure he's on Lufthansa 440, which might show as United 1457. It's scheduled to land at Bush at 2:35 out of Frankfurt."

As soon as Jay said, "Frankfurt," he regretted it. Jay could hear Bob Ambrose, a former fellow instructor at Camp Sandbox, saying, "Never volunteer information that isn't requested." It was time to start playing his A-game.

Greene looked at Reeko, the agent sitting next to Jay, who was built like a fireplug and smelled of garlic. "Jerry, make sure the dad boarded that flight, and have someone collect him if he did." Greene shifted his gaze back to Jay. "Your dad's been out of the country? What's he doing in Germany?"

You mean if he's not using an alias and flying home from terrorist central in Damascus? "It's a connecting flight. You know, before my dad's house gets mobbed by reporters, we should get my gear. Which hotel are we staying at?"

CHAPTER 7

"I EXPECTED EXCITEMENT. THIS is boring. When do I get to shoot somebody?" Jacob asked.

Sarah Bauman continued peering through her night vision binoculars. She visualized Jacob's sulk, which she assumed accompanied his childish question. The beefy young soldier in the driver's seat had just begun his mandatory service in the Israel Defense Forces and had been assigned to the National Police. He was all hers.

"Button it, soldier. If you're not up to the job, I'll find someone who is."

Their target stood in his front doorway, a half a block away from their car. Reuven Glassman's frame was powerful and rugged like Jacob, but with thirty more years under his belt. Or in Glassman's case, over his belt.

Glassman looked up and down the street like he owned it, which in a way he did. The Rechavia section of Jerusalem was a gardened enclave of the upper middle class that harbored its residents behind ageless stone walls. Jerusalem was so much more than the battleground of three defiant religions. God and humankind intersected here, and if anything, that should be celebrated. Instead it led to violence. Glassman epitomized it, ruling a branch of the Jewish mafia with a flair for bloodshed far bolder than the organized crime leaders he had replaced. He had started as a simple arms merchant who made his mark brokering the newest, most lethal weapons. Then he began using his weapons to eliminate competition. Now he had his fingers in half of the Middle East's arms deals.

"You should have listened more closely to your IDF trainers. They tell you this isn't a glamorous job." How Jacob had ever gotten detailed to her with zero experience was a mystery. "You watch too many American films. Don't believe them. This is as exciting as it gets for months on end. Then one day, wham! You'll probably pee your pants the first time it gets exciting."

"Don't bet on it. Then again, maybe we should. I bet fifty shekels you wet yourself tonight." Jacob laughed and slapped the dashboard. "Maybe you'll do more than that."

This one irritated her more than most of her other twenty-something assignments. Her job was to mentor them for a few months and teach them to be useful. She had tried by-the-book discipline with Jacob, and he hadn't responded.

She lowered the binoculars and forced a smile. "I've already seen my first bit of excitement, and my second, and more. You never get completely used to it. It's why we train. Your whole body reacts. The key is to harness the adrenaline. Make it work for you."

"I'll harness my AR-15, thank you."

"All the weapons stockpiled in our trunk will do you little good unless you control your mind and body. Firepower alone isn't enough. The mafia has more sophisticated armament than most terrorists. They rival a small army, but their greed will defeat them."

Jacob shook his head. "If it's just about greed, why would

Glassman sponsor the Black Sheikh? What's Glassman gain by supporting some clown that puts black hoods with white crosses on his dead victims?"

Sarah squeezed the binoculars till her hands hurt. "Arms merchants thrive in fear and chaos. The Black Sheikh provides that, especially after mutilating that poor Brustler woman. Before her, his victims were whipped or beaten. Now he kills and the hood is his signature."

"So do you think Glassman's involved?"

"The brass does, but it doesn't compute. One, Glassman could generate more chaos having TBS kill Jews, not Christians. Two, TBS has become a pariah among his own people, but he fancies himself an Islamic superhero. To him, Glassman is lower than an infidel. He's an Israeli occupier, and his only God is money. I don't see those two sleeping together. TBS is probably getting assistance, but I doubt it's from Glassman." Sarah shrugged. "Either way, it's our job to stop them both."

"Nothing scares you, does it? Not the Black Sheikh, Black September, or even Glassman. I heard when you were young the mafia tried to bribe you. You not only refused, you decked the lawyer who made the offer."

Sarah ignored his age slur and studied the boy-man next to her. Few people knew that story, and fewer still knew the mafia's delivery boy was a lawyer. She reacquired Glassman through the binoculars and one-handed the car's radio microphone. "This is Venus. Spiderman is on the move. White shirt and dark pants. He's getting into his Jaguar. Maroon model XK. He's alone. No driver."

Sarah squinted as her night vision optics lit up from the Jaguar XK's interior lights.

"The chief named him Spiderman, and you say I've seen too many American movies."

Her laughter shook the greened-out image, which calmed down after Glassman closed his car door. "Where's he going without his bodyguards? Usually when he drives alone, he takes the Maserati. Tonight, it's his lowly Jag."

"We should follow him instead of always passing him off. If we're never going to follow him, why are we sitting in this stuffy Skoda Superb? It's a dumb name and a miserable excuse for a car, but as long as we're in it, we should use it. It's unmarked."

"Others will pick him up, you know that. And this car—it's a lot nicer than mine. Why are you so belligerent tonight?"

"I'm not belligerent. I'm bored. This is all we've done for two weeks. Is this all you've done for twenty years? Sit in a car and watch?"

"Let me tell you something, and you better remember it. Your partner deserves your respect, whether he or she is your superior or not, and whether it is in a vehicle or on a raging battlefield. They don't owe you a justification for their choices in life. Change your attitude, or you're history." Sarah slowed her breathing. She had refused numerous promotions to stay in the field. If anything scared her, it was the prospect that her next assignment would be sitting behind a desk.

Glassman backed into the street, his car pointed away.

Sarah spoke into the radio. "Spidey is heading south, away from us. Repeat, he is heading south. Venus out."

Jacob tapped his fingertips on the steering wheel.

The radio crackled. "Venus, this is Mercury. Mars is not responding. Pursue Spiderman. Repeat, pursue target. Get your backsides moving."

Jacob started the engine. "Now we're talking."

"Okay, do it just like in training. Don't get too close."

They passed Mars's empty Kia at a decent clip. *Avi, where are you?* Avi, code-named Mars, would never leave his post without alerting someone. Sarah raised the radio's microphone flooded with concern. "Mercury this is Venus. Any luck raising Mars? I spotted the Kia. It looked unoccupied."

"Negative. No word from Mars. We'll send a car. You stay on Spiderman."

Sarah forced her mind back to Glassman. After ascending a rise in the road at the end of the block, she expected to see Glassman's sleek maroon Jaguar XK. Nothing. Minimal traffic blocked her view ahead, and none of the taillights matched the sideways teardrop of the XK.

"Drive straight and look left down the side streets. I'll search the right."

She dragged her front teeth over her lower lip as they covered the next three blocks.

Jacob let out an emphatic, "Yes! I got him. He's a block up and just turned right." Jacob slowed the car. "I don't want to crowd him."

The rookie showed flashes of competence. "Good work. I never saw him."

Thirty seconds later they turned where Jacob had seen Glassman turn. The Jag went straight. After a while, it turned left, then right again. They drove deeper into a ratty neighborhood of narrow roads. Only one other vehicle separated them from the mafia strongman. "We don't have much cover, and he might be stair-stepping us. After his next turn, turn off your lights. This is where it gets exciting."

Glassman made a left and Jacob complied as she radioed their position. Half a block later, the Jag turned right into what looked like an alley. Sarah zoomed in with their dashboard GPS. "Park on the street. This is a dead-end."

Jacob approached the alley with too much speed to pull over. "It goes through. I'm sure. We'll lose him if I park."

"Stop. Now." Her order boomed inside the Skoda's interior, but it was too late. They had turned the corner. Jacob idled the vehicle about twenty-five meters in. Her heart pounded.

The Jaguar sat another eighty meters away, gleaming under a single lamp illuminating a back entrance into who knew what. The GPS had been right. Just beyond the car, the graffiti covered wall of a three-story brick apartment building sealed the alley shut. She studied the Jag. There was no movement. She started breathing again. Glassman must have gone inside.

The lecture could wait, so she bit her tongue about his not following orders. "Back up quietly into the street, and do *not* park until we're a half-block away. I'll report in and—"

The alley lit up like day. A spotlight blinded her. She located it on the roof of the building to the right.

"Floor it. Get us out of here." She ripped her Glock from the glove box, inserted the magazine, and released the slide. The car wasn't moving. "Now! Move it."

Jacob turned off the engine and jumped out of the car jingling the keys. Leaving his driver's door wide open, he scurried toward the Jag.

What was he doing? "Jacob, no. Come back."

Behind her, the rumble of a powerful diesel engine and screeching brakes filled the alley. She twisted in her seat and looked back in time to see a garbage truck jerk to a stop across the mouth of the alley, blocking any easy exit. She quickly calculated that with no car keys the closed alley mattered less than the fact she and Jacob faced a well-coordinated trap. She swiveled back to the front where the real trouble was bound to come from. Through the spotlight's glare, she spotted Jacob ducking into a recessed doorway on the left. Was he trying to be a hero?

Something moved by the Jag.

Three men stepped out of the shadows. They spread out across the alley and leveled large caliber automatics at her. Jacob danced in the doorway, pointing to his crotch and then at her, laughing. The gunmen started walking toward her.

SOMETHING ABOUT DAD'S HOUSE looked odd.

Agent Todd Farnsleigh, who was the strong silent type and the afternoon's chauffeur, finished parking the Suburban in front of it on the tree-lined street. Reeko jumped out and gave the neighborhood a quick three-sixty. Greene was out of his seat with equal speed and appeared to study Dad's light cream stucco house. He helped Jay ease down to ground level.

The leg had stiffened up. Jay leaned on his cane. "Thanks. I can take it from here."

"As you wish."

Greene marched along a center walkway to the front door a step ahead of Jay. Overhead, the broad limbs of two live oak trees had formed a single canopy. Jay remembered when the trees were eight-foot-tall twigs.

"Nice place. What does your dad do?"

"He's retired." Jay retrieved the house key from his pants pocket.

The drapes were closed.

That's what was different. The house had a dozen windows on two stories that faced the street, and every drape and blind was shut.

"Agent Greene, the drapes in the formal living room are closed. They never are."

Greene palmed Jay's key and peered through one of two small

windows in the massive wood front door. He shifted to the second one. "I can't see much through this beveled glass." He unlocked the door and slid in sideways. Five seconds later, the agent backed out and drew a weapon from under his suit jacket.

Reeko and Farnsleigh flew up the walk.

"Mr. Hunt, how many other entrances?"

"One, it's at the back corner along the driveway. The garage is detached."

"Farnsleigh, get your eyes on the back door. Reeko, you're inside with me. Hunt, I want you in the vehicle, now. Unless your dad's a terrible housekeeper, we got a problem."

FARNSLEIGH CAME OUT OF the house with a long face and invited Jay inside, just as Jay finished leaving Doc a message to avoid her home, the hospital, and being alone. He assumed she would ignore his advice, but he also assumed it would put her on high alert. Two local police cruisers rolled up, and after proper introductions, they all walked inside. As soon as Jay stepped into the foyer, he sought out the nearest wall for support. Every seat back and cushion was slashed and gutted in the formal living room and great room.

The scene was repeated in every room. Two thoughts filled Jay's whirling mind. First, this was not a typical burglary. All the electronics were still in place, including the big screen projector, which was the size of a shoebox and easily transportable. It was worth twelve grand.

The second conclusion made little sense, but was just as obvious. Whoever ransacked the house had no worries they'd be interrupted. The burglars had been methodical, turning every room upside down. Even the lining of Jay's suitcase had been sliced open.

Somehow, they knew the homeowner was out of the country, and the visiting son would never return from the grocery store. Whether that occurred to Greene and company, Jay couldn't guess. But all question of coincidence vanished like a drop of rain in the desert.

Greene was holding court in the formal living room with the White Oaks police. They finished their hushed conversation, and the two local cops left the house.

Jay walked up to Greene. "Agent, there's a couple things you should know. I think the bomb at Kroger was targeted at me. It and this mess might both be about the Q document."

Agent Greene studied him. The furrows in his forehead looked deeper and darker than earlier. "You think three bombs were detonated across the country because of you? Why three? In case you happened to be in a supermarket, a day care center, or a bar? I don't get surprised by much anymore, but you just surprised me."

"I don't know about the other two bombs. Maybe all three had been planned from the get-go. Maybe the Kroger bomb was a last minute change of plans. How should I know? But if you're a mad bomber who's about to kill a bunch of people, why not use one of those bombs to take out an enemy that survived an earlier hit?"

"The Arizona thing? Three hours ago you didn't think that shooting had anything to do with you. Now you think you're a target of a terrorist group? Why? Who's after you?"

Jay shook his head. "I don't know, but I do know I've nearly been killed twice in two days, and my Dad was worried about his safety, and I think, mine. And it all—"

"You *think* he was worried?"

"Just send a couple extra agents to meet him, okay? If these people tried to kill me twice, there's no telling how badly they might want him dead. Look at his house."

"I think you're both—" Greene's phone rang. He answered it

with a brusque, "Greene here." The agent listened intently, nodding on occasion.

Dad's flight would land in less than half an hour. If the FBI wasn't going to protect Dad, then he had to. But how? It was an hour drive, and he had no wheels. Somehow, this time, he had to prove he could be depended on.

Greene ended his call and cleared his throat. "Mr. Hunt, your dad never boarded that flight. He didn't have a reservation, either."

Jay thought back. "In my last conversation with him, he mentioned he didn't have a confirmed seat. He liked being flexible."

"The flight out of Tel Aviv left with an open seat." The agent clenched a fist, then relaxed it. "There were two no-shows, a husband and wife from Bonn. An Israeli female flying standby got one of those two seats. What I'm saying, or trying to say is—"

"You're saying no one was left at the gate." Jay flexed his leg. He'd been standing too long. Greene was thorough. This was the moment to keep quiet or fess up that Dad could be using a different name. Whatever the consequences, Dad needed protection. "There's a chance my dad could be flying—"

Greene shook his head. "He never made it to the airport. I don't like telling you this, but we asked the Israeli National Police to track your father down. It didn't take them long. There's been an accident."

THE THREE MEN WITH automatics bombarded her with fire from the alley's far end. Sarah lunged across the car seat, bashing her head on the steering wheel. The deafening, rapid-fire attack in the enclosed alley pounded her eardrums. The car rocked and spit metal from the high-velocity impacts. Thuds and raining glass intensified the nightmare. For the moment, the engine's heft absorbed and deflected the fusillade. She had to get out of the car soon, but fought the urge to jump out and run. She'd be cut in half in seconds.

First things first.

Lying on her side, wedged between the center console and gearbox, she reached back and unlatched the passenger door. It remained closed, but ajar. Satisfied, she squirmed along the seat toward the open driver's door to access the light switch on the dash. Breaking glass pelted her face and arms. Keeping her head low, she strained with her left hand to find the switch on the far side of the steering column. Her right held a death grip on the Glock. Where was the switch? Time was running out. The hit squad had to be advancing.

She reached up and fired two shots through the glassless windshield. Between the noise and the lightshow, she wondered if her assailants even noticed.

Finally, her left index finger felt the switch. Which way was on? She twisted it counterclockwise. If the bulbs were intact, the headlamps should be on. The small victory boosted her confidence. One last job. She pulled the signaling stalk that engaged the high beams. Take that. *Sleazeballs!*

Sarah fired five more rounds through the windshield.

They noticed. The staccato of machine gun fire quieted for a heartbeat.

It was enough. She kicked open the passenger door.

The brutal firing started again. Dozens of rounds shredded the passenger door as she clambered out of the driver's side and scrambled to the vehicle's rear.

Crouching behind the car's bulk, she took out the rooftop spotlight with a single shot. Without its blinding glare, she could see again. The light from the far lamppost was dim, but sufficient. The assassins had advanced within fifty meters. They hugged the walls;

two right, one left. She shoved the pistol into her front waistband and popped the trunk's release. She thrust both hands into the dark cavity, unwilling to risk raising her head high enough to look inside. Bullets riddled the open lid. Where was it? She frisked the trunk's interior. It should be fastened in the center. It's had to be there. Everything depended on finding it.

Deeper. It must be deeper.

Sarah rose as much as she dared.

Got it! Her fingers grasped the welcome shape of the Colt AR-15. Working blind, her fingers tore at the Velcro straps that secured it. She yanked it out. A submachine gun ought to even the odds a little.

The noise and acrid smell of gunpowder was unbearable. Bullets zinged all around her.

If the men got much closer, she didn't stand a chance. How much time did she have? Every second mattered. The 20-round magazine would have to do. No time to hunt for extra mags. She dialed the weapon's safety to 3-round bursts.

The incoming spray had formed a pattern. Two men shot to the car's sides, while the third shot under the car. Moving behind the right wheel for extra cover, she shouldered the weapon, leaned out, and fired two bursts.

One man fell. The other two hesitated.

She switched the rifle's safety to full-auto and emptied the weapon in an arc, right to left. Dropping the spent gun, she ran head down for the garbage truck and drop-rolled between its giant wheels. The shooting resumed as she spun behind one of the truck's huge tires. She retrieved the Glock from her waistband, gulping breaths.

Singsong sirens and flashing blue lights lit the night. Two local police cars hurtled down the street and crunched to a stop behind the truck, short of the firing zone.

The shooting from the alley ceased.

Was it over? Sarah drew a deep breath. Her hands shook. She debated staying by the truck or running to the police cars.

She jammed the Glock into her waistband behind her. With her hands in the air, she ran for the first police car. Over the shouts of the policemen, she heard the unmistakable whoosh of an incoming RPG round.

CHAPTER 8

"SORRY FOR YOUR LOSS. I worked with your dad years ago. He was a good man."

Jay rubbed his forehead. The elderly man didn't look the least bit familiar. "Yes sir, he was. Thanks for coming. Dad would have appreciated your being here."

An old couple advanced, they were the last people in the line paying their respects. The wrinkled woman in a dark blue dress clung to her bald escort's left arm. Her perfume overpowered the floral bouquets that lined the large room's walls and surrounded Dad's casket.

The man reached out to shake Jay's hand. "I'm Johnson. I worked with your dad at the Rockefeller. Too bad I'm not a Rockefeller who worked with your dad at the Johnson, huh? Sorry for your loss. Such a shame—drivers here in Jerusalem are horrible." His eyes twinkled. "I remember when your dad packed you off to live in the desert with Nabeel's family and then to school in America. He put up a brave front, but it broke his heart." Johnson turned to his wife. "After Jay's mom died, he lived a year like a Bedouin. You were what, sixteen?"

"I was fourteen."

"Oh my."

"It was only five months, Mrs. Johnson." The smell of burning kerosene and camel dung seemed to fill the room. "The first few weeks in a village were tough, but I enjoyed every minute after that living under the stars, herding goats. I wish I could same the same about Fosters."

The wife's brow wrinkled.

"Fosters was the military school that Dad sent me to in Texas."

Johnson gave a belly laugh. "You were a handful, but I guess it paid off. Later on, this young man trained America's Special Forces to pummel our Arab enemies. Your Dad was one proud papa."

"I just showed them how to survive the desert. The pummeling they already knew."

"How long were you in the army?"

"Never was. My career was in finance, money management. I trained our forces between jobs."

"He was a good man, and I'll bet you are too. You take care of yourself."

The woman smiled and they wandered off.

Jay picked up his glass of water from a nearby table. He sipped it. Dad's long-ago sendoff at the airport filled his mind. The melancholy at losing sight of Dad. The joy of escaping Jerusalem and not having to visit Mom's grave. Somehow tomorrow at 10 a.m. he had to bury Dad next to her.

The glass of water trembled in his hand. He set it down.

A woman, standing against the wall, walked over. She was mid-thirties with a Cro-Magnon forehead and nose. Dates were probably few and far between. Tangled black hair scraped the top of her broad shoulders.

"I'm Sgt. Raczynska, Tel Aviv Police." Her voice was

impossibly deep. She stood between Jay and Dad's casket at the front of the room. She pulled back her green blazer, exposing a badge affixed to the top of her matching skirt. She handed him a business card.

He glanced at her card and pocketed it. "Do you have news on who did this?"

Her eyes took in her surroundings. "Your dad's case has been reassigned to me. I have some questions."

"I spent an hour this morning at your District Headquarters with Detective Shimon something. His last name escapes me. What is it?"

A slight smile flitted across her face. "Cohen."

"Yeah, that's it. He asked every conceivable question." All the cop knew was that Dad was found dead on a street corner in Tel Aviv—the victim of a hit-and-run. An accident. Maybe they were changing their minds. "Are you a homicide investigator?"

"No. We think the accident occurred while your father was waiting for a ride to the airport outside Tel Aviv in Lod."

"That's what Cohen said. After meeting with him, I visited the spot where my dad was killed. Cohen thought it was a truck. Did you measure the length of the skid marks to estimate its speed?"

The sergeant took a half-step back. "There were no . . . that is . . . the report didn't say anything about skid marks."

"That's because there weren't any. If it was an accident, don't you think there would be some indication that the driver swerved or broke at the last second?"

"The driver could have been drunk or asleep." Raczynska shrugged. "Shimon said you were convinced your father was murdered. You should give this murder thing a rest. Intentional or not, you'll never know what happened. Nine times out of ten, these hit-and-run cases are never solved. They—"

"Watch me." Jay leaned into her face. "He asked for my help before he died, and I was slow to react. Well, now I'm reacting. He was murdered and I *will* find who did it. Then I'll find out why, and finish what he started. And don't call him a 'case' again."

The sergeant eased back, biting the inside of her cheek. "You should leave this to us."

"Who? You and your cop buddies? Why should I leave it to you? Even you doubt that you'll find who did it."

"I was being honest about our chances. I'd like to know where you're staying."

"And I'd like to know where my Dad's clothing and possessions are. Like I told Cohen, I suspect my Dad had more cash on him than what was found in his money belt."

She dug around in her fake leather handbag and handed over a small pad of paper and a pen. Both were marked Jerusalem's Ambassador Hotel in Hebrew and English. "Please jot down your cell phone number too, Mr. Hunt."

"I already gave it to Shimon. You two should talk." Jay started scribbling the number. "Your pen is almost out of ink. I checked in at a Hilton in Tel Aviv. It's by the beach."

She retrieved the paper. "Keep the pen. Your father stayed at the Ambassador while he was here. I spoke with their management. The deceased checked out Thursday morning—the day of his accident. He spent most of that day in Jordan. Do you have any idea why he'd go there?"

Jay's heart rate zoomed. "No, I don't, but it was probably Q related. I told Cohen that I believe my Dad was here to investigate it. Cohen didn't seem to care. Do you?"

"The Q document doesn't mean much here. It's just another old piece of paper from the desert. To be honest, I never could understand how so many people today can believe Jesus was the

Jewish Messiah, but how few Jews back then thought so."

"I wasn't aware that any first century polls had been taken on the subject. Still, all I know is Jesus' impact on civilization is off the charts. I'll rephrase my question. Don't you care that a man investigating a world-altering manuscript died on your turf?"

She scratched her cheek. "I have to deal with the facts of the case, and at the moment, there aren't any."

"So why are you here? You haven't been to the crime scene."

"It's been three days since the accident. Any evidence at the site has been seriously compromised."

"We both have our excuses, don't we?" Jay inhaled a deep breath. The strong smell flowers trapped him. He never wanted to smell this many flowers again. He wanted to be anywhere but here. Home would be good. Home with Doc would be even better. Assuming she was talking. Contacting her during yesterday's layover in Newark had proved futile. Time was becoming a problem. His gut told him if he didn't get through to Doc soon, he never would.

Time was a problem here too, and what little he had was being wasted by this Tel Aviv cop. "Ma'am, I spent most of two days flying here with very little sleep. I'm pretty sure this is Sunday. I've lost track. Are we done?"

"Almost. See, the thing is, your father traveled to Jordan on a German passport under the name Huntzinger. How many passports did your father have?"

"Apparently two. My dad was born in Germany and moved to America as a kid. His father shortened the family name from Huntzinger. Immigrants used to try to fit in."

Raczynska nodded. "Yeah, they even learned English. Now the whole world speaks English except US immigrants. I know. I grew up in Jersey. Moved here eight years ago. My grandparents were

Polish Jews." She sucked on the inside of her cheek. "So did your father have any other aliases?"

"Aliases? I have a better question. Why was he found with his shoes and shirt off and lying a few feet away, near his coat?"

"The force of the truck could have dislodged his shoes and someone may have thought to steal his clothes, then changed their mind. They were . . . bloody. It happens."

"And they left his wallet?"

"Maybe someone came along. Scared the thief off. "

"You mean like a witness? Someone you could badger instead of me and solve his murder?" Jay's chest ached. He was hungry having skipped dinner, and his throat was parched. He reached for the water glass.

"Are you Pink Hummer Tours?"

He decided against a smart-aleck remark. "It's my company, yes."

"Your father called your office last Wednesday, about midnight, just hours before he left for Jordan. He must have considered it important to speak with you."

"Back to Jordan, are we? I imagine he was being thoughtful."

She tugged at her jacket's hem. "What do you mean?"

"Time zones. Midnight here is 3 p.m. in Arizona. A more convenient time for him might have been in the middle of my night. Don't you ever call New Jersey?"

Her face twitched. "According to his cell phone records, that was his last call and he spoke to you for seven minutes. It seems likely during all that time he'd have mentioned his plans. Did he say anything about it?"

Jay racked his tired brain. Dad's last call was on Thursday. It woke him at the highway rest area. It was probably an hour before his death. Why didn't she know about that call?

"I was out of the office. He left a message with my assistant."

"It must have been a long message. What was it?"

How could the details of the strange message help her? They were nearly meaningless to him. Jay wondered if Dad suspected the police were listening to his calls, but then they'd know Marge had answered that call. His head ached. *Don't lie. Don't volunteer information.*

"He gave my assistant his flight information and wanted me to call him. She was probably bored and chatted him up."

"What did he say that made you think he was investigating the Q document?"

Jay gazed over her shoulder at the casket. The reason Dad couldn't leave it alone came into focus. "It's what he did. He spent his life studying old scraps of paper, and this one disproved everything he believed. He had to do it."

"Did he uncover any information that might prove helpful to the authorities?"

"None that he shared with my assistant."

"You didn't return his call for nearly twenty-four hours, and when you finally did, you left a very short message. Why did you wait? Were you angry at your father?"

"What? This is crazy. How can you know so much about his phone calls and my business, but you don't know squat about how he died?"

The detective stared steel-eyed. "Bottom line, I gotta tell you, I wonder why an American, who's not a Jew, wants to be buried here."

Jay returned her stare. His eyes stung from the long flights and more tears than he would have expected. "The earth may not be the center of the universe, but Dad believed Jerusalem was. Now it's about to swallow him up." His voice had risen well beyond funeral parlor etiquette. "Somebody was driving the truck that killed him. When are you going to find out who it was?"

People gawked. Raczynska swallowed hard.

"What are you afraid of? That his remains will self-detonate? Dad received pre-approval to be buried in Jerusalem thirty years ago. He spent a lifetime in your desert and had more friends here than at home. Look around." Jay's heart thumped at racecar speed. "And like I told Cohen, my Mom's buried here."

"I should be delicate about that I suppose, but it only raises the same question about her. You see?"

"In case you haven't noticed, there are more than just Jews that live here. And *not* to be delicate about it, it's not his fault that none of you play nice together. Still he, or apparently they, wanted to be buried here because he believed Jerusalem will survive Armageddon. Megiddo—the end of the world—it's a Jewish valley, but it's also a Christian thing. Or at least it was before the Q document. He wanted to be first in line to fight Satan's army. Got it?"

"It always comes back to religion, doesn't it? I have to warn you not to investigate this on your own. It could have serious repercussions."

"Repercussions? You want to see serious repercussions?" Jay stepped within a foot of her heaving chest. He grasped her wrist. "Come on," he whispered. "Everyone's watching."

She yanked her hand free of his and followed. Ten feet from the casket, she stopped. "I get your point."

"Do you? I think you're too far away. Do you see his eyes? They came here wide open, looking for the truth. Now they're closed. *That* is a repercussion. He didn't find that truth, but I will."

She squinted a laser shot of animosity at him.

Jay pulled her hand again. The detective took two halting steps and froze. Was she shaking? Jay stared at his father's lifeless body; the pale skin wrinkled and made-up.

"See his hand?" Jay reached in and touched it. "It's cold. It used to be hot, and it held mine crossing streets. His arms? They used to hug me. Me! He hugged me, Sergeant Raczynska. But not anymore. I heard tonight that he cried when he sent me away to school."

Jay felt his own eyes welling up. He could barely swallow. "Now who do you think should look for his killer?"

THE SIGHT OF HER car a few meters ahead surprised Rachel. She had no recollection of leaving the funeral home, walking along Shalom Street, or turning onto the quiet side street a block later where she had parked. Her keys slipped through her icy fingers as she worked the door's lock. Once opened, she fell into the seat and slammed the car door shut. A solitary streetlight shone through the dirt-streaked windshield.

The untraceable phone vibrated in her jacket.

She jumped, then squeezed the phone out of its concealed pocket located about where her surgery-impaired left breast should have developed. Knowing only Isis would call this phone, Rachel skipped the preliminaries. "I just left him."

"You're behind schedule. I was worried about you."

"It took longer than I expected."

"Did you sense anything?"

Rachel stared at the streetlight. "Nothing to change your plan. If he knows anything specific, he isn't trusting anyone with it. It'll die with him."

"Be careful. He has already proven to be more difficult than expected. Why are you out of breath?"

Rachel exhaled sharply. "The phone jarred my thoughts."

"You've had a busy day. Tell me about the exchange. Is it done?"

"The critical phase is complete. It made it over the border in the middle of Friday's window."

"That's ancient history. Did you receive our delivery today or not?"

Rachel caught herself fidgeting with her lower lip. "No. We were there to make the pickup, but the other end refused, saying their boss was unavailable."

"That's an unfortunate complication. You're the only person privy to this aspect of my plan. Don't make me regret your recent promotion."

Rachel's stomach jumped. "You won't." The others on the team were nothing more than terrorists—soldiers, she corrected herself—and they thought of Isis merely as their general. She was much, much more. Soon, she would be hailed as the mother of their revitalized faith. Isis was a better mother than her biological mother could ever have hoped to be. "I won't let you down. It's just that I've never liked working with that criminal Glassman, and now that he's missing, his organization is a bit gun-shy."

"Dealing with the devil is never the first choice. Remind his lieutenants that *they* will be paid handsomely for their services." Isis paused. "Now tell me about your plan for the Black Sheikh's assistant. After botching Professor Hunt's kidnapping, Ammar owes me. If he had been successful, we could be interrogating an old, broken man—not disposing of a suspicious desert rat."

Rachel's hands trembled. The old man had tripped. There had been no chance to steer around him. If only she had blamed circumstances or a bystander. Isis had never terminated anyone for failure. How had it come to this?

"Your silence tells me that you think Ammar should be spared.

He missed grabbing the professor in Amman and lost him in Aqaba. Then he ruined your tracking him from Eilat and ingenious intercept of the Tel Aviv taxi. Tell me why Ammar should live."

"Those disappointments were due to the old man's skills, not Ammar's incompetence. There's no evidence that the professor knew anything that could stop us. His frantic travels suggest he didn't. In the end, we'd have had to eliminate him anyway."

"His fate was sealed, it's true. But he'd have talked. I have no doubt in your skills. We would know precisely what knowledge he possessed, and with whom he shared it."

Rachel leaned her head back against the seat's headrest. Although Jay Hunt overlooked her disfigurements, Ammar was the only man who saw beyond them. There might never be another. "I'm to blame. It's my fault. I should never have assigned Ammar to such a critical job. Make me pay."

The phone was silent an eternity. "No." Isis's tone was cold. "Never trust a man to do a woman's job. Use him to help you tonight. Forget about making the son's death look like an accident. Let me know the minute it's arranged. I'm sorry to change things on you last minute, but you're so inventive. Have the son's murder point to Ammar, and make certain Ammar can't point back. You know I hate to mention such an indelicacy, but from behind, Ammar reminds me of your father."

CHAPTER 9

THE HILTON OCCUPIED A generous portion of land in the midst of Tel Aviv's Independence Park, which was little more than a dozen acres of salt-stunted trees. But these precious acres sat on a sandy knoll that jutted out into the mercurial blue waters of the Mediterranean. Except tonight, the sea was a dark wind-whipped hammer, battering a line of modest offshore breakwaters. Jay closed his room's drapes. He slung a single-strap daypack over his shoulder, and hung the "Do not disturb" sign outside his door as he left.

The elevator whisked him from the fifteenth floor to the main level in seconds. He traversed the lobby, searching for interested eyes that might be following him. Seeing none, he stopped at the front desk and waited for a lithe strawberry blonde to complete an entry in her computer. Her fingers danced over the keyboard.

She looked up with a toothy smile.

"My name is Hunt. Do you have a package for me?"

"Oh, yes sir. Your embassy delivered it a couple of hours ago. It's in the back. I'll get it for you." She disappeared stage left with the flourish of a dancer.

Embassy? Ferguson either had a bigger sense of humor or more pull than Jay knew. He scanned the lobby using the giant mirror behind the registration desk. Two bald businessmen wandered out of the lounge toward the elevators. A short, thin woman about sixty, wearing too many pearls for her own good, approached the unmanned desk and then left in huff.

The hotel clerk returned carrying a zippered pouch as if it were a crown on a pillow. She handed the small lumpy package to Jay along with an official looking form. "You have to sign for it."

The seal was unmolested, so he scribbled his name on the form and stuffed the pouch into his daypack. Piano music from the lounge followed him across the lobby. He pushed through double glass doors and strolled through the hotel's deserted pool area. A row of collapsed umbrellas flapped in a wind gust. He plopped down on a chaise lounge at the pool's far end, near the beach access. An Easy Listening version of *Don't Stop Believin'* played from unseen speakers. Two hundred yards away, the Mediterranean kept time to the music, spewing salt into the air strong enough to taste.

Jay yanked the hesitant zipper of the embassy pouch open and removed one of two cell phones. He pressed its power button, hoping the batteries were charged. The screen came to life and Jay punched in Doc's number. He suffered through her voicemail's greeting. Intentional or not, if there was an Olympic team for avoiding his calls, she'd be captain.

Finally, he heard a beep. "It's me again. I'm not trying to bother you, but I have news that I don't want to just leave as a message. You can't call this number back, it'll dead-end. Call my regular cell, but don't leave a message. I'll know you called. You'll understand after we talk. I miss you."

The cold plastic lounge chair ate through his pant legs. He decided to call Rabbit to see if he had uncovered anything from

Dad's list of names yet. During yesterday's layover in Newark, Jay had purchased a pre-paid cell phone, which he'd used and abandoned in numerous pieces. Since it wouldn't show up in any databases for at least twenty-four hours, he was able to use it to feed Rabbit half of the list of names. No one could hide money from the Rabbit's prying eyes.

A couple walked out of the seventeen-story hotel, but stood close to the doors. They sidestepped into the shadows, huddling close to the building. Jay imagined they were debating whether a poolside chat was worth braving the nip in the air. The aquamarine pool shimmered in the low-level lighting.

Jay got up from the chaise and headed for the beach. After a short distance along a hotel walkway, he leaned against a three-foot-high cement wall under a light post and dialed. The wind cut through his sweater. Rabbit answered on the fourth ring.

"Hey, Teach. I almost didn't pick up. The phone you're calling from isn't in my database. I guessed this was you, but I can't keep doing that."

Jay smiled. Rabbit had called him 'Teach' throughout training. Neither needed their real names bouncing around the NSA's computers. "I can't trust my regular phone. I picked up a couple extra units. They use random numbers to place calls, and I'll be rotating them."

"You've got two of those? Nice." Rabbit made a tsk-tsk sound. "That'll mess with my system. I'll have to adjust my ops plan."

"Think of it as a system test."

"Right-o. Hey, that was you in Houston, wasn't it? I didn't see the footage until after we spoke. Am I hunting mad bombers? Is that why you need these peoples' finances?"

"The answers in order are; yes, unknown at this time, and probably. Are you still interested in helping?"

"Anything for a hero of the state, you know me. Bombers beware. But first, I need you to call me back on a different line. I'm changing my protocol just for you. Got a paper and pen? I'll give you the number."

Jay patted his pockets with his free hand. "Uh, no." Then he remembered Rachel Raczynska's pen and cop card in his pack. "Wait. Yeah, I do. Just a second." He pulled out her card and the Ambassador pen. "Okay, shoot."

"It's 241—"

"Hold on, this pen is worthless." Jay shook it and tried again. The ink cartridge wasn't fully extended and scraped the card. Unable to tighten the pen further, he twisted the pen open to re-align things. Something like a flat matchstick fell into his palm. Jay studied it under the light.

Whoa.

A miniature circuit board covered the top half-inch of an electronic eavesdropping device. *Nice idea, Miss TAPD. Poor execution.*

Jay rifled through his pack and drew out a clean pair of socks. He dropped the bug into one sock and began rolling it up. "This pen isn't working right. I'm not sure why, let me grab another one." Pleased that the bug would have transmitted enough of his muffled voice to be understood, he finished rolling the sock. He stuffed it into its mate, rolled that up, and jammed it in the bottom of his pack. Next, he reassembled the pen minus the electronics and doodled on the card's corner. "That's better, plus I found something to play with later. I'm ready."

Jay wrote down the new number and ended the call. He meandered further down the walkway closer to the beach and dialed the new number.

Rabbit was all business. "I started with the al Wahiri family. I

was intrigued by them living in Bethlehem. I hoped they weren't
in the tourist business, if you know what I mean. Anyway, this is
preliminary, but the old man was an antiquities dealer. He died
a month ago. I don't believe he or his wife had any accounts. If
someone slipped them a new gold chain, I'll find out, but that'll take
more time and money. Just remember, you said whatever it takes."

"I'll remember, as long as you remember to find something."

"Right-o. On to his kids. Of the two sons in Egypt, both of
whom are living in Cairo by the way, one has a clean slate. He
has a steady job, a six-year-old bank account, and precious little
money to speak of. The other son is below my radar so far. Probably
unemployed. Unemployment in the Middle East is unbelievable.
And we think we got it bad."

"Does the economics lesson cost extra?"

"Nah, it's on the house. So far so bad, right? Wrong-o. The
girl, you're gonna like. Faatina is doing all right. She's got a sweet
little bank account at a Paris branch of Credit Lyonnais. Chump
change has shown up for her there like clockwork over the last two
years, but not from an employer. At least not a legitimate one. The
source is hiding behind a few walls. Then two months ago, Faatina
transferred almost a thousand US into a Swiss account."

"Into a Swiss account?"

"Yeah. Dumb, dumb, dumb. Kind of defeats the purpose of
a secret account, doesn't it? Turns out she just may have a sugar
daddy. Someone puts lots of money into that account, nice and
regular like a Swiss timepiece."

The walkway ended on a grassy stretch, which a few yards
later, dropped down a couple feet to the beach. A mini retaining
wall kept the sand and surf at bay. Jay scanned the area. The beach
was void of people, but filled with rows of chaise lounges and more
closed umbrellas that pointed skyward like rockets. He sat on the

grassy ledge and took off his shoes and socks.

"Define lots of money."

"Ten grand a month since the account was opened eighteen months ago. Then, starting this past May, irregular deposits have totaled almost two mil. She's pretty good at using the proceeds, too. The balance never stays above fifty thousand for more than a couple days. She's either moving it beyond daddy's reach or she's doing something naughty."

The stars twinkled brighter. "Or, she's an ATM. Or all three. We need to know who's funding her and what she's doing with it."

"Yeah, you're right, that is fantastic work. High praise coming from you, Teach. Don't mention it, you're welcome."

With his shoes tied to his pack and his socks stuffed inside his pack, Jay stood barefoot on the frigid sand. The couple had ventured partway down the walkway, but they were now scurrying back toward the hotel.

"I appreciate you jumping on this thing so quickly. I don't know what I'd do without you. Is that better?"

"A little. Is that surf I hear in the background? Where are you anyway?"

"I'm on the move. It could be static. Don't keep me hanging. Do you know the money's source or destination?"

Rabbit cleared his throat. "I'm working on that."

"Thanks. I've got two more folks for you to look into. They're Tel Aviv cops. Shimon Cohen and Rachel Raczynska. The woman grew up in New Jersey and moved to Israel eight years ago. I don't know a thing about Cohen."

"No problem. How many Shimon Cohens could there be in Israel? Any others I can look up in my spare time?"

Jay pictured Rabbit's famous pout. "Yeah, but they can wait. The ones you have so far are priority items. I need them all sooner rather than later."

"You're kidding right? Tomorrow's Monday, and I do have a day job. Even the government expects its employees to work now and then." Rabbit sighed into the phone. "Should I call you when I get more intel or wait to hear from you?"

"I'll call you. I assume I should use this last number."

"Right-o."

A large wave hit the offshore breakwater, shooting a double plume of white water into the night. They looked like rabbit ears. "Thanks pal. If it helps, take an unpaid vacation day. Add it to my tab."

THE HOTEL LOBBY'S WARMTH flooded Rachel's body the moment she and Ammar entered it. She loosened her grip on his arm, but kept him snug against her side. Waiting for an elevator took forever. It suited her fine, allowing her the pleasure of maintaining the loving couple charade a little longer. If only it didn't have to end. But if she didn't complete her mission, how could she face Isis?

Inside the elevator, Ammar eased his arm free of hers and pressed fifteen. They emerged into an empty corridor. Walking along it, Rachel fought the urge to grab his arm again. At Jay's door, she removed the night maid's magnetic-card passkey from an oversized purse. Rachel inserted the card into the door's card reader. The door lock blinked red.

She exchanged a nervous glance with Ammar.

Rachel retried the card. The lock turned green with a *click*, and they slipped into a typical American-style hotel room. The short entry had a closet to the right and a bathroom to the left just past a small sink. Gillette deodorant and a cheap travel shaver sat on the sink's counter. Further in, an oak dresser and matching entertainment center hugged the right wall opposite a king-sized bed.

Rachel went back to the closet and slid its mirrored door open. The suit coat hanging in it looked like Jay's. A button-down oxford and two polo shirts plus a pair of jeans were his style and size. She closed the closet, and pulled the electronic trip beam from her bag.

She turned to Ammar, who stood near the dresser, studying her. "We're good. I'll set up the beam here just beyond the arc of the door. This little hall to the bathroom will conceal the emitter. Place the accelerant against this side of the dresser. Its bulk will direct the blast back toward the entry. He'll be covered in flaming gel in seconds. Water from the bathroom will be useless, even if he could stagger to it."

"Whatever you say." He knelt down to place the charge.

"Not whatever I say," she yelled, then lowered her voice. "You're too agreeable, too trusting."

"Only with you." His innocent eyes pleaded an unspoken request. "But, won't people question whether the professor's death was an accident, if the son is executed? Investigators will never think this is an accident."

Rachel finished setting up the mechanism. It was ready to be armed. "She doesn't want this to look like an accident."

"So why didn't we just shoot him on the beach? No one was around."

Keep thinking, Ammar. You could figure this out. I won't struggle against you.

"Unless, she wants added damage. Lucky for us, she doesn't believe in suicide martyrs." Ammar laughed. "I wouldn't know what to do with seventy-two virgins. One will be enough."

Rachel walked over to him, his concentration now on the

device. She pulled her steel police baton from her bag. Felt its smooth, cold steel as she expanded it, section by section. She raised the weapon over Ammar's head. She could inflict pain, paralysis, or death. The choice was hers. From this angle, he did resemble her father.

She made her choice.

JAY KICKED AT THE sand.

He'd walked south along the Hilton's beach until the city's marina forced him away from the water and onto the *Shlomo Lahat Promenade,* a paved sidewalk that paralleled the water for miles. Once past the creaking masts and swaying boats, he returned to the sand and occasionally strayed into the cold waters of the Mediterranean. He stopped when he neared the action at the cafes of the city's Old Jaffa port area. He opened his pack to check his Arizona cell phone. Sure enough, he'd missed Doc's callback.

He switched phones and called her cell. He'd have crossed his fingers or even prayed if he knew it would make Doc answer. He hadn't tried either technique since he'd been in Israel decades earlier. He thought she answered as a loud wave crashed behind him.

"Doc?" He ramped up the phone's volume.

"Jay? Where are you?"

"I'm in Tel Aviv."

"Israel?"

"That's the one. It's good to finally hear your voice." He slogged through the sand on an angle, away from the water and toward the street.

"Have you noticed every time we talk I need to ask where you are? And then after you tell me, I have to wonder if you're really there? I saw you on TV. On a stretcher. In Houston, I might add. Imagine my surprise."

Jay scrambled up a small sand dune. The soreness from his hook-in-thigh disease didn't appreciate the incline.

"If you don't remember," she continued, "you said you were in Detroit."

"Let me explain. Okay? Start to finish, no interruptions. I promise that you'll understand. If you don't, you can hang up, scream, yell, or whatever. Is it a deal?"

"Saturday morning I saw you on TV. I'm glad you're okay, really glad. But I worked non-stop all weekend and left my phone off on purpose. I like you Jay, I do, but honesty is very important to me. You said you had an important message. What is it?"

Jay stopped short of the street. "Remember the message my dad left for me with Marge? It was coded. He asked me to meet him in Houston, although others would think we were meeting in Detroit. The fact that he coded the message meant he believed he was in danger and that our phones weren't secure. If you think back to our conversation, I never said I was in Detroit. You—"

"I don't know what you did or didn't say, but you knew that I believed you were in Detroit. As to that other stuff—"

"Doc, I didn't have the luxury of second guessing him. I had to respect his wish for secrecy. How could I tell you I was in Houston? It would have given away his plan, which was meant to keep him and me safe."

"From whom?"

"I don't know."

He gave her time to process the information, determined not to speak until she did.

"I don't know what to think. It's all . . . hard to believe."

It did seem like a bad dream. "Right after we talked, I was

nearly blown up. And then I found his house ransacked. There's more. He's dead."

"Oh my God."

"It's why I'm here. He wanted to be buried in Jerusalem."

"I can come. I want to. When's the funeral?"

"Doc, that's nice, but it's tomorrow. Besides, it's too dangerous. Dad must have discovered something looking into the Q document. I don't know what, but it must have been significant. Someone killed him for it."

"He was murdered? How? What happened?"

"The police say it was a hit-and-run accident, but I think there's more to it. I also think the bomb in Houston was meant for me. So whoever did it has tried to kill me twice now."

"Oh Lord. In the desert . . ."

Jay shifted the phone to his left ear. "That's my guess. Plenty of people knew I was in the desert. Someone could have tracked me. Or Mike could have been bait. Innocent lives don't seem to pose a moral issue to whoever is behind this."

"I don't care. I'm coming."

"You can't possibly make it here in time for the funeral, and I don't plan to stick around long afterwards. Israel is the last place I want to be, but someone killed my father. I need to find out who and why."

"There must be some way I can help. I hate to think of you there by yourself."

He shifted the phone again. "Don't worry about me. Just stay in Evergreen. There's nothing you can do here."

"Do you really think this has something to do with the Q document?"

"Is the Pope Catholic? Never mind, we may need to retire that expression."

"That's really sick. It's not at all like you to say something so contemptible."

"What do you mean?"

She was silent again. "You haven't heard, have you? The pope was assassinated today."

CHAPTER 10

PASTOR BOB JUMPED AT the knock on his office door. He had
closed it out of habit—a habit he had developed in busier times to
help him concentrate.

"Come in, all who are weary. You can join the crowd."

Johnny Bingham waltzed in still wearing his Sunday best. He
plopped into a chair. "Sorry I'm late. I went to the sanctuary first,
but I guess I missed the meeting."

"You didn't miss a thing. No one else showed. Thanks for
coming to the service this morning."

"It's kinda different without music, isn't it? Not as worshipful,
if that's a proper word. Of course, I got a lot out of your sermon."
Johnny snorted. "After the Baptist church and the Methodist church
burned, I expected we'd have had a full house today. I only saw
three new families. We lost four of our own. That's pitiful. After St.
Paul's burned I told the pastor that he and his flock were welcome
here."

"I reached out to him too. He thanked me and said he'd find a
place. Josh over at First UMC asked the library, the High School,
and the Twin-plex to host their service this morning. All three

turned him down the second he identified himself. They're all afraid
of burning to the ground, and that was before the pope was shot. No
one wants to see a priest or a preacher get killed during a service.
It happened in Detroit last Sunday. I know it crossed my mind this
morning."

"But you were up there. I'm glad we got a combat vet for a
preacher." Johnny lit up like he always did just before quoting
Scripture. "It might be for just a time such as this. Have you heard
from Miss Ellie?"

"Yeah." Bob's thoughts drifted back to her two-sentence
resignation. He wanted to tell Johnny how his doubts had multiplied
and what a fraud he felt like in the pulpit this morning. "She's
pursuing other opportunities."

Johnny nodded. "Well, I came to see the official version of the
Q, even if nobody else came to the meeting. Can I see it?"

"I made twenty copies," Bob said, grabbing a manila folder
from his credenza. "Just like there are different versions of the
Bible, there are different translations of the Q document. I guess
you could call this the New International Version, since it was just
released yesterday by the experts in Paris." He pulled two copies
out of the folder and offered one to Johnny. The paper shook in the
pastor's hand. "Keep in mind I only copied the preamble because
that's the guts of the controversy."

Johnny's eyes danced down the page. Every now and then he
squinted or shook his head.

Pastor Bob's gaze fell to the copy in his hand, hoping a mistake
would pop out, a gloss that would prove it was a forgery. He started
reading.

Gold is the watchtower of Jerusalem's priests and
blood is the currency of the sicarii. One has sold the

*Good Teacher to the other and they in turn betrayed him
to their Babylonian masters.*

*Do you not know why? The priests of the
abomination tried to buy his silence, but he refused their
corruption. At this, I saw a vision of dry bones. The
zealousness of the dangerous ones drew Jacob's children
into battle with Babylon. None escaped with the breath of
life. The bones rattled and turned to dust that blew away
as chaff. I knew this could not be.*

*Another vision came. A man of bronze and iron, yet a
man who spoke of peace. God's wisdom shouted through
the ages and now spun wheels within wheels. I saw what
had been said about this man from the beginning. I ate
no bread. I was bidden to eat and drink only of the words
flowing from the lips of his prophets into my heart.*

*Delight surrounded me. The Good Teacher was the
man of bronze and iron. Weighed by an unfair judge, he
was nonetheless declared innocent. Born to save and
born to suffer rejection; he was bound to be lifted up as
life for all children of the light. His bloody ordeal rose
from Scripture. Like an eagle, my burden rose with those
words and many more. Use no scribe, I was told. I wrote
with a furor.*

*The providence to make him messiah is demanded of
us. Not to rise up with fools in a fight, but with the eagles
in victory. An eagle has two wings; one for us, and one
for Gentiles. The body is the tie that binds. The body that
was bound and crucified.*

*Shall we wait for the Messiah? As a deer pants for
water, but a stream now flows in the Negev to preserve
God's chosen ones. We must announce him with trumpets*

and declare him from the mountaintops. When the fateful
Day of Judgment arrives, and he is seated on high, the
faithful from every nation will bow down.

   We have need of a messiah. The Good Teacher's life
will be made as foretold and freed this day as a joyous
captive. He shall be reborn from above. His life shall
be declared as in the heavenly visions, given to me in
multiple accounts that agree in purpose, compliment
in fact, and conflict in worthless details. Zion shall be
spared. Jacob shall groan no more.

   Hear then, the story that shall unite the nations and
bring peace on earth.

As much as Bob hated to admit it, each time he read the
Preamble, it became more plausible. This time he only skimmed it,
so he waited for Johnny to finish.

After a moment, the hardware man set his paper on the desk.
"You got an mp3 player?"

Pastor Bob couldn't help but laugh at the unexpected response.
"Sure. I've got a cassette deck, a CD player, and a whole museum
of devices. Why?"

"I figured I'd show you how to hook it up to the sound system.
We need music on Sunday morning or people won't come back.
Both of the choir members who showed this morning were afraid to
sing without a pianist. That won't do it."

"That's a good idea. I can manage the wiring. I didn't know
Mary Beth had quit until I called her home this afternoon. I guess
you don't think much of the Q document?"

"It says the Gospels were written to prove an ordinary man was
the Messiah, Immanuel, God with us. The miracles and fulfilled
prophecies do that, but the Gospels also show Jesus' constant

reliance on the Father. Why would a story written to prove his godhood do such a good job of proving his humanity?"

Was it that simple?

"Okay then." Johnny dug a folded piece of paper out of the inside pocket of his plaid sport coat. "Here are the names and phone numbers for the three new families so you can invite them back next week." He stood. "Tell 'em we'll have music."

THE TEMPERATURE HAD DROPPED, and whitecaps covered the sea. Jay left his windbreaker in his pack, using the cold to stay alert. It was nearly midnight. He was walking the promenade, not far from the Hilton, when he spotted The Beachcomber Café. Painted with a jumble of soft pinks and purples, it had the carefree look of a tropical island. He approached it, looking for its hours for tomorrow's breakfast.

The sign was in Hebrew. Decades ago, he could have read it at a glance. With his Hebrew worse than rusty, tonight took longer. He finally deciphered that it opened at six. Doc and his unfulfilled offer of breakfast burritos at Lupe's came to mind. The missed opportunity seemed like months ago. At least she was talking again. He turned to walk away, then realized what else he'd seen on the door. It was a Hebrew version of the most common sign found throughout the world on a restaurant near a beach.

He screamed it into the night. "Dad, you're brilliant."

THEY HAD JUST STEPPED aboard the twenty-seven-foot runabout when Marie LeSabre's phone buzzed in her Versace waist pack. The pack was larger than her bikini bottom. A fact the fit twenty-something boat captain appeared to appreciate. Marie enjoyed his ogling stare, and if it kept his eyes off her sixteen-year-old daughter, Danielle, that was all the better.

Marie unzipped the watertight pouch to retrieve the phone and caught Danielle's grimace. They were already off to a late start for their afternoon of spearfishing at Angelfish Reef. It wasn't far offshore, none of Grand Cayman's major underwater attractions were, but they needed to get moving. Caller ID showed her assistant, Howard Brevard, was calling.

Marie took his call. "This better be important."

"Our system was accessed."

"What do you mean?"

"SecureNet called." Brevard paused. "That's the company who monitors our systems. Our customer files were accessed. Downloaded."

"Which is it, accessed or downloaded? They sound different."

"We think—"

"You think?" Marie faced away from Danielle, the last thing the teen needed was to learn a new way to talk back. "You dare call me on a beautiful Sunday afternoon unprepared to answer my most basic questions?"

"If you knew the slightest thing about banking, you would understand—"

"Was it someone in the bank?"

"No. They're certain the firewall was penetrated from off-island. SecureNet *are* investigating." Brevard loved emphasizing his British accent and idioms. Marie suspected he did it to irritate her. "Until the inspection is complete, there's rather little to be done."

Marie frowned at the captain, who was looking for permission to cast off. "That is why you are the *former* president of this bank. Which accounts were violated?"

"They're not sure. The only thing certain is that their perfect reputation is bankrupted. These fellows are the best, and so far all they've got is rubbish for information. First they said all accounts were accessed, and then they revised it to accounts M to Z. Then they called back to say only the Bs. They're rather confused, but soon their confusion will turn to anger, and I pity whoever did this. SecureNet's founders are ex-KGB. They won't take this lightly."

"Were any EFTs initiated?"

"No. Our account totals are unchanged."

"You old fool. Get someone working to confirm there were no internal transfers. Can you pull the plug to prevent further outside access until you've beefed up security?"

"Of course, but if we disconnect completely even we won't be able to—"

"Find a way." A quick calculation told Marie it was nearly midnight in Egypt. "We can wait until 8:00 a.m. tomorrow to inform Cairo of this. When I call, I want to be able to report that we're back up and running securely. In the meantime, I need a definitive list of which accounts were compromised in two hours. If it's not completed on time, tell not-so-SecureNet that more than just their reputation will be bankrupt. I don't believe I need to explain how your already precarious position will worsen."

Marie ended the call and buried the phone halfway into her waist pack. She looked across the placid blue Caribbean. Countless dive boats and red and white diver down flags bobbed in rhythm to gentle swells off Seven Mile Beach. She zipped the phone into her pack and stowed it in a compartment by the wheel.

"Captain, get us out there."

THINK OF WHAT DAD endured. Jay pushed on. An hour ago, things had started to fit. Now nothing did.

The sign at the Beachcomber Café had read: No shirt, No shoes, No service. Many times as a boy, he had waited forever with Dad for a bus, only to have one approach and roll by with an "Out of Service" placard where its route number should have been displayed. It had become their running joke. Dad must have removed his shoes and shirt on Thursday night to send one last message; his death had something to do with a bus. The euphoria of that insight had given way to sickening thoughts of his mortally wounded father, struggling with horrid injuries to remove his shoes and shirt. Jay had hurried back to the hotel, retrieved his rental car, and driven to the spot where Dad had been found. For over an hour since then, he had been walking the area, hoping to find a bus. In Israel, bus schedules were consistent day-to-day, except for Sabbath.

The screech of steel lined brakes sounded from behind him. Jay whirled around. A bus rolled to a stop at a traffic light. Chills ran down his spine. The bus sat, waiting. An eternity passed. Would it come this way? If it did, he could speak to the driver, get a bus number, and maybe inspect it for damage. The light changed. A rush of diesel smoke spewed out. The bus advanced into the intersection. Jay's pulse accelerated.

The bus turned left and motored out of sight. Cold air bit through Jay's jacket.

CHAPTER 11

JAY PEEKED AT HIS watch. Fifteen minutes had passed since
the only bus he had seen went the other way. It was 1:50 a.m. here,
which was 4:50 in the afternoon in Arizona. That would have been
just after he had talked with Dad last Thursday. Whatever happened
here Thursday night should have already happened tonight. Find
a bus, find the killer. Dad's undressing had to be about a bus. So
where was it?

A wind gust pushed Jay along the street in a mixed area of
tiny shops and small businesses near Tel Aviv's downtown. He
fought the urge to return to his car and drive away. Someone must
have seen something. If he kept walking, he'd find that person.
A powerful engine echoed in the distance. A block ahead, bright
headlights turned onto the street. A small bus, the size of an airport
shuttle, screeched to a stop and parked on the quiet street. Its
headlamps turned off, and two seconds later, minimal interior lights
were extinguished.

Jay quickened his stride and approached the darkened vehicle.
It appeared to be an oversized *sherut*, a cross between a bus and a
taxi. A streetlight illuminated a bearded male behind the wheel. He

looked at Jay and shook his head and hands, gesturing no.

Jay knocked on the door. "Please, open up." Jay repeated his request in Hebrew.

"No." The driver shouted through the closed door.

Jay pushed a twenty up against the door's window. "I just want to ask some questions."

The driver glanced around. He turned on a light and pulled a lever to open the door. He was thin and in his early thirties, with short dark hair and slits for eyes.

Fighting the urge to fly up the steps, Jay slugged up them, while verifying the vehicle was empty. He stood opposite the driver. Earlier, he had decided on the direct approach, but it seemed less wise now. He stuck with it anyway. "Tell me about your accident last Thursday?"

"What accident? I had no accident. Never." The man's "never" spilled out in Arabic.

Based on his accent, Jay guessed he was Palestinian. "A bus struck and killed a man. Right here. It was late Thursday night, early Friday morning. I think you were the driver."

"You must get out. I don't know what you are saying." The driver had switched back to English.

Jay watched the man's hands to see if he reached for a weapon. Half of the city walked around armed. "You think no one knows about it. I haven't told the police yet, but I will unless you tell me the truth. Where's your gun?"

"I don't have one."

"All the bus drivers here have one. Except you? Does your boss get many complaints because you're Palestinian?"

"I don't know." The driver, his name badge said Ibrahim, stared back. His face hardened. "Probably. Yes, I think so."

"That stinks. Trust is important. Your company must trust

you. Do you know what will happen to their trust when the police investigate what happened last week?"

The driver's eyes widened. "I saw it okay, but I didn't do it. I wanted to help. I did help. Afterward. I called the police. It's how they knew to come."

Jay could barely keep his distance. Why hadn't this man rescued Dad? "Ibrahim, you lied once already. I'm going to give you the chance to convince me you're telling the truth."

"Yes, truth only. I drove him here from Eilat. That's my run. Like tonight. All my passengers got off before here. Except him." Ibrahim rotated his right leg into the aisle and waved his arms. "See? No one is left."

"Move your leg back in front of you and turn off the engine. Then put your hands on the steering wheel. Understand? Do it now."

"Who are you?" The driver shifted his weight. "You can't tell me—"

Jay quickly stepped behind the driver's seat. He pulled the driver to him with his left arm while pushing the knuckles of his right index and middle fingers into the driver's muscle at the base of his neck.

The driver gasped in shock and pain. He rotated into a driving position. "Yes," he shrieked. "I have no gun. I swear it."

Jay released the pressure. "I can press much harder. That was a two on a ten-scale. Now, cut the engine."

The driver complied immediately, and then massaged his neck.

Jay gave him a moment. "Hands and elbows on the steering wheel. Tell me everything that happened."

"Yes, yes, okay. I tried to help him."

Jay stared at him.

The driver turned his head forward. "It's a long drive from Eilat. Five and a half hours. The bus terminal is my last stop in

Tel Aviv. Everyone must get off. Then I come and sit here before leaving on my night route. If I make good time getting here, I sit longer. Sometimes I sleep, sometimes I get coffee. He wanted to avoid being seen at the station. I let him come here and use my phone to call a taxi. This time of night there are no trains. No taxis waiting, either. Only Best Taxi is available all night."

"Where was he going?"

"He wanted to go to the airport. I went for coffee. The shop is five minutes from here. He walked part way with me and decided to come back here to wait. When I got back, I unlocked the bus and watched him pace back and forth. He checked his watch, then paced more. It was late, no traffic. Then that same white van came down the street."

Jay looked around. "What do you mean 'same' white van?"

The driver rolled his head side-to-side. "My neck. I may move one hand?" His eyes pleaded for permission, but he didn't wait for it. He massaged his neck again. "It was why he didn't get off at the bus terminal. It was a white VW van like one my brother drives. I saw it several times that night. I thought it was another sherut until it passed me, and I saw that it had no windows behind the front seats. He thought it was following him."

"What happened next?"

"The man was fifty meters away, there under the light post, on the cross-street up ahead. The van came down it from the left with no lights." Ibrahim pointed, then quickly replaced his hand on the steering wheel. "The man started walking away from the van toward the intersection. I thought he might be coming to my bus. I would have opened my door for him. The van sped up, so he sped up, but not so fast. He crossed the street and cut between two parked cars in that parking lot over there, and the van pulls into the lot. I didn't know what to do. The man went back to the sidewalk, and the van pulls through an empty spot. It drove down the sidewalk. A gun is pointing out the passenger window. I was scared—I can feel my heart racing even now."

Jay's heart raced, too. He couldn't stand to hear anymore. Or stand at all. He sat across from the driver. Jay wanted him to shut up. He needed him to talk.

Ibrahim grew animated. "The man, he starts running. The van is a meter behind him, toying with him like a mouse and cat. All of a sudden, he tripped, and it ran him over. It steered into the street, but the guy is stuck under the van. I was crying. Finally he pops out behind the van."

Jay jumped to his feet. "Stop!"

Ibrahim stared. "You knew him well? I am sorry. You wanted me to—"

"I know. Did you see the driver?"

"Not the face, but it was a woman! A woman got out of the driver's seat and checked on him. Then she pounds the side of her van, as if very angry."

Jay clamped his eyes shut. He reopened them. "What then?"

"She drove away. I went very fast to the coffee shop and called the police."

Jay's blood began to boil. "You have a cell phone. Why didn't you use it? Or tell the police about the white van and the woman? You could have called when it was happening."

"They would have looked for me." Ibrahim stared slack jawed at his lap. After a moment of silence, he looked up. "My wife lives in Bethlehem. On the other side of the wall with her parents. They have a shop near the checkpoint called Always Christmas. Her papers are from the Palestinian Authority. I'm an Israeli Palestinian. My family has lived here for generations. There are no jobs there. Why would I move there? But, she can't live here under the current law. For years we have petitioned and waited. I was afraid to bring attention to myself. I only want to live with my wife," he shouted. Tears disappeared into his beard. "I sleep thinking about the man. But the gun, and he was far away. How could this happen? I should have done something." The driver covered his ears as if he heard terrible sounds. "I just watched. You would have done something."

Jay sank back into the seat. "It might not have changed a thing. I'm sorry about your neck."

"I am sorry about your . . . he was more than a friend? He was old enough—"

"To be my father. Yeah, he was."

"Then I have something I must give you."

THE MESSAGE WAS BRIEF. Impossibly brief and impossibly true.

Rachel gulped another mouthful of Ammar's favorite brandy from the bottle. Her head retaliated, and his photo blurred in her hand. She slammed the heavy brown bottle to the table, liquid slopped out of its opening onto her blouse. Who cared? Who would look at her?

According to Hunt's message, he had found a witness to his father's death—a street punk—interested in blackmail. Hunt had gladly paid the bandit's price for his information. It would make no difference. Any minute now, Hunt would join his father. He would take his knowledge of the white van, woman driver, and partial plate to the grave.

Arrogant fool. Had he really challenged her to finish the job?

At least her bug had begun functioning again. After leaving his message, he had reserved a flight back to Texas right after the old man's funeral.

"Good riddance," she screamed into the night. She gulped down another mouthful.

If Hunt could find the punk, she could too.

CHAPTER 12

BEING CALLED INTO HER boss's office had never been a good thing. Ever.

Chief Inspector Levinson's perpetual Cheshire cat grin and scraggly beard always made Sarah want to handcuff him to a sink and shave his face off. It was worse when he sat rigid as a steel beam behind his cleared desktop, and made his pronouncements sound like they resulted from some grand scheme in the universe that only he knew. He had more years with Israel's National Police than there were locusts during the plagues, and she suspected he delayed retirement just to make her life miserable.

She crossed the threshold into his chamber of horrors. "I hammered every snitch in Israel to track down Spider. Video caught him crossing into Lebanon yesterday. He hasn't surfaced in any of his usual hangouts yet, but when he does, he's mine—ours. It's why I haven't filed my report yet."

His grin eased slightly. "Close the door, Inspector."

She did so and leaned on the back of one of two putrid green guest chairs, unable to recall any other regs she'd ignored lately. "I know that the Black Sheikh apparently died in the Hilton explosion last night, and he took a few visitors with him."

"Four others so far. Of the missing guests presumed dead, two are Americans. That's always trouble. Their FBI will offer to help, which means they'll try to take over." He checked his watch. "There were burn victims, too."

"I haven't spoken with the counter-terrorism folks yet because I never believed the connection between the Black Sheikh and Glassman made any—"

"Neither did I. Sit down."

She plopped into a guest chair, careful not to fully bend her right knee. Friday night's explosion had blown her across the pavement shredding the skin on her palms, kneecaps, and left side of her nose. Her left hand was still bandaged, but it was her right knee that complained the most. Done trying to guess the subject, she readied for the universe to speak.

"You're off the Glassman case."

She leaped up, her knee throbbing. "You can't! No one knows Spider's moves better than I do."

"He knows your moves, too, and apparently wants you dead."

"Glassman only knew my moves because he turned that little sleazeball Jacob."

"We don't know he was turned. What if Jacob was handpicked? He was assigned to you by someone higher up. That same someone is still in the department."

That unholy thought had occurred to her, but as much as she trusted Levinson, she hadn't wanted to mention it until the facts cleared him. "Then find out who it was. If you reassign me, they'll have succeeded. I'll be dead to the case."

"There's more to this than Glassman's knowledge of you. You were close to Mars. Avi." He appeared to study her. "Don't look so surprised. Everybody here knew you two were more than just partners at the office. I'm sorry for both of you, but I can't have you out for blood revenge. It's dangerous to you and the department."

She had expected a stay-objective-speech, but not this. "Avi needs to be avenged like any other officer. I'm not doing any more or less to arrest his killer. I can stay objective. I'm close, really close to pulling Glassman in. My contacts in Beirut tell me—"

"You look like you've slept two hours since Friday. You limped in and could barely sit without grimacing. I'm surprised you can hear."

"The doctor cleared me. I've got a few scrapes, and my knee stiffened at my desk." She tore the bandage off her hand. "See. It's fine, just keeping it clean."

"It looks like raw meat—"

She slammed her palm on his desk, wishing it was Glassman's head. "No one can investigate him better than me. He's in Lebanon because he knows it's too hot here. We're freezing bank accounts and monitoring his associates."

"You've done a respectable job. So much so, the department has been able to step right in. The decision to reassign you has already been made—for both of us. I couldn't help you if I wanted to. Which I don't. You've heard of the Q document?"

"Who hasn't? But what if that someone higher up is—"

"Your new job is to prove the Q is a fake."

The implied logic tumbled around her head. "That makes less sense than reassigning me. If we know it's a fake, then take the evidence public."

"We don't know it's a fake, but that doesn't change your assignment. Like it or not, despite our military hardware, the USA is still our best defense against Arab hardliners. If the Americans descend any further into the morass created by the Q document, there's a fear they may not be our friends anymore."

"I don't see why not. They call our Scriptures their Old
Testament. Once they agree Jesus was not the messiah, then maybe
they'll adopt Judaism."

"That would be logical, but polls suggest otherwise. Most are
dismissing all faith. Our intel suggests that everyone is using this
to push their own agenda, and the most successful are America's
separation of church and state atheists."

Her hand smarted. She checked it below desk level. Blood
oozed from under the splintered scab, which looked more like an
eroded desert wilderness than skin. There had to be a way to reverse
this reassignment.

Sarah pressed her palms together. "What you've said is all very
interesting, but America's anti-God movement is their problem."

"It would be, except like everything else, we're being blamed.
The Q's author all but identified himself as a first century Jew.
Personally, I think his plan was brilliant. Too bad it failed. We'd still
have a Temple. But politically, it paints Jews as the bad guys, then
and now. The Europeans have sought a good reason to abandon us
for years. We don't want the Americans walking out, too. Now do
you get the picture?"

"Sure. It's about money and politics. The brass decided the Q
needs to be a forgery. Well, I don't plant evidence. I'll scream foul
play from here to Hanukah. I know how the brass think, and if you
or they—"

"Your job is to prove it, not fabricate it. And it's not our brass
calling the shots. I'll spell it out for you. M-O-S-S-A-D. You've
been reassigned to them. I've been told you're uniquely qualified
for this assignment."

She rolled her eyes. "I was a kid."

"Maybe, but you know things. People's names. Layout of the
caves. You probably picked up more than you realized. I'll be clear.

There's no job for you here. Unless you want to input a mountain of crime data into our big, bad, new database. It could take years of staring at a computer screen to—"

"You'll haul in Glassman for killing Avi?"

"And for trying to kill you. If he's guilty, he'll rot."

"Who's taking the lead?"

"Adamchek and Rabin."

Sarah felt herself nodding. "Two of Avi's poker buddies." *They were good choices.*

Levinson tapped a thumb on his desk. "I'll throw the whole department at Glassman if I have to. I won't let them fail."

Neither will I.

A knot formed in her throat when she thought of Avi. She flexed the muscles of her right leg until her knee screamed. She flexed harder. She'd have beat on it to keep the tears from flowing.

"Will I be in the field or in some laboratory?"

"Since when do you ask me where to find evidence?" His grin faded. "Sarah, you're a good cop with a long history here. You'll be a rookie over there. Try to get along." Levinson's awful grin returned bigger than ever. He opened his desk's side drawer and removed a slip of paper the size of a gum wrapper. "Here, call this number and ask for Captain Jack."

"Now we're doing pirates?"

The Chief Inspector shook his head in disgust. "You're probably supposed to eat the paper after you call the number. Try to enjoy it."

"The paper or the assignment?"

"I doubt you'll like either one."

IT WAS 8:45 A.M., and Ibrahim was late. Jay busied himself

pretending to read a discarded copy of yesterday's Jerusalem Post. The only article he had read said that an aging cardinal from Italy admitted shooting the pope. The man was mum on his motive, so the paper interviewed dozens of people willing to guess about it. Half thought the pope was killed because he agreed to legitimize the Q document, the others because he refused to.

When did guesses become news? Where was the front-page article honoring Professor David Hunt who despised guesses and gave his life in search of the truth?

Jay wanted to rip the paper to shreds. Instead, he turned pages nonchalantly, hoping to look unconcerned by the large number of Tel Aviv police who apparently considered the Beachcomber their donut shop of choice. Last night, meeting Ibrahim here seemed a good idea. Dad's suitcase was the item that Ibrahim instinctively knew belonged to Jay. Dad had asked Ibrahim to safeguard it until his taxi arrived.

The Beachcomber was chosen as neutral ground for the handoff and a promised finder's fee. Jay had volunteered to go to Ibrahim's home to collect the suitcase, but Ibrahim nixed the idea. He lived among relatives in an ancient enclave within Old Jerusalem's Muslim Quarter. The way that Ibrahim described it reminded Jay of Louisiana's Cajun country where everybody was everyone's cousin, minus the bayous and swamps. To escape prying eyes, the bus driver had suggested delivering Dad's suitcase to Jay's hotel.

The trouble with that was Jay had no interest in divulging where he was really staying. He had sublet a small furnished flat yesterday afternoon from a scruffy Tel Aviv University student. A month's rent secured the private refuge. The mattress had proven to be as soft as a pillow, and the pillow had been as hard as a rock. More importantly though, the shower had hot water, and his daypack had enough toiletries to kick start his day.

Five Israel Defense Force members, including two young women, marched into the café, wearing olive green field dress. Three other IDF remained outside. Well armed, all but one modeled the latest in IOTVs; desert camo flak jackets with ballistic plates front, back, and sides. Seven police and plenty of civilian customers jockeyed for the Beachcomber's dozen tables amid clanging plates and escalating conversation levels. Jay sat crowded against the front plate glass window, smiling, being agreeable, and looking as American as possible.

Jay watched for Ibrahim, hoping he had the nerve to show and the smarts to be bagless. Meeting a suitcase-toting Palestinian walking with purpose into an Israeli shark's nest was no way to stay incognito. He kicked himself for failing to suggest a backup location.

Two couples, squished around the table closest to Jay, got up to leave. A dark-skinned busboy cleared it. He glanced at Jay. "They left today's paper," he said in Nigerian accented Hebrew. "Do you want it?"

"Sure. I'm waiting on a friend. At this rate, I have time to read War and Peace."

The young man squinted incomprehension and laid the disheveled pile of papers on Jay's table, then left. The five IDF barged past busy diners and took over the vacated table.

Jay considered reasons Dad would return to Jerusalem from Amman through Eilat. It was only a little less absurd than going from Evergreen to Phoenix via Cleveland. Either Dad was avoiding the checkpoints along the direct route via The King Hussein Bridge, or something tugged Dad south to Jordan's crown jewel of deserts known as the Wadi Rum. There were too many pieces to the puzzle. Jay considered calling Rachel of the TAPD to see what she had found on the van.

"Oh, no."

His outburst caught the entire room by surprise, including him. How had he missed it? The FBI had confirmed Dad had no reservation to fly home. With no plane ticket and no suitcase, how could the eavesdropping queen, Rachel Raczynska, have guessed Dad was on his way to the airport?

The words explosion, fire, and Hilton filtered into his consciousness from the IDF table. Jay tore through today's Post to find the front page. The headline, Black Sheikh dies in Hilton fire, grabbed his attention.

> *A reliable source within the National Police confirmed that last night's fire at Tel Aviv's plush Hilton Hotel may have taken the life of the Black Sheikh as he prepared to strike again. An unidentified man's body was found kneeling at the explosive device that investigators believe ignited the fire. The signature black hood of the terrorist who has plagued American Christian visitors in Jerusalem since early October was found in a scorched satchel near the body.*
>
> *Four other unidentified bodies were recovered from the hotel's fifteenth floor. A hotel spokeswoman said that management believes three guests and a hotel worker were killed in the explosion and fire, which reportedly began just after midnight. Victims' identities have not been released, but initial reports suggest a hotel detective may have surprised the terrorist as he armed the bomb. Guests unaccounted for at press time include American and Belgian nationals. Twenty-three guests and workers were treated for burns and smoke inhalation at area hospitals.*

A piercing whoop-whoop of a police siren drew Jay's and everyone else's attention outside.

Ibrahim was being forced to his knees with his hands behind his neck. Dad's suitcase lay beside him. Three IDF, with drawn weapons, stood ready to obliterate his head.

CHAPTER 13

JAY BOLTED FROM HIS chair and leaned between two of the IDF soldiers at the next table. He stared into the eyes of the soldier without the protective vest, guessing he commanded the others. "Soldier," he said, in what he hoped was understandable Hebrew, "if you're in charge, follow me. That man kneeling out there is a friendly."

The buzz-cut soldier half-choked on his coffee. His face mirrored the shock of everyone at his table.

Without waiting for a verbal response, Jay scrambled toward the entrance. At the door, he eased his pace and stepped outside the cafe. He raised his hands in surrender and stopped fifteen yards short of the soldiers and Ibrahim.

"I'm unarmed."

Someone yanked his arms down and behind him with more force than was necessary. Jay resisted just enough to keep his arms from being torn from their sockets. Multiple voices shouted in his ears. "On your knees."

He complied and spoke with a level tone. "I'm an American tourist. That man drives a sherut. He's delivering the suitcase to me.

It was left in his vehicle."

The soldier without the vest quick-stepped by and stopped a few paces past. He nodded to the men securing Ibrahim. The driver's jacket had been stripped back to secure his arms. The bottom of his shirt was up to his neck, exposing a thin, hairy chest.

The officer said, "Pull that man's shirt back down." He turned and pointed at Jay. "Check the American."

Jay's Air Strip vented travel shirt and undershirt were wrenched out of his pants. Hands jerked both shirts over his head accompanied by ripping sounds. A moment later his outer shirt was tugged back down, leaving his tee shirt wadded up around his armpits. His hands were brought back down and cuffs were slapped on his wrists. Jay gritted his teeth and looked toward the sea to slow the pressure building within. Thirty yards beyond Ibrahim on the far side of the street, Jay noticed an older Arab man in a bright green windbreaker standing, observing. He had dark wavy hair with gray streaks that ended in a neat all-gray beard. When the man's gaze found Jay's eyes, the Arab looked away.

"Everyone, ease up," the soldier in charge ordered, relaxing his stance, apparently satisfied that no one was strapped with explosives. "Check them both for weapons. I want to see IDs, now."

A soldier patted Jay down, rougher than necessary. Jay eyed his molester, but breathed deep. He'd never find Dad's killer behind bars, and a brash comment might make life difficult for Ibrahim.

The soldier yelled, "Eyes forward." He removed Jay's wallet from his back pocket. "I've got an Ezra Hunt from Arizona, USA." He twirled the wallet onto the ground. Two credit cards spilled free. The edges of several bills stuck out.

A soldier standing guard over Ibrahim called out, "This one is Israeli. Renzour. Abraham."

"Hey," Jay shouted. "It's ee-brahim. As in Israe-lee citizen."

The team leader stared at Jay, gumming his lips in thought. "I'm Lieutenant Lohrshat. We stand corrected. Koburtz, remove Mr. Hunt's restraints. Radcliffe, pick up the man's billfold. Apologize and mean it."

"Yes, sir." The soldier named Radcliffe slid the credit cards and bills back into the wallet. He waited for Jay's hands to be unshackled, then handed it over. "Sorry, sir." His eyes didn't mean it. He wheeled around and disappeared into the gaggle of IDF standing at the café's entrance.

Two cops pushed through the IDF. The beefier one of them with a thunderous voice said, "We'll take that suitcase downtown. If this guy can prove it's his, he can claim it there."

Jay racked his brain for a way to prevent that from happening. The IDF lieutenant had no civilian jurisdiction, but seemed reasonable and owed Jay something for the ripped shirt and rough treatment. The cops, on the other hand, were a wild card. Raczynska more so, if she got her paws on it.

Jay strode over to the lieutenant and cops. "So, who's in charge here?"

Lt. Lohrshat scowled. He spoke to the policeman making all the noise. "My unit and I have everything under control here. Don't concern yourself with this."

The cop balked. "The bag's going to headquarters with me."

People stared out of the Beachcomber's front window. Several patrons and a few more police wandered out. The man with the green windbreaker paced across the street.

Lohrshat motioned to the cop. "Let's talk over at the street."

Pleased that the IDF lieutenant was at least putting up a fight, Jay walked over to Ibrahim and helped straighten his jacket.

"They ripped my zipper." Ibrahim fiddle with it. "I hope my mother can replace it."

"Thanks for showing up. I'll pay for your jacket. There's a man across the street wearing a green windbreaker. He's been watching. There's something intense about him."

"That's Uncle Omar. He drove me here and told me to invite you to come to the car to get the suitcase. I should have listened to him."

"Why didn't you?"

Ibrahim shrugged. "I didn't want you to have to meet him. He is what you said. Intense. He doesn't like the English, and he thinks Americans are . . . the same."

"I think you mean *worse*. We do have a tendency to meddle."

"I should have let you meet him. I allow fear to drive my decisions." The driver shook his head. "That night, I didn't want to give the suitcase to the police and explain why I possessed it. Now I must explain why I didn't give it to them sooner. I am being punished for my fear."

"Not if you tell them it's mine, which it is. I gave it to my dad. His bags were threadbare, but his underwear would have had to fall out before he'd buy a new one."

"Threadbare? Like your shirt? I heard it rip. My mother can fix it."

Jay inspected his shirt. An armpit was now well ventilated and the fabric near two buttons was torn. "What do you know about the Black Sheikh? I've never heard of him."

"I'm glad he's dead. He mocked sharia law. He used any excuse to kill Christians."

"Was he militant Fatah or Hamas?"

Ibrahim kicked at the ground. "He was nothing. All he did was stir up hate toward us. Some think he was a Jew, since he only killed Christians."

"That's possible, I suppose, but why only Americans?" Jay

left unasked the most important question swirling around his brain, namely why would the Sheikh target him? Jay pointed to Lohrshat and the cop. "Neither one is watching the suitcase. Maybe we should take it and run."

Both laughed.

Ibrahim flicked the broken zipper on his jacket. "Maybe *you* should take it and run." He laughed harder.

"I think I will. Listen, I said I'd pay you for handling this for Dad and me, and I will. But these clowns might misinterpret it. Tell me when and where. Oh, and give me your cell phone number."

Ibrahim gave Jay his number. He added, "I'll get my new schedule tonight. We will meet in a few days when I'm off, but not for money, for dinner. You could have allowed them to arrest me. That is payment enough."

Rather than argue about the money, a better idea came to mind. "Okay, but I may be gone in a few days." He looked around. "Once I start walking with the bag, you go the other way. Walk quickly, but don't run. And don't worry, everyone will be watching me. See you later."

Jay walked to the suitcase and grabbed the handle. He pulled it past two surprised IDF soldiers, and before they could interfere, he covered the ten yards to the squabble between Lohrshat and the cop. Addressing both men, he said, "This suitcase is mine. I can't think of a single reason that would allow you to confiscate it. I'm leaving."

The lieutenant gaped at Jay.

The policeman blabbered, "But . . . you can't . . . I mean—"

Jay turned and left.

THE STRANGE FLIP PHONE with Arabic letters from Dad's

suitcase powered up, but died before it fully booted. The blank screen stared back with an uneven frown formed by the phone's dented bottom corner. Jay closed the old flip-phone and set it on the dog-eared coffee table in his rented flat's living area. Jay stared at the phone. Had it remained on, he guessed the call log would have listed his own number as the last call placed. Jay added buying a charger for it to his mental to-do list and dragged his daypack of cell phones closer.

A truck's engine interrupted the quiet. Jay twisted around on the ratty couch and peered out the curtained window behind him. A delivery truck idled in front of the three-story building. The only other window in his second-floor apartment was in the bedroom, and it faced the same direction. With only one door, the place felt claustrophobic. He turned back around and selected the LG phone from his pack. He dialed Best Taxi.

A female with either nasal problems or a cheap headset answered in Hebrew.

"Do you speak English?"

"Yes, sir. Where do you want to go?"

"It's a little late now," Jay said in an irate tone. "Your company never picked up my son who waited forever for a taxi last Thursday night."

She gathered the details and put Jay on hold.

While waiting, Jay studied the single page torn from south Jordan's Arabic weekly newspaper. It and the strange cell phone were the only unusual items in Dad's suitcase. Horrible as it was, Jay had shaken out and searched every pocket of Dad's clothes, which now littered the stained carpet. Jay had read every article in the paper as best he could. None screamed attention to themselves. That left Dad's handwritten note scribbled next to an automobile ad for Kia as the item most likely to have special meaning. As usual, his note made no sense. "Compare Quality In New Kia." Next to the note, there was a huge ink blotch the size of a golf ball.

A voice from the phone interrupted Jay's thoughts. "I'm the manager. Who is this?"

Jay cleared his throat. "My son waited forever for your cab, and it never showed. He missed meeting me at the airport when my flight arrived. Fortunately, he had me paged, but if—"

"There is some mistake. My dispatch records show that the police cancelled that fare."

"The police?" Jay didn't need to feign shock. "That's impossible. Which police? What officer called?"

"There is no name. My night dispatcher is not in, but I doubt she'll remember."

"Why not? Are you the kind of company that the police often call to cancel customers' requests? What is her home number? I need to speak with her."

"The fare was cancelled. I'm sorry for your trouble."

"Do you have a child?" Jay employed his best Jewish American accent. "If your son was in trouble with the police, wouldn't you want to know why?"

The line was quiet. Finally, the manager said, "Ask her yourself. Call back tonight."

Jay hung up. His to-do list was getting longer. Surely the dispatcher would remember a name like Raczynska. Unless she used a fake name. He contented himself thinking he could at least confirm the cop was female. Unless someone else placed the call for her. He slumped on the couch.

His regular cell phone rang. He sprinted to the bedroom to check it. The number was unidentified, but it had a 928 area code and the prefix used at Evergreen's hospital. He looked at his watch. It was 9:51, which meant it was 12:51 a.m. there.

He used his Nokia to call Doc's cell phone, an endorphin rush making his fingers shaky. She answered on the third ring. Her voice belied the late hour.

"You're up late," he said.

"I got busy and lost track of time. I know the funeral starts in a few minutes, so I won't talk long. I just wanted to say hello. I hate that you're alone. I wouldn't want to do what you're doing by myself."

"I wish we were together, too. I just finished going through my Dad's suitcase. I can't begin to tell you how strange that was."

"Oh? Are you in a limo?"

"No, I'm in a safe place where no one can find me."

"The funeral is at ten, which is in a couple minutes, right? Aren't you going to it?"

"No. I can't."

"Jay Hunt, he was your father." Her disapproval beamed through the airwaves. "I'm sorry, I didn't mean to sound so . . . what I mean is, you only get one chance at these things. People need closure. Even superman."

He pictured her stern face failing to look tough with all its delightful freckles. "I'll have closure when I finish what Dad started. He'd understand. Besides, I said my good-byes to him last night at the wake after everyone left. I knew there was a good chance I wouldn't make it to the gravesite today."

"Why?"

"A gut feeling, okay?" He exhaled to settle his stomach. "It's a good thing you're home, safe. Someone blew up the Hilton last night. It's where everyone thought I was staying. Whoever did it thinks I'm dead. I plan to leave it that way."

"They blew up the hotel?"

"Not all of it, but my floor was destroyed. They zeroed in on me, and more innocent people died. I can't stand it." His gaze settled on Dad's clothes. "The cops think some terrorist called the Black Sheikh did it. He died in the fire. But listen to this, he preyed on American Christians. It could be a connection to the Q document. I'm convinced more than ever that this is related to Dad investigating it."

"Come home. Right now."

"I've got a couple of things to do first."

Jay expected an argument, instead the phone was silent. "Doc, are you still there?"

"I'm here. It's strange, but I said a quick prayer, and now I feel better about you staying. Do what you have to. Your surviving all these attempts on your life isn't just luck. I think God is using you."

"Me?" The notion was as crazy as her praying and getting an instant response. It didn't work that way—if it ever worked at all. On the other hand, Doc prayed as naturally as she breathed. "Why would God protect me?"

"I don't know, but I believe he has a plan."

"Some plan. Why didn't he protect my dad?" His quick response sounded harsher than he would have liked.

"God may have protected your father in a way we can't conceive."

She was right about that; he couldn't conceive how dad's death was a form of protection. But it had a familiar ring to it. "You sound like my Dad again."

"I'm glad, and I have some news that might help. After we last talked, which was afternoon my time, I spoke with Officer Randy. They recovered Mike's body, but your GPS wasn't on him. They're drawing a blank on Tina, too. There's no record of credit card charges. They have no idea where she stayed. The only thing they've found is the truck that picked her up in the desert.

Unfortunately, it was stolen. They found it abandoned at the hospital of all places."

"Please be careful. If Tina is involved in this, and I can't imagine she's not, you may be one of the few people who can identify her. People are trying hard to kill me, and they don't care who gets in the way."

"Which is one reason I need to track her."

"It's a reason you should let the sheriff and Randy handle it." Jay leaned forward and absent-mindedly ran his fingers around the inside bottom of Dad's open suitcase. A small bump met his probing fingertips. He tried parting the silk lining.

"Randy's on crime prevention, and some over-worked rookie is assigned to finding Tina. But after you and I last spoke, I was searching patient files and I remembered—"

"Hold it one second. I may have found something." The bump in the lining was a latch. Jay pulled it. He lifted a solid divider that covered an entire side of the suitcase. It revealed an inch deep compartment. "Holy . . . cash." Wads of different currencies filled the partition. "I thought this was one of my old suitcases, but it couldn't be. There's a false bottom with tons of money in it. My money, I imagine. Dad withdrew thousands from one of my accounts. Ooh, and here's an ATM card. I see dollars, dinars, shekels, various currencies."

"Thousands? I didn't know you had thousands. That's great, but don't you want to hear what I have to say about Tina?"

"Absolutely." Jay continued sifting through the money, looking for anything else important. "Sorry, you were searching files."

"I remembered one night in the desert last week, Tina asked me about, um, advice from a doctor about a medical condition."

"What kind of condition? Maybe it's important."

"I can't tell you," Doc huffed. "It wouldn't be right. Let's just call it female stuff. I'll let you know if it's material."

"It's not like she paid you an office visit. It might give us—"

"Jay, she was badly abused as a young girl. I'm not saying any more, so quit pestering me and listen. Since she had just moved here, and didn't have a doctor yet, she went to the ER. I checked it out. There was no record of her, which is contrary to policy. So I checked the timing and probable diagnosis, and bingo."

Jay sat up straight. "What? Tell me."

"Her name's not Tina. It's Faatina—"

"If you say al Wahiri I'm going to kiss you right through the phone."

"How did you know?"

Jay thrust both arms skyward. He brought the phone back to his head. "This is the break we've needed. Her mother lives in Bethlehem. Visiting her is one of two things I intend to do there. I was just about to leave. "

"You forgot to say 'Good work, Doc.' How do you know where she lives?"

He made a smooching sound into the phone. "A kiss is how I say good work, Doc. In fact, it's great work. Faatina's father was an antiquities dealer. If his business included old scrolls, we're a giant step closer to finding a link with the Q document and who killed Dad."

"Could it prove the Q is a fake?"

"Not so fast. We may not have even caught up to where Dad was yet, and he wasn't convinced. But old papyrus trades like coins and art. If a shepherd finds some, who are they going to sell it to? Another shepherd? Not likely. So they sell it to a dealer, who buys it and resells at a huge profit, maybe to another dealer or maybe a buyer with deep pockets. Part of determining if the Q is authentic includes determining who found it and where. If Tina, I mean

Faatina's father was in the lineup, and she shows up in Evergreen and maybe took a shot at me, well . . . even Henson could connect those dots."

"We can prove it's a fake. Nothing can stop us, now."

"Us? That should be music to my ears, but I'd rather hear that you're leaving Evergreen for a few days. I don't think your house or the hospital is safe. Promise you'll stay away."

"I can't do that. I won't do that."

"Then at least quit calling me. Better yet, call and leave a message saying you're done with me because I never call you back. My phone's records prove that. I mean it. I'd go crazy if anything happened to you. Please promise."

"I take my promises seriously, Jay, and I won't lie."

Someone pounded on the door. Three times. Hard.

Jay stared at the door as if that would reveal who was knocking. "If you won't promise . . ."

"Police. Open up."

Impossible. Jay eased the curtains aside. An officer leaning on a police car stared back.

The pounding came again.

"I don't know how they found me, but I have to go. Stay safe, I'll call you. Don't lie, don't promise, just please don't do anything." Jay shoved the phone into his daypack and zipped it shut. He stuffed the ATM card plus two stacks of cash into his pants pockets.

"I'll be right there," he yelled. Deciding to pass off the pile of clothes as washday, he secured the secret compartment in the suitcase and then stashed it behind the couch.

CHAPTER 14

RACHEL'S INSIDES CRAWLED LIKE insects on a corpse—reminiscent of times past when she sensed more surgery coming. She didn't need to answer the phone vibrating in her chest pocket to know who was calling.

Standing weak-kneed at her desk, she announced, "I'm going out for a smoke." The noisy room of cops paid scant attention. She worked her way along the main corridor of the Tel Aviv Police Headquarters and walked outside. Alone around the building's corner, she hoped she had covered all her bases and dialed Isis.

"I've seen evidence of your work on television. I just love that the only link between the Professor and son's deaths will be an unfortunate selection by a demented terrorist. I knew you were creative, but that was an absolutely brilliant way of redirecting any inquiry away from the Q document. Well done." Isis gave a wicked laugh. "But how will you relate the Professor's death to the Black Sheikh?"

Rachel smiled. "I filed my initial investigation into the Professor's death an hour before the explosion at the hotel. I reported finding a black hood with the painted cross in bushes near the Professor's body—"

"And the world will assume the victim's hood blew off him before police arrived. The populace will be so pleased that the sheikh is gone. Unfortunately, your brilliance must beget more brilliance. Muslims killing American Christians in Israel complemented the mayhem in America nicely. We must keep up the misdirection. I can't wait to see your next move. How confident are you the son is dead?"

"Very. The hotel lists him as unaccounted for. This morning, I attended the Professor's funeral. He wasn't there. His absence caused quite a stir." Rachel heard voices approaching. She lowered her voice. "I should go. I'll keep you posted." She slid the phone into her jacket.

Two other squad members and the obnoxious Detective Rolf rounded the building's corner. "Hey, Quasimodo. Aren't you working Cohen's hit-and-run on a stiff named Hunt?"

Rachel pushed off the wall. "Yeah. Why? Your wife tell you to find out how he did it?"

The other two guys laughed.

"Very funny. I ran into somebody named Hunt at the Beachcomber this morning. This one was still breathing. He was my age only not as good looking." Rolf flexed his arm muscles. "Him and a sherut driver got me into a tussle with the IDF over a suitcase. I'm not going to write it up, but I thought you should know."

"I'll look into it. Did you get the driver's name?"

HE KNEW IT WAS crazy, but while driving from Tel Aviv to Bethlehem, Jay kept an eye peeled for the student who had sublet him the flat. It helped keep his mind off Doc. The young con man had been evicted last week and the landlord, who lived in the unit below, heard noises above. After Jay showed the landlord and policeman his receipt, they gave him thirty minutes to vacate.

A short drive brought Jay to the drab gray, twenty-foot-high wall that separated Bethlehem and the Palestinian Territories from Israel. Soldiers allowed him entry through the wall's checkpoint. It was eleven a.m. and delay-free. He set about finding the al Wahiri's apartment traversing Bethlehem's twisted, rugged streets. He felt self-conscious in his urban-cool Mazda 3. Ibrahim had been right about the city's high unemployment. The only available job at the moment seemed to be watching him drive by. The number of angry, mettlesome eyes multiplied as Jay worked his way deeper into the crumbling stone labyrinth of Jesus' now questionable birthplace.

The voice on his GPS warned of a turn in three-tenths of a mile. Jay wiped perspiration from his forehead. He made the final turn onto a residential street, nearing his destination. The neighborhood improved, and he drove past the widow's cheery four-story building. Green flower boxes hung from stone balconies. The area wasn't upscale Jerusalem, but it was far from bedraggled. Small trees dotted the thoroughfare. He made a u-turn at the end of the block, passed the apartment again, and parked on the street in front of a single-story building a few hundred yards from hers. He sat for a moment.

Traffic was sparse. A few nondescript small cars motored past. He got out and closed his door as a black Mercedes powered by. He crossed the street, watching two women at opposite ends of the block each walking away.

Everything appeared normal, but the feeling of being watched was unrelenting.

BENJAMIN HAD BEEN WATCHING the widow's apartment

152 | ALAN SCHLEIMER

for three days. No one had visited and she had stayed in. He had wondered if she were half as bored as he was. But as soon as the sporty, light blue Mazda had parked, Benjamin sensed things would get interesting. It didn't take long.

He spoke into the phone. "The guy entered the building at 11:14, and the conversation began three minutes later, so it's our guess it's the same guy we saw enter. His voice doesn't match anyone we've ever heard in there before. He's Caucasian, maybe six foot plus. Judging from his accent, I'd say an American who speaks passable Arabic. He has trouble with the woman's dialect, but who doesn't. What worries me is he's been asking about the daughter, Faatina. We got zilch on her, but he says he ran into her in Arizona. That's the US."

"I know where Arizona is. Well, I know what country it's in."

"Right. It's got Niagara Falls, I think. Anyway, the widow was none too happy to hear her baby girl was in America. She started crying and begging this guy to bring her home. I think that kind of surprised him. He also tossed around some city names that might interest you. Like Houston, Los Angeles, and Baxter, as in North Carolina."

"An American, huh? Collect him. Alive."

CHAPTER 15

RATHER THAN EXITING DIRECTLY to the street, Jay walked out the rear of the widow's apartment complex into a stone garden courtyard. After a few steps, he stopped and stretched, basking in the sun's warmth while evaluating his options. One hundred yards away at the courtyard's far left end, a large man in a red and white checkered ghutra stepped out of the shadows, his colorful head scarf drawing Jay's attention. The hulking giant put one foot on a bench and leaned over, lighting a cigarette.

Jay went right, meandering along a stone walkway through the long courtyard, which ran the length of the widow's building and extended back fifty yards to an eight-foot-high mud brick wall. At her building's end, Jay turned the corner expecting an exit to the street. A wall similar to the one that traced the property's rear changed his plan. The wall connected the al Wahiri's building to the next complex, a one-story, smooth stone affair. Jay crossed into the neighboring building's courtyard by picking his way through a flower garden still wearing summer's faded blooms. On the other side, trellises covered with passionflower vines shaded a walkway that funneled him toward the building's rear entrance. Jay used the trellis to covertly look back.

The Arab in the red and white headpiece had kept pace. He passed Jay's original position and was moving along the same walkway with his left hand raised to his ear. He appeared to be talking.

Jay assumed the conversation was about him and hurried for the back entrance. A keyless entry pad secured the door. He pushed the zero. Nothing. He punched in two more zeroes and achieved the same result. He checked on his new friend.

The Arab was plodding through the flowers dividing the two properties.

Confrontation was always an option, but never a predictable one. Jay turned back to the door and kicked it, hoping the sound mimicked it banging shut. He squeezed through a one-foot gap between the building and the trellis. Hidden from view by the vine-covered shield, he stole along the length of the building. Straight ahead, a wall matching the others boxed him in.

Gravel crunched behind him. Jay's options declined with each step toward the wall. Climbing it with speed was a low percentage, especially if his pursuer was armed. If anything was worse than being kidnapped by a terrorist, it was being a kidnap victim with a bullet hole.

A sliding glass patio door opened.

Jay dashed in.

The mid-fifties male resident bellowed unintelligible protests, dropping some sort of sandwich and spilling a cup of tea. Finally finding words, he yelled at Jay to stop.

"Sorry, can't do that," Jay shouted over his shoulder and flew through the man's apartment, which required only a few strides. The kitchen was to the right. In most apartments that meant a way out was nearby. For some reason, Jay pictured a stereotypical New York

City apartment door with a million deadbolts and chains.

Please, please, no locks.

The door beckoned. One chain dangled free along its doorframe. A twist of the doorknob, and Jay was out of the smelly apartment and into a smelly hallway. A quick right and a left led him out the building's main entrance; the last place he hoped anyone watching would expect him. Hurrying without being too obvious, Jay spotted his car fifty yards up the street. He beelined to it, jumped in, and checked his mirrors as he accelerated away from the curb. The red- and white-scarfed pursuer ran into the street. A white sedan pulled out of the line of parked cars. It broke hard beside ghutra-man, who jumped in. The car roared off in pursuit. A gray van fell in behind it.

Speeding down the street, Jay decided an American in a Palestinian jail was probably only a half-measure better off than one in a terrorist torture parlor. He slowed his speed to match traffic. At a busy intersection, he swerved onto a four-lane street that travelled in the general direction of the Israeli checkpoint.

Midday traffic was building, and Jay hoped to work that to his advantage, though he wasn't sure how. Crashing red lights and going the wrong way on one-way streets were popular options on TV, but he wasn't sure Bethlehem's drivers would notice, or that those chasing him would hesitate to follow suit.

The gray van was half a block back. Two dozen cars separated them. He didn't see the white sedan, which meant it was hidden from view, lost, or doing something sneaky. The next traffic light had been green for a while and became a decent candidate to crash. Jay increased his speed. The light turned yellow, then red, and three cars in front of him stopped. He swerved left over the centerline. An oncoming truck had the audacity to crash its red light, occupying the outside lane. Jay threaded the needle. Cross traffic hesitated for the truck, allowing him to make a screeching left turn onto the two-lane cross street.

"Woohoo."

When his sanity returned, he noticed the back of his shirt was damp and his heart was in his throat. He tried swallowing it back down to where it belonged. Neither the van nor the sedan appeared in his mirrors, although several trucks behind him blocked his view. He drove straight for a block, made that light on green, and began looking for a suitable street to aim him back toward the wall. What he spotted ahead was even better.

At the end of the block, he entered a parking garage and backed into a spot that gave him an unobstructed view of the intersection. A minute later, a white sedan with a passenger in a red and white ghutra sped by. Jay was glad to see that the back seat was unoccupied. The gray van with two men in front tailgated a BMW that separated them from the sedan. Five long minutes later, Jay made a right out of the garage. The wall wasn't hard to find. A block short of it, he turned left. His mirrors showed he was clear of any tails. The main road to the checkpoint was in sight. Freedom and safety was one block to the right. He swore his rental car almost turned by itself at the next intersection.

Instead, he cruised straight through it and patted the dash. "Easy, girl. One more stop, then we'll go back to the barn." Several shops later he saw his destination. He circled the block. There was no evidence of his pursuers or a place to park. Once more around, and a spot opened on the backside of the block. He parked in front of a grubby tee shirt store. He hustled inside it and picked out a hiking hat with a wrap-around floppy brim, a dark brown "I heart Bethlehem" sweatshirt, and the nicest zip jacket in the store. He walked to the counter.

"Is there a back entrance?"

The aging woman shopkeeper looked up. An Arabic soap opera, suffering from poor reception, hissed with static from a portable television on the counter. "No, door is that way." She pointed to the street.

"Do you have a restroom I could use?"

She started to shake her head no.

Before she could say anything, he slapped eighty dollars on the glass counter. The price tags on his three purchases totaled sixty-five dollars US, and with over a month until Christmas, he could probably make her day paying thirty. "Keep the change," he said, jiggling up and down just enough to give the impression he urgently needed the facilities.

She smiled and pointed to the back. "It's on the left."

As he hoped, a rear exit was just beyond the lavatory. He entered the rest room, put the sweatshirt on inside out, added the hat, and then walked out the rear door into an alley. He walked a bit, guessed where he was, and cut through to the next block.

He emerged one shop south of Always Christmas. Advancing quickly toward it, he noted several tourists walking leisurely, but otherwise the street was clear of his new Arab friends.

Jay entered the store, unprepared for the dazzling display before him. The garage-sized tourist shop was filled with a dozen fully decorated Christmas trees. An attractive older woman, standing at a cash register, watched him enter. A younger woman came forward from a back room, walking through the sparkling stand of trees. She wore a black dress with red embroidery, and except for the age difference, could have been a clone of the lady at the register.

He took off his hat and approached the younger woman. "Are you married to Ibrahim?"

Her eyes lit up brighter than the festive trees.

"Why do you want to know?" the older woman asked, moving

closer.

He held out the jacket to the daughter. "I owe this to him. Are you his wife?"

The young woman smiled. She reached for the jacket. "I don't recognize it."

"I helped ruin his, this is a replacement. I hope you like it. I doubt Ibrahim cares one way or the other." Jay handed it over and reached into his front pants pocket. The Travelsmart pants boasted pockets that reached to his knees. Normally, their depth bugged him, swallowing keys and coins beyond reach of all but orangutans. Today they proved useful. He withdrew a sealed envelope and extended it to her.

She stepped back, concern etched on her face.

"Please, take it. In his own way, he asked me to give it to you."

She hesitated, and then accepted it.

Jay turned and left. He might not have solved Dad's murder today, but he had given an old widow hope, and now he'd done something nice for a lonely young wife. *Not a bad day.* He emerged into the overcast day and glanced at his watch.

A hand with a steel grip squeezed his right shoulder.

Jay reached around with his left hand and held the man's hand in place. He pivoted ninety degrees to the right while raising his right arm. He crashed his elbow down on the backside of the attacker's extended arm, snapping it. A back fist to the howling assailant's face finished him, but not before a punch from an unseen second man pounded Jay's side. A back kick connected with this second man. The man in the ghutra rushed up like a linebacker. Jay spun to his left and front-kicked the man's chin. A hopping sidekick to the man's mid-section hurled him through the shop's glass door.

The first man leg whipped Jay as two more attackers in thobes rushed up.

Jay fell to the pavement. A boot came at his head. The man's long robe slowed it, and Jay avoided it by rolling left. He jumped up and blocked a punch to his head. Another man rammed Jay with a shoulder to his gut, battering him into a brick wall.

Someone shouted in English, "We are Israel Defense Force."

The IDF didn't attack tourists or wear thobes. Jay smashed both hands on the back of the man's head as he kneed the man's face from below. The attacker fell away.

Jay spun left just in time to see the bloodied ghutra-man swing at his head.

Jay blocked it. He returned a flurry of punches. They didn't faze the man, who proceeded to double Jay over with a vicious kick to his stomach. A chop on the back of Jay's neck splayed him to the ground face down. Jay rolled over and kicked straight up into the man's groin.

Another twisting roll to the right brought him into a position that stared straight up the barrel of a massive handgun.

THE TWO GOONS LOOKED none too happy.

Mafuss, a short thick-necked guard, who didn't speak much, hovered five feet away. Thanks to Jay, the thirty-something Jewish thug sported a taped nose. Benjamin, a bearded and less high strung man, was the one that had brought the gun to the party outside Always Christmas. He sat by the door ten feet away in a padded chair—lucky guy.

Jay shifted in his rigid wooden chair, which was permanently redesigning his backside. Standing wasn't an option. His wrists had been poked through the chair's back slats and handcuffed. He faced the door of the Spartan room. The only window in the pale green hellhole was behind a heavy black drape. It probably had security bars; he couldn't tell. With nothing else on the walls, the mirror next to the door had to be a two-way number. Jay attributed the duo's bad moods to having to babysit him in the freezing cold home on the outskirts of Jerusalem. After several hours of this cruel and unusual punishment, his fingers and toes were frozen. He hoped theirs were too, not so much out of spite, but in case an opportunity to make a fast break surfaced. Although the chance of that looked slim, at least he was out of Bethlehem.

The door swung opened, and Benjamin stood.

She stood in the doorway, looking sharp and well dressed. After a perfunctory glance at Jay, she strode into the room favoring her right leg. That she had studied him through the two-way mirror was a given. He wondered how long. Her suit was inexpensive, but finely pressed and fit well. Despite a scab on her nose and bandages on her palms, her natural radiance showered the room.

Jay cocked his head toward Mafuss, no longer wearing a thobe. "Did you bring your kid sister to work with you today?"

The guard's shoulder telegraphed that he was about to throw a punch. Jay tensed his abs and drew a quick breath to inflate his stomach. Mafuss's jab to his ribs expelled the extra air, but had little power behind it. Jay maintained an uninterrupted smile, which disappointed his assailant, brought a grin to Benjamin's face, and earned everyone a glare from the woman.

Mafuss explained, "He put Levi and Ben Meier in the hospital."

Jay felt bad about that. "You should have identified yourselves."

"We tried," they deadpanned in stereo.

"You should have tried harder and sooner."

The beauty rolled her dark brown eyes. She turned her attention to Benjamin. "I switched off the video camera. When you two get in the other room, leave it off." Neither budged. She added, "You can leave now."

"Yes ma'am." Mafuss joined his buddy at the door and they left.

Jay studied his captor. "Should I leave too?"

She walked closer, towering over him. "Don't get up." She backhanded his cheek.

The force surprised him. "What was that for?"

"You said you'd write. I got two letters."

"I think I sent more than two, but however many it was, I should have written more. We were only fourteen, Princess."

"Besides my mom, you're the only person I ever let call me that. I'm not sure you're entitled anymore."

"That stings more than the slap, but I guess it's fair." He studied her gorgeous face, wondering what scrape she'd been in. It looked recent. "You could give me some credit for saying how young you look."

"That's why I didn't punch your lights out." Dark shadows under her eyes competed with the light inside them. "You owe me a lot of letters."

"I can't write with these bracelets on. Aren't you going to remove them?"

"Why should I?" She straightened her jaw. Her lipstick appeared to be a fresh coat. "I prayed this day would come. So far, it's better than I could have hoped."

"What's with Israel and handcuffs? This is the second set I've worn today. You and I both know I haven't done anything to warrant being arrested. This whole ordeal smells like a government operation. Which part do you work for?"

"You're not under arrest. You're being *detained*."

"There's a difference?"

She smiled. "Oh, yeah, there's a big difference. See, in my old job, I would have needed a good reason to arrest you. In this job, I don't need any reason at all, and I can detain you as long as I like."

"So who do you work for? You never answered my question."

"When you're wearing my handcuffs, I'll ask the questions." She ran a hand through her short hair, which she parted in the middle. It was coarse, kind of kinky, and still black as a desert night. "You hurt two of my guys."

"They were dressed like street toughs and attacked me. They might have been terrorists. Getting kidnapped didn't appeal to me. I've got things to do." He stamped his feet to warm them. "You haven't asked me what I'm doing here, so I'm guessing I wasn't your target. Why was the widow's place staked out?"

"Where did you learn to fight like that?"

"It's a long story."

"You're not going anywhere until I say you can."

Jay glanced around the room. "I love what you've done with this place. Who's your decorator?"

She twisted her full lips into a coy smile and produced and a small key from her jacket. "Let's start over."

"Can we skip the slap this time?" He wanted his privilege to call her Princess reinstated too, but he knew that would have to be earned.

"Deal." Sarah circled behind him. She continued talking while unfastening his handcuffs. "You always could make me laugh. Apparently, you've acquired several additional skills in your old age."

He pulled his hands through the chair and rubbed them. "If I'm old, you're older. By fifteen months, if I recall correctly."

She came back around, dragging the padded chair across the hardwood floor, and sat two feet away, facing him. The sparkle in her eyes was as alluring as always. They had always telegraphed pure joy during their cliff-side explorations so many years ago.

He swore he could feel the sun's heat and smell the fragrant desert breeze of springtime in her breath.

A knock on the door reminded him of the room's chill. "Ma'am?"

She twisted toward the door. "I'm fine, guys. I moved a chair." She turned back and shrugged. "I locked them out of the viewing room. Your skills . . ."

Jay rubbed his wrists. "The short version is after living a few months with Nabeel's desert relatives, Dad sent me to military school in the States. The other kids thought I was cool because I had lived like a Bedouin. One kid, whose father later made general, remembered my desert stories. The father recruited me as a civilian to teach desert survival skills to his commandos. All I know is they taught me a thing or two while I was teaching them. Our Special Forces are definitely special." He studied her injuries. "You know you were special to me, too. I can't explain why I didn't write more. Maybe it reminded me too much about the car accident that took both of our moms."

The memory of the scorched wreck at the bottom of the cliff surfaced. His mother's lifeless body lodged half-way down the rocky slope. Princess's mother had remained in the car, looking like a burnt statue with hands still grasping the steering wheel. It had haunted him for months.

He shook the thought away. "Can you forgive me?"

Her eyes were misty, and he wondered if he was forgiven. He banished the thought, knowing he didn't deserve it, and added her to the list of women he had let down over the years.

She pushed her hair behind her ears. "When you left for America, your Dad never told me where you were. I wished you'd have written to me. You were my best friend. I was so lonely with Mom and you gone. Some nights were nothing but tears."

Her gaze fell to her lap, then returned to him.

A hollow pain ate at his gut. "I don't know what to say, except I'm sorry."

"Maybe I should thank you. I swore then, no more tears—ever. The last few days have tested that, but I've succeeded." She bit her lip. "I wrote to you, but I couldn't address my letters. Your Dad kept making excuses for not giving me your address. I hated him for it. After a while I quit asking."

"I don't get it. He was crazy about you, but it was like he tried to keep us apart." The muddy water of time cleared. He recalled losing Sarah's address when he moved stateside and sending a couple letters to Dad to forward. Dad must have burned them. Jay considered mentioning it, but two or four letters didn't matter when it should have been forty. "Parents. They think they know best. Still, I should have been more persistent. There's something you should know. Maybe you can help." Jay's chest tightened so much he had to drive the words out. "Dad's dead. He was murdered. In Tel Aviv. I'm going to find out who did it and why."

She leaned over and hugged him. "I'm so sorry," she whispered. "I didn't know. I'm sorry I said I hated him. I didn't really. I don't know where that came from. My dad's gone too. It's hard losing your last surviving parent."

After another powerful squeeze, she pulled back. "I'd help with the investigation if I could, but I can't right now, and the first few days are really critical. I'm leaving the country tonight. I've just been reassigned to a case that will consume my every minute. Plus, I'm still working one of my old cases. I can give you several names. Let the police handle it. They're good at what they do. We don't have many homicides in Israel—at least not without bombs. The homicide guys will be all over this."

Jay shook his head. "They're calling it an accident. A hit-and-run. But there's more to it. Much more. Have you ever heard of the Q document?"

CHAPTER 16

ACCORDING TO THE CAPTAIN of the Boeing 767, the bumps they were experiencing resulted from an arctic cold front racing them to Houston. The pilot reported that Dallas/Fort Worth's temperatures had plunged twenty-two degrees as the front passed, leaving it an icy, snarled mess of roads and power lines. He assured them that Houston would be spared that extreme, but their on-time arrival at 10:53 would find late morning temperatures in the upper-thirties. Jay hoped the pilot was right about missing the worst of the storm. There was nothing but gray soup out his window.

A "bump" dropped the plane five hundred feet. Sarah dug her nails into Jay's forearm. He inspected the collection of half-moon dents his arm had accumulated over the last half-hour. "You could register your nails as lethal weapons, Mrs. Chase." The Mossad's ever-efficient document department had produced the marriage cover and fake passports to spirit Jay out of Israel without challenging anyone's assumption he'd died at the Hilton.

"Sorry, I'm not a very good flier."

"Yeah, I got that *impression*."

"Pun intended?"

He smirked. "For someone who doesn't like flying, I'd say you're doing pretty well. I feel like we're in a rowboat in a hurricane."

The plane shuddered as the hydraulics jerked the landing gear into position. Sarah's eyes widened.

"The wheels are down," he said, trying to reassure her without being patronizing. "We'll be on the ground soon."

The wrinkles around her eyes intensified. "I hate that expression."

Princess with wrinkles. She wore them well. Her beauty came from her Egyptian mother, reclusive to a fault, fond of face veils, and reportedly quite beautiful. Her father was a French Jew and no extrovert himself. The combined gene pool gave Sarah a permanently tan peaches-and-cream complexion.

Sarah swallowed hard. "Let's talk again about the message that your dad left with your assistant. Read the part to me about the letter. Start with his code word that reverses everything."

Jay located the message's text in his phone. "It says, 'Remember our arrangement? Well, ignore my letter, and don't meet me at home in Houston. Meet me in Detroit. I want to go to the U-P to fish and get away—'"

"That's enough. He asked you to ignore a letter he sent, which you say meant read it—a letter you've never found. I'm beginning to think finding it will help us unravel his other clues, but something about it bugs me. Why would he tell you to read it? Remember his state of mind. He believed someone had bugged his and your phones. By mentioning it, he risked informing those people the letter existed."

"That's true. What are you getting at?"

"If you got a letter from him, wouldn't you read it without being told?"

"Yeah, I would." He tapped the left armrest nearest the window and looked out. Nothing was visible but dense clouds. Tiny water droplets streaked across the glass. "Do you think it contained misinformation that he wanted them to read?"

"That's one possibility, but he could have provided that during his phone message. I think there's another explanation."

The plane dipped.

Jay's stomach caught up a few seconds later. His brain caught up with Sarah a second after that. "I see what you're thinking. He didn't send it to me. He said, 'Ignore *my* letter.' He sent it to himself. That makes it his letter. He was telling me to find it."

"Right. He didn't send it to you because he didn't want you to know its contents unless it became absolutely necessary. Maybe something embarrassing, who knows."

"It's a good theory, and it'll be easy to check. He lived in the Houston area." He looked sideways at her. "What else is going on in that pretty little head of yours, Mrs. Chase?"

"I hate that expression more than the other one. Let's keep going. What in the world did fishing in the U-P mean? What's a U-P?"

"They're initials. U-P is the abbreviation for Michigan's Upper Peninsula. Do you remember the message's ground rules?"

She nodded. "Everything after 'arrangement' means the opposite of what is stated. The expression 'you should know' means the information is no longer reversed. An uncommon word used twice means it's very important. It's a simple but devious system. I like it."

"That's it, except reversing requires some creativity. Michigan's initials are MI, just like Mustang Island where he loved to fish. It's just down the coast a few hours from Houston. It was probably his way of saying if we miss connections in Houston, he'd meet me at his condo on Mustang Island. I'd say that part of the message is no longer relevant."

"I'm sorry." Her understanding eyes held his until the storm's edge shook them. "As I recall the next part of his message was to ID his flight info. What's after that?"

"Two things. First, he said, 'I can't get in Friday, the picture's not clear, but I'll see you on Saturday.' That meant he'd see me on Friday. That was simple, but then he added, 'You should know I'm trying to avoid Heathrow, shooting at JFK first, National next. You can bet on one of them to get the right picture.' Notice he said 'picture' twice and used the 'You should know' expression."

"So what's it mean?"

The plane banked hard right.

"I don't know. No picture comes to mind, and he already established that his connection would likely be through Hamburg. So why mention those three airports? I doubt it's about his itinerary, and if it is, then the grammar is incorrect. Proper English would be shooting *for* JFK, not *at* JFK. It's exactly the kind of nuance he would expect a non-native English speaker to miss, but one that would alert me to an alternate meaning. I just wish I knew what. Avoiding National is strange too, since most international flights in Washington pass through Dulles. I hope you're right about the letter containing a key that will unlock these clues because I'm lost."

"Does anyone besides your secretary know about the message?"

"A friend."

"Can he keep his mouth shut?"

"He's a she."

"We're toast." Sarah studied his face and smiled. "What kind of friend? A lover? Have you been cheating on me, Mr. Chase? Spill it, I want details."

"She's not my lover, and we're not toast. If a patient had a hangnail she wouldn't tell a soul. She'll keep it quiet."

"Is she a nurse or something?"

Jay searched for a graceful way out, fearing he'd already said enough to lead to Doc's identity. "Yeah, or something. I'm worried she'll be the next target of whoever is after me. We need to find Faatina and put an end to this."

Sarah glanced at her watch. "Well, I meet with Agent Greene in forty minutes. I'd like to tell him everything I know about Faatina. Is there anything else you want to tell me about her?"

"Isn't it enough to know she recently moved to Evergreen, was new to Search and Rescue, bails on the search just before I get shot at, and her father is an antiquities dealer who died about the time the Q document surfaced? And then, there's all the money flowing through her Swiss account. What else is there to know?"

"That is the question, isn't it?" Sarah stared a hole in him. "In my experience, people that conceal their sources are also holding back other information. Greene will feel the same way. If I could tell him how we know all this, we could gain his trust."

Jay looked out the window as they dropped below the clouds. He considered his options while watching a golf course rush by a thousand feet below. Uncovering Rabbit was a non-starter, at least prior to Sarah's meeting with the FBI. Doc's unauthorized search of hospital records was probably a minor breach of protocol at worst, but he wasn't sure, and so he couldn't breathe a word about her either.

He looked back at Sarah. "This meeting's objective is to find out what the FBI discovered about Faatina. Besides knowing who is after me, I think she can tell us why my dad was killed, and how it relates to the Q document. Faatina should already be a person of interest to Greene. I doubt he'll know about her accounts. Why would he suspect you're holding anything back?"

"This meeting's objective is about all the deaths and making sure neither you nor anyone else is killed. Faatina and her father tie the Q document to you, which ties it to the bombings. Greene needs to know that link exists. My problem is I can't explain how you know Faatina's real name and family occupation today, but didn't know any of it last week. He'll want to know. Heck, I want to know."

"Greene already knows the Q is connected to me through my dad, which links it to the bombings. Plus you said that Greene has peppered you with questions about the Q document."

"Because he suspects a link. That's different than knowing it."

"True, but it seems to me he should investigate her all the same." Jay could tell Sarah was less than happy. "Look, I'm all for full disclosure. I tried that with him earlier and was almost incinerated. Greene said he'd have someone keep an eye on me in Israel. Somewhere between him and the State Department, it didn't work out very well. My embassy had no idea who I was or that I was coming. I'd rather be lying in the morgue than be the reason one of my friends is there. So forget about sources. But, what if we cooperate in stages?"

Her eyes widened at the prospect. "Enlighten me."

"Skip the Swiss account, since that begs source information. It's also blockbuster stuff worth saving. If the FBI shares anything at all, then you provide her name and father. Instead of holding back a source, let's give him one—Faatina's mother. Tell him you were alerted by Imaad al Wahiri's untimely death, bugged the family apartment—"

Sarah held up her hand like a traffic cop. "It was a directional microphone. They're perfectly legal."

"Fine, in fact that's better. You had ears and no video. Your guys heard the widow being quizzed about Tina, Houston, and

Arizona by someone unknown to them. As childhood friends, let him assume we ran into each other at the wake. We chatted about my near death experience in Arizona and Houston, and you made a connection worth checking out. The blast at the Hilton was only a few hours after Dad's wake. Since I'm officially unaccounted for in the rubble, he'll have no reason to think we had a subsequent conversation. Greene will know everything he needs to, and you learn what tons of FBI agents have uncovered. If he's all gung-ho to find Faatina, I'll come out of the woodwork. I'll share everything I know that will help him."

She puckered her lips in thought. "And either way, you'll still tell me everything later that you're not telling me now, right?"

The aircraft fluttered left and right and increased its speed as it neared the ground. They were only a hundred feet off the tarmac and descending fast. The plane's left side hit home with force, eliciting gasps from a number of passengers. An eternity later the right side of the plane also landed in Houston. First class came down a second later. And, of course, softer.

Jay smiled. "I flew coach for you, didn't I?"

"THE BOMBING CASE IS closed? That's great, I guess. I'm a little surprised."

Sarah followed Greene into the plush third floor conference room at the FBI's Houston Field Office. The sensor-operated lights popped on. She sat in the closest seat at the giant oak table, needing it more than she let on. On the drive from the airport Adamchek had told her they'd made no progress tracking Glassman. Now this. Greene sat opposite her. His baggy eyes and sagging shoulders looked like he had been awake for days.

He leaned back. "I was surprised, too. But if I said closed, I misspoke. It's closed for me and this office. The case is wrapping up in our Charlotte office. Everything points to Arab fanatics called the Seventh Day Islamic Nation. They have a slogan, 'Your Christian god rests, but we never will.' Well, they're resting now, under lock and key."

"I've never heard of them. Have you?"

"Not until this."

"I had hoped to exchange information. Do you mind if I ask several questions?"

"Not at all. My time is yours, but I think we can finalize our conversation in a few minutes."

"When I said that I was surprised the case was closed, you said you were too. What surprised you about it?"

"It all came together pretty quick. Evidence led us to a mosque just outside of Baxter, North Carolina—our third bombsite. At a status meeting with my new boss in DC on Sunday, I reported it. He relayed the intel to a team that had the mosque under surveillance for years. They moved in yesterday. The Imam has been spouting hate since 9-11."

"What led your investigation to the mosque?"

Greene sat up straighten. "Good old fashioned shoe leather. My guys determined the bomb was detonated remotely. Video from a store across the street from the bombsite picked up who we think did it. A car pulled in, sat there for eight minutes, then left five seconds after the bar exploded. They drove as easy as you please, like they were going out for a Sunday drive. A Saturday drive for you, I guess. Anyway, most people would hunker down, but if they leave, they cut and run in a panic."

"If it could be detonated by remote, why did they risk being proximate? What kind of remote was used?"

Greene clucked his tongue. "That had me scratching my head

for a while because it was rigged with a cellular receiver."

"They could have activated the bomb from anywhere, and yet they sat in the parking lot across the street? Who was in the bar?"

Greene smiled. "That's what I wondered. I think the bomber showed her face inside the bar earlier and didn't want someone leaving early." Greene mugged for her. "That's right. The camera recorded a woman driver. The car windows distort the image too much to ID her, but our software says it's a female face."

"So you tracked a license plate to the mosque?"

"Indirectly. It traced back to a rental car leased with a stolen credit card. We traced the card to a mugging by a gang. We sweated a couple of the punks and found they routinely sell stolen cards to an Arab named Hosni at the Baxter mosque. The gang knew him as a front man for his group—the Seventh Day Islamist Nation."

"I can see why you were surprised the entire investigation was moved to Charlotte. The connection is kind of weak, if you don't mind my saying so."

"On its own, it would be. The bomb was hidden inside a jukebox. We found the jukebox company's owner dead, and one of his maintenance vans missing. The same camera picked up the missing maintenance van in the bar's parking lot that morning. The distance is too great to ID the driver, but the perp walked like a woman. No offense, but y'all walk nicer than us males. We think that was when she installed the device. Plus, it matched the religious theme."

"Religious theme? You mean because of the mosque?"

"That and who was inside the bar. A group of Jewish students had lunch there every Friday to study Scripture. There's no synagogue nearby. They had an online group that advertised their meeting—they called it the bar mitzvah."

"Clever."

"Maybe too clever. Anyone in the world could see their meeting time and location. It was lunch on Fridays."

"I read that the other bomb was at a daycare. What's religious about that, or a grocery store?"

"The LA bombing was at the King David Daycare Center. It catered to Jewish parents. Kosher snacks, Hebrew studies, that kind of thing. I'm not sure why they picked Houston, but our guys will find out everything soon enough. Any other questions?"

Sarah's stomach flipped. From what she'd heard so far, these so-called terrorists shouldn't have been capable of blowing up a firecracker in secret. "Well, it's great work and fast, but I don't see . . . I hope this isn't too impertinent, but I don't see case closed in Baxter let alone anywhere else. You were interested in the Q document, but I haven't heard you mention it today."

"I appreciate your honesty. My original interest in the Q document was based on our lone survivor from the bombing here. Jay Hunt. I understand you knew him. He claimed there was a connection. I didn't see it before, and I sure don't see it now, but I wanted to look at it. I'm a Christian, and a big part of me won't accept the Q document until I have to. We think the Q document put their plan in motion to capitalize on the chaos. Nothing more."

"So you believed Hunt initially?"

"No, not really. But it made sense. I mean, who has a better motive to shoot down Christianity than a bunch of Arabs?"

"I presume you mean Muslims. Some Arabs are Christians, you know."

"No, I don't know. But you get the idea. As for Hunt, he was a little too nice, but never really helpful. Do you know what I mean? He never gave decent information until it served his best interests. You know he fingered a woman as the possible Houston bomber, who we call the Arab Beauty. She's never turned up. We've identified all the victims and none match his description of her. Only two people left the store just before the bomb went off, and both were male. I'm not sure she ever existed. And then there was the globetrotting father of his. Hunt just kind of raised red flags, if you know the expression."

She not only knew the expression, she could see Greene's point of view. Poking around the edges wasn't getting her anywhere on Faatina. "Have you found Tina?"

The FBI man wrinkled his lip. "The possible shooter in Arizona? I never looked into her. Leaving early from a search party you volunteered for isn't a crime, federal or otherwise." He stood and smiled. "If this case weren't virtually closed, and if Hunt were still alive, I'd grill *him* again before looking for her. I hope I was of some help."

Sarah remained seated. "What if I told you her name wasn't Tina. It's Faatina al Wahiri. She's here illegally, and her father, who dealt in ancient scrolls, died four weeks ago. Faatina disappeared just after his death."

"Tell ICE. I'd have been interested two days ago, but I've got a boss who thinks he knows what happened."

Besides her hole card about the Swiss account, Sarah had one giant button left to push, and she punched it. "Has he promised you a promotion yet?"

Greene pushed back from the table like a rocket propelled him. His sleepy blood-shot eyes awakened ready to rumble.

She stared back. "What's Jewish about a Kroger? Who is after Hunt? He's come under fire three times since last Wednesday. Twice in the U.S. and once in Tel Aviv. How did your mosque's Imam explode three bombs in precisely two hours right under your watchful noses? I'm glad he doesn't train our terrorists because even Hamas lacks that sophistication. Do you really think a bunch of weekend wannabes could do all that?"

"This would be a good time for you to leave, ma'am."

CHAPTER 17

THE ENORMOUS CONSOLE IN front of Jay had more TV monitors than an electronics superstore. One high-res video feed showed a column of heavily armed men trudging through knee-deep snowdrifts on a rugged pass near the Afghanistan border.

"This is live, right?"

Major Danny Ferguson nodded. "Live as it gets from 7,900 miles away. I've already called this in to the commander in the field. We're flying at 22,000 feet and 120 mph. Want to take the stick?"

"I've never flown anything before."

"You were never blown up before, either, but you survived that okay. This is my last offer."

"Try stopping me." Jay took over the former F-16 pilot's seat and grabbed the twin joysticks. He marveled at the technology that allowed him to guide a Predator over a war zone from Houston's Ellington Field.

The female Sensor Operator, seated at the console like a co-pilot on Jay's right, demonstrated how to control the targeting laser.

After a few minutes, Danny thanked her and called a relief pilot over. He turned to Jay. "Let's go down the hall."

The frequent migraines that had grounded Danny appeared absent today. Since Jay last saw him, Danny's salt and pepper hair had turned the color of cement. With a pro wrestler's build, the Irishman resembled a silverback gorilla. They walked out of the room past dozens of the large consoles.

"Why the empty stations? That's a lot of unused expensive hardware."

"We have guys AWOL. This Q thing is affecting more than just cops and firemen."

Jay followed Danny into a vending room and beat him to the coffee machine. He fed a dollar bill into it. As the first cup finished filling, Jay said, "We can do something about that and end the grief it's causing."

"I know." Danny accepted the cup with a nod. "I'll just turn our Middle East satellites around a few times looking for a white van. I don't suppose it has an 'x' on top?"

Jay bought a second cup and they sat at a small round table. "You make it sound difficult. If you can pilot a drone in Afghanistan from here, you should be able to find a van. You delivered all those cell phones to me in Israel on a day's notice. Through our embassy, no less. Thanks, by the way. They helped."

"Thank Mendez. He owed me. Even still, he balked at the idea until he found out the phones were for you." Danny tapped his paper cup. "I'm glad that worked out, but this is different."

"I gave you a partial license plate."

"Oh, yeah, the plate. That makes it a piece-of-cake. In case you forgot, we fly drones here, not satellites."

"True, but you can redirect the sats when needed. I don't expect to need a drone until later. How long do you think this'll take?"

"Without better intel, it'll depend on how lucky we get. And that's not the way I like to run a mission. I'll have to work on that."

"Does that mean you'll do it?"

The major stirred his coffee. "I'll need a reason."

"If I'm right, this van could lead to whoever is blowing people up back here."

"I mean an official reason. This will require more than a cursory glance on my lunch break. I'll have to work on that, too." Danny turned toward the room's only window as a jet roared down a runway. He stared awhile before looking back. "They bombed my country and killed our babies in LA. If I didn't sign up to stop that, what am I doing in the military? I'll find a way."

IT WAS A QUICK five-minute drive south to I-610 from the FBI's field office. Merging onto the freeway was relatively easy, but to stay on it, Sarah had a tenth of a mile to fight her way left across four lanes of uncooperative Houston traffic. If she failed, the signs told her she'd be on her way to San Antonio. She made her final assault on the correct lane at the last possible second and squeezed in. She thanked God that she had made it alive, and that in his wisdom and providence, her unintended maneuver had probably shaken anyone tailing her.

She exited at Westheimer Road and soon thereafter pulled down a ramp into a multi-level underground parking garage at the Galleria. The place was jammed. She slogged up and down myriad rows glutted with fancy cars and SUVs.

Don't these people have jobs?

It took a few more laps, but she secured the ideal parking spot that would allow her to watch her car from inside the ritzy mall's entrance. She walked quickly to the gleaming glass doors. A smiling young Hispanic man held the door open for her. She thanked him, and he returned to cleaning them from a bucket of filthy water. She stood behind him, moving when he moved, and stared back into the garage.

"I'm waiting to meet someone," Sarah told him, but he paid little attention other than to smile larger.

After ten minutes, no one approached her rented white Malibu, and she considered delving deeper into the mall to eat. There was a strong smell of pizza and Chinese food, but she decided against letting her car out of sight. She pushed on the door to leave. A boxy black sedan rushed up to her rental, and then slowed. It stopped several cars past. A well-groomed male passenger jumped out, and as soon as he closed his door, the sedan left. The man walked along her Malibu's passenger side. He bent over by the front end, hesitated, and then continued walking through to the next row of parked cars. The black sedan timed its arrival as the man emerged into the driving lane. He got into the black car, and they drove up the ramp and out of the garage.

With her senses on full alert, she walked to her car, pitying anyone that looked at her the wrong way. No one came near. After a moment, she located a small transmitter attached to the underside of her car's frame. She reattached the tracking device to a white Lexus three cars away and hoped that driver's next stop was San Antonio, wherever that was.

A second ramp led back to daylight. Driving in Houston reminded her of traffic in Rome, only here the vehicles were bigger and more lethal. Jay had given her his portable GPS. According to the GPS, her ETA at the White Oaks Marriott was at 1:47.

She beat it by one minute.

Sarah checked in as Mrs. Chase. The desk clerk informed her that Mr. Chase had not yet arrived with the kids. Sarah collected the key cards to both inter-connecting rooms. Jay had thought up the kids as cover for renting two rooms. He'd always been clever, and even Greene noticed he was "too nice." Now in his old age, Jay had added cautious and wary. She laid down on the bed wondering if she was glad about that or not.

A knock on the door woke her. She checked her watch on the nightstand. It was 4:35. Jay walked in.

"Sorry, dear. I didn't know which room you chose. Do I need to look away?"

Can a guy be too nice? "It's okay, I'm dressed." She kicked back the sheet and fluffed her hair, wondering how bad it looked.

"Would you like me to duck into the other room for a few minutes?"

"Do I look that bad?"

"Not to me, Princess."

That bad, huh?

JAY GUIDED THE RENTED Jeep Patriot onto Palm Royale Boulevard. Like him, Sarah wore dark clothes from head to toe. She looked great in the black form-fitting workout top. Pity she had covered up with a dark jacket they purchased ten minutes ago at the Oak Place Mall along with a few other necessities. He dialed back the heater's temperature. "Well, you learned a lot today. Too bad none of it makes any sense."

"Welcome to my world. How did the conversation with your flyboy buddy go?

"I flew a drone. I want to be a pilot when I grow up."

She shook her head. "You look like a little kid that just ate a bag of cookies. Can he do what we want?"

"I feel like a little kid. It's not a bad feeling." Jay turned into the Garden Oaks subdivision. He leaned into the turn as if flying a plane. "Danny's a patriot, and he loves a challenge. The LA bombing pushed him over the edge. After I tell him that the FBI has gone squirrelly on us, he'll be unstoppable."

"I'd love to know how he can do this without violating our airspace."

"He might be under the impression that you'll take care of that little problem."

"Jay!" Sarah's quick lunge at him engaged her seatbelt. "You didn't!"

He leaned away and spoke fast. "You said this was a national security issue, and you have the highest authority to complete your mission. Right? We won't need that phase for at least a few days, and he'll verify before he engages." He gave her a second to relax. "Until we know whose side the FBI is on, we can't handle this through normal channels." Jay tapped the steering wheel. "Besides you getting blown across the pavement, did anything odd happen in the Middle East last weekend?"

The muscles in Sarah's face went limp. She looked away. "I lost a good friend."

"I'm sorry. What happened?"

She continued staring out her window. After a moment, she sighed. "Some other time."

Jay turned down Dad's cul-de-sac in silence. At the end, he negotiated the tight circle and coasted past a dozen mailboxes clumped together. Halfway back up the short street, he slowed. "I hate to interrupt your thoughts . . ."

She patted his arm. "It's okay. What?"

"The house on the right is my Dad's. I don't see any movement inside. We'll park on the block behind it."

Jay took the first right followed by another one. He slowed again. "Dad's property backs up to this stucco house. I'll park by those other cars up ahead. We'll walk back and cut through to his yard."

The chilly walk stirred a few dogs into haphazard barking spells. He could see his breath. No one appeared to be home at the stucco house. They quick-stepped up the driveway and circled around their backyard pool before ducking behind the garage. Jay climbed the six-foot cedar privacy fence that separated the neighbor's yard from Dad's. Sarah followed close behind, managing the fence with little effort. They stood in a grouping of Texas palmettos and ornamental grasses at the back of Dad's pool. Submerged pool lights sparkled through the blue water.

One by one, the dogs quit barking. Sarah and Jay emerged from the palms and a motion-activated floodlight lit a cobblestone patio.

"Was your father concerned about security?"

"The light? No, this is a safe neighborhood. I installed it. This was my house before Dad moved here. It was strictly crime prevention."

"You sold your house to your father? That's so typical of America. It's the exact opposite of Middle Eastern practices. There, the oldest male inherits the family home from the parents."

"I didn't sell it. I gave it to him."

"You gave him this house? It's huge."

"It was before I knew he wouldn't give you my address."

Sarah punched his arm.

Jay unlocked the back door and entered a step ahead of Sarah. They each turned on a flashlight. He knew the place would still be a mess, but seeing it made his stomach turn. "Let's find the letter."

After a thorough search of the house failed to find the letter, they sat at the dining room table. She looked as exhausted as he felt.

Jay patted the table. "This is the only piece of furniture these criminals didn't cut up or ruin. It has quite a history. If these chairs weren't solid wood they'd have slashed them too. I can't believe, even after seeing this mess, the FBI essentially closed the case."

"Greene didn't completely roll over. He worked the break-in here, until discovering a house at this same address a street over was hit the next night in this same manner. Something about lawyers stealing case material from each other."

In the glow of a single flashlight, Sarah looked years younger, much the way Jay remembered her. "The supposition being that the thieves hit my Dad's house by accident. That's a smart cover. We're not dealing with dummies are we?"

"Someone wanted to find something quite badly. Do you still believe this has to do with whatever your dad stole?"

Jay leaned the chair back on its rear legs. "I'd say either that or they intercepted his call and were after his letter. If it was here, it's gone now. I really hoped we would find it. His mailbox is at the end of the cul-de-sac along with everyone else on the block, and I checked it last Friday to empty it. It already was. This afternoon, I called the post office, thinking he must have had his mail held, but they said it wasn't."

"When I left Israel, I asked a neighbor to look after my mail. A friend and I do that for each other. Could there be—"

"That's it. Mrs. Fenton! She might have his mail, assuming she's still alive. She was spry, but eighty-something when I moved away. Dad and I used to look in on her periodically. Let's go." Jay grabbed their jackets. "I hope you like cats."

DAD'S MAIL FILLED TWO plastic shopping bags and made the vehicle smell like cat pee. Jay drove to the subdivision's nearest community pool. He parked under a decorative lamp that illuminated the small parking lot and partially lowered all four windows to coax in fresh air. He turned off the headlights, but left the engine idling to run the heater. He and Sarah each took a bag and sifted through the bills, junk mail, and magazines.

Sarah announced, "I think I have it." She offered a brown letter-size envelope to Jay.

"You found it, you should open it."

She tore into the envelope and withdrew a single sheet of paper. "It's addressed to you. I think you should read it."

Jay took the letter from her outstretched hand and angled it to catch the light. "It says, 'If you're reading this, I've finally joined the scrolls' whispering souls. I've heard them for decades, speaking to me, not thru mere paper and ink, but thru time—thru eternal life. Maybe our family tree will finally be important to you now that I'm dead as a stump. Although even a stump tenaciously holds on to life, and hidden within may be the key to saving mankind's soul. Picture that!' It's signed, Dad."

"Is that it?"

Jay felt a huge grin expand across his face. "It's all we need."

"That *means* something to you?"

He nodded. "We have to go back to his house."

ELEVATORS, FAATINA DECIDED, SHOULD go straight up and straight down. At the Luxor hotel in Las Vegas, they followed the angled sides of the pyramid. The Pharaohs would never have approved. A bald, potbellied man stared at her and her dripping wet bikini. She hummed Love in an Elevator until she arrived at her floor. The doors opened. A couple in their mid-thirties stood ready to board, poised for a night on the town. It was nearly ten p.m. She skipped past them, still humming.

Her suite was decorated in gaudy golds and purples, but it felt homey all the same. She headed for the all-marble bath. Gold fixtures accented the white stone with gold and pinkish swirls. The bathroom was big enough to live in. Faatina had no idea what excuse Sheriff Henson had dreamed up to leave Evergreen tonight, but it no doubt involved helping a poor, lonely, scared woman— provided she came clean. She was running the bath now to show how cooperative she could be. She fluffed the extra towels and tucked a stiletto into their midst. A girl could never be too careful. He was due in fifteen minutes.

Her phone vibrated on the marble sink top, which surprised her. Reception in the room was horrible. It was Isis. Faatina answered the call as she walked out of the bathroom and sat on a couch by the window.

Isis's garbled voice strengthened. "I asked you to discredit Jay Hunt's memory."

"Yes, and I'm about to accomplish that. I'll say I overheard him arguing with the dead hiker."

"That may have worked, if young Hunt was dead, but that's no longer a certainty. I want something more positive, more direct, and irrefutable. I believe he's in Houston. Can't any of you kill him?"

Faatina winced at the reprimand. "Should I continue with the plan?"

"Yes. It will be a good backup, but your primary mission is to dispose of him."

Flying to Houston risked being spotted. Reza came to mind. The scar-faced Palestinian had rejoined her in Arizona. She was a first-class pain to live with and a lousy marksman, but she could handle demolitions. "Reza is here. She knows Houston, and we have another bomb. Should I assign the job to her?"

"No," Isis shouted. "That's the last place I want her. Besides," she said, calming down, "assuming Hunt is alive, he'll likely come looking for you. I suggest you find him first."

"That should be easy."

"Please . . ."

"I'll take care of him. You'll see."

"Faatina, we are so close to success. American Christians are the Pharisees of the 21st century—white-washed tombs who go to church, but wouldn't know their God if he sat in the pew next to them. The battle we are fighting is in their media. It's run by snobbish elites who wouldn't dream of embracing the faith of their parents. They want the Q document to be real. It validates their self-centered lives and purges their fears. Faatina, you must persevere."

"I am strong, Mother Isis."

"I know you are. But Christians are not our only nemesis, merely our first victory. We must also defeat the Muslims and the Jews. Religion has corrupted the world."

"Your words are a beacon to us all."

"Let's discuss Mr. Hunt. I have an idea of what he and the hiker argued over in the desert."

CHAPTER 18

THE WOMAN HOLDING A Sarah Baumann passport and boarding pass to Chicago entered Bush Intercontinental's Terminal C at 7:09 a.m. Houston's Wednesday morning traffic on the beltway had eaten up every second of margin she had allowed. She stepped into the TSA screening line at precisely 7:10 a.m. and relaxed. The time-sensitive part of her assignment was accomplished. Except for flying to Chicago, all she had to do now was get through security. That was never a problem.

The line snaked up and back three times through the retractable belts and posts. Fellow travelers inched along. To relieve her boredom, she tried to guess which of the fifty or so women in line might be Sarah. She and Sarah probably didn't look much alike. What mattered was that the real Sarah was videoed going through Security about the same time that her passport did, and that airline records showed Sarah flying somewhere that she didn't.

About twenty people ahead, she spotted a woman around forty years old dressed in a stylish navy blue business suit. A black microfiber jacket that was anything but business or stylish was slung over her bag. *Gotcha.* The woman had flown Lod to Newark and on to Houston yesterday. Only three other female passengers had done that, but this woman had done it draped on the arm of a dreamy-looking man. Eva turned to see if any of the other three women were in line behind her. She blushed when she stared into Mr. Dreamy's eyes.

He was four people behind her and smiled.

If only I was Sarah Baumann. I could use a little excitement.

AFTER CLEARING AIRPORT SECURITY, Jay went to the Terminal C food court and sat near the Chick-fil-A with a coffee and a Wall Street Journal. He was flying to Vegas, and Sarah was headed to the University of Arizona in Tucson. She had an appointment at one of its special labs. The university and the National Science Foundation jointly operated the world's foremost radiocarbon dating laboratory known as the Accelerator Mass Spectrometry, or AMS lab. The lab had evaluated small fragments expertly cut in Paris from the Q document's edges. Sarah was meeting with the AMS director. Jay stirred his coffee, hopeful that she would get the man's personal insights—the kind that wouldn't show up in a starchy scientific report.

When she approached Jay, the only thing recognizable about this morning's dark-haired beauty in a business suit that had waded through the TSA line was her smile. Sarah's blonde wig, silky black cowgirl top, and tight blue jeans screamed, Welcome to Houston, y'all. Glossy black-framed eyeglasses completed the makeover. Jay watched her sashay closer. They might have overdone it. Throngs of passengers dragged briefcases, suitcases, and kids in and out of lines at a dozen fast food counters, but every guy was watching her.

She stood at his table and half-whispered, "Does everything look okay?"

"You are easy on the eyes, miss, um . . . would your last name be America? Or Israel?"

"Cut it out." She looked wantonly at his coffee. "Any insight on the key we found? It's obviously important. Like the table it was hidden in. I still can't believe you're going to sell that table. What a marvelous heirloom, a dining room table made from a giant oak on your grandparents' ranch. You really have a family tree."

"No, I haven't the foggiest idea what it's a key to, but I'm sure one of Dad's clues will make it all clear. I was going to sell the table, but I've seen the light. On the way here, I called the auction company and told them to put the table in storage."

Sarah smiled and glanced around as she sat. "What is that wonderful smell?"

Jay tugged his polo out at the neck and sniffed inside. "Me?"

Her head-tilt suggested she wanted a straight answer.

"It's called Cinnabon. They're addictive. Especially with coffee."

She looked at his coffee again, then her watch. "I need to get going. My flight to Phoenix was scheduled to begin boarding two minutes ago. You charged that Arabic phone over night, correct? Read me the numbers in it. I'd like to get my guys tracing the phone's owner and call log."

"I can't. It's in my checked bag along with my spares. If going through Security with four cell phones doesn't earn an automatic frisking, it should." Jay reached for the coffee on the unoccupied table next to them. He handed it to her, grinning. "Here. Black with sugar and one ice cube."

"Ah, you remembered. How sweet. I wish you were flying with me to Phoenix. You could rent a car and drive to Evergreen when I drive to Tucson."

"I can't, my Jeep's in Las Vegas."

"You still have a thing for Jeeps. That's kind of cute." A far-away look glazed her eyes. "Those were good times. Oh, one more thing. After I'm done in Tucson at the university, and before I join you, I want to see Niagara Falls. Can you give me directions to get there?"

"From Tucson?"

"Yes, from Tucson."

"To Niagara Falls?"

"Jay, my flight is boarding, I need to hurry. Just give me the directions."

"Okay. Head north to Interstate 80, turn right, and then drive a couple thousand miles east. That'll get you pretty close." He studied her face as she scrambled to write down the directions. He added, "It'll be on your left."

She looked up, eyes wide. "How many miles?"

AFTER LANDING IN VEGAS just after noon, Jay left for Evergreen. It was a little over three hours southeast. He cleared the Hoover Dam's new bridge and was on a stretch of Highway 93 that was one lane in each direction. Lumpy chocolate and vanilla-striped hills whizzed by. The radio blasted out Radar Love, and he found himself singing along. Traffic heading north was light but constant. He checked his mirrors. A southbound Buick Riviera was passing a car a half-mile back.

From this distance, he couldn't tell the car's color, but it reminded him of the green Riviera he'd seen last week on the way to the airport. The big old Buick ducked back into its lane behind a few pickups and cars.

Another good song came on that Jay liked but couldn't place. The Riviera was passing again. Between the hills, curves, and traffic, it took the Riv five minutes to catch up. When it did, it rode Jay's bumper. The car was green, but the sun's glare prevented him from seeing who or how many were inside it. A small break in oncoming traffic appeared. He expected the big Buick to pass.

Wham.

Jay's Jeep surged forward. His head whipped back against his headrest. His eyes darted to the rear view mirror. The big—

The Buick rammed him again. The Jeep lurched left toward a line of oncoming traffic. A pickup truck rushed at him. Jay jerked back to the right. The rear of the Jeep threatened to spin out. He corrected again. He looked in the rear view mirror. The dented front end of the Riviera was speeding toward him.

He's going to do it again.

The old Buick had a low center of gravity and probably outweighed his Jeep Cherokee by five hundred pounds. *What is this madman doing?*

The green battering ram hit him again.

Jay was ready this time and steered slightly right to keep his vehicle straight. It worked, but he couldn't take many more hits. He floored the accelerator. His speed neared 90 mph.

The Riviera was closing the gap without breaking a sweat.

What his Jeep lacked in speed, his heart rate more than made up for. It was pounding in his ears. He needed an edge, a way to end this nightmare. The Riv was faster and heavier. *On the road, but not off!* He had to get off the pavement. The Jeep could take a beating off-road, but not at high speed. If he slowed, he'd get hammered again and risked rolling over. Especially at this section of highway. The desert dropped off several feet from the shoulder into a wide and uneven ditch.

He looked back. The road was clear. *Where are you?* An object on his side attracted his attention. The driver of the Riviera had swung left into the open northbound lane. It drew abreast. Jay looked again—he could barely see through the smoke-gray window. The driver had long hair. A woman?

She planned to shove him into the ditch. Jay stood on his brakes.

The Buick flew by and its driver swerved right at the last second, sideswiping his front end.

The glancing blow angled him toward the ditch. His ABS brakes, already engaged, pulsed, trying to stop him. Not enough. He bucked and bounced across the ditch. A pile of rotted wood loomed dead ahead. If he steered around it at this speed, he'd flip. He plowed through it. The Jeep skidded over hard rock and sand. At least he was slowing.

The Jeep limped forward, now crawling across deep sand. Jay's whole body shook. He gave the Cherokee enough gas to keep from bogging down, but he bottomed out with every bump and couldn't push the Jeep too hard. Blasting across the ditch must have blown out the rear stabilizer and leaf springs. He looked back to the road.

The Riviera wasn't giving up. She fishtailed across the sand coming after him.

Who are you? What do you want?

He heard a crack. A gunshot? Yes, and another. It wasn't enough to kill him with her car, now the psycho was shooting at him. It was time for a new plan.

A couple hundred yards away, a long line of small overlapping hills ran parallel to the highway. He turned the steering wheel. It barely budged. His power steering had died. He manhandled the Jeep toward the hills in a wide arc. If he could get there without getting shot, he could climb the hills, which would be impossible for the heavy Riviera.

She was gaining on him, driving like a kamikaze. He heard

another gunshot.

A deep swale loomed just ahead on a diagonal to his direction. It would be a disaster to tackle it full-bore on this tack. He sped up.

At the last second, Jay broke hard. Unless she copied his move, she'd never make it across. No longer needing speed, he shifted into four-wheel low. His front end bottomed out and his rear tires ate into their wheel wells. Deep sand and a sharp exit angle threatened to hold him. The Jeep clawed its way out. He fought his way up the hill, hoping the back side wasn't too severe. *At least the four-wheel drive is still working.* He crested and steered straight down the hill.

He was in a mini-valley between brown rows of rock and sand hills. He couldn't see out or up. If the Riviera had somehow managed to get to the hill's top, the armed driver could pick him off.

Fighting his steering wheel, he aimed for a hill that was lower than most. He parked the Jeep at its base and scrambled up the hill on foot. Hugging a rock formation at the top, he peered back. The green machine had entered the swale and overturned onto its roof. A black Silverado pickup had stopped near it, but was too far away to see any detail. The Riviera's driver hoisted herself into the truck's passenger seat, and it sped off across the sand, angling south.

Since the Jeep was in no shape to give chase, Jay watched the pickup enter the highway. He planned to circle back to the overturned Buick to poke around inside and check the license plate, until he spotted a highway patrol car speeding toward it across the desert floor. Playing dead had disadvantages.

THE TORTUOUS DRIVE TO Evergreen ended at Dean's Auto Repair just before five o'clock. Dean gave Jay a lift to his trailer, which was just outside of town and situated a hundred yards off the paved section of Washboard Road. A mile later the pavement

ended and the road earned its name as it wound through the foothills
and washes that led into the Cerbat Mountains. Dean had barely
left when Jay's personal alarm sounded. Nothing seemed out of
the ordinary other than the soft breeze and pleasant temperature,
but like at Dad's, something unidentifiable had changed. Jay's
property included two hundred dusty acres out back, but it was the
homestead area that felt wrong. He dropped his bags and climbed
the three steps to the wood deck without a sound. He crossed to the
front door.

The wood frame was splintered.

Jay stood and listened. Hearing nothing, he pushed the door of
his doublewide open a few inches and peered into the living room.
The air left his lungs. It was Dad's house déjà vu. The leather pit
group and a side recliner were sliced and their stuffing yanked free.
Chair bottoms in a tiny dining room, wedged behind the living area
and kitchen, had received the same treatment.

He let out a yell. These people had to be stopped.

It didn't take long to inspect the bedrooms. Nothing had
escaped the wrath of whoever did this. In his bedroom closet, he
opened the fake wall that concealed his safe and removed his laptop.
At least it hadn't been violated. He took the laptop to the kitchen
and picked up the phone to call the sheriff. There was no dial tone.
His cell phones were still outside in his bag, but the odds were
high that none of them would work. It's why he had a landline. He
powered up the hard-duty computer that he used for Search and
Rescue soirées to check on a theory. It was bulkier than most PCs,
with military-style grips and dirt guards. After it booted, he opened
the GPS tracking program that had failed to locate his transmitter in
the desert. When Doc lost his signal last week, everyone assumed
the transmitter he carried and put on Mike had quit working. There
was another possibility. Jay opened the software to check the list of

IDs being tracked. His identification number was gone.

When he and Doc packed up camp Thursday morning, they didn't delete any IDs. Even if she had reset the list without him knowing it, she'd never delete his number. He reviewed the list. Doc's number was listed. So was Faatina's.

He input his identification number and went outside to the deck. It took a minute to locate the satellite, but three signals appeared. Two were together. Those would be the transmitters Doc and Faatina had used. The screen showed that he was almost on top of them. That made sense. Their units were with the S&R gear in his shed, a hundred yards behind the trailer. In their haste to leave camp, he and Doc must have left them turned on.

The third beacon on the map, the far more interesting blinking dot had to be coming from his transmitter that someone had removed from Mike. It was on the far side of town.

Jay jumped off the deck to retrieve his bags and took them into the trailer. He stuffed his gaggle of cell phones into his daypack and collected a few goodies from his closet safe. Ready for anything, he slammed his defenseless front door shut, grabbed the laptop from the deck, and jogged to the shed.

The oversized shed predated Arizona's statehood. It didn't look like much, but it had character. Jay hoped his destructive visitors had left it alone. He walked beyond the shed's small front door to the large re-engineered barn doors on its extended back end. His stomach settled down seeing that neither Jeep parked inside had been disturbed. He climbed into his Wrangler Rubicon, which was parked nose-to-tail with his 1978 CJ. The Rube fired up. He plugged in the laptop and backed out.

Jay debated whether it was a good idea to let law enforcement know he was alive. Once he concluded that Sheriff Henson probably had no idea he might be taking up space in a Tel Aviv morgue, Jay reasoned Henson would have no reason to broadcast the news. Besides, Dean already knew he was back, and Evergreen was a small town. Jay reached the Jack-in-the-Box on the edge of town where his cell phone always worked. He parked in the lot and dialed the department's general number. It was a little late to call 9-1-1.

Sophie, the sheriff's assistant, answered the phone and Jay began filling her in.

She stopped him. "Another break-in? If the intruders are gone, you don't need the sheriff. I'll connect you to Sergeant Alvarez. He's handlin' break-ins. We're kinda backed up on them, just so's you know. Who is this, please?"

Jay informed her.

"Wow. Mr. Hunt. Um . . . you hold on for me, okay? I'll get Sheriff Henson straight away."

Special treatment wasn't anything Jay was used to, at least not in Evergreen.

Henson came on the line. "Mr. Hunt, good to hear from you. Sophie says your place got busted into. Sorry to hear that, but we'll get right on it. Are you there now? As long as you're safe, I need you to stay put. I understand the scum that did this is gone. Is that right?"

"They're gone, but I want you know that it looks just like—"

"I don't need the details now. I'll be right out to see them for myself."

Henson's keen interest launched a boatload of concern in Jay's swamped brain. Six days ago, the guy didn't want to discuss an executed hiker messing up his desert or the ridgeline sniper. Now he wanted to play detective at a home invasion. Jay wondered if an election was coming up, but he kept his mouth shut.

The sheriff continued, "In fact, I'll have a couple other boys come out with me. So don't get excited when you see all of us rollin' up."

Some interest could be explained. But rolling multiple units?

Jay moved the phone away from his mouth. "Sheriff? Sheriff? I can't hear you. Are you there?" He pressed the 'end' button.

For the first time, he wished his Jeep wasn't bright red, or new. There weren't many of either in Evergreen. Jay took the loop road around the city and in ten minutes he sat parked across the street from the source of the blinking dot. The GPS technology had been adapted by the military to work in rock canyons, steamy jungles, and dense forests.

Jay could now vouch that it also worked from inside seedy motel rooms.

CHAPTER 19

GAINING ENTRY WOULD BE tricky.

The Chieftain Motor-In had six units on either side of a central office. The efficiency motel reflected the era of housewives in pearls and cars with fins. If built today, the Chieftain would have had a more politically correct name and called itself an all-suite hotel. The place was hardly impregnable, but the clerk was a thin man in his fifties who took frequent outdoor cigarette breaks. Jay thought about the busted doorframe at his trailer and racked his brain for a less noisy way in. Driving around to the back of the motel turned up small, hard-to-crawl-through windows and no back doors.

It was 6:40, dark, and getting darker. Jay watched the motel from behind a Wash-a-Load across the street. His objective was unit 112, and so far, it had shown no movement, lights, or TV flicker. The motel's only traffic in the last half-hour was three pickups and a cherry picker, all with Mountain Electric plastered on their doors. They had arrived like a military convoy at 6:10 and four men in grubby tan work uniforms went straight to four separate units. They had reappeared twenty minutes later in grubby casual clothes, joined into pairs, and left in two trucks.

While Jay had waited on Mountain Electric's finest to refresh themselves, he had called and fed Rabbit the numbers from the Arabic cell phone's call logs. He recognized one, Rachel Raczynska's. He had put off calling Doc, uncertain how long the men would take. Thinking about her reminded him that the last time she rode in the Rubicon she had left a package of clean scrubs on his rear seat, and that provided the idea of the century, which now occupied him.

The inside of the Jeep was tight, but he managed to don her loose-fitting medical garments, which after cutting the waistband, fit better than expected. He hung a surgical mask from his neck and walked to the motel. Just outside the office, he adjusted the mask over his face, tied on the medical head cover, and walked in.

The clerk sat watching a small TV. He looked up the instant the door moved and nearly jumped out of his chair. Realizing the guy thought he was being robbed, Jay spoke up before facing a double-barreled invitation to leave. "I'm with Med-STID," he blurted out, "the medical scrub team for infectious disease. We have a patient at the hospital that isn't communicative, but had a key to your unit 112. I hope you didn't have any contact with them. I'm here to test the air in the unit. I may have to check some of the others as well."

"Tricia rents it. I haven't seen her in a few days. Is she sick?"

Jay looked around in a slow wide circle. "I'll need her full name and particulars. Can you describe her? I want to be sure we're talking about the same person."

The clerk's description centered on Tricia Smith's Arab features and womanly characteristics. *Faatina?* Jay couldn't believe his luck.

"It sounds like a match, but I'll need DNA to be sure. We don't need a panic on our hands. But if it is her, well . . . she's in a secure containment zone, in case she's contagious." Jay eased his conscience thinking Faatina did have an infectious smile. "I'll need her credit card information and driver's license."

"She paid cash for everything. The room, security deposit, you name it. She said she didn't have a license. Most people staying here aren't keen on leaving tracks, you know. My boss don't care if they got ID, as long as they got money."

"I see. I also need to know who she saw, ate with, what restaurants she may have gone to, whatever you know about her. Make a list while I check out her unit."

"I'd be lying, if I said we talked a bunch. Though, I sure admit to trying. If you've seen her, you know."

Jay smirked and looked at the clerk sideways. "I'm not supposed to notice things like that. Patients are uncomfortable as it is in those hospital gowns. But one time, well, oh man. You know what I'm saying?"

The clerk rolled his eyes and made a whooshing sound.

"So, can you hand me the key, please."

"I thought you come here because she had a key."

"She did. It's in decontamination segregation. You don't want it back. Trust me."

"I don't know about giving you her key, mister, um, what was your name?"

Jay didn't want rumors decimating the town, but he needed a clincher, and he needed it now. "We could be talking about an airborne pathogen. Chances are she brought it with her when she moved to town, but we can't be sure. The other possibility is she caught it while she was staying here at the Chieftain. I'm authorized to request approval for a full quarantine. That'll shut you down for who knows how long. And I can do it right now. It's your choice."

The clerk hesitated.

"See this mask I'm wearing? I'm worried about the air in this office. You've talked to her without benefit of a respirator. Have you been in her unit, cleaning it, maybe scoping it out? Maybe touched her stuff, by accident. If I were you, I'd sure want to know if the air in there is breathable. But like I said, it's up—"

"I can let you in. You won't take nothin', right?"

"You can come with me. You got a mask around here somewhere? I really shouldn't let you in without one, but if you insist—"

"No, you go." The clerk spun around, talking while he fidgeted with the clasp securing a small cabinet affixed to the back wall. It was the size of a woman's upright jewelry box. "I gotta stay here and watch the front desk." As he swung the door open, keys on a dozen teacup hooks jingled and swayed. He grabbed one labeled 112 and passed it to Jay. "Tell me if you find something."

BEFORE ENTERING, JAY PUT on cloth gloves that he kept in a roadside emergency kit. It was a good move.

The unit had hosted one too many biker parties with dents and gouges interrupted by occasional patches of smooth wallboard. Even with the mask over his nose, Jay could tell this unit wasn't well ventilated. The question wasn't if the air had pathogens, but what kind. If Faatina had stayed here, a musty S&R trailer must have seemed like a palace.

Except for the minor things like appearance and odor, the main room had a standard motel room feel to it; an unmade bed to the right, a chest of drawers missing significant pieces of its corners, and a 19-inch TV chained to its top. What wasn't standard, at least in his motel rooms, was the bra and a woman's button shirt on the bed. The light blue top had stains on it. He poked at it with a pen from the nightstand. Dried blood splatters caked the sleeves. He turned his attention to the drawers. They were all empty. No phone books, not even a Gideon's Bible.

So far, there was no sign of his GPS unit or anything else to help his cause. A bathroom and an extra sink occupied the right side of the unit's rear. To the left, a drunken door knocked off one hinge led to a mini eat-in kitchen. He explored the tub and toilet area first. The sink's yellow linoleum countertop, besides holding a drug store's worth of beauty products, had reddish brown streaks that looked like blood. They continued into the sink. The curtain to the tub was drawn closed. Jay readied the pen to pull it back, hoping not to find the source of the blood. He pulled slowly at first. A few inches revealed only a filthy tub. He tugged it a bit further and froze when he thought he heard someone in the room. After an eternity of listening to the pulse in his ears, he quit the tub in favor of peaking into the main room.

Empty quiet greeted him. He returned to the tub feeling foolish and worked the curtain open. Like the room, no body was present, but apparently the maid had taken the year off. He moved on to the kitchenette.

Once again, a nice floor plan had yielded to age and neglect. There were enough grease spatters on the wall behind the small cook top to fry an egg. It looked like someone may have tried. The kitchen table's red and black checkerboard top must have been original equipment from the 1950s as was an equally old white refrigerator with rust trim. The area around the door handle had more fingerprints than the FBI. He couldn't imagine putting food in the thing, let alone eating whatever came out of it. He noticed the door was latched, but bulged out an inch at its base. If it hadn't been used in a while the air exchange could be a good thing. It might also be contributing to the room's assorted smells.

He felt compelled to look inside it.

SHE WIGGLED THE LOOSE tooth with her tongue, enjoying the taste of her blood. Faatina's stomach growled as she snapped on a pair of latex gloves. Thanks to Jay, she'd likely be eating with one less tooth tonight. She cheered herself thinking it could have been worse.

Downtown Evergreen's square was pitifully quiet for seven o'clock, and with no security system, her entry into his offices would be easy. She retrieved her lock pick set, selected her tool of choice, and concentrated on the door's lock. Within a ten-count, she had defeated it. She picked up her bag of goodies and slipped inside. All in all, the day had paid luscious dividends. There would be no more yap from Reza tonight. Reluctant as Reza had been to remain in the US, now she really had cold feet. Later tonight, she'd be in a nice warm desert grave, and Jay's complicity in the far-reaching reign of terror irrefutable.

After a moment, Faatina's eyes adjusted to the dark interior and multiple desks became visible. She wondered which one was his. Guessing correctly was important, so she took a full inventory before deciding. She followed a narrow hallway to the building's rear, losing what little light came through the front windows along the way. Deciding it was safe to use the torch in this area, she pointed the light down and continued along the hall past stacks of smelly boxes into a back office.

As dashing as he was, this was quite a dull room. But there was no mistaking his scent, or that this desk was his. She removed the handgun from her bag and slipped it under several papers in a bottom drawer. She pulled the rolled drawings out of the bag and looked for a proper place to put them. The desktop appeared as good a repository as any. Even this sheriff would be able to find them there.

Now, what do you have for me, Mr. Hunted?

She rifled through the other desk drawers, but found nothing worthwhile and headed back toward the entrance. She bumped into the boxes in the hall. Pulling back a flap on a top box, she found tons of files. Why would a tour driver have so many files? Grabbing several, she went back to his office.

She couldn't stop herself from humming as she read them.

On the way out, she blew a kiss into his office. "This Hunt is over."

CHAPTER 20

PREPARED TO SEE BLACK and green fuzzy containers, Jay
hooked his trusty pen on the refrigerator's handle. He yanked it.
The pen slipped off the hard-to-work handle and fell from his loose
grip to the floor. Bending down to pick up the pen, he noticed more
blood streaks at the base of the refrigerator. It had been swirled
in a haphazard attempt to clean it. He left the pen there. From his
new vantage point, he saw under the kitchen table. Wire shelves,
probably from the refrigerator, had been stacked underneath it.

He grabbed the door's handle with a gloved hand.

It resisted opening like an overstuffed suitcase. He pushed on
the door while pulling on the handle. It jerked open.

An arm flopped down, followed by the rest of the Arab Beauty.

Black and fuzzy would have been better. Her eyes, too wide-
open in life, were the same in death. Her contorted mouth was very
different. She had no teeth.

Jay retreated to the main room. He leaned against a wall and
slid down it until he sat on the carpet. He stared into the room
without focus. And he saw it. His GPS transmitter was under the
arched base of the nightstand. He grabbed it and his brain restarted.

He had a problem.

The front desk clerk had seen him. The sheriff was already overly interested, so calling him didn't seem like a winning strategy. On the other hand, case closed or not, the FBI needed to find the frigid babe now sprawled on the kitchen floor. Calling them seemed a better choice. Jay's heavy breathing into the mask reminded him of his medical costume. He got up and looked in the mirror. What looked back at him from behind the mask and under the hat was unrecognizable. Height, weight, and Caucasian were the only descriptors the clerk could provide.

Jay's brain wandered back to this woman and the chances she'd be in Evergreen. The clerk's description of the guest in 112 could have fit this woman or Faatina, except he had specifically commented on her flawless brown skin. The scar across this lady's right cheek didn't fit. So this wasn't the person the clerk called Tricia. Unless he killed her and his description was meant to throw Jay off. No, he'd never have given over the key, knowing her body was inside.

Concentrate.

If Faatina rented this room, then this woman could tie the Houston bombing to Faatina. He had to inform the FBI. Except, even if he called anonymously, they'd know he had called. He was the only living person who had seen her in the store and could make that connection.

That meant Henson must get the tip. But not until he was clear of the scene.

DOC'S VOICE HAD SOUNDED unsettled, speaking in short, clipped sentences and weighing every word. She had promised to meet him at eight o'clock, which alleviated some of his concern.

Maybe he read too much into her tone, but he couldn't help wonder if this was going to be the big kiss off.

She had suggested meeting at his trailer, but he declined, since the police had an abnormal interest in him. She suggested her house, but he didn't want to drag her any deeper than necessary into this latest wrinkle in his life. They settled on the hospital. If the police spotted him, at least she would have a good excuse for being there.

With that settled and a half-hour to kill, he found an outside pay phone at another Wash-a-Load. This one was near the hospital. It was time to call in the body. The police dispatcher was most interested in his name. When she got too insistent, he hung up. Problem solved. A plan to involve the FBI fell together, too, but carrying it out would have to wait until tomorrow after the news of the body was all over town. Another anonymous call, saying the lady at the motel had boasted about "things" she had done in Houston, should do the job.

Jay arrived early at the hospital and dropped his scrubs in an exchange closet. Doc's office was in the hospital's new wing near the OR, but she'd insisted on meeting in the employees' commissary in the east wing. Nobody called it the old wing, but that's what it was. It dated back to the 1940s. The hallways and rooms were cramped by today's standards. Jay peaked inside a window into the mess hall and didn't see her or recognize any of the three workers. The rest of the wing had a deserted feel about it.

At 8:00 sharp, Doc walked through the connecting corridor about fifty yards away. She didn't look anywhere near as happy to see him as he felt about seeing her. He walked toward her away from the commissary. The closer he got to Doc, the paler she looked. He wondered if she was ill.

He heard the employees who had been eating in the commissary enter the hall behind him. Two male employees behind Doc passed around her, walking in his direction. The realization dawned that the two groups of men were set to converge about where he stood. His internal alarm system shrieked.

It was too late. Hands grabbed him from behind as the men in front pounced on him. They were all yelling, "Police. You're under arrest."

He didn't resist.

As the five men wrestled him to the ground, he locked eyes with Doc.

She was crying.

JAY SAT HANDCUFFED ON the floor against the wall. Two of the undercover crew guarded him. Doc froze when the action started about fifteen yards off and had stayed there. Her chin hung down to her chest and her hands were folded as if in prayer. On occasion, her lips moved.

Sheriff Henson appeared from within the employees' cafeteria. Late thirties with a boyish face and wispy mustache, he had starred on Evergreen High's basketball team, taking them to the state 1 A title two years in a row. He straightened his uniform.

Jay looked at him. "Your guys won't tell me what this is about. Why don't you give it a try?"

Henson stared down at Jay, and began reciting his Miranda rights. An undercover deputy radioed that the suspect was under arrest. The sheriff was nearly done when Jay saw Randy and another deputy enter the hallway from an exit at the far end.

Doc had drawn near. Her face was red and tear-streaked. "I'll tell you why," she said in a cold monotone, "because you would've killed me. You used me to worm your way into the hospital so you could blow it up too."

Her rage-filled eyes hurt more than her words, and neither made sense.

"I don't know what you've heard, but it's all lies."

The sheriff stepped toward her, smirking like he had just beaten four jacks with four queens. "He's dangerous, you should stand clear." The sheriff reached for her hand.

Doc recoiled.

Jay said, "Touch her, and you'll regret it."

Randy hustled into the space between Doc and the red-faced sheriff. "Let's move over here," Randy suggested. He steered Doc by her upper arms. Trance-like, she walked off with him to her earlier spot.

Henson stepped closer and glared down at Jay. "You threatened me?"

Jay nodded, imperceptibly slow. "That's right—with a charge of official oppression. And if you make any other unwanted advances toward her, it'll be more than a threat. Now, tell me why I'm under arrest."

The sheriff chewed on the apparently unexpected counter-charge. "Humph. You're under arrest for the death of Mike Williams from Ohio, and on suspicion of murdering eighteen others in Houston. There'll be specific charges concerning your terrorist activities later from the Feds."

"Why do you think these things? Who has been talking to you?

Henson shook his head. "Talk? The gun we found in your desk matches the caliber used to kill the supposed hiker from Ohio, who you were pretending to save. The state ballistics lab will confirm the match. Architectural drawings for this hospital and the Kroger in Houston were also found in your office. We know for a fact that all this bomb activity was paid for with money you embezzled from former clients. We have the files and a huge recent withdrawal from your account to prove it. This isn't about talk. You are going to rot in jail a very long time."

PASTOR BOB UNWOUND THE chains on the church's side door. It was quarter after ten when the ringer at the church's side door had buzzed. Johnny Bingham stood outside under the intense light of the new mercury vapor lamps. A former football player, Johnny looked the part under the harsh glare of stadium-style lights. Pastor Bob fumbled with the key ring to unlock the deadbolt. After succeeding, he ushered Johnny into the library.

Johnny's upbeat attitude gave way to a determined look. "I heard that you're sleeping in the church every night."

"Is that what people think?"

"It's what they're saying."

"That's good."

"They say you sleep with a loaded shotgun, too."

"I'd rather they didn't say that." Pastor Bob looked away. "But I'm glad they're thinking it. I'd strike the match before I'd allow a weapon in here."

"I don't mind taking turns bunking down here. I'm just as single as you are. Maybe more. Nobody misses either one of us at night. That's a shame, isn't it? Two studs like us."

"It's a darn shame. How can you be more single than me?"

"I'm old and ugly. You're still a handsome young pup."

"You're not either one of those things and neither am I. If I'm young, I sure don't feel it. Not anymore. Did you hear about Chuck Kravitz?"

"He's in a better place. How's Martha?"

"Like you'd expect. I met with her this afternoon. She's questioning everything. Having the new baby may help keep her

mind off things, but she's going to need help. Two months ago
this church would have rallied around her. But there's hardly any
church left. I could hardly look at her. They beat her pretty bad."
Pastor Bob turned away when he couldn't see straight through his
tearing eyes. "Chuck came home and walked right into what they
were doing to her. She's blaming herself for his death. They stabbed
him over a dozen times. Right in front of their kids. How he ever
found his gun after that, I'll never know." He blinked his eyes dry.
"I failed her. My words were hollow. She'd been teaching children's
Sunday school since she was seventeen. They stopped coming to
church, but she said she wants a funeral service for Chuck's benefit.
I don't know that I'd have had the right words before, but now . . ."

"If you were with her, you didn't fail her."

Pastor Bob smashed his fist on the conference table. "I just want
to march down to the hospital and unplug the cords keeping those
two thugs alive. How's that sound coming from your preacher? She
asked how could there be a heaven if there wasn't a resurrection.
What was I supposed to say? So I said what I always say. I don't
know if I believed a single word. I was a used car salesman today.
That's what I am now. I acted like I believed every word. Don't look
under the hood, just believe. Can there be a greater sin?"

"Giving comfort is no sin, and neither is doubt. John the Baptist
had doubts, so he dealt with them. I once heard a young pastor
preach on the subject." Johnny eyes twinkled. "Remember? You
said it wasn't an accident that the Baptist's doubts came while he sat
in prison. From the depths of his cell, the Baptist sought answers to
ease his mind. Son, spending twenty-four hours a day in here isn't
doing you any good. Especially when your nights are spent behind
locks and chains. You need a break. I got my stuff in the truck.
I'm ordering you home for the night, soldier. If you can't settle
your doubts here, and if home won't work, then you go where you

need to. In the weeks and months ahead, we're going to need your leadership not your salesmanship. The Holy Spirit's in charge of sales, we just have to do the advertising."

THE MOLDED PLASTIC REAR seat of Randy's cop car was even less comfortable than it looked. Jay shifted. "I like how my handcuffed arms fit behind me into the seat's channels. Believe it or not, this is the best part of my day. How's yours going?"

Randy responded without turning around. "Better than yours. I'd say you're having a bad week. I know you were almost blown to bits in Houston, and Doc told me about your dad. I was sorry to hear it. Tonight, I saw your place. What happened over there?"

"Randy, I don't know where to begin, but I can tell you it's all related. My dad's place in Houston received the same treatment. All I can conclude is that someone thinks my dad or me has something that could challenge the authenticity of the Q document. I don't have a personal stake in whether Jesus was divine or not, but I see what it's doing to the world. If it's a fake, it needs to be exposed."

"I have a stake in his divinity, and if Jesus was divine, then so do you. What have you found?"

Jay made a quick decision. "The woman's body at the Chieftain—"

"How do you know about that?"

"I phoned it in. The FBI calls her the Arab Beauty." Jay explained about seeing her in the Houston Kroger and how the GPS led him to the Chieftain. "A woman whose description matches Tina rented the room. Her real name is Faatina al Wahiri, and her father dealt in old scrolls like the Q document. That's what I know. Now why do people think I killed Mike the hiker?"

"Everything you said fits better than you know. This morning

the sheriff said he got a tip that'll make him the next Governor."
Randy pulled his cruiser into the dark parking lot of a vacant Dollar
Store. Four-foot-high scraggly weeds grew from cracks in the
buckled blacktop. He parked and said, "Give me a minute," as he
began texting a message.

"No, I want you take me to jail faster."

Jay heard a chuckle from the front seat.

The deputy faced rearward. "Okay. You know Sophie, Sheriff
Henson's assistant? She told me that Henson went to Sin City
last night to meet with a tipster. Turns out it was Tina. She told
Henson that Mike and you met late Tuesday night near base camp
and argued. She overheard you both boasting about being in the
militia and all the bombings you had planned. You were headed to
Houston, and he was supposed to target Evergreen. Mike argued
against making Evergreen's hospital a fourth target. You walked
deeper into the desert together and came back alone. Scared, she left
camp the first chance she got the next day, and wandered the desert
alone. She went into hiding."

"And then I dragged his body five miles into the box canyon?"

"She guessed you marched him there and then shot him."

"And Mike just cooperated? Why would I have taken him half
that distance or told you where he was? Why didn't she alert anyone
about a possible bomb at the hospital?"

"Yeah, she was sorry about that. Then, less than an hour ago,
we got an anonymous tip about the gun in your office. The caller
tried to sound old and gruff."

"No! Can you check on Marge for me? Make sure she's all
right?"

"Relax. I talked to her. She's fine. I figured we were supposed
to believe she was the caller. Anyway, we found maps of Houston
and drawings of the hospital lying on top of your desk. You don't

strike me as that dumb. Especially not if you did a Madoff on a bunch of clients. We have all the files on your victims. Why didn't you quit when you were ahead?"

"Victims? Call them. You'll hear a different story."

"I don't have time to call them."

"That's the trouble with the world, everyone's in a hurry."

Randy shook his head. "You're making my decision difficult."

"So was mine, Randy. So was mine."

"I need to know more, and now would be real helpful."

"I wasn't always a tour operator. I was a money manager. First in Zurich, then in Houston with a couple government jobs in between. I crushed the market year after year. Then when the market tanked, I had a terrible year. To make up for it, I tried hitting for the fences. I lost even more. People with me from the start still did extremely well compared to their original investment, but newer investors lost money. I personally covered their losses. I expected that it would cost me a ton. As it turned out, all it cost me was my fiancé."

"You were engaged?"

Jay watched a dirt devil blow toward them, then collapse. "Yeah. Her dad was a recent investor. When I closed his account and handed him a fat check to make up his losses, I was a big hero. After she found out I did the same for all my new clients, and that it had cost me millions, she left me. Funny, but to exit the business completely, I couldn't sell everything at once, so I cashed everyone out and laid on puts—options that guarded against the market getting torpedoed. A huge market correction occurred, bigger than before. It made my options worth all the money I had paid out, and then some."

"I figured you'd have a pretty good story. Most con men do." Randy turned the cruiser's engine over.

Jay started thinking of lawyers to call, but Doc was the only person he really wanted to speak with.

The deputy pulled into traffic. "Of course if Mike was militia, even from Ohio, he wouldn't wander around the desert in shorts. And the timing in Faatina's story doesn't fit the condition of Mike's body, which makes me think the babe in the fridge might have been its second occupant. There were no prints on the gun in your desk, which is odd, and when you left town last week, you told me to keep an eye on Doc. I don't know why you'd do that and then try to blow her up. So I've got one more question. Did you do it?"

"No."

Randy lifted his cell phone from his console and spoke into it. "We're live. I'm on Main crossing Airport Highway. I'll be at Blackjack Avenue in one minute." He turned to Jay. "You might want to tighten your seatbelt."

Jay looked around. "There aren't any."

"Then you better lean left and hang on." Randy winked in the rearview mirror and raised his phone again. "Crossing Blackjack. Yeah, okay." Randy slowed his cruiser. "Jay you're going to have to fend for yourself. I'll be unconscious in a minute. Here's the key to your cuffs. It'll save you some time. Oh and here's the keys to a red Mustang half a block up Perdido Street. It'll be reported stolen at oh-eight hundred hours tomorrow, so you better ditch it by then. I figure if the bad guys can make things look like accidents, so can we."

Jay worked behind his back to release his handcuffs. "Randy, don't let Faatina slip away." The tiny key refused to find the lock. He kept at it. "How do I thank you and the Mustang's owner?"

Randy listened on the phone. "He says by ditching the car nice and leaving the keys under the mat. Thirty seconds. I'll move your Jeep. Wreckers enjoy being nasty to new cars that belong to escapees. Don't forget your bag on my front seat. I took the liberty of removing it from your Jeep. That's a lot of cell phones. They better be legal. Fifteen seconds." Randy set the phone down and put both hands on the wheel. "Ten seconds."

An old model pickup truck with one working headlight barreled down Perdido on Jay's right. There was no way it could break in time for its stop sign. Jay worked one wrist free and raised his arms so that a forearm rested on each ear. The handcuffs dangled from his left wrist. He laid across the seat with his feet against the right door and his knees flexed.

Randy plastered his head against his headrest. "This was a bad idea. Find those—"

CHAPTER 21

THE MUSTANG MIGHT NOT be reported missing until tomorrow morning, but felony suspect escapees are chased right away, and hard. Knowing his face would be sent around the state at the speed of fax and email was less than comforting. It was half past eight and it wouldn't be long before the state troopers and nearby counties would be looking for him. It was also an automatic in Arizona to alert Customs, Border Patrol, and he assumed in his case, the FBI. How the FBI would react was hard to guess, since the accusations against him ran counter to their public thesis that the bombers were from the Baxter mosque. Jay supposed the worst case was they would claim he was a Muslim convert, or if they pushed the militia angle, that mutual enemies of the US government had combined forces. Either way, he was a bug headed for a windshield.

On the positive side, he wasn't in jail and the Mustang drove like a dream. Keeping it under the speed limit was nearly impossible, so he was doubly glad that he had grabbed the ultimate fuzz buster from his safe before he'd left his trailer. It not only detected radar and laser guns, but defeated them as well. As confused as his brain was, one thing was certain; if he ever had kids, he would never let them own a Mustang. Randy had failed to mention that the car came complete with a police scanner and a list of the most common frequencies different state agencies used. That was a nice touch.

The back roads to Las Vegas through Nevada beckoned. They could provide a quick exit from Arizona, and with his Mossad identity, Jay Chase, he figured he could fly anywhere. TSA wouldn't pose a problem with his authentic docs. There was even a made to order flight to Houston at 1:05 a.m. But every cop and air marshal in Vegas would be sitting at the boarding gate with his picture. No disguise would be adequate. Driving to Albuquerque was tempting, but he'd be driving in Arizona as long as if he drove south to Mexico. Crossing the U.S. border, at least through a legal point of entry, was too risky. He hoped the state would pour its resources into those most likely alternatives because he had a better option.

He dialed the first of two people who could help pull it off.

NEITHER RICHARD CLEARWATER NOR his tribe split hairs whether the desert surrounding Evergreen should be spelled Mohave, as it was by Arizonans, or Mojave, as Californians preferred. To Richard the desert was mother, god, and freedom rolled into one, and nobody knew it as intimately as he did. It's why Jay had spent many nights around a campfire with Richard, and why Jay felt safe asking him for help. Not only did Richard know a great place to stash the low-slung Mustang off-road, but he volunteered to drive Jay south to Phoenix to meet Sarah, who was driving up from Tucson. Three hours later, they united at a Denny's off Phoenix's Highway 101 Loop. They ordered three Grand Slams to-go and ate them in an RV-style van that Jay recommended Sarah rent in Tucson.

After Richard left, Sarah drove southeast on US 70 toward New Mexico, while Jay slept in one of two twin beds in the van's rear. Just south of Franklin, a mile from the New Mexico line, she woke him as they neared a highway patrol checkpoint. He put on Sarah's blonde wig from Houston and had wire-rimmed reading glasses available. Up close, it wouldn't fool anyone besides a drag queen, but in the dark van, it might work. He pretended to sleep.

An officer studied Sarah through her rolled down window and shined a powerful flashlight into the rear. "You ladies have a nice trip." He waved them past the orange cones.

Sarah wanted to keep driving and Jay obliged. Thirty minutes later in Lordsburg, New Mexico they connected with I-10, and Sarah said she'd had enough. Jay drove them to Las Cruces where he stopped at a rest area overlooking the city. It was 6:40, and sunrise was an hour off, but its beginnings peppered the horizon. Purplish-gray clouds mushroomed over the Organ Mountains ten miles to the east. Sarah stirred in back. He invited her forward to enjoy the sight. The red in her eyes reminded him of the pain in Doc's.

In town, Sarah bought donuts and coffee, which they elected to eat elsewhere. The tantalizing smell of jelly, fried dough, and powdered sugar overtook the van. Jay drove, while Sarah called her team. She hung up half an hour later as they crossed into Texas.

A road sign told them Houston was another 728 miles.

Sarah squinted at Jay. "If we're in Texas, that sign can't be right. Can it?"

"Afraid so, but Dad's condo on Mustang Island won't be quite that far." He punched the address into the GPS. "It's only 695 miles."

A few miles later, just north of El Paso, they found a spot perfect for eating donuts and taking in the scenic Franklin

Mountains. They each swiveled their seat around and ate at a table located in the van's center aisle.

Sarah had bought three coffees for herself and started sucking the third one dry. "We have a problem. The Q document's sanctioning is in a week, and science isn't on our side. My Mossad team includes an expert from the Israel Antiquities Authority. Lizabeth is coordinating with various scholars at the Rockefeller and Israel Museums. She says that the papyrus is definitely from the first century and very likely to be in the 30 to 40 AD range. PIXE analysis, I forget what that stands for, confirmed that no metals are present in the ink samples."

"Particle Induced X-ray Emission analysis. It's a test for metal oxides. If it uncovers molecules not used for inks back whenever the fragment was theoretically written, it points to a forgery. The real trick for the forger is making the ink set up correctly on the ancient paper. That's why testers like to have comparable period pieces available for comparison."

"I should have let you talk to her."

Jay shrugged off the compliment. "Your mom was the expert. After she passed, you didn't have the opportunity to stay immersed in this jazz. Even after I left Israel, Dad and I talked. What about the script, syntax, vocabulary—"

"It's passing every test. Historians, theologians, and physical scientists are all falling into line. My team says every test so far is failing to disprove that the Q document is a forgery."

He wiped sugar off his shirt. "That seems backwards doesn't it? The burden of proof should be on proving the Q's authenticity."

"There's no doubt the papyrus is first century. Experts in Paris tested the Q's age with non-destructive techniques and sent it to Professor Albright in Tucson. It was his tests that confirmed it's from the first century. By the way, he knew your dad and sends his condolences. Albright's worked with the BBM since its inception."

"BBM?"

"That's what he calls his room full of equipment. Big bloody match. To count the fragment's C-14 ions, it has to be converted to graphite, so they burn it. Ergo, big bloody match."

"If the experts can't disprove this thing, how are we going to do it?"

"Well, Nigel mentioned something that isn't exactly proof, but it tells me we're on the right path."

"Nigel, huh? Why were you late leaving Tucson?"

She blushed. "Professor Albright, who is pushing seventy, said that he tested a piece of papyrus that your dad gave him on the sly nearly ten years ago. He recalled that the results were similar, so he looked them up. The results were an exact match. He thinks your dad may have had a piece of the Q document."

Jay gulped down the last of his coffee. "That's when Dad retired and moved back to the States. If Nigel has a remnant of Dad's sample, he could match the fibers or something."

"He thought of that. Your dad's entire fragment was consumed during the original test. All he had was a record of the results. Even if they were a match, he said it only proves that your dad came across the document before the rest of the world. Do you think your dad knew about the Q document way back then?"

Jay tapped his empty coffee cup on the table. "When the news first broke that the Q document had been found, Dad was shocked, then in denial. That all argues no. But there was his confession that he stole something. Small. Inconsequential at the time, but one that could save mankind's soul. What if my dad had—"

They finished the thought together. "Another piece."

Jay retrieved his daypack from a drawer under a bed and returned to his seat. He pulled out the key they had recovered from Dad's dining table. He tossed the key in the air and caught it. "This must be to a safe deposit box. Let's compare Dad's letter to his message that Marge typed." He pulled them from his pack and placed them next to each on the table. "Dad's letter speaks of 'the key to saving mankind's soul' and added, 'Picture that.' His message from Marge says, 'the picture's not clear,' and 'you can bet on one of *them* to get the picture right.' I think his 'them' refers to the prior sentence about airports, which we already concluded has nothing to do with his itinerary. That part reads, 'I'm trying to avoid Heathrow, shooting at JFK first, National next.'" Jay stared at the paper, trying to decipher the clue.

"Let's assume saving mankind's soul means proving the Q is a fake and do what your dad said and 'avoid Heathrow.' That leaves 'shooting at JFK first, National next.' Does that help?"

"Maybe. Dad said, 'You can *bet* on one of those.' He hated gambling. I don't think he'd say 'bet' unless it meant something."

Sarah shrugged. "What's another way to say it? Maybe he needed to *avoid* saying something."

"Uh, you can bet, you can wager, gamble, risk. You can depend, lean on. Sarah! You can *bank* on it. We think the key is to a safe deposit box. Okay, let's see, 'shooting at JFK first, National next.' This is the sentence where he uses the word 'at' incorrectly." Jay clapped his hands. "I've got it!"

Sarah looked at him. "What? Tell me."

"We need to alter course. We're not going to Mustang Island." He grabbed the GPS and tapped in the destination so Sarah couldn't see the letters. "It's only 620 miles. Nine hours and thirty-one minutes."

CHAPTER 22

FOR SOME REASON THE GPS showed the FedEx copy center on the wrong side of the highway. Jay spotted it and drove there. They were in Grand Prairie, Texas, just a few minutes north of Cedar Hill State Park where they had spent a cold night and frigid morning.

Sarah let out a long sigh as they pulled into the lot. "If Dallas is best known for JFK's assassination, why is their sports team called America's team?"

"Because it sells more jerseys. That's it. It's all marketing. No one really thinks of them that way. Let's hope your package is in. Remember, now you're Sarah Bennet."

With one foot out the door, she sighed again, this time with a smile. "Who's the spy here? You or me?"

"You mean ever since Sunday? That would be you."

Sarah was in and out in a flash. She jogged to the van, clutching the overnight delivery package. She slipped into the passenger seat, waving a photocopy of a page from the local phone book.

"There are fourteen Dallas First National Bank branches. This could take all day and we're not even sure we figured out the clues correctly." She looked down at the page. "It's Friday, Jay."

"I'm feeling it, too." Jay dumped the package in his lap, placed their new identity documents aside in favor of the more pertinent sheaf. "These legal documents from your Embassy will relieve some of the pressure. This one shows that you're executrix for my estate, and these say I was the executor for my dad. Taken together that gives you power-of-attorney over his affairs. There are two death certificates and everything is notarized. All we have to do is call the bank's main number and ask where he kept the box. What could be easier?"

SARAH'S HANDS WERE CLAMMY. She couldn't help wondering if Professor Hunt's accounts and safe deposit box had been flagged.

At 9:35, five minutes after the branch opened, she had waltzed through the front door and into the spiffy white marble lobby. The woman in charge of safe deposit boxes was new on the job and had never dealt with letters of authorization from a probate judge. She deferred to the assistant branch manager. He said that all of Sarah's papers were in order, except he wasn't sure if it made any difference that Sarah was an Israeli citizen. Then he wondered if Israeli death certificates were valid. The branch manager was off, and the assistant manager's call to the main office went to voice mail. A couple other calls failed to elicit a firm answer, and he'd gotten busy.

It was 10:45.

The current nonsense coupled with profuse apologies could have been a stalling action until the FBI arrived. Sarah had avoided looking into the cameras scattered around the lobby, but that was getting more difficult as she was shuffled between cubicles. She was about to call Jay, expecting he was at wits end, when the assistant manager walked in.

"Can you come back on Monday? My manager will be—"

She lost her temper.

HE ASSUMED SOME SNAFU had snagged Sarah, so Jay busied himself as best he could. He sat in the driver's seat, which was turned backwards to face the handy little table behind him. He called Rabbit to see what his friend had discovered about the Arabic phone from Dad's suitcase.

Rabbit sounded excited. "I've got some really good intel from those phone numbers. I'll start with the owner. It belonged to Hassan Tariq al Rhaheem. You should recognize the name. It's another dead guy on your father's financial shopping list. I'm glad I'm not on his list."

"Dad said he was a Jordanian. Have you found out anything about him beyond that?"

"Very little. I've concentrated elsewhere. What I can say with certainty is that Hassan didn't have an account at Faatina's Swiss bank, which by the way is Sitzweiller United. He also doesn't have an account at Island Bancshares in the Caymans."

"I came across Sitzweiller when I worked in Zurich, but I never did any business with them. What does the Cayman bank have to do with this? And how do you know where he doesn't have accounts?"

"I have lists of all the accountholders at both—"

"Their names? You have their names—like spelled with letters?"

"Right-o. Kinda cool, ain't it?"

"I don't know about cool, but it is impressive. You better watch yourself. Obtaining those cross-lists is no way to make friends. Are you still wheeling around in a black tee shirt?"

"Whenever I use the apartment." Rabbit made a tsk-tsk noise. "The accounts work as follows. Faatina's Swiss account gets fed big money from the Cayman bank, and periodically she passes some back there again. They don't seem to have a clearinghouse function, but get this. IB, that's what I call Island Bancshares, does have accounts for two other guys on your father's list who also appeared in the phone logs. I'd say that's more than a coincidence, and as far as I know, they're both alive."

"Great. Who?"

"Claude Duvert and Jean Veillon. And they're tied together by more than the phone. Stay with me here. Faatina's Swiss account receives money from an IB account identified by the letters SLLC. Faatina has made two transfers to Duvert and routinely puts small deposits into Veillon's account. SLLC has never transferred money to Duvert directly, but funds pass back and forth all the time between SLLC and the Society Duvert controls. It's like a feeding frenzy down there."

Jay's mind raced through the possibilities. "My dad knew both of them. I heard him mention Veillon. I've met Duvert."

"You realize the Duvert we're talking about is *Doctor* Claude Duvert at the—let me look it up—the Société des Antiquités Archéologiques. He's in charge of the eggheads looking into the Q document and Veillon's the guy who—"

"Supposedly found the scroll. Yeah, I know. This is incredible. They're not very careful, are they?"

"Are you kidding? These lazy intra-bank transfers have given me several leads, including transfers from SLLC to the bank's president, a Marie LeSabre. This is like amateur hour. By the way, Veillon opened a local account in George Town in the Caymans. He may have taken up residence."

Jay tapped on the table. "Do you have any ideas on SLLC's

identity?"

"No, but it's someone in Egypt loaded to the gills, and I'm getting closer. One last thing. When you gave me the list of numbers, you said that you recognized Rachel Raczynska's phone. If she's in with the cool kids, I haven't seen proof of it."

"Meaning what? She doesn't have an account at either bank?"

"Right-o. But I'm still working her. The other two numbers in the call logs are Hassan's relatives. I don't expect to find much on them."

A car parked two spaces over from the van. "Is that all the phone numbers? It seemed like there were more."

"That's all you gave me, but you have the phone, check it."

"The phone died yesterday. I'm lucky if the battery lasts eighteen hours in standby. I'll charge it when I get a chance and get back to you."

Jay looked out the windshield and saw Sarah marching across the parking lot. A young bank guard with a swagger and a cocky sneer kept pace a few steps directly behind her. His hand rested on his holstered sidearm.

"Great work. I'll be in touch." Jay reached for the door handle. "Milady's coming, and me thinks she may need a knight."

TWO DAYS WITHOUT EMAIL was all Agent Greene could stand. He had taken his wife to a B&B in the Texas Hill Country to celebrate his upcoming promotion and Yvonne was out shopping. He checked it and found two priority alerts. Jay Hunt was wanted for murder, terrorism, and escaping custody in Arizona. Greene leaned back in the rickety chair. He stared at a picture of bluebonnets hanging on the wall above the small desk. Fugitives often turned up dead, but it was rare that the dead turned up as fugitives. A second email alert signaled that the body of the Arab Beauty suspect in the Houston bombing was found mutilated in Evergreen, Arizona. The alerts had been routed to Green even though he had signed off on the case on Monday. The Bureau's administrative wheels turned as slow as a pig on a spit.

Greene called Houston. Reeko's voicemail said he had been reassigned. Todd Farnsleigh was away from his desk. Greene left him a detailed message.

Once again, he'd been taught the dangers of a mid-week vacation and listening to his boss, Waters. The investigation's imminent close was looking premature, as was his promotion celebration. Waters declared the investigation wrapped, but Greene was the name all over the case file.

Yvonne returned from shopping with a couple of twenty-dollar knickknacks that she'd sell at a garage sale for fifty cents in two years.

"Aren't these darling?" she asked.

"You sure have an eye for finding those things. Hungry?"

They left for lunch and ate at a funky corner café on the small town's square. His phone jiggled on his belt. It was Farnsleigh. Greene took the call.

"You know that Israeli cop Baumann that you asked about? She flew to Chicago on Wednesday."

Greene looked at his watch. He had only left that message thirty minutes ago. "That was quick. You must need work."

"I checked on her yesterday. Some DC grunt wondered if she was still in town. Waters wanted to verify that we treated her well and answered all her questions. I told him that you sent her away crying."

"I doubt that gal cries." A dirty look from Yvonne sent Greene from the table to the sidewalk outside. "I wonder what's in

Chicago."

"Besides a big lake and lots of wind? Remember, the University of Chicago came up a couple times when we looked into radiocarbon dating old documents."

"That's right. The big dog was in Arizona, though." A truck pulling a rickety horse trailer passed the restaurant. "Find out where Ms. Baumann is now. If she's still in Chicago, ask Jolene Peterson in our office up there to find out where Ms. B is staying. Have her ask our Israeli friend the same questions you got. You know, did we treat her well, any other questions, whatever. Call me when you know."

"We're not on this case anymore, remember?"

"That's why you're calling Agent Peterson. Besides, I'm already in the soup. I might as well do something to deserve being there. The Arab Beauty is real—real dead."

Greene ended the call. Sarah Bauman was right. Waters reassigned the case too soon.

And I let him.

"JAY, THERE ARE THREE pictures. I couldn't help myself, I had to flip through them. I couldn't believe it—I still can't. They're faded, but they're black and whites photographs of a scroll. One while it's rolled, one unrolled, and one in-process. I can't wait for you to see them."

Jay contented himself with hearing about them and drove out of the bank's parking lot toward DFW. "What happened in there?"

Sarah explained in minute-by-minute fashion how her frustration had exploded. "After I accused the assistant manager of sexual harassment, he began softening. I got kind of loud and demanded to speak to the bank's president, whose name I then discovered was Rosenfeld. I threw in discrimination against Jews, and the wise young man couldn't get me into the safe deposit vault fast enough. That's when he assigned the guard to me to be sure I wasn't disturbed. I think he just wanted to be sure I left. Besides the pictures, there's $500 cash and a diary."

"A diary? In his safe deposit box?" The GPS instructed Jay to turn left ahead. "I hope it's not more clues."

They had been driving for twenty minutes and were entering a part of town where cars with tired paint and smoking tailpipes were the norm. He made a u-turn the GPS didn't like and pulled into a strip center. He parked in front of Big Wigs of the West. "I'm going to need one of these. We're flying to the Cayman Islands."

"Why?"

"I think Veillon is there, and it's sort of on the way to Paris."

"Since when?"

"Since I became a fugitive, and you became an accomplice. Plus, we've probably just committed bank fraud. There's a bank on Grand Cayman that may specialize in that sort of thing. Maybe they can improve our technique."

A NON-STOP TO THE Cayman Islands wasn't possible, so they settled for a connection through Miami. Shortly after their flight left DFW, Jay pulled Dad's faded black diary from his daypack and set it on his tray table. Fifteen minutes later, still unopened, he stuffed it into the seat pouch in front of him. It stayed there until the chatty co-captain said they were passing over Atlanta. Jay retrieved the diary and gingerly folded back its worn leather cover. He felt Sarah's gaze and turned to her.

"Do you want to read it with me?"

"If you want me to."

Jay slid the diary toward her. The first page read, "Dear son, You are embarking on an adventure of a lifetime. Don't let the details slip away." It was signed, "Dad." The handwritten note confused Jay until he realized it had been written by his grandfather, a man he had never met. Jay turned the page carefully and read silently. Dad was a single, 22-year-old doctoral student joining an internationally renowned team in Egypt. He wrote about the long flights and his assignment to work on the Cairo Genizah Collection. The depository of ancient Jewish writings dated back to the eleventh century, but covered Jewish history for a thousand years before that. Even for a promising young scholar, it must have been heady stuff. After his first few entries, Dad stuck to the spiritual highlights of his journey. He wasn't much of a daily chronicler. Then he mentioned working closely with an Egyptian girl of similar age, skills, and interests. She was a Coptic Christian and they had lively debates about Scripture. Their common interests turned toward each other and within weeks of meeting her, Dad had a crush on a married woman.

Jay and Sarah looked at each other. Neither breathed. They looked back down at the handwritten pages in tandem.

Dad lamented his unholy feelings for the woman he called Z. A few entries later, he wrote of his shame. He had acted on his impulses and was powerless to stop his ongoing affair. Dad concluded that entry with "Romans 7: I do what I hate."

Jay looked at Sarah, who stared back. "The Romans 7 thing is a reference to Christian Scriptures."

"I figured."

He closed the thick black book with a smack. "What if Dad forgot the diary was in the safe deposit box?"

Sarah patted his arm. "We can read more later. Or you can read it alone. If you want, you can burn it, that's your choice too. I'm glad you closed it, but from what I remember of your father, he didn't forget it was in there."

THE CONNECTION IN MIAMI went like clockwork. The diary remained shut, and they landed at 8:25 p.m. in George Town on Grand Cayman, home of Island Bancshares and the Lucky Parrot Saloon. Mossad intelligence had verified that Veillon exercised his credit card heavily at the legendary George Town bar.

From the airport, Sarah and Jay's cabbie avoided downtown's harbor front, which he said was a zoo for Pirates Week and its Friday night fireworks. By the time they checked in to the Marriott a few miles outside of town, it was ten o'clock. They dropped their bags, freshened up, and lit out for the Lucky Parrot. Another cab took them to the edge of downtown where the crowds and blocked off streets formed an impenetrable barrier. Sarah and Jay hoofed it to the harbor front. Families with kids of all ages, most dressed like pirates, clogged the streets, enjoying face painting, street dancing, and a food festival.

The Lucky Parrot was on a side street in the main shopping district. A green and yellow parrot painted on a wood sign hung over a raucous doorway jammed with as many people entering as leaving. Once inside the smaller than expected establishment, Jay worked his way up to the bar. Its entire length was three-patrons deep in snarling pirate talk. Jay accepted an eye patch from a buxom wench named Amanda who insisted he get in the spirit.

"Thanks, I've been wondering where to get one of these. We just got here and didn't expect any of this. What do you have that could dress up my wife?"

"Wife? No one is married tonight, matey."

Sarah begged to differ, and the three had a good laugh when the lady's husband, Franklin, showed up, questioning who was stealing his wife. The bartender said Jean Veillon wasn't in yet, but promised to point him out. Veillon, he said, preferred to go by the initials JL, as in Jean Lafitte. Sarah and Jay stuck around until midnight. Veillon was a no-show, but the small bar's turtle soup was a big hit.

Back outside in the fresh seventy-five-degree night air, the children were gone and the streets were more crowded than ever. It wasn't over the top like Mardi Gras or Carnival, but it was definitely the adults turn to play.

CHAPTER 23

THE MALAYSIAN WOMAN PUSHED the wobbly cleaning cart down the hall and stopped to mop the floor for the third time. It was 7:20 a.m. and Yeta and her friend Eva should have already left. The Israel Museum didn't open until 10:00, but its legitimate employees would arrive before long.

"Maybe this is the southwest corner." If Yeta stared at the sun long enough, she could tell east from west. Underground, she was hopeless.

Eva shrugged. "If not, there's only one corner left."

Both giggled nervously. Thirty years in prison wasn't Yeta's idea of a new future. It turned out neither woman was very good with determining points of the compass once they had trudged into the bowels of the museum's Youth Wing. It was the closest building to the parking lot at the sprawling complex and had the added advantage of a basement. Not all buildings at the museum did. It's why the device had been positioned there in the first place. But it wasn't for Yeta to understand why it was being moved, or why they couldn't tell Rachel.

She continued mopping and watched Eva unlock the storage

room door.

"Okay, cardboard box, rear wall, bottom shelf, left side." Eva repeated her instructions as she disappeared inside. She came out beaming. "Bring the cart."

Yeta knew the nuke wouldn't resemble a bomb or have flashing lights and hazardous material stickers, but she was disappointed all the same. Who would guess the frumpy water-stained cardboard box contained a suitcase stuffed with a mushroom cloud? She immobilized the cart and pulled back the curtain that concealed the cart's reinforced bottom and oversized wheels. She and Eva pulled the heavy box off the shelf with care. No matter what Isis said, jiggling it seemed a bad idea. HEU was a terrorist's dream, effective and transportable, but why risk fate?

SEVEN MILE BEACH LIVED up to its paradise hype. Crystalline waters lapped at powdery sand in both directions as far as Jay could see, and sand dunes the size of buildings blocked everything manmade from view. With twenty minutes of hard open-water swimming completed, Jay toweled off and walked back to his and Sarah's room through a garden overflowing with hibiscus and orchids.

He entered the room relieved that Sarah had left. Sharing sleeping quarters in the van had been a necessity, but last night was optional and had felt awkward. So had slipping out this morning. He walked toward the dresser and found a note on it that asked him to join her in the Red Parrot for breakfast. Parrots appeared to be popular on the island. He showered and hurried to the restaurant.

The hostess directed Jay to Mrs. Bennet's table past an endless breakfast buffet. A curvy Australian waitress took his order of oatmeal. She filled both coffee cups and left.

"You look rested," he told Sarah. "When did you get up?"

"Right after you thought you snuck out."

"Did you sneak a peek?"

"No." She frowned. "You're so disgusting." She softened her appearance. "Actually, you were quite gentlemanly, changing in the bathroom. I almost joined you for a swim, but I wanted to call my boss during his office hours for once."

"Any news?"

She nodded in the affirmative. "Outing the Q document as a hoax is a long-shot getting longer. Your pope was negotiating to hold the Q's sanctioning event in the Church of the Holy Sepulcher."

"He was never my pope. Mom and Dad were non-denominational, which coming from Texas pretty much means Baptist."

The waitress brought a huge bowl of oatmeal with blueberries on the side. "I thought you might like a little something extra." Her accent added to the laidback island ambience, but it didn't penetrate his sense of mission. He had an appointment at Island Bancshares at 11:15 a.m. and a couple errands before that.

Jay spooned the berries onto his oatmeal. "Why would the pope even try to hold the event there? Even if the Roman Catholic Church was convinced that the Q was authentic, what are the odds the other five Christian creeds sharing the church would agree?" He sipped his coffee. "Christ's crucifixion, burial, and resurrection are all celebrated as happening at that location. The symbolism . . ."

"It would make a powerful statement. According to some experts, the pope was angling to be the 'Ayatollah of the West' and convert his church to Islam overnight."

"What experts? Judaism makes more sense."

"Judaism has no equivalent to his position as pontiff."

"I'm a cynic, but even I can't buy that one." Jay checked the time. "I need to pick up my new suit."

"Oh, the printer called. Your business cards are ready. At the bank, you'll be Richard Wise of Wise Wealth Management. It's got a nice ring to it. Are you sure you can make them believe you're an investment expert?"

"My story is simple and impossible to verify. I've been out of the business a while and exploring getting back in. I've got an appointment with Marie LeSabre, the bank's president. She shouldn't be busy on a Saturday, and I know all the buzzwords plus every name in New York worth dropping. What could be easier?"

He ignored Sarah's sideways glance.

JAY WAS DETERMINED TO turn Marie LeSabre's disinterest to his advantage. Forced to settle for lunch with Howard Brevard, the two men sat in a corner booth at the Yardarm Restaurant. If a customer missed the nautical theme from the restaurant's name, management rammed it home with dark plank paneling, miles of rigging, and wrought iron lamps.

Howard, as he insisted on being called, ordered his second scorpion. Having downed the first rum cocktail faster than a pirate on shore leave, he asked that its replacement be a double. The only thing his bulbous nose and pockmarked face was missing was an eye-patch. Jay would have lent him his, but he'd left it in the room.

Jay nursed his ice tea. "Ms. LeSabre was rather dismissive. Is your boss like that with all potential customers?"

"Yes, to be honest, and I trust our conversation is in confidence." Howard kept his voice low even though their nearest fellow diners were several tables away. "The bank is constantly adding new accounts, but I haven't a clue how she's winning them with her snippy attitude. I remind her she can't push clients away forever. 'A new world order is coming,' she says. But let me assure you, Mr. Wise, I welcome your business. What you offer Island Bancshares would hardly be paltry accounts."

"What does she mean by a new world order?"

"Haven't a clue." Howard grabbed his drink from the waiter's tray before the young man could set it down. "Most of what she says is half-baked."

"You're not filling me with confidence in the bank, Howard."

"The bank is stable. When I was its president, I put us on very firm ground. Our capital ratios are a study in conservatism. Our balance sheet is rock solid. One executive can't muck that up this quickly."

"What happened that changed your fortune at the bank?"

"It was a corporate decision, old man." Howard saluted the air with his glass. His words emphasized his clipped British accent. "The bank was taken over by Suez. They brought in Marie to run things in a modern way."

"Who is Suez?"

"It's not a who, it's a what. Suez LLC, a wealthy outfit out of Cairo."

That tidbit was worth the price of lunch. Jay imagined Suez was SLLC. It would be nice to feed Rabbit information for a change. "Your boss sounds French. Is she?"

"Who knows?" He laughed and swilled his scorpion. "The devil's own, if you ask me. She believes in using what the Almighty gave her. I'm sure you noticed he gave her plenty. She's making quite a name for herself around the island. And it's not about banking."

"So where's the Suez money come from?"

"Oil money I believe."

Jay was ready to order and caught the waiter's eye, as the young man worked another table. Jay turned back to Howard. "There's not much oil in Egypt."

"True, but oil was the origin of the money. From bits and pieces I've gathered from Marie, it's leftovers from a Saudi prince. Of course, there are hundreds of them."

Thousands actually, Jay thought to himself. "With your banking background and years at IB's helm, you could be valuable to me. When I get back into the business, I'll have accounts looking for a home. I would prefer to park that money in something I own. I have partners waiting in the wings to fund a buyout."

"Suez won't sell. You can forget that."

"Never say never, Mr. Brevard." Jay leaned in to the table. "Marketing practices aren't the only things that appear to be irregular here. Your quiet little bank has come to the attention of certain authorities."

The former bank president gulped the last of his drink. The ice cubes clunked against the glass's bottom as he set it down. "I am completely in the dark when it comes to her operations. I'm not aware of any irregularities."

"I believe you, of course. But overcoming the taint of scandal can be difficult for someone so intimate to the business. Island officials can only look the other way for so long. However, if I became privy to details surrounding certain irregularities that I have come across . . . well, Suez might find it desirable to move on to greener pastures and sell at a reduced price to exit quickly. That would make me grateful, and it would leave you in a unique position. I can see the PR release now. 'We wish to reassure the substantial base of our customers that solid banking processes will again be carried out under the able stewardship of President Howard Brevard.' What do you think?"

"Perhaps I could look into—"

Jay leaned in. "The time for 'perhaps' is over. Many of your customers have less than pristine histories. Several of your new customers play with bombs and others have mysteriously come into fantastic wealth. It's time for you to decide how much longer you can stand being her assistant and whether you wish to go to jail for the privilege."

Howard looked around nervously. "Well, there is Monsieur Veillon—"

"Doctor Veillon, actually. We can start with him."

SOME PEOPLE'S JOINTS PREDICTED the weather. Greene's lumbar predicted trouble. Last night, Farnsleigh reported that Sarah Baumann was found dead in her Chicago hotel room. That, combined with Jay Hunt's resurrection in Arizona, set his spine tingling something awful. He had dismissed the feeling last Monday when Waters transferred the case. Greene wouldn't make that mistake again.

He opened Jolene Peterson's morning email containing three photos of the crime scene. Dead bodies were never pleasant to look at, but this was less so. Sarah Baumann had straightened him out when he needed it, and she had done it in a professional manner. He owed her one. Relief washed over him when he saw that the strangled young face didn't belong to Sarah Baumann. He picked up his desk phone and called Farnsleigh at home.

"I hope you don't have any plans for the rest of today."

"You mean like a life? Are you trying to wreck my marriage, too?"

"That's not funny. I got Peterson's photos. The dead woman in Chi-town is not that Israeli cop Baumann, at least not the one

I met. One of those two ladies is not who she claimed to be. I want to know which one was lying and why. I need you to pull up TSA video at Bush Intercontinental for Wednesday starting three hours in advance of Ms. Baumann's flight to O'Hare. Use the facial recognition software to compare it with arrivals in Chicago and match that against the video we got of Ms. Baumann here on Tuesday morning. I'll forward Agent Peterson's email to you with the pictures of the dead woman they found in the hotel room in Chicago."

"I can do that."

Greene appreciated Farnsleigh's agreeable nature, if not his humor. "I wish that was all, but there's more." He paged through the timeline on his desk. "Hunt escaped Wednesday night in some cow town called Evergreen, Arizona at 20:30 Mountain Time. Adjust it for driving times and scan airport security tapes for departures in Vegas, Phoenix, Albuquerque, and El Paso for common faces."

"I can start the process rolling, but this could take a while."

"I'll see what I can do about getting Reeko back here. And Farnsleigh . . . thanks."

"The three Amigos. We hang together."

Greene hung up the phone, thinking he could have done without the gallows humor. Then the more he thought about it, he realized he had a bigger problem. He poised his finger over the speed dial button for home, then instead pushed the intercom. "Maria, please call Yvonne and tell her I won't be home for dinner tonight."

AT 7:30 A CALYPSO band kicked off the evening's street dancing. Jay wore his eye patch, a red bandana headscarf, and a ripped pale blue tee shirt. He swayed to the sound of steel drums near the main stage. His bare left shoulder was the identifying mark Veillon would

recognize. Sarah was somewhere in the crowd watching from a distance. Brevard was unaware of her presence on the island, and in case he had Jay followed from the Yardarm, Jay and Sarah had checked out of the Marriott and acquired a rental car.

A man with a Jolly Roger flag draped over his shoulders and a black pirate's hat approached like an old friend. He introduced himself as JL. Veillon was a delicate man with a pleasant face and a lightening quick smile that flashed with every breath.

"Pleased to meet you, Mr. Lafitte. I didn't know you plied these waters. I'd love to get your story of how you acquired the Q document."

"Who wouldn't? Brevard said you would pay me $5,000. I'd like my money up front."

"Who wouldn't?" Jay parroted back. "I agreed to one thousand in advance, which Brevard has already received. If he hasn't given it to you, take it up with him. I'll pay four more when we're done. It's too noisy here, let's move away from the crowd."

Veillon nodded, his black hat sliding forward across his eyes. He pushed it back. "I know a place we can talk."

They elbowed their way through the crowd and turned on Fort Street. Although the serious ruckus was behind them near the harbor, every street had its share of marauding locals and tourists. Jay hoped Sarah had been able to keep up with them. Five cruise ships were anchored in the harbor and had added 7,000 passengers to the mix. Amanda at the Lucky Parrot had said her ship wasn't departing until this evening's festivities wound down. Whenever that was.

Veillon veered left into an alley. "There's a bar a block from here that will be quiet. It's too refined for this crowd."

A dozen restaurants and shops' back doors emptied into the dark alley. The smell of fried seafood mixed with the stink of dumpsters.

It wouldn't be a highlight on the Visitor Bureau's walking tour. Two pirates, mock sword fighting, entered the alley at its far end fifty yards ahead. As they drew near, Jay realized their swords were too shiny to be fakes.

Jay pushed up his eye-patch and restrained Veillon. "We should turn around."

The pirates ran at them. The man in the lead brandished his sword overhead.

Jay turned to run, but Veillon froze. Jay pushed him out of the way. "Run," he yelled, then ducked under the first attacker's arm and flipped him over his back. The trailing pirate ignored Jay and made a wide slash at Veillon, who slunk out of the way. Jay kicked the slashing pirate in the back, which knocked the man into a wall. His fellow pirate had regained his feet. Both attackers raised their swords and spun around.

A shot rang out from behind Jay. Sarah was running towards them. "Stop, you're under arrest."

The pirates ran.

Sarah stopped next to Jay, panting. "Are you two okay?"

Veillon stood with his back plastered tight against the building, holding his upper arm.

"Where did you get the gun?" Jay asked her.

She smiled faster than Veillon.

"You know her?" It was Veillon. He moved away from the wall clutching his left arm.

CHAPTER 24

THE RUSTY SCUPPER WAS a thirty-six-foot yacht that Veillon moored in North Sound, and the threesome was motoring out to board her. North Sound was a wide bay that extended from Rum Point to West Bay and made the north side of Grand Cayman look like a shark had taken a bite out of it. Veillon's skiff plodded toward the Scupper's sleek all-white hull, which rested steady in the evening's calm water. A flying helm above the main deck increased the boat's appeal. They tied up at the transom, where a generous diving platform off the stern provided easy access.

Tonight, the Scupper was Veillon's residence and hospital of choice. He opined that his cut wasn't bad, and unlike hospitals, the medicine on his boat tasted like rum. It appeared to Jay that what the man credited with finding the Q document appreciated most was Sarah dressing his wound. That is after he learned she wasn't a cop, but an ex-cop. With his arm bandaged, Veillon laughed off the attack as drunken hooligans and went below to put on a clean shirt.

Jay watched Sarah pack up the extra gauze and tape. The clear water provided extraordinary visibility during the day but appeared black tonight. It lapped at the boat's hull in a constant rhythm. The moon reflected off the water and backlit her. "I think I'll have a talk with Howard Brevard tomorrow."

Sarah re-stowed the first-aid kit in the compartment under the wheel. "I don't think Brevard sent those men to attack you. I watched them follow Veillon into the harbor area. When he dodged around in the crowd looking for you, they matched his every move. Brevard knew where your meeting was to take place. If Brevard had sent them, they wouldn't have had to follow Veillon so closely."

Jay sat in a chair near the controls. "Then who sent them?"

She motioned Jay toward the bow. He followed her, shimmying between the rail and the helm and navigation station's enclosed cabin.

Her voice was low. "They were sent by whoever Veillon's afraid of. He lives on a boat moored in the water a half-mile from the expensive slip he rents at the marina. When we started from shore tonight, he hesitated, as if he had to remember where he had parked. I think he moves frequently. He doesn't want to go to the hospital, which would have been a good idea, and he refuses to report the attack to the police. He's scared."

Veillon came topside with a bottle of wine and Jay's blood-soaked bandana that Sarah had wrapped around his cut. He joined them up front. He flashed his smile, extending the bandana and the bottle. "Thanks matey, here's your bandana. Let's celebrate. " He sat on a deck chair across from Jay and Sarah who stood against the railing.

Jay shook his head. "Keep it, JL. You're going to need it again. Next time it won't be a flesh wound."

Veillon's head jerked back.

"Do you know how many people have died because of the Q document?" Jay asked. "I'm not talking about the crime or the suicides. I mean those directly involved. The first death I know of was Imaad al Wahiri. Then there's his fellow antiquities dealer Hassan Tariq al Rhaheem and their mutual friend Professor David Hunt. The three bombs in the United States killed sixty-four more. And then there's the taxi dispatcher who disappeared, a hiker in the desert, and—"

"Who are you?" His eyes narrowed. "What do you want? You're not a reporter."

"I've been doing a lot of digging, doctor. Let me show you something." Jay pulled out Dad's photos from his back pocket. It was time to ad lib and see what Veillon confirmed. "Look at these pictures. This is the Q document rolled up nice and tight. Now here it's unrolled and in five or six pieces. Who did you buy it from? What state was it in, rolled or unrolled?"

Veillon stood.

Sarah clicked off the safety on her weapon.

Veillon sat back down with a shrug. "You saved my life to kill me?"

"Don't count on our generosity out here," Jay said. "Who did you buy it from? Imaad died first. Was it him?" Jay watched Veillon's darting eyes. "You never bought it from anyone, did you? How long can you hide before the people running this scam find you? They will kill you. You know that, don't you?"

"You are guessing. I bought it in February from a boy in a souk, a bazaar. I knew it was precious, very old—"

"We don't know all the details, but the truth is leaking out. Your story won't last. Do yourself a favor and tell us now. Did Duvert put you up to this? Is he trying to kill you? You know someone is. The next time we won't be around to save you."

Veillon shifted his gaze toward the photos. "Those pictures. Where did they come from?" He looked back at Jay's face, and waved a dismissive hand. "It doesn't matter. They prove nothing."

"They show it was blank," Jay insisted, fanning the photos. "Did you know that? Have you even ever seen it? Are you willing to die for something you've never seen?" Jay turned to Sarah. "He wants to die."

"Hassan is dead? How?" Veillon's resolve was crumbling.

Jay realized he had no idea. "It wasn't old age or drinking too much green tea."

"I bought it from Hassan." Veillon rubbed his face. "He obtained it from Imaad."

Sarah quickly asked, "Who gave you the money?"

"No one," Veillon answered. He stared at the deck, then up at Sarah. He nodded. "I received a key in the mail to a hotel room in the George Cinq. A suitcase was there. It was all cash, US dollars. I don't know how much, at least 50,000. I grew weary of counting someone else's money." He flexed his injured arm. "Professor Hunt is dead too, you say? I didn't know he was involved. I'm surprised at that. But Claude would never send anyone to kill me. He told me to hide."

"Why would he tell you that? What has he discovered? Is he being bribed to fake his tests? Are they bonafide?"

"The tests are real." Veillon shook his head. "Claude told me to buy a scroll from Hassan. A simple deal, he said. I didn't know what it was, or why he wanted it. The scroll was nothing. Nothing! Maybe a few hundred years old. Even Hassan could not believe what price was being paid him to hand over a worthless scroll. He practically laughed in my face. I think Claude burned it after people saw it delivered." Veillon stood. He looked at Sarah. "Will you shoot me, mademoiselle? For what? I delivered nothing!" He began laughing and gave the corkscrew protruding from the wine bottle a tug. It came free with a *pop*.

Something to starboard attracted Jay's attention. "Doctor, do you have underwater lights?"

He shrugged. "I only rent this thing."

The light flashed again near the stern. "Sarah, get down." Jay pulled Veillon to the deck. "Unless you're expecting someone by aqualung, we have uninvited guests."

He and Sarah scrambled to positions in front of the main cabin where they could watch the boat's stern through the windshield. Jay waved Veillon closer. Sarah readied her weapon. Jay looked up to the flying helm eight to ten feet overhead. It would have a commanding view of the boat, but the only way to get there was an aft ladder a few feet from where the intruders were coming aboard. He needed another way up.

Jay turned to Veillon and whispered, "Stay here."

Sarah looked at him quizzically.

He pointed to the flying bridge, then climbed the windshield and flopped onto the upper deck. He raised a cushioned seat top and looked inside. Empty. He noticed a forward louvered door. He opened it. It held just what he'd hoped to find. He scrambled back to the rear and peered over the bulkhead to the stern.

The boat's rear weighed down, shifting ever so slightly. Two pairs of hands came over the transom. Two men with weapons of some kind at their sides slipped onto the aft deck.

Spearguns.

The man on the left took to one knee. He leveled his weapon and moved it in a slow arc, sweeping his field of vision. The other man advanced two steps with his speargun up, and scanned the deck.

Jay steadied his aim, resting both hands on the upper rail. His gun had no sight, but Jay stared down its barrel at the man crouching. He decided the man standing made a better target for Sarah. He wished there was a way to communicate to her what he was about to do, but she'd know soon enough.

He squeezed the trigger.

The hissing jet trail and the burst of bright light propelled the flare straight for the kneeling man's chest. He had no way to escape its impact. It happened so fast Jay couldn't tell if the man screamed before or after it hit him. It continued to burn, lodged in the base of his neck, like someone had stuck a roman candle into a bowl of Jell-O. The burning trail gave away Jay's position to the other assailant, who had taken a defensive position behind a chair molded into the deck. Jay heard someone, he assumed it was Sarah, brush along the port rail toward the rear.

If Jay could get the man to fire at him, then Sarah would have a decent chance of taking him out. Jay grabbed a life preserver and prepared to hoist it over his head when he heard a commotion at the wheel behind him. The attacker stood and fired.

Sarah fired multiple shots. The assailant fell silent.

Jay looked behind him. Veillon leaned back against the upper deck's controls, wobbling and looking at his gut. He dropped the photos, which fluttered overboard, and with both hands grasped at the end of a spear sticking out of his stomach. Its barbed end protruded from his back.

Jay lunged at Veillon to keep him from falling on it and making the wound any worse. If that was possible. The man couldn't lay on his back or front. Jay laid him on his side and propped up his head with the life preserver. It was the least he could do. Veillon was about to die knowing a friend had used him. No one deserved that. "We'll get you to shore, don't worry."

Blood drooled across Veillon's chin. "It wasn't even old," he repeated twice. "The scroll was nothing. The real Q document arrived over a year ago. In long flat pieces over the course of a week. Sandwiched in glass between sheets of dry wall delivered during a renovation. The scroll I bought was a ruse. Duvert only claimed to spend months painstakingly unrolling it."

Sarah climbed the ladder. "They're both dead." She looked at Veillon. "Oh no."

Veillon coughed. Blood bubbled out of his mouth onto the deck. A large pool collected at his stomach. "Stay far away from the sanctioning event." He took a long rasping breath. "Isis." His head collapsed onto the life preserver. The muscles in his face released.

Sarah hovered over them. "Do you think he meant—"

"A bomb?" Jay rose and searched the locker next to the wheel. "Whoever's pulling the strings in this thing sure seems to like them." He retrieved a diver's flashlight and shouted to Sarah as he flew down the ladder. "The photos blew into the water. I'm going to see if I can find them." The flashlight's spot on the water covered minimal surface area. Hopeful, he removed his shoes and slipped off his jeans while searching. He thought he saw a photo floating fifteen feet out. He dove into the cold water. But when he got to the spot, there was nothing there.

After a few circles, he knew it was hopeless and swam back to the diving platform. He was about to hoist himself up when he saw a small black box clamped under the platform. Curly cue wires stuck into and out of its end.

"Sarah," he yelled, "we need to leave." When she didn't respond, he yelled louder, dread lacing his voice. "Sarah, where are you?"

She still didn't answer.

Thoughts of additional spearmen raced through his brain. He jumped onto the deck and rambled down the steps into the cabin, calling her name. If he drew fire, so be it. He had to find her. They might only have seconds to leave. He ran into the forward cabin. She was there, rummaging through drawers and cabinets.

"I found a bomb. We need to get off the boat."

She delayed for a second, and then appeared to grasp what he'd said. He ushered her up the steps to the rear deck. Sarah jumped into the skiff and began untying it. Jay suddenly realized he had no pants or shoes on. He grabbed them, jumped into the tiny boat, and started the outboard engine.

He pointed to the device. "That has got to be a bomb. Agree?"

"Agreed. Let's go."

The small boat crawled away from its big sister, seemingly an inch at a time.

Sarah sat in the bow, hanging on to the gunwales on either side. "Can't you go any faster?"

"This is it. It's a row boat with a one inch prop."

"I could paddle faster. Wait, we should have detached the bomb. Thrown it somewhere. The police need to check the identity of those men."

"You are *not* suggesting we go back, are you? Maybe they'll be blown clear."

A giant fireball lit up the sky. The shock wave of the blast rocked the small boat.

Jay looked back. Debris littered the water where the Rusty Scupper had been. Small fires dotted the area, rising and falling with the sea. "There won't be much for them to identify."

They had made more progress than what it had seemed. The shoreline was a quarter mile distant. A speedboat left a dock about a third of a mile from the marina. An onboard spotlight scanned the water as the boat raced for the disaster. The light's strong beam settled on Jay and Sarah. The boat changed course to intercept them.

Jay waved them off. "We're fine."

"I doubt they can hear you. Why are they so interested in us?"

Shots rang out.

"Even spearfishermen have friends."

"I'm down to six rounds," Sarah said.

The boat kept charging at them. The gap dwindled.

Jay hunkered down as much as he could and still steer. Bullets hit the water nearby. "They don't seem to be conserving ammo. They're also moving five times faster, and will catch us before we reach the dock. Any ideas?"

"There's a driver and a shooter. With their speed, the one can't aim well because of the turbulence. If they slow to shoot, we'll outrun them. If they keep up their speed, then they'll soon be within my range." She lowered herself even further into the center of the skiff. She patted his calf. "I'll take them out."

"Okay, how about when I'm sure, *absolutely* sure that they're about to overtake us, I'll idle our engine. That should give you a steadier shot. Agree?"

Several more shots landed close by. "Agreed."

The onrushing boat showed no intention of slowing. It raced on a diagonal toward them.

"Are they going to ram us?" Sarah's question mirrored his thoughts.

"They have all the cards, why would they risk it?" He considered their alternatives. "They're going to swamp us. Then they'll slow their speed and pick us off in the water. We have zero chance of getting to the dock before they get to us." He swung the tiller so they angled away from the dock and paralleled the course of the boat chasing them.

"Jay, what are you doing?"

"It's like sailing. I'm tacking us into shore. When they circle us, I'll have to turn into their wake to keep us upright. I'll use the opportunity to point us back to the dock. Their circle to return is so large, we'll gain more net distance on the dock. I won't be able to cut the engine, though; I'll need the power to get us through the wake. Fire while we're in the dead zone."

"You couldn't think of a better term than that?"

The roar of the approaching boat was deafening. It was at full throttle and kicking up a geyser behind it. This was going to be rougher than Jay expected. "Sarah, protect yourself from our boat's edges, we're about to get tossed around hard."

Jay saw a boat leaving the dock where he had hoped to arrive. He saw two more people running down the same pier toward another boat.

Sarah yelled above the engine noise. "Come and get us, sleazeballs."

The speedboat's wild turn around them was on a dime, and within twenty feet. Their maneuver created a six-foot trough. Jay heard shots fired, too numerous to be from Sarah.

Jay turned into the wake. "Here we go."

Their little skiff fell into the trough like they crested a waterfall. A wall of water as unforgiving as concrete slammed them. Their small propeller clawed forward. Water surrounded them. They popped out the other side like a cork. Sarah squeezed off two shots. The windshield of the speedboat shattered as it sped away. The little skiff stayed the course. The pounding had jammed Jay's ribs into a crosspiece. Sarah, lying deep in their boat, must have smashed into something. She was groaning.

Jay looked behind him. The speedboat had begun a wide circle back at them.

The two assist boats rushed from the dock in Jay and Sarah's general direction. With any luck, a commodity that had been in short supply all night, these two boats were Good Samaritans drawn by the Rusty Scupper's explosion. The ball of fire would have been visible for miles.

The circling speedboat abandoned its mission and swung out to sea.

The first boat from shore slowed as it approached, and Jay waved it off. The helmsman waved and gave his boat full throttle. It was gone in a flash, followed by the second responder.

Sarah sat up. "I guess not everyone on the island wants to kill us."

MARIE HAD NO IDEA that Captain George was such a whiner. She toweled off as she spoke into the speaker phone. "Stop complaining. I don't want to hear about your windshield. It was your incompetence that let Wise escape."

"He hasn't escaped yet. I left someone on the road near the docks just in case."

"Good. Are you sure Veillon is dead?"

"I haven't seen the body, but he didn't leave with Wise and the girl. I'm sure no one on board the Rusty Scupper survived. That boat is *gone*."

"Did you get a look at the woman? Is she a local?"

"It was too dark, but it's probably the same woman that saved his bacon in the alley. Someone fired back at us from the little dinghy. We put enough lead in that thing to sink a battleship. My guess is one of them took a hit."

"Have your people watch the hospital plus the airport and downtown. You have photos of him from his appearance in my bank. I have someone waiting at the Marriott. Wise didn't register under that name, but if he slips past you, I'll nail him when he returns. Find him."

Marie hung up. There was no sense waking Cairo. She went back outside to the pirate swashbuckling in her hot tub.

THEY HAD NO SOONER left the small marina and turned onto
Safehaven Drive when Jay noticed a gray SUV parked along the
golf course in a No Parking area. He sped by it and watched it in his
mirrors. Sarah hadn't said one word of complaint, but he could tell
by the way she moved that she was sore, bruised, or worse. Both
of them were soaked. Sarah had put on two of his shirts to fend off
the cold, and insisted he drive. That was easier said than done. He
had bashed his ribs on the edge of the boat's seat and hyperextended
his left elbow and shoulder. His pants were back on, but one of his
running shoes had been lost at sea. Sockless, he was wearing dress
shoes to drive.

The SUV pulled onto the road with its lights off.

Until now, Jay had been driving right-handed and resting his
left arm. He positioned both hands on the wheel despite the pain.
"Do you have any bullets left?" he asked Sarah, hoping her answer
was in the double-digits.

"Three. Now what?"

"There's a Land Rover with no lights following us. It joined our
little parade from the side of the road." He glanced back. "And it's
in a hurry."

Jay turned left on Esterly Tibbetts Highway, which was a
highway in name only. It had one lane in each direction. Speeds
were slow but faster than on the hotel-clogged West Bay Road,
bordering the beach. He sped through a right-hand turn onto Canal
Point, thinking he could lose the Rover in The Strand's parking lot.

It stayed on his tail only fifty yards back, so he nixed the idea of
parking and hiding. Instead he extinguished his lights and rounded
the end of their row, then reversed direction one aisle over. As they
crossed by the Rover, someone shot at them through the parked cars

separating them.

The shots sent everyone in the lot scrambling for cover. People started screaming.

Jay swerved around a MINI Cooper that was backing up. Sarah stiff-armed the dash in front of her as he avoided the small car.

"Whoa," she yelled. "That was a little close."

The Range Rover made it around the aisle and sped to catch up. The MINI Cooper, which had jammed on its brakes, blocked the aisle. The Rover stopped, but not soon enough.

Sarah was watching behind them. "They're stuck on the far side of that tiny car you nearly smashed into. I think they hit it."

More shots were fired. It must have been to encourage the driver to unblock the aisle.

Jay accelerated back to the highway, fishtailing through the berm until his tires caught traction and they burst into a short gap in the traffic. Horns blasted them, but it beat bullets hands down. "Is the Rover following us?"

Sarah turned around. "No." She smacked the dash. "Yes. They're wedged behind a couple dozen cars behind us, but they're coming."

"Then the race to town is on. If we can keep our lead, maybe we can lose them in the festival's crowds. Worst case, we get stopped by the police. Best case . . . I don't know if there is a best case. Every time we lose one batch of bad guys, new ones take their place."

"Normally I'd recommend driving to a police station, but they're more likely to slow us down. They might even arrest you. We need to get off this island and find Duvert. Whoever is sensitive about us talking to Veillon might assume he implicated Duvert. Do you know how to get to the airport?"

"I don't see the airport working out. We'll be sitting ducks waiting on a flight. There may not even be a flight out until tomorrow. We're at most five minutes from town. I think we ditch the car and get lost in the crowd."

"Maybe five minutes with no traffic, but it's already getting heavy. We can only hide in the crowds if we can get to them. Once traffic stops us, our new best friends behind us can run after us." Sarah turned back to look again. "They're still back there."

"Then we won't stop."

Jay maintained their distance ahead of the Range Rover, but it was a constant battle. He worked his way down to the water and North Church Street, which was the best route into downtown. Further up, he could see that traffic was impassable.

"Grab everything together you want to take with us," he suggested. "I'm going to park as soon as we bog down in traffic. I'll grab the bags in the trunk. We're hoofing it through town."

The traffic light ahead turned red. Jay turned off the car's lights and bounced them over a curb to squeeze into a darkened parking lot hidden by a long, tall hedge. He snuggled the car up against it. "We've got a three to four minute lead. If the Rover didn't see us park, it might give us a few more minutes before they realize what's happened." Locked in by the hedge, Sarah struggled out of the driver's side, while Jay grabbed both bags. He slammed the trunk before the line of traffic moved again. He slung his suitcase onto his back, since it had shoulder straps in addition to its wheels, and he carried hers. They ran through to the next street. The crowds were minimal until they worked their way closer to the area with the stages. Steel-drum music assaulted his ears and made their situation seem surreal.

Jay surveyed the area. Two men crouched on rooftops. He doubted they were cops putting on a show of force, and even if they were, it was hardly a comforting feeling. To the left, the Range

Rover was nosing its way through the protesting crowd. It parked. Three men jumped out and scattered.

Jay directed Sarah to the back of a large group. She was having trouble keeping up. "Let's slow down and move with the crowd," he suggested. "The Rover's here and they have eyes up high." Jay pulled Sarah deeper into the group undulating with the music, excusing his way into their midst. When the group stopped, Jay and Sarah bolted out in front of it. Someone grabbed Jay's arm.

A deep voice yelled, "I got him."

Jay spun and front kicked the guy in the groin. As the man bent over, Jay raised Sarah's suitcase. He crashed it onto the man's skull, wheels first.

The assailant crumpled to the ground. Two other men ran at them from thirty yards on the right, hampered by the crowd.

"We can mix in with the crowds at the waterfront." Jay pointed her to the south terminal, where long lines of passengers waited for the small tenders that would ferry them back to their cruise ships at anchor.

"I'll keep up," Sarah said in a weak voice.

Jay was about to jettison her bag and hoist her over his shoulder when he saw a waving female arm at the front of one of the lines. It wasn't for them, but a plan came to mind. He guided Sarah between the lengthy weaving lines to a chorus of complaints.

Sarah croaked out her words. "Are you thinking what I think you're thinking?"

"Do you have a better idea?"

CHAPTER 25

BEING ALL WET WASN'T all bad. When they neared the front of
the lines, the last thing Jay expected was lady luck. But there she
was, waving at them. Not the original arm that got them over there,
but an arm all the same. Amanda from the Lucky Parrot shouted at
them to join her and Franklin at the front of the line.

With Jay dripping and Sarah shivering, no one objected. Their
wet clothes also provided a great excuse for how they both had
lost their boarding documents. If that was good luck, then Amanda
vouching for them was pure poetry. Although a few of the ship's
crew wore pirate clothes, there were no signs of men with swords,
rifles, or spearguns. For the first time in hours, Jay relaxed. Franklin
insisted on toting Sarah's suitcase. Knowing that dry clothes were
only minutes away heightened the anticipation of being warm again.
Sarah's lips had turned blue.

Amanda walked between them. At five-foot-three she wore
a modest version of pirate-wench with a billowy white silk top,
black bodice with strings everywhere, and leather pants. The couple
looked about the same age as he and Sarah. Amanda's mouth never
stopped. Franklin's rarely started. "Something tells me I fibbed to

that nice young officer on the launch who asked for your passes. Last night you said you were staying in a hotel on the island. Care to tell us what you're up to?" When neither said anything, Amanda filled the silence. "You're stow—"

"Shush."

"—aways," she finished her thought in a whisper. "This is even more fun than I guessed."

The ship's horn bellowed, signaling they were leaving the anchorage.

Jay confessed. "We need a steward who knows of an empty cabin and won't mind earning a big tip."

"Our steward is your man. Come to our room. He's always hovering close by. He'll find one."

"And a ship's doc—" Sarah's knees buckled.

Franklin and Jay caught her before she hit the deck.

"THE DOCTOR SAID YOU were lucky. The bullet just grazed your arm. He told me to keep you full of liquids and off your feet." The advice reminded Jay of his college days.

"I know the routine. I've been shot before."

"Yeah, he told me that, too."

"So much for patient confidentiality." Sarah squirmed deeper into the overstuffed armchair bolted to the floor under the porthole of their stateroom. She looked the picture of contentment, in dry clothes and a thick terry robe with a giant "R" on it, signifying Regal Cruise Lines. "Sorry about the blood on your shirts. I didn't think I was bleeding that much."

"Why didn't you tell me?"

"Going to the hospital wasn't an option, and you'd have insisted on it."

Jay knew she was right on both counts. "Next time, tell me anyway."

"Next time, don't take me to a party where there's shooting."

"Deal." Jay freed Dad's diary from his suitcase and pulled a small desk chair over to her. "I'm starving, but I don't want to push our luck by charging meals to the room. The midnight buffet won't start for another hour." He thumbed through the book. "Are you up to more light reading? We should push through Dad's diary."

"When you get to something that will be useful, read it to me." She tucked her legs under herself on the plush armchair and closed her eyes.

Jay skimmed about twenty pages before he spoke. "His affair with Z continued on and off for almost a year. Then in 1966, he was nominated to join the team working on the Dead Sea Scrolls at the Rockefeller Museum in East Jerusalem. He was a pretty confused guy. Happy to leave, but sad, too. Mostly over her, but also due to an anomaly in some documents they'd found. Anyway, he moved on, and there's not much until June 1967."

"The Six Day War was that June."

"Yeah, listen to this. He took some of the fragments to Amman to protect them before the war began, which he felt partially responsible for. He questioned if he had done the right thing. If he took them, why would he only feel partially responsible?" Jay looked at her. "I don't get that."

Sarah sipped her coffee. "The Arab countries massed troops to invade Israel, but when we learned an invasion was only hours away, Israel struck first. That's when Israel captured East Jerusalem and the west Bank from Jordan. The Rockefeller Museum came under our control along with the largest portion of the Dead Sea Scrolls. Maybe your dad corroborated that intelligence trying to protect the scrolls."

"Amazing. Then just after the war, he met my mom. The summer must have been better than what he wrote because they got married in September. The following July they had me." Jay counted the months on his fingers. "Ten months later. That's pretty quick work. I'm going to read a little more. We have twenty minutes yet, and I don't want to be first in line."

After five more pages that covered ten years, Dad's writing became more frequent. The reading turned interesting in a hurry. Jay backtracked through the pages to fill Sarah in.

"Get this. There's no date, but the timeline would be late 70s or early 80s. Z joined the scrolls team in Jerusalem. They worked together platonically, but Dad was worried. He wrote, 'She has wormed her way into Nancy's graces.' She must have been quite a babe. He fought off her approaches, he wrote, 'despite my desires for her.' A year later, he and Z found something in the desert. They had spent weekends scouring the caves near Qumran and found a clay jar in the tiniest fissure. They were both at odds with the head of the team. Z had other issues with the team too, mostly because she was a woman. Remember all the bickering between factions and the conflicting news releases?"

Sarah was all attention. "How could I forget, but how is this useful?"

"For background. Listen to what he wrote about their find. 'We could see the front end was blank. We continued, convinced of our spectacular find. Z and I unrolled it with delicate caution for days on end, much to Nancy's chagrin.' That was my mom."

"I remember her. She was beautiful. Keep reading."

"Okay, it continues, 'She doesn't understand my and Z's need to keep our work secret. She must suspect an affair. How do I admit it, but convince her it was long ago? I bury myself in my work. This magnificent scroll would be the greatest find in years, except the more we unroll it, the more we see it is blank. Our euphoria has turned to nauseating disappointment. The scroll is not the worst of it. Z is lying to rekindle the gravest sin of my life. If true, I'm sure she'd have told me sooner. I fear my resolve has caused her to become unbalanced. Her failures with me, the scroll, and the team have devastated her. I fear for her life. I have no idea what to do. How can I pray about such things?'"

Jay rolled his neck and turned to Sarah. "That's as far as I've gotten. I don't understand half of it, it's like he wrote in Greek in case my mom found the diary." He leaned back, closed his eyes for a second, then sat up straight ready to dive back in. "I'm glad you're here. I'm sure it's important to read more, but I can't do it alone." He began reading the new material aloud. "It says, 'Z is worse off than I thought. Her fragile state of mind scares me. She's thoughtful and scientific one day, coy the next, then without warning she becomes threatening. I blame myself, but am powerless to help.' Some of his entries were dated, some not. This next one doesn't need one. 'My love and my life are gone. All I want is to be buried beside her tomorrow. My heart aches, and I find consolation that my problem with Z is over. It feels so wrong.' The next says, 'The huge scroll is gone. I've looked everywhere. I don't know what has become of it. I suspect Z hid it to hurt me, not anticipating—" Jay stopped himself.

"Not anticipating what?" Sarah opened her eyes.

"It's not that useful. I'll skim ahead."

"You saw something. Let me see it or read it out loud." She reached for the diary.

Jay pulled it away, beyond her reach. He wished he had noticed it sooner.

"Tell me what it said."

He handed Dad's journal to her open to the page where he had stopped reading one sentence too late.

Sarah looked up and down the page. "I found where you stopped reading. 'I suspect Z hid it to hurt me, not anticipating her *demise*.' The next entry reads, 'I had a frightful thought this morning. What if Z destroyed the scroll and killed herself? Could I have driven her to kill? The police said it was an accident. How can they know? I should have done something when I had the chance. But what?'"

Jay stood and paced the small room. The memories of his role in his mother's death resurfaced as raw and fresh as if it happened yesterday. Memories of things Dad didn't know because he was away that weekend. Illogical things. *You were a kid. Focus on the present.* Anything was better than being back there. "Do you know what this could mean?"

Sarah closed the diary and set it on the bed. She wrapped the robe tighter around her. "I don't want to think. Read it to yourself."

The diary's handwriting, its mix of inks and smudges, drew his eyes like a magnet to metal. He read further and had to share it. "There's more. Let me read one part to you."

"Will it torture me?"

"I think you should hear it."

The resistance melted from her face. "Go ahead."

"It says, 'I'm resigned to the fact the scroll is gone. But I no longer care. I don't want to see it or my fragment ever again. It reminds me of who I found it with. Her insane intense pain and what she might have done. There is only one thing to do. I could never smuggle it out anyway.' There are a few blank pages, before he starts again, but I haven't read those." Jay looked up. "Do you think, I mean, what if—"

"No *what if's* tonight." Sarah stood. Her soulful eyes were dulled by pain. "Hold me."

THE INSPIRATION THAT PASTOR Bob needed escaped him at home. He was trying an all-night pancake house along I-65 in one of Indianapolis's look-alike suburbs. So far the Li'l Peep's coffee wasn't helping. He had high hopes for the omelet, if it ever arrived. For the second night this week, Johnny Bingham was holding down the fort in Colville, while he worked on tomorrow morning's sermon.

A check of his watch made him mutter out loud, "today's sermon." It was 1:33 a.m.

None of the dozen or so patrons in his section paid him any attention. Even though a glass partition separated them, a loud bunch in the smoking area drowned out his words. With the nine o'clock service fast approaching, he wondered if anyone would attend. The only way he had made it through yesterday's Kravitz funeral was by stealing from his Sunday sermon. Somehow he had made it applicable.

His mind drifted to the bishop's resignation email. She asserted that the Q document must be genuine. The Gospel's favorable casting of Pilate and Roman soldiers, which had always seemed odd to her, were designed to induce Romans to accept the Q's fake messiah. Could she be right?

The bedraggled waitress approached in a huff. She bounced his plate onto the table. She took a step away and returned. "I'm sorry. I've had it with that bunch in there." She pointed to the rowdies.

Now that he stared at them, Pastor Bob thought a few might be from Colville. All had shaved heads and it was hard to tell. "What's the problem? I could talk to them for you. I'm a pastor."

At that moment, the loud group scraped their chairs back and rose en masse. There were only seven. The small number surprised

Bob given the noise level. Two ducked their heads into the No-Smoking section. The one in a skin-tight black tee announced, "Don't expect any tip, witch."

Bob pushed his chair back to stand.

The waitress put a hand on his shoulder. "Let it go. Being a pastor won't help you with most folks anymore. That group just might shoot you."

The young man in the black tee glared back. "You better sit back down, old man." He laughed and his friend pulled him away, while talking in his ear and pointing at Pastor Bob. The two joined their friends outside. They left, squealing their tires into the night.

Five minutes into his omelet, which he poked at more than ate, Pastor Bob was still bothered by the unruly men's faces. Then he remembered. He threw fifteen dollars on the table and bolted for the door. Driving like a wild man he dialed Johnny Bingham's cell phone and got voice mail. "Get out now," he yelled into the phone.

He dialed 9-1-1 and was told to call Colville PD's general number, since he was in Indianapolis. He did so, but an answering machine said to call back during office hours.

He redialed 9-1-1. The words poured out. "I think some kids are going to burn down my church." He realized his error the moment he said it.

The dispatcher couldn't get past the words, "I think."

Pastor Bob prayed like he was back in Iraq. He redialed Johnny without getting through. Inside Colville's city limits, he called 9-1-1 again. They answered as he turned onto Main Street.

But it was too late. Flames crackled high into the sky.

IT WAS JAY'S LAST lap around the open deck. Seagulls swooped breakfast from the turbulent water churning behind the immense ship. Jay was as clueless this morning as last night about what had been expected of him. He had done what Sarah asked. He held her. No more. No less. She had laid on the bed and spoken of love and death and Avi. He'd laid next to her and listened. That's when he realized that his feelings for Doc rose beyond his memories of Sarah. He wondered if Doc was as gone for him as Avi was for Sarah. He finished his lap and returned to their stateroom. He knocked and was invited to enter.

Sarah was all smiles and fresh perfume. "You're a good listener. Thanks. That discussion of a fragment has got to be why your dad put the diary in the safe deposit box. I looked at his pictures while you were gone, but I can't tell what fragment he might have stolen. Do you think it was that little piece that Professor Albright burned in the dating process?"

"I don't think so. Directing us to the diary makes no sense if there's no other piece. How did you look at the pictures?"

"I took pictures of his pictures with my phone at the bank. I meant to tell you yesterday on Veillon's boat, but things got a little hairy." She picked her phone up from the bureau and showed him the photo of the unrolled blank scroll. "I count five or six pieces. It's hard to tell. As soon as we get into port, I'm going to send these to Jerusalem. Maybe they can map the dimensions and pieces to the existing Q document."

"That's good, but even if these are pictures of the Q document, how do they help? They raise doubts, but don't prove it's a forgery. For some reason, people want to believe this thing. We need the actual fragment. A photo of a photo isn't going to do it."

She straightened the covers on the bed, and then sat on it. She motioned him down beside her. "I agree, but the mapping has to be our first step. It will confirm that the scroll we have pictures of could be the Q document. Otherwise, we might be chasing a fragment of an unrelated papyrus. And I've been wondering about something else. What if this isn't about the fragment?"

"It must be. Nothing else fits."

"Then why didn't your Dad show it to the world instead of feeding you a bunch of clues to find it?"

"That bothers me, too. His diary said he never wanted to see it again. If he destroyed it, he couldn't show it. If he kept it, why wasn't it in the safe deposit box? If he hid it some other place, where? We've exhausted all his clues to get this far."

Sarah bounced onto her feet. "That's why I want you to think about other possibilities. Consider too that Faatina may not be the only femme-fatale new to Evergreen. Only Doc knew or could have guessed where you were each time you were nearly killed."

"And she understood the GPS software."

"I'm glad you're agreeable." Sarah pulled the gun from her purse, checked the safety, and tucked it back inside.

"I've been wondering about something, too," he said. "Do you think your mother was—"

"No. I don't. For one thing, she wasn't unbalanced. Let's go."

"She worked on the Genizah Collection. The timing fits. Didn't you move to Jerusalem in the late 70s?"

"The diary identified Z as a Coptic Christian. Mom was a Jewess, *not* an adulteress. So drop it. Unless you know where your dad's fragment is hidden, our next step is to visit Duvert in Paris. We probe for weaknesses and hit him where it hurts most."

When Sarah said to drop it a second time, Jay knew it was time to move on. "For me, 'where it hurts' would be just about everywhere. How are your aches, pains, and gunshot wounds this morning?"

She continued as if he hadn't spoken. "And I don't see how the woman's identity is important no matter who she was. The poor thing is dead and can't help us. Leave her be." She marched to the door. "There's a flight to Paris this afternoon. We need to get off this boat at the next port. That's Montego Bay at nine o'clock. Let's find the breakfast buffet. The doctor said I should eat well to boost my blood supply."

CHAPTER 26

JAY'S FOND ANTICIPATION OF returning to gay Paree caved in
under a cold reality. This particular morning, the City of Light was
the City of Dull Gray. Their Sunday departure from Jamaica arrived
at Charles de Gaulle International at nine a.m. Monday, Paris time.
Wednesday's sanctioning event was approaching at light speed, and
they were spending half their time in a plane, ship, or airport.

Their surly taxi driver pulled up to the *patisserie,* nearly
knocking over a neat line of parked motorbikes. Sarah went inside
the bakery to meet her Mossad contact. Jay corralled their luggage
on the sidewalk. The aroma of baked dough and cinnamon invited
him to hurry. He tipped the Afghan driver more than he deserved
and wheeled both suitcases inside where it smelled like a donut had
exploded. A couple dozen people with sugar-high smiles relaxed
around small tables, oblivious to everyone but their tablemates.
Sarah sat at a table along the wall opposite a young man with curly
black hair, bushy eyebrows, and a tan suede jacket. He jangled
several keys over her open hand and dropped them into her palm
with a lustful grin.

Jay approached the table.

The contact appeared wary of Jay until Sarah approved his presence. She offered to buy her fellow agent a *pain au chocolat*, but he declined and left.

With her own lustful grin, she told Jay, "I'm not leaving without one."

Sarah dragged Jay to the all-glass counter; he dragged the suitcases. A million calories stared back. A middle-aged woman with straw for hair efficiently filled their order, and they sat at a rear table.

Sarah swallowed a bite of her chocolate croissant. Looking pleased, she said, "I have the keys to a gray Citroen parked out front and an apartment in the *Quartier Latin.* Wherever that is, it sounds nice. The directions are in my purse along with our new IDs."

"It's another name for the Left Bank. I can get us there. Staying at a company apartment doesn't thrill me even if it is a great location. Who else knows we'll be there besides Mr. Jingeling with the keys?"

She shook her head. "I'm not sure, but I don't think it poses much risk. My department knows all of the names we might use. They could find us wherever we stayed."

"That depends. Not all hotels collect passports. I've stayed in that area at a quiet little hotel called the St-Joan. The staff could be very discreet. Has your department confirmed your afternoon appointment with Duvert?"

"Four thirty. It's when he conducts all his interviews. I'm writing for the Jerusalem Post."

"I'm still not crazy about you interviewing him. There's a chance he'll recognize you."

"True, but I'd peg it at less than ten percent. On the other hand, we know he'll recognize you, so I don't see any choice. Besides, what can happen in his lab?"

Sarah finished her pastry and the remaining third of Jay's crumbly, puffy selection that scattered powdered sugar with every bite. They left in the Citroen and arrived at the apartment just after noon. Neither was hungry for lunch, so they opted for placing phone calls. To avoid a telephone shouting competition, they chose separate bedrooms to call from. She picked the large master bedroom with a domed-ceiling. Jay's tiny room didn't have a chair, so he went out to the main living area and opened heavy maroon drapes at the room's far end. It revealed the fifth-floor corner apartment's *coup de gras.* French doors opened to a balcony with a great view of Notre Dame. Jay stepped outside. The dome of the Pantheon floated over the city to his left. Sun or no sun, Paris could still dazzle.

He was itching to call Danny and Rabbit, since he hadn't spoken to either in days. It reminded him to plug in Hassan's phone, which he did back in the living room. He verified that Rabbit had given him a name for every number in the phone's logs. Jay phoned Rabbit and told him about Suez LLC. It made his day. While Rabbit talked, Jay turned on his Arizona cell phone. There was one missed call and a strange text from an odd number.

Rabbit finished his guesswork on Suez and added, "One last thing. Rachel Raczynska has no hidden money. Anywhere. But she has a past. She was abused for years by her parents. Her father was a plastic surgeon and apparently wanted a boy. The sicko tried his best to change things. She was removed from their home when she was twelve and spent the next six years in and out of foster care and hospitals. More interesting is that six months after she moved to Egypt, both parents were grizzly homicide victims."

"Egypt?"

"Yeah, Cairo. She didn't arrive in Israel until a few weeks after her parents' deaths. Somebody really made them suffer. A buddy with Newark PD said nobody pursued it very hard. She was an ex-cop and had a solid alibi. Everybody figured even if she was involved, the parents got what they deserved."

"That they did." Jay studied the short text, 'StJ1400.' It started to make sense. "How fast can you run a phone number for me?" Jay read him the phone number where the text originated.

Rabbit's answer surprised him.

RANDY SOUNDED GROGGY.

Jay hoped it wasn't too early to call. "Can you talk? I wanted to catch you without a bunch of your compadres around. I hesitated calling you at this hour."

"It's 5:37. You should have hesitated longer."

"Any problems with . . . *things?*"

"No. Everything's good. The car was fine. Abandoning it at the Havasupai Res worked well. I assume you didn't stick around, which is exactly what I told Sheriff Henson. He hates advice. He's got half the county and the FBI crawling all over that reservation on the assumption that you've gone to ground out there."

Jay laughed. "Nice work." It was a doubly funny turn of events. Richard Clearwater was Hualapai, not Havasupai. He must have guessed the cops and feds would be tramping all over his lands for weeks, so he repositioned the Mustang on rival tribal lands. What a joker.

Randy yawned into the phone. "There are a couple other things you should know. Two different FBI teams have contacted our department. There's some kind of battle brewing between them. One team wants to hang you."

"And the other?"

"They think hanging is too good for you."

"Gotta love competition."

"Wherever you are, keep your head down. Get out of the country if you can. If you're already gone, stay gone."

"You said a couple things."

"Yeah, the other is about Doc."

"Is she okay?"

"Yeah, she's fine. I think. But, well, I'm not sure how to tell you this . . ."

Jay pictured Randy at the hospital helping Doc deal with his arrest, stepping between her and Henson, leading her away. At the time Jay was glad Randy was there to assist her. Now he wasn't so delighted, recalling that she hadn't recoiled from Randy like she did from the sheriff. He decided to make it easy on the deputy. "Look, if you and Doc are—"

"Forget that. How disappointing . . . I figured you for a fighter. But it's not me you have to worry about in the department."

"Henson? He's married."

"I guess he's not happy, and you sort of challenged him. Look, this is not what we need to be talking about. I'm trying to tell you Doc has disappeared. There's no reason to suspect trouble. She told the hospital she was taking time off to join the manhunt for you. But the teams in the desert have yet to see her. I think she's hunting you down, brother. It's just not with them."

"I think you're right."

JAY KNOCKED ON SARAH'S bedroom door. "Are you decent? We need to go out."

He heard mumbling that sounded like come in. He eased the door open enough to peek in. She was talking on her cell phone and making notes while sitting at a walnut campaign desk that

Charlemagne might have owned.

"There's been a development," he told her, opening the door completely. "Can you finish your call?"

She flashed five fingers on her free hand twice.

Five minutes was stretching it. Ten were too many. He shook his head and flashed back four fingers. "Bring the gun," he whispered. The fully-furnished Mossad apartment included a Jericho 941 handgun. Jay didn't like the idea of taking it on this mission, but since Sarah would have to go in alone, he wanted her prepared for anything. He grabbed his daypack and stuffed two phones and the GPS inside it. He knew where they were going. The problem might be getting back.

Sarah emerged from the bedroom. "I'm ready. What's the hurry?"

"I'll fill you in on the way to the St-Joan. You have someone to meet there at 1400 hours."

"That's twelve minutes."

"That's why we're hurrying. I'll drive, so I can drop you at the door."

Two buildings up the street, they jumped into the Citroen. It stood to reason that a secret agent car ought to have something special under the hood, so at the first traffic light, he floored it. Besides noise, little else happened. "I can run faster than this. It better have machine guns behind the lights."

She rolled her eyes. "Guys believe too many movies."

Jay turned off Boulevard Saint-Germain onto a small side street. They were a block away with six minutes to go. "Here's the deal." He laid out the simple plan for her.

NOTHING IN THE ST-JOAN'S elongated lobby looked anything

like what Sarah had expected. Strawberry, plum, and orange from the 60s colored everything from the window treatments to the furniture. A wall of windows that looked out to the street was lined with curved sofas and plush chairs grouped around glass-topped tables. Impressionist art graced the opposite wall. Three older eastern Europeans studied a map in one of the conversation pits. Sarah walked slowly past the woman and two men, memorizing their wide faces and stodgy clothes. A single elevator, located at the far end of the lobby between the registration desk and a lounge, dinged its arrival. Sarah stopped halfway to it, pretending to search her purse.

A woman wearing a babushka stepped out. She joined the others reviewing the map.

Sarah pulled several brochures from a rack near the unattended front desk, and smoothed her windblown hair using the window behind the rack as a mirror. She backtracked through the lobby and took up residence on a plum couch. After fifteen minutes, the tourists had gone and Sarah had left a phone message for Adamchek to see if he'd nailed Glassman yet. They'd talked from Jamaica, and although he was doing all he could, Avi's friend hadn't accomplished squat. The hotel's revolving door began turning. An elegant man in a blue pin stripe suit entered. He crossed the lobby, glanced at Sarah, and proceeded to the elevator.

On Sarah's third trip to the brochure rack, she saw her. It was 2:35. Sarah left the hotel and entered the bistro across the street where the subject sat at the window. Sarah bought a coffee at the counter and chose a table near the woman, who never took her eyes off the hotel's entrance.

After a few minutes, a male patron approached the subject's table. He was late-twenties and energetic. "I can show you my marvelous city for no charge."

"No thanks. I'm here on business," the redhead told him.

"But you can still enjoy the sights, no? Have you been to Paris before? We can go to Notre Dame. I know its history intimately."

"I went to school here. I'm busy, please leave me alone."

The man pulled out the extra chair at the woman's table and sat. "This city is not dangerous, but it is a city nonetheless. Someone as beautiful as you should have a male escort. I would be honored to protect you."

"She doesn't need your kind of protection." Sarah rose and walked over to the table.

The man looked up with a wry smile. "We can all three go. You'll see I mean very well."

"She asked you to leave." Sarah flashed her badge. "I'm telling you to get lost."

"The only crime here is that we will not all become friends." The man left.

The redhead shook her head. "I forgot how forward men behave here. Thanks. I hate to appear rude or unappreciative, but I really am busy."

"You've been staring out the window. Are you waiting for someone?"

The subject laughed. "Are you going to offer to show me around Notre Dame?"

"I would be honored to protect you." Sarah laughed with her. "Actually, you could show it to me. This is my first time in Paris. Where did you go to school?"

"I studied two years at Paris VI. It's also called Pierre and Marie Curie University. It's a mouthful."

"You sound American. What do you do in America after only two years of schooling in Paris?"

"I went to other schools, too. I'm a doctor."

Doc was even prettier than Sarah had imagined.

"I think I've been stood up." Doc looked at her watch and bit her lip. "I was waiting for someone. Someone special, you know? It's crazy, but . . . I was hoping to make up for something I did. Maybe tomorrow. Would you like to see Notre Dame? I haven't seen it in years."

"I have a car and a driver just up the street."

JAY HAD POSITIONED THE Citroen for an unobstructed view of the St-Joan—not for whatever shop Sarah had entered eleven minutes ago. When she crossed to his side of the street, it reduced his angle of vision and placed a long line of parked cars between them. He crossed the street on foot to regain his angle. The problem, besides the icy wind funneling down the narrow street, was that he hadn't seen where she had gone. A perfume shop, bistro, and leather goods store were each good candidates. He kept an eye on all three entrances from outside a Greek delicatessen. His ears felt as a cold as the meat in the deli case. He turned his collar up against the wind.

Sarah emerged from the bistro. She looked up and down the block before stepping onto the sidewalk. Traffic was non-existent. Another woman came out and joined her.

Doc? Sarah was supposed to just observe her.

The two women advanced toward the car, walking and talking like old friends.

Jay stepped off the curb.

A bicyclist broke hard. His tires skidded on the pavement. The rider shouted a rash of French. "Imbecile" was the only recognizable word, and probably the kindest.

"*Excusez-moi. Pardon.*"

The biker rode off. Sarah and Doc gawked from thirty yards

away.

Jay stared back, picturing Doc's tears and rage at the hospital. He recalled the St-Joan coming up in past conversations about their separate days here, but had she come to help or hinder? He shuffled into the street on an angle to intercept her.

She dashed into it.

He raced to meet her. They embraced. He held her tighter than he had the right. She returned it in-kind.

"I'm so sorry," she spoke in his ear. Her voice quivered. Their hands entwined by instinct as they separated and remained facing each other. "They told me you were a con man. That you could make anyone like you. I thought—"

"You don't need to explain."

"I want to. When you called Wednesday night, the sheriff was in my office. He had just told me everything that you were accused of, and he could tell from my face it was you on the line. He said if I helped you get away, I'd be committing a federal crime. I didn't know what to do. You insisted I stay away from the hospital. Twice. I didn't tell Henson, but . . . I thought you had lied a couple other times, and even though you explained them, those memories flooded back. I began doubting your explanations and your motives." She took a deep breath. "I should have trusted you."

"Why? You don't really know me. I've had doubts, too."

"I can imagine."

A small car motored by.

"Let's get to the sidewalk," Jay said. "Even Paris may not be romantic enough to shut down a street just for our happy reunion."

"We're reuniting? You don't hate me anymore?"

Jay stopped cold. A lump rose in his throat. "I could *never* hate you." He took her arm and led her toward the sidewalk.

Sarah met them at the curb. "This is cute, but I have to

THE Q MANIFESTO | 289

interview Duvert in ninety-three minutes. That means wig and makeup."

"Dr. Duvert?" Doc asked. "I figured Jay would show up near the Q document eventually, but how'd you two arrange a meeting with him?"

"He's a friend of the family," Jay told her, as they hustled to the car. "We think he's also friends with whoever faked the Q document."

"The same whoever that's trying to kill Jay," Sarah added.

They piled into the car. Sarah sat in the backseat and grabbed her bag of wigs.

"Confronting Duvert is the quickest way to learn what he knows. Since he met Jay as a kid, I was elected to do the interview. There's a slim chance he'll remember me, so I'm going in disguise." She maneuvered a dark pixy-style hairpiece into place. "What do you think?"

Doc turned to her. "Do you speak French?"

CHAPTER 27

DOC DIDN'T NEED A stethoscope to monitor her out-of-control heart rate. "I know you don't want me interviewing Duvert. It's mostly because of the danger, but it's partly because you don't trust me." She stared at Jay, while they sat at a traffic light a few blocks from the Archeological Society's offices. She waited for him to look at her. When he finally turned, she recognized the conflict in his face. "Based on the facts, you could suspect me of half your problems. I know that. I also know you must trust me a little, or I wouldn't be here. What I'm saying is that it's okay that you don't trust me completely for now, but I need to know that you'll give me a chance to regain it."

Jay groaned. "I'm pulling my hair out over this. Over you." He shook the steering wheel so hard she thought he'd break it. "There's this battle raging in my brain," he said. "Those thoughts—the memories—they keep surfacing. I don't know how to silence them."

"I understand. I've fought that battle. The difference is trust."

He parked on the side of the road. "Why did you change your mind about me?"

"In a word, Randy. The sheriff had looked for shells on the

ridge top. He didn't find any, which he said showed that you killed the hiker and were never shot at. The next day, on his day off, Randy took me there with a metal detector. We found a cache of spent casings a few inches under the sand."

"So the facts convinced you?"

"No. I changed my mind before we found them. I saw that Randy believed you. Rather than accept circumstantial evidence that pointed to the worst, he challenged it. It embarrassed me to realize that I wasn't doing the same."

"Is it that easy?"

"It's that simple. Stepping off a cliff is never easy."

Jay groaned and looked away. He pressed both palms to his forehead, then looked back. "It's getting late, we should get moving. This isn't exactly the sendoff I wanted to give you."

"You're being honest. I prefer that."

Two minutes later they approached the Société des Antiquités Archéologiques near the Sorbonne. A familiar black wrought iron fence surrounded the Society's building. As a student, Doc had admired the building's architecture and thought the fence completed the look. Not anymore.

Razor wire curled atop its posts. Behind the fence, a dozen armed guards in blue uniforms patrolled with Dobermans and Rottweilers.

SARAH WAS READY TO copy down the list of linguists alive today that could pull off imitating a first century Jew writing in an unusual Hebrew dialect. The Q document's phrasing, vernacular, and grammar all appeared genuine to every expert who analyzed it. Unanimous opinions were rare. So rather than beating the dead horse of hiring yet another expert to find fault with the document, it made more sense to see who could have pulled off such a convincing fake.

The Mossad expert began her list. "The foremost authority is Professor David Hunt."

"Lizabeth, he died a week ago Thursday."

"That's too bad. I think you'll see that doesn't leave us much to work with. The next name is Dr. Horace Stansfield of Edinshire. Unfortunately, he suffers from dementia. He's had the disease for a number of years."

Sarah wrote the name down. "How many years?"

"Let's see . . . nine. He doesn't seem to be a very likely candidate, does he?"

Sarah put brackets around Horace's name. "Give me the rest of your list."

"Dr. Irving Stonemyer."

"He sounds familiar. I wonder if I met him as a child."

"You might have, he's quite old. It's more likely that you remember the name because he's Director of The Israel Museum. Before my assignment to this project, he was my boss's boss's boss."

"Oh, that Stonemyer. He stays on the list. Who's next?"

"That's it."

Sarah tapped her pen on the desktop. "We need more names. Expand the criteria."

"How?"

"Easy. Include the deceased. You already have your first name, Professor Hunt. Catalog anyone who could have done it."

"Ever? It's 2,000 years old."

"Work backwards to the seventies, then let's review your list." Sarah ended the call and checked her watch. It was 4:28, almost time for Doc's interview with Duvert. Doc was a quick study, but probably as nervous as a sheep on Yom Kippur. Ideally, she would get Duvert to confess. That wasn't likely, but Doc was bright enough to find a chink in his armor.

Good luck, lady. I like your chutzpah. Sarah wondered if she meant that. It had been hard watching Doc's obvious pleasure in being around Jay. That he didn't fully share it sent ripples of mixed emotions through all three of them. *Baumann, you're a cop. Act like one.*

Her phone rang. It was Adamchek.

"I have news," he said. "It's not good, but it's not all bad. We picked up Jacob at 3 a.m. last night. He was spending a little too freely at the Navartz. He and his friends got too rowdy, and the Tel Aviv district picked him up along with half the bar's occupants."

"That's great. Even if he hasn't talked yet, he will." Sarah settled into the deep cushions of the apartment's sofa. Notre Dame rose in the distance. "He'll lead us to Glassman."

"Nobody knew we had Jacob. He was in a holding tank with the general population. Sarah, he wasn't ID'd until this morning when his body was discovered with a shank in his neck. Trust me, no one in there is going home until we find who did it. Someone will cough up Jacob's killer, and then we'll sweat him. I'll stay in touch." He hung up.

Sarah stared out the window. The hit man would fear Glassman's retribution more than the law. She needed another way to get to Glassman.

Her alarm rang, reminding her that the package from Jerusalem was due at a nearby copy center at five o'clock. With fifteen minutes to kill, she remembered she hadn't finished the last part of the diary. It was important to get two sets of eyes on it. Jay had resisted, but eventually agreed. She trudged into his room. Her stomach grew queasy. Touching the diary made it worse. She grabbed the diary and returned to her bed to read it. A sealed envelope fell out of it with Jay's handwriting on the outside. He had written, "Read the diary before this letter." She speed-read the diary's ramblings until her name jumped off the page. She read the entry. The handwriting blurred. She set the diary down, and wiped a tear from its cover, wondering how much more she could take.

She tore the envelope open.

> *Sarah—now you know the full truth. It still doesn't excuse my behavior, but consider this letter the first of many letters to come. I don't intend to lose contact with you ever again. Jay.*

At long last, she cried. All twenty-eight years worth. Jay had been a better friend and son than she knew. The trouble was knowing what to do about it. And what exactly did Jay mean by ever again? Did he harbor romantic feelings for her? It was like he wrote the note in code. Just when she thought she was done crying, she remembered how Avi wrote her love poems, and she cried again. Catching her breath, she realized she needed to quit crying, and start asking the right question. What did she feel for Jay? That was becoming clear.

THE DEFENSIVE MEASURES SURROUNDING the Société des Antiquités Archéologiques kept several hundred protestors at bay. Doc wanted to join them. They waved homemade signs in French and English and shouted in numerous languages at passing cars. Jay parked on the street opposite the building, and wearing a medium length black wig, he escorted her into the throng of protestors. She wore Sarah's brunette wig. Slogans supporting Jesus' divinity rippled through the crowd as people parted to allow Doc and Jay to pass.

Chills tingled her spine each time she responded, "Amen," to a protestor's declaration that Jesus was real. She prayed for guidance and strength. As they made their way deeper into the group, Jay stopped and faced her. He rubbed her upper arms and then held them.

"I can't let you do this just yet. You once told me that people think with their brains, but they know with their hearts. I've been relying on my brain, and I don't like the results. All I know is that I hate, really *hate,* the thought of you going in there. I think the hate is coming from my heart, if that makes any sense, because it knows." A smile burst across his face. "Yeah. My heart *knows*. It's screaming at me louder than all these people." He grabbed her and kissed her with more passion than all of Paris.

Her heart screamed, too, and she became aware that the crowd was clapping and cheering at them.

Jay backed up. "I trust you more than I trust myself." His face looked like it was made of steel. "Now you can go. If you don't come out in one hour, I'll break down those walls with my bare hands and rescue you, fair maiden."

"Amen," she said, squeezing his hand. He'd slay a dragon for her, and she'd do the same for him. *That's the strength I prayed for. Now, about that guidance . . .*

They headed for a gate at the front of the protestors.

Jay stopped her again. "I just remembered something. Duvert was placed on the Dead Sea Scrolls team because of his special expertise, but he didn't perform up to expectations. They sent him packing. It probably still smarts. Maybe you can use that."

"Do you recall his specialty?"

"Cultic practices during Israel's Kingdom period around 1000

B.C."

"King David and Solomon. Got it."

Guards at the gate checked her credentials and swiveled a barricade aside, granting her access to the property. A former carriage path with barren rose bushes on either side led to the dark stone structure that housed the Q document and Dr. Claude Duvert. The building seemed to grow in size and complexity as she approached. It had four floors under a central dome with twin two-story side wings. The door to the main entrance opened as she approached it. A guard ushered her inside toward a metal detector and x-ray machine. A glossy white marble interior rose to an intricately molded ceiling twenty feet overhead.

Before passing through the metal detector the guard instructed her to place her purse, phone, and notepad in an open gray bin, which he x-rayed. He returned her notepad, but placed the bin still holding her purse and phone on a shelf by the x-ray machine. He instructed her to step down the hall to a second security station where another guard hand-wanded her. He remarked favorably to a partner in graphic French about her anatomy. She assumed they were testing her French language skills, so she smiled and acted as though they had commented on the weather. One of them escorted her to the building's east wing, and yet another guard station just outside a waiting room. According to Sarah, there were four interview rules; no viewing the Q document, no photos, a maximum of twenty minutes with Duvert, and all interviews would be videoed for the sole benefit of the Society.

The waiting room had that old school smell that reeked of history. Butterflies in her stomach reinforced the feeling she was about to take a major exam. Which, she reminded herself, she invariably aced.

ISIS WAS SURELY A prophetess. She always called at the worst possible time.

"I have news." Her voice was free of suspicion, but Isis must have known things had gone wrong. "But first, tell me about Victoria Case."

The woman's proper name surprised Faatina. During their days together in the desert, Faatina had grown accustomed to calling the blanch-skinned woman Doc. "As you know—"

"Don't bore me with what I already know. That shall be first among my new commandments."

"Sorry. Doctor Case has disappeared. I don't know how, but she left her hotel without my noticing. I checked a bistro that she spent hours at yesterday, but she wasn't there. I'm sorry."

"Where are you now?"

"Hotel de l'Ouest. It's where she's staying. The moment she returns, I'll know it."

"I'm sure. In the mean time, Jay Hunt has materialized in Paris. You know how to find him. I suspect she won't be far away. It's time we end this."

"I won't disappoint you again."

"I'm glad to hear that, but don't be too harsh on yourself. You know I love you. If not for your vigilance, I would not have known she flew to Paris. Your strategic placement of the final U.S. bomb will ensure she has nowhere to run."

"She won't leave Paris upright."

"I will take you at your word. However, there is a problem in the making with her and Hunt both showing up in Paris."

"Duvert."

"*Exactement.* I've alerted him to Hunt's presence. And hers.

Duvert will recognize Hunt, but even I don't know what Case looks like. Fill him in and make sure he doesn't talk to her. Faatina, don't relax. The world will thank us for our victory."

"You speak as a prophetess."

UPON ENTERING, DUVERT NODDED to her. He wore a starched white shirt, which was open at the neck, and corduroy pants. "I understand you wish to conduct this interview in English. It will be my pleasure to converse with you in any language."

"Thank you. I'm looking forward to it." From television, Doc had expected his studious face, Roman nose, and bald head with an ear-to-ear band of gray. In person, though, she had also expected anti-Christ evil to ooze from his pores.

Instead, he beamed like a Frenchman in a winery. "Pardon, but your lovely green eyes are filled with surprise. Did you expect a beast? A demon, perhaps? Do not lie to me, I will know it."

She didn't doubt that for a moment. "Thank you for speaking English. Actually, I've heard you are very charming."

He reached for her hand to help her up, and then kissed it. "Whom should I thank for spreading such a wonderful tale?"

A herd of butterflies invaded her stomach. He was not going to be easily bluffed or manipulated. "Barbara Landis. She closed a CSN interview with those words."

"*Mais oui.*"

"I know that '*oui*' means yes."

"That is the only word you ever need use around me."

Doc felt her face flush.

"After we finish with this business, I will take you to a most intimate restaurant."

"I'm sorry, but that would be inappropriate."

"Congratulations, you have passed your first test. We can speak Hebrew, if you prefer. Would you be more comfortable in your native tongue?"

"English is my native language. I'm a stringer. I only received this assignment at the last minute from the Jerusalem Post."

"So then, Mademoiselle Stringer, what story would you like to hear? I will tell it on the way to show you the document."

THE BUILDING THAT HOUSED the Société des Antiquités Archéologiques had multiple points of entry, but the fence surrounding it only had one gate. Jay and Sarah had cruised the building's perimeter earlier, so Jay was comfortable that Doc could not be spirited off the grounds except through the front gate. From his vantage point across the street, Jay walked west. Nothing but lawn surrounded the west wing. He traipsed back east. Four vehicles were parked in a gravel lot not far from the fence by the building's east wing. Two black Mercedes had smoked-out windows. He pulled Hassan's phone from his daypack to photograph the vehicles' license plates. He was glad he had Hassan's phone, since his Arizona camera phone was about 0.0001 megapixels and its photos were generally worthless. He waited on the guard at this end of the property to clear the frame, and snapped the picture. He reviewed the picture.

Six of six?

Jay navigated the camera's photos. There was a woman in a burqa taken from behind, a rolled scroll on a table, and a photo of Veillon taken at an odd angle. Jay guessed the camera had been waist high and directed up at his face. All were taken in early February, several days apart. Two other shots had been made the day Dad was murdered. One was a Bedouin woman cooking something, and another showed the same woman trapping smoke from incense.

Compare Quality In New Kia.

Jay stared at the phone in his hands, then sent the photos to Rabbit plus a text, locate geotags. thanx. If Jay guessed right, Dad took the picture of a woman making ink in Jordan's Wadi Rum. Dad's big blotch on the newspaper was a sample to compare with Q ink.

What else was in this phone? He fooled with the phone's messaging icons and found one saved text. Speaking Arabic was one thing, reading it was something else. The gist of the message was send more money. It had been sent to a different number than any of those in the call logs. He forwarded the text to Rabbit. He repeated the process, sending everything to himself.

Jay hiked partway back to the Citroen and nestled in the doorway of a low-rise apartment out of the wind. The inconspicuous spot allowed him to observe the Society's front gate and the east wing exit that led to the parked cars.

DURING AN EXHAUSTING TOUR of rooms, Doc depleted her repertoire of prepared questions. Nothing useful had turned up during Duvert's bragging, and the Q document had yet to make an appearance. The staff was gone for the day, and Duvert was a bore who inched ever closer. She needed a diversion and noticed a thin carved statue through the window of a closed door. It was a female with a spiked headdress, standing five-feet tall.

"What is that interesting item? I love ancient cults."

Duvert backpedalled to the door and pulled a large batch of keys from his pocket. His fingers immediately selected the correct one and opened the door. "They're only called cults by nonbelievers."

Doc looked in from the hall. "Is that an Asherah pole? I've seen pictures, but don't know much about them."

"It is indeed. Asherah was Baal's consort and the Canaanite fertility goddess. This one dates back to 1400 BCE. It's carved from ivory."

"Ivory, how is that possible in Canaan?"

He maneuvered around her and walked to the statue. He ran his fingertips along its midsection. "Come feel it. This find helped me uncover her origins. In my humble opinion, Asherah was borrowed from Egyptian religious beliefs surrounding Isis. I won't bore you—"

"Isis? She of the Throne. Correct?" Doc strolled into the room, gazing at the fine lines of the lustrous statue.

"That is but one name and meaning." His eyes burned like torches. "Isis has as many powers as she has worshippers. She is the goddess of nature and magic, of slaves and the rich, of limitless rulers and powerless children. She protects the dead, and maidens— like you."

Doc looked away from his stare and turned to leave. She stood face-to-face with a small bronze of an Egyptian woman with an elaborate wishbone headdress nursing a baby. It occupied the wall next to the door. This female statue sat on a large rectangular box, something like a coffin. "Is that Isis?"

He nodded. "Nursing Horus. Quite a piece, no? The original is in the Musée du Louvre. Do you know of Isis and her sister Nephthys? Or perhaps their two brothers, Osiris and Set?"

"Osiris sounds familiar."

"Isis was sister and wife to Osiris." Duvert arched his brows. "Set, their evil brother, killed Osiris and put his body in a box similar to that one. Then, Set cast the box into the Nile to deprive

Osiris of a proper burial. Isis retrieved it, and hid her husband's dead body. Alas, Set found the hiding place and chopped Osiris's body into forty-two pieces. Set scattered the remains so they could never be found. However, with Nephthys's help, Isis found every piece, but one. Fish had eaten—how shall I say this—his manhood. Being the goddess of magic, Isis conjured up a replacement, and the happy couple conceived Horus."

"She brought Osiris back to life?"

He smiled. "Such is her power. There is another piece at the Louvre you would appreciate. It is captivating, a terracotta of Isis mourning for Osiris. Her hair is long, dark, and flowing, much like yours. If you would permit it, I will introduce you to her someday."

"The statue or the goddess?"

He smiled and moved toward the door, then stopped, blocking three-quarters of it. He faced her and ran his hand along the back of her hair. "Your hair is very similar."

She jerked her head away. "That too, is inappropriate."

Duvert spoke as though he was in a trance. "She has no freckles, which you possess in abundance. It's an unusual and striking combination. How do you explain it?"

Doc advanced to the door and brushed against him to exit. "I don't." She shuddered at the contact and remembered Jay reminding her about a well-placed knee to the groin. His advice had seemed silly at the time, but she realized now that it was poor strategy to take her eyes off Duvert. She stopped and faced him. "When do we see the Q document?"

CHAPTER 28

THE ROOM SMELLED LIKE a McDonalds. One-fourth the size of a high school biology lab, it didn't look scientific at all. A moth or insect collector might have been more at home in it. Three eight-foot-long wood counters were arranged around the room's windowless walls. Computer equipment and miles of snarled cables occupied the lab's center. The monitors shared space with heaps of food wrappers, paper cups, and plastic utensils from Le Grand Croissant. A wonderful eatery she had frequented as a student.

Doc shifted her gaze to the counters and away from the mess. Each white-topped counter had glass panels resting on ancient papyrus. She moved closer to the counter on her right and peered through the glass.

The paper was yellowed and spotted with age. Rough edges appeared scorched as though they had been saved from a fire. Rows and columns of Hebrew marched across the blemished paper in perfect alignment.

"There you have it. *Magnifique*, no?"

The words dribbled from her mouth. "It's beautiful. I never thought—"

"We should reserve that word for describing you, but I admit it. The Q, she is beautiful."

"It's in pieces. I expected torn edges, but it's . . . so incomplete. The gaps between some sections are small, others large. How can you know the amount of paper that is missing?"

Duvert stepped to a section. He traced his fingers across the glass along the document below it. "You can see here where it has a precise match where even the eye can visualize its orientation. Thus this gap below develops into a trapezoid of sorts. But over here, what would have been an educated guess, the computer assists us with placement. The software considers the words, paper shape and size, even texture of the papyrus. Notice this streak?"

"Yes, I see a darker swathe through the paper. It's slight, but it does look as though it connects with those others. How many pieces are there?"

"We would call them fragments. Ancient scrolls are always missing fragments. The Q is actually more believable because it is incomplete. What you see here is nothing in terms of complexity. Had it been purchased in its original jar, all the fragments would likely be available, even if crumbs. Amazingly, the Q is in fantastic shape, nearly intact. Look over here." He walked to an adjacent counter. "These two pieces have a minor gap between them, but in reality they mate perfectly. We have kept them apart for unbiased mapping. Also, placing them against each other might cause an edge to crumble. With today's technology, we can safely manipulate them on the computer."

"I can see the writing appears to jump over the gap. Here I see the edge was torn right through the writing."

"Unfortunately, yes. And the wonderful message was lost in antiquity."

"How long did it take to unroll it?" She studied his eyes.

"Close to a year of painstaking work. It was extremely laborious, but exciting all the same. I worked on it alone." He stared straight at her, never blinking.

Doc marveled at how convincing a liar he was. "It's a shame it didn't just show up sandwiched between pieces of glass like this."

"Wouldn't that be nice."

"Dr. Duvert, we covered all the usual details. What was most uncharacteristic about this find, aside from its earth-shattering content?"

"The ink. What an insightful question, Anne. It is time you called me Claude." He reached for her hand that rested on the glass.

Anticipating his move, she flitted further down the counter.

He continued. "The ink is tested by lifting a sample with a very pointed tungsten needle. We expected to find fragile carbon ink. As such, it would rest on the surface rather than soak into the papyrus. We found it had soaked in somewhat. It gave us the first hint of an anomaly. However, once we determined that the writer was likely to have been an Essene, but not necessarily from Qumran, we compared it to scrolls from an Essene community in Egypt. It had similar qualities."

"So you don't think it was written at Qumran?"

"The location is uncertain. This finding points to the possibilities of an imported papyrus or of an ink technique learned in Egypt or an exceptional vintage of gum Arabic or incense." He laughed. "It will give the experts something marvelous to argue over for hundreds of years."

"But what do you think?"

"I won't make unsubstantiated guesses, but it reinforces my finding that this document is legitimate in two ways. First, a forger would not have strayed from the expected. It would bring light to bear on a situation that may not have been cleared up except for

our passionate investigation. Second, replicating this minor degree
of seepage is astronomically more difficult to accomplish than the
expected result."

A phone rang. The sound came from under the fast-food rubble.

"It will go to voice mail," he said.

Doc flipped through her notes. It was time to open up. "Why
did you leave the Scrolls team when you did? Was it amicable?"

The phone on Duvert's belt vibrated with a subtle buzz.
He looked down at it, then back at her. "It was time. There was
a mutual mistrust with the person I reported to. Voice mail is
wonderful, no?"

"You mentioned that funding for your organization is primarily
from private sources that desire to remain anonymous. What about
the French National Library? What is their interest? Except for
Islamic states, most countries are trying to stay neutral on the Q
document."

His posture straightened. "Our research here is absolutely
neutral. As to France, a French Dominican named Father Roland de
Vaux of l'École Biblique was among the first recognized scholars
to study the Dead Sea Scrolls. There are no less than one hundred
thousand fragments in existence. Our national library has but 377.
That is a crime they wish to see rectified."

A tall guard came in. "*Excusez-moi*, Doctor Duvert."

The *Directeur Général* turned and faced the security man. "Is
this important?"

The guard replied in French, "I must have a moment with you
in the hall. I was ordered to give you this message immediately."

Duvert smiled at Doc. "Excuse me."

Doc eased along the counter to a spot where she could hear
better, though only the guard's back was visible. He asked Duvert to
return an urgent call and slipped him a note. He also said the device

had been in position, but an alternate location was being planned for security purposes. The guard's conspiratorial tone during the next minute was too hushed to hear well, but it had to do with visiting a convent before his trip to Jerusalem.

Duvert reappeared and picked up a wayward food wrapper from the floor near the door. He tossed it into a trashcan.

A single high-pitched bark filled the small room. Doc looked under the tables holding the computer equipment for the source of the bark.

"Karnak, shush. This is my guest. Get out of there, that's not your box."

The strangest looking animal with wonderful brown eyes stared back. Tufts of fur protruded from the head, tail, and paws of an otherwise hairless dog. It had dappled pink skin.

The tiny dog ventured out and sniffed Doc's extended hands. "Karnak, you're so cute."

"She is a terrific judge of humans. Consequently, she doesn't like many people."

The dog licked Doc's fingers. "What breed is she?"

"She is a Chinese Crested, but like the Asherah pole, her true origin is Africa. The breed was a favorite of the fifth Dynasty pharaohs, and I would posit she is Egyptian to the core. Now Karnak, get in your box."

The dog scampered into a corner behind the centralized equipment tables. Karnak whimpered in front of an ornate bronze metal box about a yard long and a couple feet deep and tall. The box's lid had a set of angel wings mounted on each end. Their wingtips pointed toward the center.

Duvert walked over to Karnak. "Did someone close your house? Poor Karnak." He opened the box, which was hinged in the back like a casket. A red chenille cloth lined the interior. Duvert stood and faced Doc. "It's a sisterhood funerary box. Isis and Nephthys were often depicted on coffins with wings outstretched as protection."

"If it were larger, it could be used for you. Jean Veillon needs one. Did you know that?"

The smile drained from Duvert's face. He leaned a hand on a computer table. "He is on vacation. Why would you say these things?"

"Because he's dead. Killed by your people. Did he choose the Cayman's or did you suggest it so he could be watched?"

"Who are you?" His words had no force.

Doc moved closer. "There have been a large number of deaths associated with the Q document. Surely you know of the other loose ends that are no longer loose. Is the goddess and protector of the dead enlarging her collection of souls to guard? Will yours be next?"

He sat in a chair at a workstation. Sorrow filled his eyes. "You should leave."

She fought her instinct to comfort the hurting man, and reminded herself that pain can bring about healing. "Who is Isis? What is her real name? Veillon didn't like her much. Do you love her as much as her statues? Does she know the true reason you were asked to leave the Scrolls team? Is she holding that over your head?"

Duvert reached for a phone under the food wrappers. His trembling hand knocked over an empty soft drink cup. He cleared his throat and pressed a button on the phone. He spoke in its direction. "We have a problem."

Doc ran out of the room and into two guards. She twirled around. Another guard approached from the opposite end of the hallway.

Hands grasped her from behind, pulling her around. She kneed one guard in the groin. He cursed her but held on. His partner yanked her arms behind her and bound her wrists with something sharp.

Duvert cursed her in French and tore off her wig.

"HEY, BOSS. I HAVE a video of my kid's first soccer game on my PC. You want to see it?"

Maria and the other agents standing nearby rolled their eyes at Farnsleigh's request. Greene put on a distressed face, and turned to Farnsleigh. "I'd love to. It's not long is it?"

Inside his office, Farnsleigh kept his voice low. "I found our three flyers—Jay Hunt, Sarah, and the dead Sarah—all in the same TSA security line in time for that flight to Chicago."

Greene dragged a guest chair behind Farnsleigh's desk. "Nice. Start the soccer video in a separate window. I've confirmed that I met the real Sarah, but we need to know where she and Jay went from here, what names they used, and who died in Chicago. Cross-reference folks on Sarah Baumann's Israel to Houston flight with passengers on outbound flights around the time the three were in line together. Let's find common names."

Farnsleigh started the video, then pulled up passenger lists. A moment later he announced, "Three hits. Sarah Baumann went to Chicago, a Sarah Chase went to Phoenix, and Jay Chase flew to Vegas."

More questions than answers filled Greene's head. "So Jay Hunt survived the Hilton fire, and the Israeli government sends him to the US with their Q document strategist under false passports. So why did she have a shadow?"

"If she flew here as Sarah Chase, how could Sarah Baumann

meet you?"

"Alright, that's good. Why send her shadow to Chicago?"

"Either to surprise someone in Arizona that might be monitoring flights, or they thought someone was trailing her, and they didn't want the real Sarah interrupted."

"I think you should go to Arizona. I'm going to find out who wanted her dead. Did you notice that no one gives a whit about Baxter, North Carolina? We've been chasing our tails."

THE EAST WING'S DOOR near the parked cars burst open. A guard in a blue uniform similar to those walking the fence advanced to a Mercedes. He opened its rear door and held it. A second guard backed out of the doorway. He was pulling something. No, someone. Doc. Jay raced for the front gate, while watching yet another guard emerge to help shove Doc, writhing and kicking, into the car.

Jay barged into the crowd. "There's a car about to leave. Don't let it out. They're devil worshippers and are kidnapping a woman. They'll sacrifice her. Don't let the car out. We have to stop them."

A man blurted out in English, "Are you sure?"

"Yes. It's the woman that went in. They'll kill her."

"I'll repeat it in French." He shouted his translation to the crowd.

The car came down the path from the main building. Guards at the gate began swinging the barrier out of the way as it approached.

Jay took up a position on the passenger side where Doc would be. He shouted, "Lock arms. They won't run anyone over. Stick together. They'll stop. We have to make them stop."

People were yelling in various languages and began interlocking arms across the driveway. Some sang, "We shall overcome." Someone yelled, "Be strong in the Lord." Everyone pulled together. They formed an immense human blockade, ten or more deep.

The Mercedes crept out of the gate. It pushed its front end up against the leading edge of the crowd. The car inched forward. Gravel crunched under its tires. It was pushing into the crowd. Protestors screamed and shouted. All stood their ground. Some at the front released their locked arms and pounded on the hood. The car stopped.

Guards pointed their M-16s at the protestors from inside the perimeter, except one who had advanced with the car's nose and was cut off from the others by the swarming protestors. Jay front kicked him, and grabbing the man's weapon, smashed the rifle stock up and into his chin. The guard flew backwards onto the ground. Jay smashed the rifle butt into the car's rear passenger window, shattering the safety glass. He reached in to pull Doc through the window.

Instead, she pushed the door open. "Let me out, let me out," she yelled, forcing her way clear.

The crowd cheered.

Duvert leaned toward Jay from the other side of the rear seat, balling a length of duct tape in his hands. "She was a willing occupant, *monsieur* . . ." His smirk turned to recognition. "Jay Hunt. We were delivering her to you."

Jay pointed the rifle inside. "And I have a delivery for you."

Duvert's face paled. He squirmed into the corner against the door.

Jay dropped the M16A2's magazine onto the ground and speared the weapon into the car. Its barrel banged against Duvert's closed window.

CHAPTER 29

"PRIVATE PROPERTY AND NO proof. What a crock." Jay pictured Duvert speeding away to points unknown. The police had taken hours to interview witnesses who all confirmed that Doc's door opened and she jumped out. It was almost nine o'clock and they'd just gotten back to the Mossad apartment. "How are your wrists?"

"Would you please stop asking every five minutes? They hurt, but I'll survive." Doc was looking in the bathroom mirror and wiping alcohol on the last of the glue from the duct tape on her mouth. She turned and faced him. "I'm proud of you."

"He was going to kill you. I'd have done anything to get you out of that car."

"I'm proud that you didn't shoot him after I was free. You could have."

"Yeah, well . . . I had lust in my heart. Besides shooting him, I wanted to smash the rifle into his face and ram the duct tape down his throat with it."

"You're lucky the rent-a-guards didn't shoot you." Sarah joined them in the bathroom. "They didn't know who was in the car. If

316 | ALAN SCHLEIMER

they were better trained they might have fired to immobilize you.
You definitely provoked them. My bureau chief confirmed what
the cops onsite told you. They can question the inside guards on
assault, but it'll be Doc's word against several of them. The French
National Police Commandant pledged to prosecute the driver for
bumping the protestors, but as a passenger, Duvert's in the clear.
He's also disappeared. The Mossad is watching his apartment and
his laboratory. Don't worry, it won't end here. Assuming Duvert
accompanies the Q document to Jerusalem for the sanctioning
event, he better not even spit on the sidewalk."

Jay asked, "What about the device comment that the guard
made? It reinforces what Veillon said about avoiding Jerusalem
during the sanctioning event."

"Our police are always on the alert for bombs. With nothing
concrete to go on, there's nothing different anyone can do."

Doc turned from the mirror. "I appreciate all the news and
everyone's concern, but I could use a little privacy in here."

Jay led the way out. Sarah followed him into the living room,
then ducked into her bedroom and came out waving the diary. "I
read the last of your dad's entries, and your note. Why didn't you
tell me?"

Jay sat on the sofa. "About the letters I sent from the States?"

"Yes, the letters." Sarah sat in an adjacent chair facing him.
She opened the diary to a page marked with his envelope and began
reading. "I tossed another of Jay's letters to Sarah. I feel bad, but
his fondness for her must stop. I could never explain why to him
now. If he asks when he's older, I pray he'll understand. I pray even
harder he won't know to ask." She looked up from the page. A tear
broke free from the corner of her eye. "Well? You took the heat, and
it wasn't your fault."

"When I moved stateside I lost your address. I sent a couple letters to him to forward. When you didn't write back, I figured . . ." His throat knotted. "I thought you had moved on. I shouldn't have given up so easily. But I did. I never knew what he did until I saw his diary." He looked out over the River Seine and the floodlit Notre Dame, then back at Sarah. "I'm sorry if you think I should have told you this at your safe house. There was no point in blaming him. He didn't let you down, I did. It's something I excel at."

"Please don't say that. I see now I played a role, too. I wish I knew why your dad felt that way. I guess we'll never know." Sarah moved to the couch and hugged him. She released him and patted his leg as she sat beside him. "By the way, what you stuffed into the diary was a note. It doesn't count as a letter. Letters are much longer, and I will expect them once this is over. Come on, we have work to do."

"May I join?" Doc tiptoed into the room. She sat in the chair Sarah had vacated. "He's let me down a few times."

Sarah chimed in, "Now that you mention it, there was that night in the desert when you were thirteen and—"

Jay interrupted. "I thought we had work to do."

Doc snickered. "Interesting, there was that night when *we* were in the desert and—"

"This is totally unfair."

Both women laughed.

"I think we better keep him out of the desert," Sarah said. Her expression turned business like. "While you two were out goofing off, I received a fax of your dad's Mossad file. I was hoping for a clue to Z's identity. I thought it might help us find out if there is another fragment and how to use it."

"They have a file on my Dad?"

Sarah nodded. "They probably have one on little Jay too. But your dad's is definitely more interesting." She smiled. "It turns out your father was a triple agent. He worked for the U.S. They allowed him to be used by foreign governments, including Israel and Jordan."

Jay slunk into the sofa. "I don't know a thing about that man. He stole things, destroyed letters, had affairs . . . Next, you're going to tell me he was a double-o and not my father."

"Stop being so melodramatic. He couldn't very well tell you he was a spy, which he really wasn't. His job was simply to tell the Americans which nationals contacted him or asked for favors. If approved, he was allowed to do what they asked. The Israeli's didn't know at first, but your State Department had some major leak."

"That's a surprise." Jay leaned forward. "So what exciting thing did he do?"

"Oh, nothing much, he just won the Six Day War."

"My dad?" Each new revelation shocked Jay more than the one before it. But, spying and war? "That can't be right. He was a peaceful man."

"According to his file, he frequently traveled between Jerusalem and Amman and sometimes Damascus. He reported the massing of Syrian and Jordanian troops before they actually moved to the borders. Because of his intelligence, Israel knew where to watch. The extra few days of preparations probably led to our quick success. It saved a lot of lives."

"Saving lives was more his style." This was interesting, but it wasn't identifying Dad's killer. "Did you find any hints about Z?"

"No such luck. I figured if he'd had an affair with her in Israel, they'd have documented it. Basically, he was squeaky clean. Now we know how he obtained approval to be buried anywhere in Israel he chose. He was an unsung hero."

Jay stood and paced to the window and back. "We need our own pre-emptive attack. A way to identify Isis and bring her out in the open. We know that she's planning something major, and it's related to the Q document. So we use the Q document to find her."

"Who got hit in the head with a rifle butt, you or the guard?" Sarah asked.

He smiled. "To find the source, we reverse the Q's money trails. In a nutshell, we bring Isis out of hiding by framing Duvert for stealing from her." Jay stared at two blank faces. "We've been running down the money trails to the accomplices. If we go up the chain, we find Isis. We'll use Duvert because he hasn't taken much money. The fact he has taken some tells me he needs it. That he hasn't taken much says he has other motivations."

Doc jumped in. "That fits with what I saw. Duvert absolutely worships the ground Isis floats over. People with strong mythological obsessions tend to act them out. He definitely has other motivations."

Sarah leaned forward in her chair. "We don't know their relationship. If he hasn't taken much money, then she knows he's in it for other reasons. I don't see any way it'll work using him. Try someone else."

"I've worked for years with people who have tons of money," Jay said. "They never have enough, and they can't imagine everyone's not after theirs. She'll believe he was being deceptive all along because of the money."

Doc spoke up. "In this case, their relationship may not matter. If it's weak, she might believe he's acting out of greed or unrequited love or blackmail or even revenge. If their relationship is strong, and if the evidence is convincing, she'll feel betrayed." Doc took a deep breath. "Betrayal is horrible. It makes you crazy. I believed something I never should have even considered." She patted Jay's hand. "It took a big man to forgive me. I think this strategy works either way."

"If it's convincing." Sarah stalked off toward her bedroom. "I'll call in the Cairo phone number that Hassan texted his demand for more money to, and have my team monitor it and Duvert's phone. If Isis surfaces, we don't want to miss it. Should we switch rooms? Jay's bed is rather small."

Jay stammered, "Uh, I'll be on the phone, too."

"And after he's off the phone, he'll be on the couch."

AFTER COMPLETING HIS CALL, Doc insisted they flip a coin for the bed. It was a long shot, but Jay was hoping the quarter would land on its edge. She won, and arranged blankets and a sheet for him.

"Our plan is looking good," Jay told her. "The friend I called in Washington said our timing was excellent since Island Bancshares's reporting period just ended, and their reports would be generated at the end of business today. It was only 3:05 p.m., which didn't give him much time, but he felt he could get his part done."

Doc finished tucking in the blanket. "No money will actually be stolen, right?"

She sat on the sofa, and Jay joined her.

"Not a penny, that's the beauty of this. Like most banks, IB has strenuous safeguards to prevent tampering with the actual accounts, but their reporting system is like a poor cousin with obsolete security. He'll doctor the reports to show dozens of transactions that only Duvert could have initiated. See, his Archeological Society's account is linked with Suez LLC's main account. Either party can initiate transfers, but only Duvert is authorized to act on behalf of the Society, so any transfers faked between the accounts will point to Duvert. As owner of the bank, a suspicious Suez will see that excess Society funds were siphoned into Duvert's personal account, then subsequently moved to another bank."

"What if whoever runs Suez orders him shot or something?"

"That would be terrible. It'd ruin our plan." Jay smiled, but Doc didn't seem to appreciate the humor. "Assuming Isis is Suez, she won't. Duvert controls the Q document, and he appears on the world stage too often. She's stuck with him."

"So what's next? We're running out of time. The sanctioning event is the day after tomorrow."

"For us, shut eye. We need Isis to surface."

"Even if she does, how will we know?"

"We find Duvert. My bet is she contacts him, and with luck, insists on a face-to-face meeting."

RABBIT STARED AT HIS array of computer monitors. "No, no, not today. This is not happening." He kept working.

The skull icon rose again on his leftmost monitor. "Juliya, this better not be you," he yelled at the screen. If he sent an impale order at her, she'd be sorry. He sent her a quick message.

An automatic response reported, *Off line.*

"Are you really?" He needed a way to verify it. This wasn't playtime. He sent a text. "Not funny, trouble coming at you in five."

He clacked away on the keyboard and finished falsifying the first account's report. One down, two to go. He needed to finish fudging all three before sending any. All by five o'clock, which left forty-four minutes.

Again the black skull rose. It sped through green and hovered in the yellow zone. At least it wasn't a red skull. "No, you can't be reaching that deep into my layers."

Juliya sent a text back. "Fire at will."

"Okay, cretin, you're not Juliya." He sent the Impaler. "Good riddance."

He studied the statement for the Society account and planned his changes.

The Impaler returned.

"What? No way. No way." His fingers danced like lightening. He resent it with a twist.

The Impaler was back before he could cross his fingers. Sweat beaded on his forehead. To be ready, he pulled up PowerPoint—a re-programmed version just for this eventuality. RabidPowerPoint was ready. How had this happened? How would he explain to Jay, whose past business not only paid for most of this equipment, but who needed the faked reports in thirty-eighty minutes?

An idea hit him. He sent a time bomb to Island Bancshares that should delay their reports for an extra hour. He hoped it worked. There was no time to check.

A red skull rose. Then another. Both red.

Two at once? Both in the black zone. He had sent the time bomb just in time. Two seconds later and they would have seen what he did. Not only was this cretin recording and stealing his keystrokes in real time, but a resident program just embedded for later recall if he cut the connection.

"Okay, this is war."

He cleared his programs. RabidPowerPoint required every ounce of RAM. It would look innocent enough to whoever was working him, but the program was anything but harmless. His fingers trembled, poised over the keyboard.

A third red skull rose. They were augmenting his hard drive.

His stomach squeezed. *So this is what it's like to be hacked.* Rabbit controlled his emotions and opened the MonthlyPresentation. ppt file. It would run for an hour and look as though he was still typing. In reality he would be flying out the door, never to return.

Every byte on his computer would be switched to random mush. It would take the cretins hours of encryption time before they figured out what happened. In the mean time, a secondary program was eating his remaining data. Best of all, it was shredding data on the hacker's system.

"Hoo-ah!"

Not just anyone could have found his address and penetrated his outer defenses, let alone installed the fundamental data capturing programs. He stared at the most secure modem, firewall, and software creation ever harnessed together. Soon, it would all be rubbish.

How did they do it?

What have you seen? The cutouts between his system and whoever hacked it were probably enough to safeguard this single-purpose apartment's physical address, but nothing was certain. They could be driving down the block at this moment. Teach had told him to let it go, if it came to this. He'd replace it. It was only equipment, he said. A hundred grand worth of equipment was nothing to a guy worth zillions, but Teach didn't appreciate that this equipment had personality.

Live to fight the next battle. It was superior military strategy, but backing off never sat well. He slipped the black tee shirt on over his regular shirt.

He launched it.

Rabbit hustled into his wheelchair, which was parked at the apartment's door. He looked back. "Bye, y'all." He slammed the door behind him.

Right-o. This will not happen in my next setup.

There were two underground parking levels. Rabbit punched P-2. The doors opened to the dim garage. He maneuvered his wheelchair out backwards. Going front wheels first almost always got them stuck in the gap between the elevator and the garage floor. Over his shoulder, he saw a boxy black and white Crown Victoria, sitting in the handicapped spot two inches from his specially equipped van. It blocked access to his rear side door and power lift.

The Crown Vic's dome light turned on.

Rabbit stopped his momentum and wheeled back toward the open elevator.

The gap swallowed his left front wheel. He heard the car door slam shut. Rabbit jerked his body back to take the weight off the jammed front wheel.

Still stuck. The first shot was a silenced whisper. The bullet pinged off a metal piece of his wheel chair.

Rabbit dove into the elevator, kicking the wheel chair free. He hit P-1.

NOW THAT SHE KNEW where to look, it practically slapped Lizabeth in the face. At twenty times magnification, the jagged gap looked like a craggy mountain range. Only a thin thread connected the fragment to the main body. She could have kissed the computer. This could explain the dimension and fit problems.

Okay, photo-shopping the end piece away.

Her eyes liked the result. Now for the computer software's objective analysis. She reran the photo-shopped image against of the Q document. The ten-second wait lasted forever. Sixty-two percent. That was more like it. The simulation should raise the probability of a match even higher. Lizabeth set the parameters and let the computer crunch away.

She rubbed her eyes and waited while the computer simulated every conceivable reorientation of the scroll's fragments. She walked to the end of the Israel Museum's lab to stretch her legs. The windows reflected her image against the dark night beyond them.

Her computer *pinged* like an old stove timer. She ran back to it. The histogram showed one spike at ninety-six percent.

Lizabeth danced and spun in a full circle. She dialed Sarah's drop box and left a message.

"Sarah, the Q document looks like an unfinished jigsaw puzzle. Most of the edges are intact, but a number of pieces are missing. Based on background images in your photo of the blank scroll, I estimated its length and scaled the Q document to fit. Nothing made sense until I discovered there weren't five or six fragments in your scroll, but seven. An end piece is so well aligned and your photo quality so poor that it's hard to tell it's connected. Removing that end piece and rescaling produced excellent statistical results. There are three things to know. First, despite missing pieces in the middle, the Q document still has more fragments than the blank scroll in your photo. I assume the blank scroll broke into additional pieces in the rolling, unrolling, and writing process. Second, the Q's spacing tells me the forger knew the original dimensions and purposely lost, ruined, or pitched the missing internal fragments and one end piece. Third, the program says it's a match. *Mazel tov.*"

RABBIT TORE OFF THE black tee shirt, folded, and stuffed it under his red one. The elevator doors opened onto P-1 of the underground parking garage. He walked casually past the hulking cretin in the sunglasses and a blue sport coat. A curly-cue earpiece completed his outfit. The man's jacket did a poor job of covering a bulky shoulder holster. With luck, the guy was too busy watching for the computer geek in a wheelchair to study any face walking by.

The killer fidgeted with his keys, bending over the door latch of a Ford Edge.

326 | ALAN SCHLEIMER

Rabbit gave a slight head nod, wishing he had a sport coat of his own to hide his thumping heart. He marched past the man's gaze to the old Camaro. With keys in hand, he hoped it turned over. Juliya had started it for him on occasion, but it hadn't been driven since the day he parked it nine months ago.

The green machine roared to life. He drove up the ramp and into a rainy Washington DC traffic jam. Rush hour in the rain. "This isn't helping," he yelled.

There were friends who would assist, but the gunplay at the apartment complex nixed that idea. As much as he hated it, there was only one real option. Rabbit directed the Camaro toward his office in direct violation of his most sacrosanct rule.

CHAPTER 30

SARAH OPENED AND CLOSED every kitchen cabinet door and drawer. At home, she put them by the dishwasher. Where would these people put them?

"What's going on?"

She jumped. "Oh, Jay. You scared me. Was I noisy?"

"Any louder and the neighbors will be pounding on the walls. What's bothering you?"

"Nothing. Why do men always think something is bothering us?"

"We don't always think it. Just when you're destroying a kitchen."

"The U.S. has done it again," she yelled. "You reneged on a missile system delivery to Israel. Contracts should not be political."

"Agreed."

"Half your population may go Muslim on us, and your government refuses to let us protect ourselves. Votes. Every single thing your leaders do is about votes."

"I'm sure that never happens in Israel." Jay wandered deeper into the kitchen. He opened a drawer and handed Sarah a spoon.

"Does your cereal need one of these?"

She grabbed it and a bowl of cereal, then banged the bowl back down on the sink's counter top. Milk splashed out. "Yeah, thanks, but it's already soggy."

"I've noticed you're not much of a morning person. You hog the covers, too."

"Should I go back into the other room?" Doc stood at the entrance to the kitchen and gave Jay a disappointed look. "And I felt bad you were sleeping on the couch."

"He didn't sleep with me last night. He's talking about a couple nights ago."

"Oh, that explains everything."

Jay rubbed his temples. "Can we start over?"

Doc puffed her cheeks. "Okay. Good morning everyone. When did you two sleep together? Is that what all the noise is about?"

Jay left, shaking his head.

Sarah dumped her cereal down the drain and refilled the bowl, while watching Doc twist and stretch her shoulders. Her ponytail swished side-to-side.

"Those guards yanked me around more than I realized. And I don't care what you and Jay did two nights ago or two decades ago."

"That would be a great attitude, wouldn't it? I don't think either one of us could maintain it for long." Sarah poured milk on her cereal and turned to Doc. "Sleep yes, but other than that nothing, ever, anywhere."

"Thanks. I heard about the letters. Men don't write much."

"No they don't. Plus where his dad first sent him, they don't exactly have mailboxes on every corner. They don't even have corners. Bedouins aren't big on paper, but they make their own ink. Go figure."

"That reminds me. Duvert made a big deal about the ink saturation proving the Q's legitimacy. I don't buy it. Setting new ink on old paper wouldn't be that tough using photobiostimulation. There's a medical laser, some call it a cold laser, which penetrates deep into tissue to stimulate it for pain relief. It operates in the 830 nanometer range. With some tweaking, it could sink the ink into the papyrus to whatever level was desired."

"Nice insight."

Jay showed up in clean clothes and wet hair. "So what was all that noise really about? It wasn't spoons or missiles."

Sarah decided to spill the beans. "My boss called this morning. The suspected Isis phone never rang, and Duvert's vanished. He's probably left the country. We're finished."

Doc flipped her ponytail. "Not as long as Karnak is around."

LE GRAND CROISSANT RESTAURANT was doing a brisk business for such a brisk day. Jay leaned back, lifting his front chair legs inches off the floor.

"Sarah called this a stakeout of a third kind. We've been here so long she's drinking decaf. What kind of dog are we looking for again?"

Doc answered, "Chinese Crested. Trust me, you'll recognize it. I know you both think I'm crazy, but Duvert's lab was full of wrappers and cups from this place. Wherever he's hiding, he'll want a delivery of this food, plus his dog."

Sarah entered and strode over to their table with a big city grin. Throughout the morning, they had taken turns in pairs, sitting, watching, and drinking lattes.

Jay checked his watch. "Noon. Right on time. You look perky."

Doc laughed. "Is that a coffee pun?"

Sarah's eyes beamed with confidence. "The Q document was definitely written on the blank scroll in your dad's photo. I just spoke with Lizabeth. She's certain of it. That should raise plenty of eyebrows, though the rest of my team says the photo is such poor quality that people will claim it, not the Q, is the fake. Of course, we know better."

Doc stood and hugged Sarah. "I knew the Q was a fake." She pointed to her heart. "In here. We have to tell people."

Sarah sat, as did Doc. Sarah said, "It would be better if we could prove it first, and that may be more doable than it sounds. Lizabeth's breakthrough came with the discovery that a big piece from the end of the blank scroll is missing."

Jay leaned forward. "How big is big?"

"More than enough. It's triangular. A foot wide at the base, a couple inches at the top. It's much bigger than what Professor Albright recorded testing."

Jay counted on his fingers. "Okay, mission one is to locate Duvert, and with luck, an unhappy Isis. Number two is finding the missing piece. If Dad didn't show it to the world here, it could be in the States. We have to split up the team."

"Has your friend in Washington reported in yet? None of the phones my team are monitoring have been used."

"Not a peep, but he didn't fail unless his world fell apart."

Doc's eyes widened. She whispered, "Here comes Karnak."

Sarah gawked at it. "You were right about it being unique. I'll wait outside in case the lady makes a break for it."

Jay stared at the small hairless dog. "A Karnak should be big. This one couldn't weigh more than ten pounds soaking wet."

Doc laughed. "I'll let you know."

A cute college age brunette with a bowl-cut hairdo and a lavender ski vest led a prancing Karnak to the counter. Karnak sat quietly at the end of her red sequined leash. The girl paid, collected a large pre-bagged order, and headed for the door.

With their well-choreographed moves, Doc bumped into Jay as the girl walked by. Jay dumped a cool latte all over the dog, making sure he soaked the six-inch plume of brown and white hair on its head and tail. "Oh, I'm so sorry."

He was again on the receiving end of "imbecile" and other such words. Whatever they meant, the tone should not have come from such a cute young girl's mouth. Then she set her bags down and cried.

That wasn't part of the plan.

Doc took over in French. In theory, she was offering to shampoo the dog at her nearby grooming studio. The offer didn't appear to be well received, but the crying stopped.

The conversation turned to Jay. After a lot of pointing, Doc spoke to him in English. "The girl's afraid I'll steal the dog. Put your wallet and passport on the table over by her. It's collateral. Feed her anything she wants until I get back." She looked at the girl, who was studying Jay with a friendly smile. Doc looked back at Jay. "Remember, you're old enough to be her father."

She turned to the girl and struck a deal. Doc walked out with Karnak.

THE FULL SERVICE SHAMPOO included a blow dry, comb out, and complimentary GPS chip injected near Karnak's shoulder. Just under the skin, her mane hid it. Like an RFID identifying microchip, the GPS chip was the size of an uncooked grain of rice. Its signal was leading Sarah and Jay along a busy country road an hour beyond the sprawl of Paris. Splitting the team had proved necessary, but Jay was thinking it should have been him on his own, not Doc.

Sarah turned the car's heater down. "Snap out of it. Her flight was at 1:45. She's probably over the channel by now. Remembering your dad's condo was brilliant. She'll be safer in Texas and may find something. Worst case, we'll know it's not there."

"Yeah. What if Duvert is driving this stupid dog all the way to Israel?"

"We have plenty of croissants in the back seat," she responded a little too quickly, and much too bubbly.

Before he could say anything that would get him in trouble, her phone rang and she answered it. Her face lost its exuberance the longer she listened.

"When *exactly* did it go out?" she asked sharply. "Okay. Did her flight leave on time? Find out. If she's still in France, hide her. I know, but they're wrong. Yes, about him too. He's with me." She ended the call and started dialing.

"Is it about Doc? Tell me." The Citroen strayed near the road's edge. Jay brought it back into the lane. "Is her plane okay?"

"Shush, the plane's fine. I need to call her." Sarah finished dialing. "Nuts. I have to leave a message." She hesitated, and then spoke into her phone. "Doc, if you're still local, do not board. Cover your head and go to the apartment. If you're in the U.S., don't use your name for *anything*." Sarah flipped the phone closed.

"I'm almost out of my skin. Talk to me."

"Doc has joined you on INTERPOL's Wanted Fugitives list. They circulated a Red Notice on her this morning. Your FBI found an unexploded bomb in her hospital locker. They think she and you were some kind of terror cell. I imagine they'll bring her plane down in England."

"What have I gotten her into?"

"Whatever happens, remember she volunteered." Sarah laid a hand on Jay's arm. "We'll clear both of your names. As much as I'd like to not like her, I can't. I want you two to grow old together."

"I didn't know it, but that's all I've wanted since the day I met her. She better be safe." Jay looked at Sarah. He could tell her things he'd never admit to himself. "I love you both, you know. It's different kinds of love." He rounded a sharp turn. "We should stay focused. The best way to help Doc and Jerusalem is to capture Isis."

"Agreed. Speed up, the chip's signal is fading."

"You said its range was five kilometers."

"It was when we started. It loses range and power quickly. It could be a hundred feet by tomorrow. You have to be right on top of a standard RFID, so quit complaining. Hey, it stopped moving."

Three kilometers later, Karnak's chip signaled from within a small walled city of more than a dozen stone buildings. The compound covered five or six acres in the middle of flat pastureland. Several brown workhorses were keeping it mowed.

Jay drove past. "What is that place, a medieval fortress? All it needs is a moat and a drawbridge."

"There's no cover within a kilometer of those walls. I should call in the troops."

"And do what? Duvert's untouchable. We've got less on Isis, and we don't know what she looks like. Without the scroll's end piece, we can't prove the Q is a fraud, or that she forged it. We don't even *know* if she did it. Sarah, we got squat unless Isis talks. I'll go in. She's been trying to kill me for weeks. My guess is she'll want to see me die up close and personal. Wire me. Maybe I can get her to admit what she's done."

"Or maybe she uses you for long-range target practice."

"She already tried that. I'll tell her I have a blank piece. That should keep me alive a while."

"Why would she believe you? You could just show it to the world. Why talk to her?"

"Revenge? She killed my father."

Sarah chewed on the possibilities. "You worked on the Ambassador Hotel pen. Do you have it with you?"

"No. It's of no value without a paired receiver. I gave it to Doc with Hassan's phone to take home for safekeeping. Look, all I know is I have to go in there. Surround the place with the French Foreign Legion. If I don't walk out on my own, you can arrest her for killing me."

"We need a better plan B than that."

THE VILLAGE PLUMBER HAD the only van in town with local markings. For three hundred dollars, the man had been happy to rent it while the Citroen was supposedly being repaired. Jean the plumber had explained that the fortress they had seen was Le Sanctuaire; a fifteenth century monastery that had served over the last hundred years as a convent, an orphanage, and now as a refuge for abused women.

Dust swirled behind the van as Jay approached the old monastery's walls along a gravel roadway. He slowed as he and Sarah drew near its ancient rock walls of weathered gray and black boulders. Sprigs of dead grass stuck out of cracks in the wall's mortar.

Sarah eased into the van's rear from the front passenger seat, while phoning in their location and plan to her team. "Pull up a satellite image of the monastery. A local gave us a mini tour of the place on the Internet. It's like a little town with sixteen buildings encircled by a stone wall. There's a large central building he called the quad. The building is open in the middle, so its four sides surround a cloistered grassy area the size of a square soccer field. You can't miss it."

A woman wearing a navy blue winter coat and matching knit cap walked outside the wall near its entrance. Jay angled down the bill of a baseball cap that Jean had left on the passenger seat. The woman glanced up, raised a white cross bar, and waved them inside.

"We're in," he told Sarah. "I'll find a place to drop you. It looks deserted."

Karnak's chip blipped ahead and right. Jay turned a corner and stopped.

"According to the plumber's information, we're on the backside of the old machine shop. I've got Karnak's signal. Are you picking it up, too?"

She replied, "Got it," and jumped out the back of the van. She closed the door and disappeared up an alley on the right.

The GPS blips convinced Jay that Karnak was in the quad. Jay drove deeper into the compound past well-maintained stone buildings; some the size of double garages, others like small sheds, but no people. The place combined the look of a Disney movie set with the unease of a horror flick. He parked near a dormitory closest to the quad. He waited, making sure no one was around, then got out. Emptiness festered in his gut. All three of the tiny team were on their own with no sure means of communication between them. Jay turned up his jacket collar to ward off the cold, and started walking.

"LET'S KEEP THIS BRIEF," Adamchek told her.

"That suits me better than you can imagine," Sarah whispered. She huddled inside the corner of a dank tool shed where she could watch the compound's entry through a frosted window. Maybe it was Adamchek's lack of progress, but he sounded less thrilled than ever that she had phoned. "I appreciate you keeping me informed," she said, trying to mollify him. "I know it's hard on you too. Did

Jacob's killer lead you to Glassman yet?"

"The short answer is no. As to Glassman, he's been spotted all over the Middle East. He never stays anywhere long. Last night, he was at The Mlaendri Resort in Byblos. It's this year's in-place for all the rich and famous slugs."

"Living it up, while Avi . . . doesn't. I can't stand it." She shook off her gloom and focused. "Glassman can't hide for long and still run his empire in Israel."

"That's what I thought, but I'm not so sure anymore. He's sold every one of his properties in Jerusalem and transferred his other Israeli assets to family. He receives protection from the terrorist groups that he supplied with arms."

"But we froze his assets. How could he sell or transfer—"

"It was done last month. As if he knew he'd be on the run."

Sarah breathed across her icy fingers. "He also might know land values in Jerusalem are about to plummet. I've informed my new employers, but those spooks don't always share intel. Listen, there may be a bombing planned for the Q document's sanctioning event tomorrow."

"I'd be surprised if there wasn't."

"I mean worst case scenario. Alert Levinson and tell him we need Glassman to talk."

"I'll pass it on and send your love, but we don't know where Glassman is. He moves around like the wind. If he's still in Lebanon, there's nothing we can do."

Sarah stomped her feet. "There's nothing *you* can do."

"Be careful. I know you. Even in your new role, you can't just show up and shoot him if he won't talk." He paused for a moment. "I've moved to where I can talk openly. Listen to me. Keep your head down. You've joined your friends on INTERPOL's fugitives list. If you cross any borders, you better be bald, chomping on a cigar, and using a new name. Your picture's everywhere."

Sarah hung up. Cigars were so gross. Wigs, on the other hand, were a thing of beauty. It was 2:48. With a little luck, the Mlaendri would have a new guest tonight, and tomorrow, she could be interviewing slugs on the beach.

FEMALE VOICES CHANTED UP a storm to the slow beat of a dull bass drum. Faint at first, the rhythms drew Jay to a stone chapel on his left. A row of evergreen cypress bushes obscured brilliant stained-glass windows near the chapel's rear. He squeezed between the fresh-scented shrubs and the ancient windows. He found a fist-sized clear piece and peered in. The thick glass distorted the image, but women stood swaying to the drum's monotonous beat. An individual up front, wearing red vestments and a tall pointed bishop's hat, led the chanting. It could have been Duvert. The leader moved like a man, but was too far away to tell. There wasn't anyone being worshipped like a goddess.

Jay slipped out from behind the unforgiving branches and followed Karnak's blip down an alley, hugging the shadows cast by a tool shed. At the building's end, the two-story quad rose from a dormant lawn. Karnak was stationary, and somewhere inside. The quad's exterior was weathered stone interrupted by small hatched windows on the second level. The ground floor had but one massive wood door and the only way to it was across seventy-five yards of lawn or along a crushed stone path. Jay took the path.

The huge door opened easily. Inside, a spotless slate floor reflected the light of dull lamps. He stood at the door letting his eyes adjust. When they had, he noticed a blinking red light opposite him near the ceiling. *A camera. Great.* He hoped the security staff was whooping it up at the chapel. He crossed to the wall with the camera and stood under it, listening for footfalls on the stone floor. The building remained silent. The electronics reminded him to turn on the pocket recorder from Jean the plumber. Karnak was on the building's far side. Jay headed left.

Everything was shiny slate floors and closed wood doors. At the hallway's end, it made a hard left to follow the quadrangle. He crept around the corner. Light seeped into the hall from an open door ahead. He moved to it and peeked inside a well-stocked library. Arched windows looked out to the central courtyard, but a thick hedge blocked his view. He followed the hall until he came to Karnak's blip behind a closed wooden door. Jay pocketed his receiver and listened.

All was quiet. With his right hand, he pulled a dog treat from his pocket. He squeezed the thumb-latch handle with his left hand. He cracked the door open an inch and put the treat at ground level. There were no nibbles. Unable to see much, he opened it all the way.

She was seated on the floor up against the wall opposite him. Her mouth was duct taped.

Doc?

He rushed in.

Her eyes tried to convey a message. Something hard hammered his lights out.

CHAPTER 31

CHICAGO SWAT ESTABLISHED AN exterior perimeter around the squalid Southside apartment building. Greene and an FBI SWAT team secured the hall and stairwells. The hallway looked and smelled like most Greene remembered from his days at the Chicago Field Office. It was how he knew Agent Peterson. She was dependable then, and she broke this case wide open eight short hours ago.

Greene pressed his back flat against the filthy wall with his Remington 870 pointing skyward. The door to Veccio's unit, the hit man Peterson fingered from security footage for killing the fake Sarah Baumann, was on his left. Six other agents stood between the door and Greene, with four more beyond it. Peterson was on his right. Greene's escalating pulse reminded him he hadn't done this in a while.

The finger countdown expired and the unit's doorframe splintered into matchsticks. A dozen agents flooded into the unit. The shouting started and ended before Greene made it inside.

Veccio lay sprawled on his stomach on the floor. His fingers were interlaced behind his neck, and his legs were spread eagle.

Two shotguns pointed at his head from three feet, while two agents frisked him.

"All clear," sounded from the other rooms in the small apartment.

Peterson holstered her weapon. "Your poor boss. First, an Evergreen deputy shows that the Arab Beauty's probable killer resembles the woman driver in the Baxter bombing, and then neither woman has an affiliation with the mosque. Now, you go and do this. He isn't going to like it."

"He isn't going to like it a lot more when his mosque theory goes completely up in smoke. At least everything he can depend on came from me, Farnsleigh, and you. Your phone tap told us plenty." Greene knelt next to Veccio. "We know an Israeli arms dealer hired you. I want you to start remembering how to find him. The sooner you remember, the less time I'll have to think up charges against you."

A SPECIAL OPS INSTRUCTOR had once said that when you regain consciousness in enemy hands, keep your eyes closed, listen, and evaluate your situation. When Jay came to, his eyes opened automatically, and he realized he'd missed a crucial how-to session. He made a mental note to ask Bob Ambrose about it, if he ever saw the man again. Like Doc, Jay was seated slumped against a wall. His wrists were hog-tied with a rope tied to a rusty metal ring screwed into the floor between his legs. Jay clamped his eyes shut in case no one noticed.

"Nice of you to join us." The voice sounded familiar.

He opened his eyes, and Faatina stared down at him, victorious. He tried to say her name, but his lips wouldn't move.

Doc was on his right, petting Karnak double-handed. The left side of her face was bruised. Her mouth, like his, was sealed with duct tape.

Jay struggled to kick or stand.

"We call this the no-no-bad-monk room."

Jay looked around and noticed additional floor rings along three walls. Faatina occupied a slat wood chair, the only piece of furniture in the windowless room.

"This is your lucky day. Soon you'll have an audience with Isis. She's making a special guest appearance." Faatina tossed Hassan's phone in the air and caught it. "Recognize this? Whether it's turned on or off, it sends a GPS signal and really sucks power. Thanks for keeping it charged." She grinned and pocketed it. "I'm going to leave now. Don't say anything bad about me." Faatina laughed and slammed the door behind her.

Jay couldn't look at Doc. Having been blind to the problem with Hassan's phone, he might as well have hand delivered her to Isis. He yanked on his restraints until his wrists had paid for his crime. The knots held firm, as did the bolt securing the metal ring to the plank floor. He stared at Doc who stared back. Muffled words failed, and they exchanged thoughts with their eyes. Jay tried to look hopeful. She looked tired and scared.

Before long, his back was killing him. He slumped onto his side toward Doc. She did the same, and they touched heads. Laying there felt too much like he'd given up. He jerked upright. Seeing Doc shift Karnak gave him an idea. He grunted at Doc to sit up. There was enough length to the ropes that tied them to their metal rings that he and Doc could nearly touch hands. The gap was shorter than a Karnak. Jay grunted SOS in short and long grunts, then pointed at Karnak. He said, "Sarah," as best as he could. Somehow Doc got the idea. They passed Karnak back and forth between them three times fast, three times slow, and three fast again. They thrust poor

Karnak as wide as possible. With luck, Sarah's GPS would register the pattern. Doc's eyes looked hopeful.

They stopped signaling after ten minutes when they heard two sets of footsteps in the hallway.

The door opened.

Faatina walked in with a hook on a six-foot pole. Before Jay could think of a single positive purpose for it, she outlined his thigh with its tip, then tugged at his ropes. Satisfied he was still tied, she checked Doc's. Faatina placed the pole on the floor in the far corner and left.

A woman in her sixties entered. Strictly a class act, she had neat black hair arranged in a smart do, tasteful gold earrings, and a pearl necklace around a graceful, but aging neck. Except for wary eyes and a revolver in her hand, she was beautiful. Why did she look so familiar?

The woman studied them. "We need two volunteers for tonight's sacrifice."

This must be Isis. Jay glared at her, showing as much antagonism as possible. Maybe she'd settle for one.

"No wonder you were so hard to kill. That will change soon enough. I hate to cut this short, but I have a problem in the organization to deal with." She raised the gun. "I have good news and bad news. The good news is you're not really tonight's sacrifice. I already have someone. He thinks he's the emcee. The bad news is one of us is going to die now."

She removed a bullet from the revolver and dropped it to the floor. It rolled along a plank to a far wall. She spun the cylinder. "How about once more for good measure? I need one of you alive." Isis laughed and spun it again. "If there is a God, don't you think that *she* will kill me and let the two of you live? Well, I think she will. Let's see."

She held the gun under her chin. She laughed, then aimed at Doc's forehead.

Jay yanked as hard as he could on his ropes. Pain lashed at his wrists. "No!" His yells went nowhere. "I have a piece." The tape ate at his lips. Guttural sounds were all he managed.

Doc struggled. She thrust her head side-to-side.

He couldn't stand to watch. He pleaded, "Please, use it on me." The words drowned in an ocean of tape.

Isis grabbed a fistful of Doc's hair. Still, Doc shimmied. She screamed wordless rants.

"What, no faith, my little darling?"

The lunatic pulled the trigger.

The gun clicked.

Doc's chest heaved.

Isis shrugged. She looked at Jay. A hint of a smile creased her eyes. "You're next."

A muted, but long and understandable, "No," roared from deep inside Doc.

Isis studied the gun for a second and fanned its revolving mechanism. She lifted it and aimed at Jay. "Are you ready to die? Do you think your God will save you?"

The barrel was aimed straight between his eyes.

He could fall one way or the other to make her miss. But then what? This game was no way to discover if there was a God. And no way to die. His brain yelled, Stop, until he realized this was what he had asked for just a moment ago. Had he prayed that a bullet be spent on him so Doc would live? Was it an answered prayer?

"I asked a simple enough question. Are you ready?"

"No," echoed in his bones. "I'm not ready."

The gun clicked.

Isis tilted the gun in her hand. She stared at it. "Humph. Some would call that a sign. I don't. I do need one of you. And I really don't want the other."

"Wait. Wait." Jay had to get her attention. "Listen to me."

"Do you have something to say, little man?"

What did she say? His mind whirled. Why had she used that expression?

"If I allow you to speak, do you promise not to bite me or something equally desperate?"

Jay nodded and sucked in his lips.

She tore his tape free and scooted back.

"I have the missing piece from the blank scroll."

She frowned for a split second, and then gave him a sideways glance. "That's it? That's what was so necessary to tell me?"

"My dad had it. Professor Hunt, who you killed, was my father."

"Oh, I knew your father. Biblically, to be honest. He called me Izzy. He had nothing, and neither do you. I'll let you in on a little secret, little man. Yes, I wrote the Q document. And I burned every piece that I damaged in the writing process or didn't want."

"All but one fairly large, triangular—"

"Liar," she screamed. She aimed the gun at Jay's chest. It trembled in her hands. Her eyes were as wide as the Grand Canyon. She muttered, "The end piece . . ."

"Correction, the blank, perfectly mated end piece that when laid next to your handiwork, will prove it's a forgery."

She staggered to the sidewall. "Give it to me," she said, reclaiming her composure. "And she lives."

Doc shook her head and body violently, blurting out a muffled, "Don't you dare."

Isis shot just above Doc's head. Both ducked. Wood splinters showered down on them. The crazy woman fired again, high into the wall.

The door burst open. Sarah tucked and rolled into the room. She leveled a gun at Isis.

"Drop your gun or they die." Isis pointed her gun at Jay's head. "He goes first."

Sarah's mouth hung open. "I . . . you . . ."

Jay yelled, "She's confessed. I got it. Shoot her."

"She can't shoot me," Isis strung out her words. "Can you, Princess?" Gloating, Isis added, "Listen to your mother. I will kill him."

Sarah's arm lost its tension; it collapsed to the floor, as did her countenance. "You left me." She shoved the gun across the uneven floorboards toward Isis.

"But you're dead," Jay shouted.

"No, only the little hussy who stole my David, and who you called mother is dead. She's my sister for eternity, Nephthys. She and Ishabel died so Isis would live. Mama's little man couldn't keep his promise to her, could he?"

Sporadic gunshots erupted outside the building.

Jay sat frozen to the floor. "Ishabel. Izzy? You're Z?"

The shooting outside grew fierce. It crept closer.

Faatina ran in. She stared uncomprehending at the gun lying near Isis's feet. She scooped it up and trained it on Sarah. "We should go," she told Isis.

"You abandoned me and Dad for a scrap of paper? I should have shot you."

Isis frowned and turned to Faatina. "Check him for a wire. Remove it and any piece of flesh it's attached to. He must be punished like my High Priest." She looked at Jay. "I came because of his thievery, and I find he consorted with my girls in 'special rituals' for his pleasure. *My* girls."

"Listen to the shooting. You're trapped." Sarah pleaded.

Faatina shifted the gun to her left hand and ordered Sarah to back up. She pulled a knife from her ankle scabbard and pressed the point under Jay's chin. "Too bad it's not around his neck." She flicked the blade down and cut open his shirt. She sliced the microphone and cord free from his chest. It scraped open a wide wound across his abs. He felt nothing for a second, then searing pain accompanied by rivulets of blood. Faatina laughed. "Is that a recorder in your pocket, or are you just glad to see me?"

Sarah cried out. "Mother, stop her."

"What has he done to you? I hated that you had a brother."

"What are you talking about? Do you have any idea what *you* did to me?"

Isis's eyes glazed over. "Incest isn't wrong, if you're a goddess, like me. All my girls here had a brother that . . . worshipped them." Her eyes regained their focus. She spoke to Faatina. "Leave Anubis functioning, if that is what Princess desires."

Jay assumed that meant him, though he had no idea what she was ranting about.

Faatina sliced Jay's pants pocket open, drawing blood from his thigh. She took the recorder.

"Bring Doctor Case. Leave the other two alive." Isis turned her attention to Jay. "The perfect Christian professor wasn't quite so perfect was he? His lying nature, sorry for the pun, must have passed to you. I believe you're bluffing about an extra piece. But if I hear even a hint that you're seeking out the press, what Faatina did to you will be nothing compared to what she'll do to this fair beauty. Don't let her down . . . too."

Isis looked at Sarah. "My dear, I'm afraid I must leave you. Again. I do hate it."

Faatina left Doc's hands bound, but untied her from the ring, leaving several extra feet of rope. In seconds, she wrapped the length around Doc's throat and drew it tight. "This is how my brother *worshipped* me." Isis left, and Faatina backed out of the room, pulling Doc behind her with Sarah's gun in her back. The door swung shut and something jiggled on the outside.

Sarah ran to Jay.

"Leave me tied," he said. "Help Doc. You have to save her."

"It's my fault she has her. I'm sorry." Sarah moved to the door and began shaking it.

"No. I should have figured out days ago I was being tracked through Hassan's phone."

Sarah scrambled back to Jay. "I can't open the door alone. Maybe both of us can break it down." She began untying his ropes. "The gunshots must be the French Police. They have a photo of Doc. They'll stop her. I can't imagine they won't stop two maniacs leading her by a rope." She loosened Jay's final knot.

He wrestled the ropes from his hands and stood. "The pole," he said, rushing to it and jamming the hooked end into the simple latch until it broke. The door sprung free, and Karnak scampered away. Jay bolted into the hall.

Sarah followed and yelled, "Go left. There's an open door two rooms down that leads out."

They ran into the room as a strong engine started outside. A door led them to an outdoor colonnade and the grass courtyard in the quad's center. They ran across it as a small Bell helicopter's rotor reached full speed. The back, then front ends of the skis, lifted into the air before they neared it.

Jay's heart threatened to explode, watching Isis fly away with Doc. For all the adrenaline surging through his body, he was helpless.

Three French police ran into the quadrangle's interior. "*Arret.*

Stop. *Alto.*"

Sarah whispered to Jay. "Remember, we're wanted."

"What do you mean, 'We're wanted'?"

SARAH LOOKED AROUND WILDLY. There was no chance she and Jay could both escape. One of them would be sitting in jail, which meant either she couldn't hunt Glassman, or Jay couldn't track the helicopter.

The cops were moving closer and spreading out.

If she could just get Glassman to talk . . . assuming she found him. So what if Glassman moved around like the wind? She looked at Jay. He was waiting on her. She had to choose; chase the wind or protect her brother. *I have a brother!*

She turned to Jay. "We can't let them take you. I'll distract the police, while you slip away. Take care of your wounds. I'll watch the Citroen, every hour on the twenty until you show. If you get to it first, leave without me. They'll be expanding the search radius for you, so keep moving. I'll call you when I can. Go."

Jay opened his mouth as though he wanted to argue, but then nodded and turned.

Sarah watched him walk away from the police and toward a large hedge on the courtyard's far side. Good choice, she thought, then turned and walked at an angle toward the gendarmes, which made her the easier target to overtake. They changed course to intercept her, which pulled their attention away from Jay. But he'd need another twenty to thirty seconds to reach the hedge without running. She babbled at the local constabulary in Hebrew to reinforce her identity. They closed in fast and forced her to the ground. She squirmed around, forcing them to handcuff her.

"Why are you arresting me?" she shouted in English, hoping

Jay could hear. "The man and woman fugitives you are chasing escaped in that helicopter. You can still track it."

"They won't get far," one of the Frenchmen replied. "And you, Sarah Baumann, will be returned to Israel. We are only too glad to be rid of a cop turned terrorist." He kicked her in the side.

To keep their focus, she spit on his pant leg.

It worked.

THE HEE-HAW OF A French meat-wagon echoed off the old stone chapel. The shrill sound wrenched Jay's attention back to the present; disrupting his replaying of the day's events, and what he should have done differently. He scrambled behind the gnarly cypress shrubs wedged against the chapel's colorful windows. An ambulance stopped and backed up to the chapel's entrance. Jay had gravitated to the chapel to quiz Duvert on where Isis might be taking Doc and what kind of device was being relocated. Everything pointed to tomorrow's sanctioning event in Jerusalem, but guesses and clues, not to mention time, were running low. Jay peered inside the chapel.

Duvert wouldn't be talking much. The party had gotten out of hand.

The man hung high over the chapel's altar where a crucifix should have been. His shirtless bloody body mimicked a grotesque cross with outstretched arms tied to the sanctuary's sides. The bishop's hat lay below his lifeless feet.

CHAPTER 32

LAST NIGHT'S PRIVATE FLIGHT to Jerusalem had been a shot in the dark, but then as now, Jay couldn't imagine Isis missing the sanctioning event. He fit right in with thousands of others in a sour mood, milling around the wrong side of Jerusalem's Jaffa Gate. It was quarter to nine in the morning, and even though the big event wasn't until 5:30, the entrance to the walled Old City was closed. An unprecedented action, the Old City was choked with people striving to attend the event of the millennia at the Church of the Holy Sepulcher.

A strong grip squeezed the shoulder he had injured in the Caymans. Jay wrenched the unknown hand free and twisted the tendril-like fingers under and backwards. It extended the attackers wrist just short of snapping, which drove the man to the pavement and pinned him there.

A weightier version of an old friend stared up.

Jay gasped and released the pressure faster than he had applied it. "Captain, I'm so sorry. I didn't know it was you."

Jay helped Captain Bob Ambrose to his feet. "Are you okay?"

Ambrose rotated his wrist. "I will be. Nice to see you again—I think." His features relaxed. "I see you still remember how to disable an enemy. I'm glad you weren't in lethal mode."

"My brain was a million miles away. I'm sorry. You surprised the heck out of me."

"That's mutual. You're a little jumpy."

"Yeah, I am." Jay's heart slowed to normal. "You shouldn't be seen with me."

"Now you've got me curious. It sounds like you need someone to watch your back. I'm available."

"You need to finish your business and leave. Unless you can get us inside the Old City. What brings you here?"

"It's a long story, but this town helped me clear my head a few years ago. After two tours in Iraq, my faith needed a boost. I drifted to Israel after I discharged and just being here . . . I felt God's presence. I needed it again. So here I am."

"Is it working?"

"To be honest, the jury's still out. I reminded God not five minutes ago that he said seek and ye shall find. I'm waiting on him to come through. I didn't expect to be brought to my knees quite so literally. So what about you?"

"Mine's a long story, too, but if your problem is Q-related, you'll like it." Time was short, but he could use a fresh perspective. Jay boiled the history down to its essentials. He added, "So basically, Isis is going to blow up a fraud. I can't prove it, and I don't know where to turn next." He looked around. "I need to save these people. And Doc and Sarah. I knew they couldn't depend on me."

"I hear a story behind the story. I'm in a different service now. I haven't earned my pay in a while, but they call me Pastor Bob."

"*Pastor* Bob? Whew."

"I'm a pretty good listener."

A woman in a blue dress with huge white buttons and a white belt squeezed past.

Jay collapsed onto a bench. The woman could have been his mother thirty years ago. "My dad went on a business trip and my mom told me I was the man of the house. She beamed at me with the prettiest eyes. Shafts of light from heaven. I told her I'd protect her. But I didn't, Bob. I didn't." Jay covered his head with his hands. It hung to his chest. "She died that afternoon in a car crash. I failed her. My brain knows that's just a kid's way of thinking, that it wasn't really my fault, but . . . my heart won't budge. I *hate* it when people depend on me. I see her lying on the hillside, a tarp covering her body, the smashed car at the bottom of the ravine. I want to smell her perfume. All I smell is burnt rubber."

Bob nodded. "A good man is in the hospital because of me. I didn't strike him, but I feel like I put him there. We took turns protecting my church against vandals. I was weak when I should have been strong. Let's make you strong."

Jay looked up. "Iron sharpening iron. I bet it was his church, too."

They punched knuckles.

Bob set his jaw. "I admired you for teaching kids how to live. You told them don't fight the desert because the desert always wins. To survive, you said respect the desert, and use what it gives you. What has Isis given us?"

"Us?" Jay looked up in surprise. "You like lost causes?"

"There has to be something."

"Our only leverage is the missing piece and guess what? It's missing."

"Then let's pray for an answer."

"I knew you'd say that. I can't remember the last time . . ." Jay hesitated.

"It was answered, wasn't it?"

A patrol car cruised by. "Hey, I just thought of somebody who can help."

"I think somebody just did."

DOC SAT UP IN the bed with no idea where she was. The room was austere and cool, but not like a fifteenth-century monastery. No, we left. A scattered memory of floating in the air, the distance from the ground growing . . . a helicopter. Jay running toward her in the courtyard. Faatina sticking a needle in her arm. Now here. When was that?

The contents of her purse had been dumped onto a small table near the bed. Everything except her phone was there, including the pen that she hoped to find. She inserted it in her sock, snug against her ankle and noticed dried blood on the tip of her right index finger. She used spit to remove the evidence, except for a speck under her nail. She bit it off, then checked her pants pockets. *Good.* They had been left alone. Light seeped in from around the edges of window. She crossed to it. The window was nailed shut from the inside and boarded up on the outside. Resisting the urge to shatter the glass, she tried the door. It was locked. She shook the knob, then pounded on the door. When she stopped, nothing happened. She beat on it again until the pain made her stop.

Thirty minutes passed before the lock rattled. The door opened and a heavyset woman in a blue pantsuit entered. She maintained her position by the door, appearing ready to bolt on a moment's notice. "Sit on the bed," she said. The white woman's English carried a thick South African accent. "Cooperate, and I'll bring your breakfast."

"Are you from near Durban?"

The woman's face lit. "I can't speak to you."

"I could use a friend, a smiling face. That's all," Doc said.

"Sit on the bed."

Doc complied.

The woman rolled a cart into the room with a tray holding a small carton of milk and a dark biscuit. She set the tray on the floor near the door. After a tight-lipped smile, she backed out of the room with the cart and locked the door.

Doc called after her. "I could use water, please." She ate the dry biscuit and sniffed the milk. Her throat was parched, but she opted to wait on the water. It would be easier to smell test for drugs.

A few minutes later, the door cracked opened.

Doc sat on the bed.

"Don't you like milk? It's organic." Isis set a clear plastic pitcher of water and an empty plastic cup on the tray still lying by the door. She placed two pills by the cup and carried the tray to the nightstand. She poured Doc a drink. "Those are aspirin in case you have a headache. Taste them. I have no desire to drug you again."

Doc left the pills and water on the tray. "Why are you doing this?"

"What do you think I'm going to do?"

"Kill people. Kill Christianity. Blow up a city."

"Oh, I'm doing much more than that. I'm fulfilling your Christ's prophecy. He should thank me. Frankly, he made a mess of things." Isis gazed at her. "You think I'm anti-Christian, but I'm not even anti-God. I am, however, anti-religion."

"The Q document won't end religion. There are still Jews and Muslims. Former Christians will join one of those religions or start a new one."

"That's why there's a bomb. I'm fulfilling the prophecy of Armageddon. First, I'll rid the world of hypocrites. You call them

Christians. They spout pleasantries like love thy neighbor while they sip their lattes and watch three-fourths of the world starve. Muslims confuse love with weakness, and those that know the difference, elect their radical leaders with votes of silence and fear. They will never allow women like us into their exclusive club. Jews can't decide if they should be warmongers or sheep led to the slaughter. They're stuck in time three thousand years ago. Why should anyone be forced to live in a world like that?"

Doc scratched her thigh, then her calf. "What's the alternative?" She reached down to the Ambassador Hotel pen in her sock, which Jay had re-jiggered to turn on and off by pressing the top. She coughed and simultaneously clicked it on. Her sense of success was fleeting as Isis narrowed her eyes. Doc cleared her throat, coughed again, and for good measure sniffed at the water glass. She drank from it.

Isis smiled. "The alternative is quite simple. A few diehard Christian extremists will blow up Jerusalem's Old City, and with it, most of the city. You and your friend Jay will share that blame. The Muslims will be outraged at the destruction of Haram esh-Sharif, as will the Jews over the loss of the Temple Mount and their Wailing Wall. Needless to say, Muslim reaction will be swift. Your wonderful U.S.A., the formerly Christian and psychologically impotent superpower, will be pouting in isolation. Its oh-so-slow reaction will neutralize its military advantage. I call it Definitely Assured Destruction. Forgive the unfortunate initials in English. Without America to counter Islamic extremists, Arab states will become Islamic states. Israel will soon be a bad memory, and a faithless America will have no friends and a battle royal on its hands. China will receive all the cheap oil they can stand, and America will be forced to use their long-range nuclear weapons. Armageddon. Christianity and Islam will duel to the death and join

Judaism in the trash heap of history."

Doc forced her eyes to focus. "Let me guess. As architect of the new world order, you'll agree to be the world's new supreme leader."

"Please. Save the hysterics. Survivors will recognize religion as the cause of the calamity and outlaw it. My girls and I will survive, free from the dictates of this unpleasant male-dominated religious world."

"So where's the bomb?"

Isis wagged a finger at Doc. "I won't tell you everything. I've seen that movie."

The woman's blurry finger should have stopped moving, but it continued and left a trail in midair.

Isis nodded and her speech slowed. "I'll tell you where it was. Rachel, one of my girls, planted it near the scrolls at The Shrine of the Book. She had no idea it would have done more than destroy that complex. Rachel's not very bright. Have you seen her? Her father tried to make her look like a boy, and I'm afraid he succeeded. She never really fit in among my girls, yet I accepted her. Despite my love, she disobeyed and failed me at every turn. She could no longer be trusted, so I had the device moved."

The glass slipped from Doc's hand. Water spilled on her pants. She wondered why she didn't care and leaned over to sleep.

NORMALLY, BREAKING AND ENTERING a cop's apartment would not have struck Jay as a terrific idea. Ambrose, ever the older and wiser instructor, wanted nothing to do with it, so he had charged off looking for Sarah. That left Jay feeling like a cat burglar prowling a dim hallway on the second level of Rachel's two-story apartment building. He stopped at unit 24's brass marker and stared at the Mezuzah nailed to the doorframe's left upright. Every door in the hall displayed a similar Jewish mitzvah. It gave him pause as though trespassing beyond it magnified his crime, but zero activity in the hall, and the odds it wouldn't stay that way, reinforced his now-or-never attitude. Rachel was involved in this in too many ways not to know something useful. With any luck, some tidbit of information was lying around that would lead him to Doc and Isis. He twisted the doorknob. To his surprise, it turned.

He crept inside, wishing he knew what he was looking for. The living area and kitchen held nothing unusual. He walked down a short hall.

Muffled sobs froze him mid-step. He resumed, inching along.

At the end of the hall, he peeked into a bedroom. Rachel lay curled in a ball on the bed, crying onto the chest of a dead man whose bearded neck had been slashed. A black hood with a painted white cross had been pulled up to his forehead, revealing an ashen face.

She looked up. "You."

A holstered gun lay on a dresser to Jay's right. He moved between it and Rachel, opposite an open closet. Dozens of black hoods littered its floor.

Rachel said, "Shoot me. I don't care." Her masculine voice as deep as ever.

"Was he the Black Sheikh? I don't understand."

"If you're not going to shoot me, leave."

"I don't want to shoot you. Who killed—"

"She did. Isis hates me. She thinks I look like a man." Rachel looked toward an alarm clock on her night table. "We're all going to die soon. I thought it was a small bomb, just enough to blow up the Israel museum's wing with the scrolls. She said it was to make her fragments in Paris more valuable." She turned and spoke to the dead man on her bed. "We'll be together again soon."

"Isis is holding a friend of mine hostage. It's to stop me from revealing a blank piece that will prove the Q document is a fake. I'm afraid she'll kill my friend no matter what I do. Do you know where Isis is, or where she might hold a hostage?"

"A blank piece? All her work . . ." Rachel looked back at the man on the bed. "She told me to kill Ammar with you at the Hilton. We grabbed a man from the hallway. I shouldn't have done that." Rachel stroked Ammar's lifeless leg. She looked back. "Isis doesn't have to worry about your proof. An hour after she leaves the ceremony, it'll all be gone. The Q document, us, everything. I heard her talking. You should leave the city. The pen I gave you is transmitting again. Isis has a nuclear bomb."

"The pen! Doc—my friend—has it. What's its range? Can we track it?"

"No, Isis found the pen and smashed it. She could be anywhere in the city. Originally, she wasn't planning to attend the sanctioning. I don't know why she's here."

"Duvert's dead. I imagine she's filling in for him. It's one reason I came." Jay paused in thought. "A last-minute change of plans causes problems. There must be some way to use that to our advantage."

Rachel lifted the dead man's head and pulled the hood free. She lowered his pale head gently back onto the bloody pillow. She walked to the far side of the bed and placed the hood in an open metal box on the floor. A red lining made the box look familiar. She closed its lid.

"Wings." Jay moved closer to inspect it. Two seraphim with outstretched wings were mounted on the lid. "That box. It's what Doc saw at Duvert's. She described it to me, and it sounded familiar, but I couldn't place it. My mother had one. How did you get this?"

She turned. "All of us have one."

"All of us? Who's us? It's the mercy seat from the Ark of the Covenant."

"Hardly. It's a watertight ossuary for bones. It's Isis and Nephthys protecting the dead. It's—"

"That's what Doc called it. That's why it didn't register. My dad must have left it when he moved back to the States. No . . . he couldn't have just left it. I know where the blank piece is." Jay bolted for the door, then stopped and faced Rachel. "If I find the piece and prove the Q is a fake, Doc and Jerusalem will be destroyed. If I save Doc, Christianity is doomed. I'm not sure the world can survive either result." The agony of his decision rose within him, knowing what choice he had to make. Just when he was learning to trust his heart, he had to break it. At the moment, finding Dad's blank piece was the only realistic option. *At the moment.*

"Rachel, we may not know where Isis is now, but we know where she'll be at 5:30."

"She'll never cooperate."

"Don't be so sure. She's given herself an hour to leave Jerusalem. That gives me sixty minutes to make her sweat and get some answers."

"That's possible, but only if the bomb's on a preset timer. And wherever it is, your friend is near it. Isis screamed that into the pen as she smashed it. She'll use her for leverage."

"So I'll have to find an edge, but first I need the piece." Slim as the odds were, going after the blank fragment wasn't abandoning Doc after all; it was the first step in saving her. "The police are looking for me, and they're all over the Old City. How can I get into the sanctioning event?"

Rachel shook her head. "You can't, and it's not just the police you'll have to worry about. I might be able to arrange it, but are you sure you want my help? Do you know what all I've done?" Her eyes pleaded, her whole face begged.

What did she need from him? Her lack of success investigating Dad's . . . the pieces tumbled into place. She never found the van and *woman* driver for a reason. Jay sagged against the dresser unable to breathe, think, or feel. Anger, even relief at finding Dad's killer, would have been better than numb. "Dad was alive when you left him. He suffered."

"Not as much as he would have." Her voice was barely a whisper. "Isis wanted him taken alive. She had really nasty plans for him."

Doc was right. Dad was protected in a way I couldn't conceive. Jay picked up Rachel's gun and turned toward her.

"Go ahead," she said, her lifeless eyes no longer seeking forgiveness, but inviting death. "I understand hate and revenge."

"So do I," he admitted. "But we can change. What a person is willing to do is more important than what they've done." Jay handed her the gun.

Rachel hesitated, and then accepted it. "I don't know if I can change, but I can help stop Isis and maybe save your friend."

JAY LEFT RACHEL'S APARTMENT with far more success than he ever could have dared to hope. She had already been a huge help, but there was still a lot to do to make their plan work. The traffic light gave Jay an opportunity to return a call to Danny.

"I've been trying to get you for an hour," Danny bellowed into the phone. "I have a fix on that VW van as we speak. It parked at the Risen Gardens in Jerusalem, and it just left."

"How did she find it?" Jay looked up and down the busy

divided road, but didn't see any vans. "Don't mind my ramblings. I'm on my way there, two minutes out. I have to stop that van. Direct me to it." Jay read Danny his coordinates off the GPS. "I'll be easy to spot. I'm driving a small red pickup pulling a backhoe. Are you watching on satellite?"

"It's how I found the van. No way I could get a drone there fast enough. Plus I needed clearance. Some countries I could risk, but not Israel."

"What about the Israelis? See if they'll put one in position."

"They're on some kind of high alert."

"Good, I think. They must be listening to Sarah. Do you have me yet?"

"Affirmative. Turn right in about 750 feet. Then right again. By the time you get to that intersection the target will be just a tad in front. Better speed up."

Jay weaved around two cars. Sway from the trailer and backhoe was bad. He made the turns as instructed. "I don't see it. This isn't easy dragging a backhoe."

"They're lugging one, too. Is there some kind of special on backhoes today? I got a little work to do in my garden."

"Could be. I got mine out of a police impound lot."

"Sorry I asked. Okay, the one you're chasing is immediately in front of a bus. Five hundred feet ahead."

The bus stopped. "I see the van. I'm putting you on speaker. I suspect I'm going to need both hands on the wheel."

The VW van was stuck at a light. When the light changed, it turned left onto a two lane road, then stopped first in line at another light. Jay passed it and corralled it with his own truck and trailer. Jay was half out of his seat when the van backed up. It smashed its trailer into a parked car and battered another. An oncoming car jammed on its brakes, causing a second car to smash into it. The van peeled out and around Jay.

He jumped back into his pickup and floored it. His tires spun. He released pressure on the gas pedal, and gained traction.

The van was several cars and a hundred feet ahead. At the next street, it bounded over a crowned boulevard, down an incline, and jumped a curb turning right onto another four lane boulevard. The van's backhoe slid part way off the trailer. Sparks flew from its bucket dragging on the concrete. The tie straps released and the backhoe skidded and somersaulted onto its side. A delivery truck plowed into it, setting off a chain reaction involving three cars. The van kept going with the empty trailer bouncing and wagging.

Jay made the turn and avoided the car wrecks by vaulting over a curbed grassy median. Somehow his truck and rickety trailer stayed upright, but he was driving against traffic. Cars coming at him squeezed right, blowing their horns. He swerved back to the right side of the road at the next intersection, cutting off a number of vehicles. He was half a dozen cars behind the van and empty trailer.

The van lurched left and jumped the divider. Olive trees lined the median. The van caromed between two trees, scraping both sides. It tried making a u-turn, but turned too hard too soon, snagging a tree at the hitch connecting the van and trailer. Immobilized, the van stuck out into oncoming traffic. A semi-truck slammed on its brakes and air horn. The semi's jackknifing rig swung wide and looked like a building skidding down the street. Smoking tires smelled like his mom's accident scene. It smashed into the helpless van.

Jay stopped, as did a number of others. He ran toward the van. The truck driver tried opening one front door, then the other, without success. Jay pried open a rear cargo door enough to look inside. The van's front was crumpled, trapping two women in their seats. The passenger side was hammered inward three feet and

364 | ALAN SCHLEIMER

pinned the woman sitting there against the driver. Her head was a mass of blood. The driver's long hair was filled with glass.

"Hey, can you hear me?" Jay asked.

Neither moved or spoke. Police sirens blared.

The van was empty. No box, no papyrus. Whatever the two women were up to, they didn't leave the cemetery with anything. Two police cars screeched to a halt. Jay retreated from the van and picked up its license plate, which had torn free on the tree.

CHAPTER 33

JAY'S HANDS TREMBLED AS he drove into the Risen Gardens Cemetery, past sand-blasted mausoleums and rows of faded headstones. Scraggly trees, small yuccas, and meager patches of grass competed with barren ground amidst an unkempt collection of graves. He parked where Danny told him the van had been, and ended the call. He knew the area. Too well. Mom, and now Dad's graves were fifty feet away. If not for Danny directing him, Jay doubted he could have forced himself this close.

He sat quiet, glued to the driver's seat with closed eyes. Tears seeped under his clenched eyelids. Memories flashed through his mind. In the darkness, Mom lay under the tarp just above the burned out car at the bottom of the rocky slope. The wind blew the tarp off of her blood-soaked blue dress. Her neck and head were twisted at a horrible angle. A policeman moved him away from the road's edge.

When Jay's eyes opened, his hands were squeezing the life out of the steering wheel. If Isis had her way, how many kids would see their parent's bodies burnt and twisted from an incomprehensible explosion? How many kids would die?

The answer would be none, if he could end his pity party; so he shoved the door open and hustled to the trailer's rear. He dropped its gate, which formed a ramp, and drove the backhoe to ground level and then along a stony path to his parents' graves. In position and ready to dig, the dirt-crusted knob that would engage the backhoe's shovel waited, vibrating in his hand.

"Mom, I'm sorry. I'll try not to disturb you. I know that's crazy, but it's from my heart, and I've been learning to pay attention to it lately. You'd like the girl who's teaching me that. Dad's next to you. It's freshly dug. He stole something, and said you took it to your grave. I need it to finish what he started—the world has to know the truth. I've discovered some truth myself lately. I know that I didn't kill you and neither did God. Isis, who you knew as Ishabel, did. I have to stop her before she kills more people."

Part of him wanted to add, "Amen." He settled for, "Here we go."

The first few scoops barely dented the hard earth. Eventually, the digging became easier. At 3:08, after digging for an hour and a half and managing to carve out a three-foot-deep trench, he began dragging the blade. The sun glinted off metal, doubling his heart rate. He jumped in with a hand shovel. The gold wings showed first. He dug around the box and pulled dirt away with his hands until he could lift it out. The wings had not held up well, but the box had. He took it to the truck, and retrieved his daypack from the front seat. He pulled out rags to wipe dirt from around the seal before opening it. The GPS locator, which he and Sarah used to find Karnak, tumbled out with the rags.

The signal was going nuts. It said he was twenty feet from the little dog.

Did those women come out here to bury Karnak? When a more obvious answer dawned, his heart sank. They buried someone with the dog, and it wasn't its master. Doc had been petting the dog.

Tears welled up, blurring his vision.

"No," he shouted, remembering Karnak running off at the monastery. Doc must have removed Karnak's chip. If she thought to do that, then . . . "Doc, I'm coming. Please be alive."

The signal was strongest at Dad's grave. Jay retrieved the truck's tire iron and gingerly stuck it into the recently turned earth near the grave's edge. Nothing stopped it. He tried again a few inches away. About a foot deep, it hit something hard. Further poking along the edge and the center also stopped a foot deep. Convinced it was safe to dig with the backhoe, he mounted it and scraped back the earth.

"I'm coming, Doc. I won't let you down."

The backhoe's large bucket made quick work of the new mound and uncovered a three-by-six-foot wood crate. Jay knelt beside the grave and tried pushing the pointed end of the tire iron under the lid. It was too tight. He jammed it in a quarter inch and hammered the bent end with his palm. Ignoring the bruising pain, he hammered the point in deeper and pried the lid open a crack. Moving along the lid a few inches at a time, he forced the lid open enough to shove his fingertips inside. He pulled up until he could peek inside.

Doc lay there.

"It's me, Doc. I'm here."

No number of nails could have resisted his yanking. She lay on her side, scrunched into the upper two-thirds of the mock casket with her legs bent at the knees and her feet wedged against an armored suitcase. Jay leaned in and placed his cheek near her mouth. Feeling no breath, he pulled on her chin to open her mouth and leaned closer. *Come on.* A faint kiss of warm air brushed his cheek. Unsure if it was his imagination, Jay watched her chest rise to take a breath. "Yes! You're breathing. Thank you, thank you, thank you." He collapsed onto her; hugging, then shaking her shoulders.

He scrambled back to his daypack and rifled through it. Grabbing the first cell phone he touched, he called 9-1-1, knowing that in most countries it would be automatically redirected to the local emergency number. The male operator promised an ambulance. Jay turned his attention back to Doc. She refused to respond to her name or taps on her cheek. Her color looked okay, and she was still breathing, but he couldn't stop worrying that she passed out from lack of oxygen or from fright. He shook off the negative thoughts and caught sight of the heavy-duty suitcase at her feet. Its contents were suddenly obvious and sobering. He pounced back onto his phone, this time dialing Israel's 012.

A no-nonsense woman operator asked the nature of his emergency.

As calmly as possible, he said, "This is not a prank. There is an armed nuclear bomb in the Risen Gardens Cemetery."

"It's illegal to—"

"You can be a hero, or you could be blamed for contributing to a huge tragedy. The bomb will detonate soon. Get someone here now."

"Sir, I'll need your name and how to contact you. Your caller ID is blocked."

"My name is Jay Hunt." In case she doubted his story, he added, "I'm wanted by INTERPOL and your national police. I'm in section 131 at the Risen Gardens Cemetery." Even if she only sent the police to arrest him, he figured he accomplished his mission. As a backup, he phoned Ambrose—Pastor Bob—and gave him the bomb's location. Ambrose ended the call when his call waiting ID showed that Sarah's Israeli Police headquarters was calling.

The call ended as a boxy ambulance sprinted through the cemetery's arched gate and headed for Jay standing on the backhoe's seat waving. It pulled to a crunching stop on the gravel road. Two paramedics bolted out of the ambulance with military precision. Jay directed them to Doc. They exchanged odd glances when they realized their patient occupied a grave, but that was nothing compared to their blood-drained faces when Jay advised against jiggling the suitcase with a nuclear bomb. The paramedics assured Jay that Doc's vitals were good and predicted she would wake on her own after whatever drugs had been administered wore off.

Jay kissed two of his fingertips and touched them to Doc's lips. "I can't stay with you. Forgive me when you wake up alone. I'm willing to make sure that never happens again."

JAY THOUGHT IT WAS fair that this time, he was late and Ibrahim had been waiting. Last week, when Jay had waited to collect Dad's suitcase from him, the bus driver had wound up on his knees with the IDF ready to blow his head off. Hopefully, today would go better. Ambrose had already helped in that department. He'd involved somebody in Sarah's chain-of-command that knew of the found nuke, and they provided Jay with a get-out-of-jail-free card.

"One last bolt, and we're good to go." Jay finished attaching the license plate from the wrecked VW van onto Ibrahim brother's lookalike van. They piled in with Ibrahim at the wheel, and sped toward the Old City.

"I told my wife to take her family far from the city."

"Good. Better safe than sorry. But don't worry. The bomb unit arrived as I was leaving the cemetery, and they were the A-team. They suspected the nuke was an updated version of Russian suitcase technology that the Chinese have been fooling with. If they can't disarm it, some brave soul will fly it deep into the desert. They thought thirty miles would be far enough, so they have time to think it through. Of course, none of that matters if it's booby-trapped."

"Do you think it's booby-trapped?"

"They wouldn't hazard a guess without toying with it so neither will I, but if it is, our distance will be just enough to know it's coming before we're vaporized." Jay smirked. "The only thing I asked was that they take Doc to a hospital outside the destructive zone." Jay hoped she'd recover on her own like the EMTs had suggested. "All I know is we've got our own job to worry about. So, brother Ibrahim, get us to the church on time."

"What is this you say? Why are you laughing?"

"It's an American expression. Put the pedal to the metal."

Ibrahim knew that expression. Before long, they approached an IDF checkpoint rerouting traffic away from the Old City. They were pre-cleared and passed through it. On most days, the church was a ten-minute walk from the Jaffa Gate. Today was not most days. They approached a reserved area just outside the Lion's Gate, one of two direct entrances into the Old City's Muslim Quarter. One of Isis's security detail, a stern woman in a blue uniform, compared the van and its license plate to a checklist before allowing them to park.

Uncle Omar greeted them inside the gate. "These men will escort you to the church." He turned and pointed to a half-dozen men that looked like they escaped from a bodybuilders convention. Jay motioned for Uncle Omar to follow him a few steps away.

"Before you help, you should know that the bomb has been found. The Dome of the Rock and El-Aqsa mosque are probably safe. If we prove the Q document is a fraud, you may not be too popular."

The grizzled man stared, unfazed. "I am not helping to protect buildings. They are holy, but of no consequence compared to men and honor. You showed me what kind of man you are," he pounded

his chest, "when you gave Ibrahim's wife that money. The amount
is one thing, ten thousand American dollars, but you risked your life
to deliver it. Now that you wish to restore the truth, how can I not
help? Truth leads to paradise."

Uncle Omar returned to Ibrahim and asked one of the
musclemen named Baasim to join them. The man carried
professional video equipment, which Rachel had suggested for their
cover. Ibrahim received a quick demonstration of its use plus twice
as many warnings not to break it.

Jay tapped his watch. "It's 4:10. We have an hour and twenty
minutes until the big event, but no one gets in or out of the church
after five. I'd like some margin."

The escort formed a human wedge, which moved through the
impossibly crowded and narrow Via Dolorosa. TV monitors were
set up along the ancient street at frequent intervals. As they neared
the Church of the Holy Sepulcher, its two blue domes danced in
and out of view over nearby buildings. Still over a block away, the
wedge halted behind a solid wall of humanity.

Jay looked around. "Even your Neanderthal cousins can't get us
through this crowd."

"That's not why they're with us." Ibrahim moved up to the front
man and pointed left to a doorway about five people deep in the
crowd.

The wedge excused and pushed their way to the door. They
entered the building and took steps down to a small room with solid
stone walls. Two hefty chains hung on both sidewalls. The wedge
split into two groups and pulled the chains. Muscles bulged. After
numerous grunts, a grinding noise filled the dusty room. The rear
wall rose like a curtain on a stage.

Ibrahim ducked under the elevated wall and into a dark narrow
passageway. He set down his video gear and lit a torch in a wall

bracket. "This is where they leave us. Follow me. Hurry."

Jay scooted under the wall, and the stone barrier slammed down. "Okay, I'm impressed. How does an Arab guy know about a secret tunnel in the Christian Quarter?"

"The city wasn't always in quarters. This is an ancient access to an underground cistern. The Old City has several of these. Few people outside my family know of this one."

The sickly sweet smell of kerosene filled the small enclosure. Jay removed the torch from its holder and looked down the one-way tunnel. The direction wasn't hard to guess, so he took the lead, carrying the torch while Ibrahim babied the video gear. There was barely room for elbows, so they walked single file. "Does this end inside the church?"

"No, but we'll be close."

They walked downhill on an uneven and rutted floor. Every ten feet, Jay swiped at thin cobwebs with the torch, the flame warming his face with each pass in the cool, bone-dry air. "I hope there's not another set of chains at the other end."

"Me too, my hands are full."

"Very funny."

About the time it felt like they should have covered the distance to the church, the corridor appeared to end. Jay slowed. The light flickered off irregular hand-carved walls. The end was a T-intersection. "Now what?"

"Uncle Omar said to go left."

Jay looked right. There was nothing but a downward slope that disappeared into an earth-bound black hole. He turned left into an equally dark passage that rose at a slight but steady incline. Thirty paces later, a draft sucked at the torch's flame. The wavering light picked up shadowed holes in the passage's dead-end twenty feet away. They reached it and Jay secured the burning torch in a metal cradle. "There are toeholds cut in the rock. It looks like we go up."

"Uncle Omar says there's a cover overhead. Push it up and slide it over."

Jay tried. "It won't budge."

"He said it might be heavy."

Jay climbed a step higher and tried again, using his legs and too much of his back. Nothing. "Are you sure we should have turned left? What was in the other direction?"

"The cistern."

Jay readied for another assault on the gritty stone cover separating them from daylight.

"Um," Ibrahim's voice was apologetic, "did I mention you must push a release button?"

"Did I mention you're paying for my chiropractor?" Jay found a small rectangular recess a couple inches deep and probed it with his fingertips. There was no lever to pull, so he pushed at its rear. It moved inward. Another attempt on the overhead cover increased the airflow sweeping past his sweaty forehead. A final all-or-nothing shove produced a circular opening. They clambered out into a ten-by-ten room filled with rakes, brooms, and dust. After replacing the ancient manhole cover, they exited into the harsh sunlight of a small courtyard that encircled the stone shed they'd been in and an ancient building it was tacked onto. It was nearly five o'clock and they rushed out a gate onto St. Helena alley. The church was in sight and close, but half of humanity separated them from it. They squeezed through.

Two Israeli National Police stopped them at the arched gateway into the Church of the Holy Sepulcher. One cop checked their credentials. "You're not on the list."

"Check it again," Jay ordered, hoping Rachel's revised list had made it to these guys. She had lost sway with Isis, but she still held weight with the cops downtown. "We were added this afternoon. There was an error in the original."

The two sentries argued about whether there was another list. The wind blew the top sheets of their clipboard back, revealing the updated list. The sentry holding it spoke up. "Huh, I thought this was just a copy, but they're on this one."

That was permission enough and Jay escorted Ibrahim past them into the church's large private courtyard. Devoid of a single soul, its emptiness eerily contrasted with the surrounding jam-packed streets. Television monitors were set up here as well, and they currently were showing the myriad of rooms, altars, and chapels within the venerable place of worship. Having toured the church as a teen, Jay wondered which area Isis had chosen for her grand event. None of the areas were very big. Even the great Rotunda lacked sufficient floor space for today's spectacle, since Jesus' briefly-occupied tomb dominated its center.

They hustled to the church's main entrance and entered through a wide iron-strapped door. Partially propped open, it ushered them into a collage of smells distilled from centuries of incense, candle wax, and tears. The Rotunda was to the left, and with no true anteroom, they stood in The Stone of Anointing, a smallish area named after the polished limestone slab lying at its center. The three-by twenty-foot flame red stone occupied the spot where tradition held Jesus was anointed after his crucifixion. The room was more vertical than horizontal, but there was no doubt it was ground zero for the Q document's unveiling.

TV camera crews lit the confined space like a sound stage. A mural of Christ's anointing on the wall behind the stone glowed from the intense lights, especially Jesus' gold halo. Overhead, hundreds of crimson and blue banners hung from the multi-leveled arched ceiling several stories up. Cameras pointed at an eight-foot-long table behind the stone. A solid burled wood front hid its legs. Two similar tables about six feet long each flanked it, forming a u-shaped perimeter around the anointing stone. Heavy purple drapes covered the top halves of the tables. Lamps that Jay recalled hanging over the stone had been removed.

"Ibrahim, we need to look under those drapes. I have to know which table has the fragment that matches my blank piece. When my moment comes, I may have to move fast."

Jay explained his idea to Ibrahim, who frowned at his role. Jay continued, "If you have a better idea, I'm listening."

Ibrahim stared at the floor.

THE GUARD TAPPED A key on the cell door's small wire-reinforced glass window.

Sarah looked up from her bunk in solitary, hoping all her information had gotten into the right hands. She had been moved overnight from France to a jail on Jerusalem's outskirts, and wondered if this would be her chance to escape. If the city was about to disappear in a flash and a mushroom cloud, she preferred not to be sitting on her butt when it happened.

The guard opened the door. "You have a visitor." The guard walked Sarah to the end of the corridor. The security door buzzed, and Sarah was led through it and into a meeting room.

Chief Inspector Ira Levinson looked up with his ridiculous grin. He sat behind a metal table and slid a pile of clothes toward her. It included what she had worn in France plus a blue pantsuit. "Don't bother sitting," he said. "We have a ride waiting for us. You're invited to the big show at the Holy Sepulcher, and you'll want to be wearing this blue suit. I'll explain on the way there."

Sarah reached for the pile. "What about the bomb and the

American woman, Dr. Case?"

"Both have been found. Let's go."

The weight of the temple lifted off her shoulders. Changing clothes took less than no time, although the pants were too short. On the way past the final guard station, a guard asked them to sign out. He handed Sarah a clipboard and a pen. She glanced at it and turned to Levinson. "The date and time on my form are blank."

"Just sign it. They'll fill that in once a judge approves your release."

She smiled and followed her ex-boss out of the building and into the sunshine. They hurried to the perimeter fence and were buzzed through a double gate. When their *ride* fifty meters away became obvious, Sarah's feet dug into the concrete.

JAY STOOD WITH HIS back against Jesus' mural behind the short table nearest the Rotunda.

Ibrahim strutted into position behind the long center table and clapped his hands. "Attention everyone. Attention. Take your assigned places. You and you—" He pointed to two men standing idle. "Get behind the two shorter tables. It's 5:10 and time for our scheduled run through. We're going to lift these drapes and give our cameramen an opportunity to focus and frame what they've come for. On the count of three. Everyone ready?"

People scrambled into position.

"One . . . two . . . three." Ibrahim and the two men pressed into service lifted the coverings. Protective glass sandwiched the ancient papyrus on top of the tables.

The Q document on the short table nearest Jay was virtually intact. He hurried to the other side table. Intense glare from the glass almost blinded him. *Come on.* He moved around to the table's front.

There it was. Unmistakable. *Gotcha.* He nodded to Ibrahim before slinking into the shadows of a hall to the far right.

"What's going on here?" A large woman in a blue suit yelled from the direction of the Rotunda. She rumbled into the room and addressed the man closest. "What are you doing?"

"It was time. That man . . ." He looked toward the large table, but Ibrahim had already replaced his drape and was moving back under the lights to his camera equipment. "Someone told us to do it."

The woman supervised recovering the tables, and walked over to another woman in blue, who had followed her into the room.

Jay wandered back to Ibrahim. "Well done. You should be directing news programs or movies."

"Maybe I will. I need a job. I decided life was short, and I moved to Bethlehem to live with my wife."

"In twelve minutes, you're going to own valuable news footage. There are only five news crews here. Your video could be worth its weight in gold."

Ibrahim looked around, nodding, until worry lines formed. "Where is your satchel?"

"I wedged it up against the wall with the camera cases and our jackets." Jay went to the spot. The briefcase was gone. He glanced around the room without seeing it, then surveyed every inch in slow motion. The two women in blue suits were inspecting it by the entrance.

Jay hurried over to them. "That's mine. May I have it please?"

The large woman responded. "Our instructions said nothing comes in or out besides cameras and microphones. Why did you bring this?"

"For cords and microphones."

"Then what is this?" She pulled out the preamble's English

translation.

"It's from the Internet. I have this in there, too." Jay produced a photo of Duvert. "Autographs. I'd like his signature and others. Would you care to sign one?"

"Dr. Duvert will not be here. He's taken ill." She handed him the open briefcase and text.

He put the photo back inside and secured the clasps. "If Duvert's not coming, who will conduct the event? It's in ten minutes."

"Eleven. You'll know then."

BOLWYN WATCHED THE MAN who had asked for her autograph until he disappeared around the corner toward the Chapel of Adam. When she looked back toward the Rotunda she noticed Faatina signaling to her. Now what? The guard hobbled over to her. "I should be in the Stone room watching things. What do you need?"

"There are six camera crews. There should only be five."

"Are you sure? It's so crowded, how can you be sure?"

"Fool. Count the cameras, not the men."

"Well, six crews were invited, but one wanted to shoot down onto the ceremony from the second floor balcony." Bolwyn turned and counted. "The crew on the balcony must have changed their minds. The banners probably—"

"Go up there and make sure it's empty."

The circular stairwell to Golgotha and the Crucifixion Altar was near the main entrance. Bolwyn made her way there and limped up the steps, favoring her right ankle.

At the top, a cameraman glanced at her from behind his equipment, and then looked back at his small monitor. He spoke into his headset.

"There is an extra camera below," she muttered.

"It's okay. I approved the extra crew."

Bolwyn spun around. She smiled at Rachel. "Faatina doesn't know about them."

"She's in charge of security for Isis, not cameras or us," Rachel assured her. "Carry on with what you were doing. I'll take care of Faatina. Where is she?"

CHAPTER 34

AT 5:22, JAY KEPT out of sight in the Chapel of Adam, which was just around the corner from the Stone of Anointing. He leaned over an ornate three-foot-high partition and peered into a window behind the small altar. Inches beyond the streaked glass stood what was left of Golgotha, which had been excavated to build the church. A shiny object, moving toward his head, reflected in the glass. He sidestepped left and tripped over the briefcase between his feet. A gold candleholder grazed his head and landed with a thud on his shoulder. He slumped to the ground.

The candle base clanged onto the ground. Faatina stared down at him, pointing a handgun at his bleeding head. "Sit right there. I don't want to fire this in here, but I will."

"Why not? Are you tired of hitting on me?"

Faatina chuckled and knelt down to Jay's level, staying clear of him. "You should have quit in France. The Q document might be a lie, but that doesn't mean there's a god."

"I think you're missing the point."

She shrugged. "If ever a god should be working to help noble causes in a pinch, it seems like this would be it."

That thought had occurred to him more than once this past week. "Maybe he's giving both of us a chance to do the right thing."

While keeping the gun steady, she unsheathed her knife. "Maybe he doesn't like losers who let their mommy and girlfriends down."

"If you're planning to kill me, you're going to need more than that knife."

ONE GRIN FROM LEVINSON got Sarah moving toward the squat military helicopter. Armed to the teeth, it looked like an angry hornet. The handsome copilot nodded at her through his window. It slowed the churning in her stomach and she boarded with bravado. She strapped in opposite Levinson facing rearward.

The faded green contraption took off in a jerk. She tightened the lap belt beyond reason and focused her eyes on her former boss. From the corner of her eye, she saw the ground fall away in a blur.

"Shouldn't we close the door?"

"We'll need it open." Levinson shouted over the engine noise. "The suit you're wearing will identify you as a guard at the Q document's sanctioning event. A Tel Aviv district cop named Raczynska left it for you. I'll tell you more about her later. Your buddy Hunt should already be inside the church as a cameraman. He found the blank you two have been looking for. Your job is to help him show the world the Q is a forgery. Incidentally, he's the one that found the bomb."

"Another Hunt, another hero of the state."

"What?"

"Never mind," she shouted. "Do I work for you again?"

"No. There are three things to remember. One, you're still in jail. I haven't exactly asked a judge to approve your release yet.

Two and three are remembering which organization put you in jail, and which one got you out."

"What I'll remember is who *ignored* procedures."

"If you think you can blackmail me, forget it. I'm retiring at the end of the month."

The helicopter's nose tipped forward as they ratcheted toward the Old City.

Levinson checked his watch. "Mr. Ambrose, come on back here." The copilot unbuckled and worked his way back, while the Chief Inspector turned to Sarah. "This man has been catching me up on your situation and developments within the FBI. An Agent Greene has rescinded the INTERPOL Notices on your friends. Greene also passed along information that allowed us to arrest Glassman."

Sarah punched at the air in victory.

The copilot jerked his head and avoided her fist. "Ms. Baumann, my pleasure. Nice right jab. I hope you won't need it anymore today. The event starts in five minutes. Sergeant Raczynska says an entrance on the church's roof will be the only avenue into the building at this late hour. I've done this with first-timers before, so relax. I'm going to secure you in a harness and lower you by steel cable onto the back side of the building . . ."

JAY PUT ON HIS best poker face, but the thud from the candleholder smacking Faatina's skull made him wince anyway. Faatina registered shock, then pain. Her knife and gun clattered onto the stone floor. She staggered for a second and then collapsed at the foot of the altar, holding her head. Jay kicked the gun toward Rachel, his unexpected liberator. He retrieved the knife and his briefcase. Rachel scooped up the gun and pointed it at Faatina in a single efficient move. She tossed the candleholder down the hall.

"Your chest is bleeding again, and so is your head." Rachel kept her eyes plastered on Faatina, but offered a quick smile in his direction. "It's 5:27. You're going to look terrible on camera."

Jay handed Rachel the knife and eased along the hall into the event room, stepping over miles of cables taped to the floor. He knelt behind a waist-high portable stage light that was as bright as the sun and would blind anyone looking in his direction from the tables. Heat radiated from it in waves. Jay opened the briefcase and removed the blank piece of papyrus secured under the lining.

Isis emerged from between two massive columns that supported the Rotunda. In a floor-length navy blue skirt, she glided along a red carpet and into the wash of camera lights. A lily-white blouse glowed under a navy jacket. At the end of the carpet, she stopped and mugged for the cameras, then strode onto the polished marble floor that surrounded the anointing stone. She stepped onto the holy stone, which was several inches above the floor, and opened her arms with a grand sweep.

Three petite women kneeling at the back wall moved in unison to the back of the Q document's tables. As Isis slowly raised her hands over her head, the three women pulled the heavy drapes off the tables. They dropped them onto the floor and scampered off to the Rotunda.

"Thank you for coming," Isis said into the cameras. "You have just witnessed the uncovering of truth. Hidden for two thousand years, the Q document's light could not be extinguished. Peace on earth and good will toward men was the author's objective. Let us not fault the writer's subterfuge for such a noble goal. He wrote that you can know a tree by its fruit. Despite good intentions, the fruit of his gospel has been war."

Jay stood.

Isis jerked her head in his direction. Her face froze.

He moved to the short table nearest him and thrust his blank piece over his head. "This fragment speaks of a different deception—not from the first century, but one committed today."

Isis tried to swat the papyrus from Jay's hand.

He twisted away.

The room filled with confused shouts. Rachel ran in and grabbed Isis around the waist. Her momentum pushed Isis off the stone toward the Rotunda. They banged into the furthest small table. Rachel pinned Isis there.

Jay placed the blank piece on his table and aligned it. "I have a blank fragment that is an exact match to a jagged edge of the Q document that's torn through the writing. I also have photographs showing them next to each other when both were blank."

Isis squirmed away from Rachel and dove to the floor. She yanked at electrical cords like a madwoman, unplugging them. Several lights at the top of ten-foot-high stanchions went dark. Two others crashed to the floor, sending glass and sparks flying. The long, red carpet ignited like a river of gasoline. Flames climbed an overhead banner.

Cameramen and assistants grabbed equipment. In seconds, the fire spread to other banners. Fire dripped throughout the room like hot wax. The TV crews scrambled for the single doorway, abandoning equipment. Isis's blue-garbed followers joined the pushing and shoving at the exit. A light near Ibrahim exploded. Its ten-foot tripod crashed onto him. He shoved it off, and wobbled away with blood spilling across his face and his video gear clutched to his chest.

Jay rushed towards Ibrahim, and steered him to the door. All the newsmen had escaped. Rachel and Isis were wrestling behind the Q document's leftmost table on the far side of the flaming carpet. Fire swept through the room with a whoosh and the temperature became unbearable.

With his lungs protesting, Jay yelled to Rachel, "Drag Isis out. I'm going after Faatina and the matching Q document."

Rachel screamed and Isis broke free. Coughing and stumbling, Isis lurched toward the large table. Jay hurried as best he could through the debris strewn floor to help Rachel. Halfway there, she rose and tackled Isis. A flaming banner rained down onto the large table between Jay and the two women.

More lights exploded. Tripods crashed to the ground. Thick electrical cables hissed and snapped like whips. One smacked the back of Jay's head, knocking him onto the Anointing Stone. Looking up, he saw another fiery banner barreling down on him in a spiral of flames. He dove toward the doorway and avoided being buried under twenty yards of fire. He picked his way around the flames through piles of video gear, lights, and scaffolding to go find Faatina. Halfway to the hallway where he'd last seen her, he spotted her running into the room toward Rachel and Isis, who remained locked in a two-woman scrum under the back wall's mural.

Faatina swung a candleholder at Rachel, who deflected it with her arm and a grunt of pain. A guard in a blue suit rushed in from the Rotunda on the left.

Sarah? The room was spinning, but through the flames and falling debris, the guard looked like Sarah.

"Get out," he yelled, certain now it was her, running to her mother. Changing direction to help Sarah, Jay bulldozed his way over the center table, burning his palms on its hot glass.

Faatina swung at Rachel again, but she ducked under Faatina's arm and shoved her away.

As Jay caught up to the melee, Faatina kicked the back of his knee, which collapsed his leg. He fell backwards onto the large table as Faatina spun past him and drove Sarah into the back wall with a vicious hockey check. The table collapsed, dumping him, glass, and Q fragments into a pile of burning fabric. His shirtsleeve ignited as he rolled through it. Continuing his roll quenched it and took him to the room's front. He plucked two pieces of broken glass from his left forearm, not bothering with smaller bits.

Part of a burning banner dropped onto Rachel and Faatina. Arms flailed from underneath it, and then its top portion released and engulfed them. Faatina emerged with her hair and jacket burning. Rachel was aflame from the waist up. Screaming, they tripped and collapsed behind the crumpled center table. He lost sight of them, but behind where they went down, he saw Sarah rise from under the mural, trying to drag Isis toward the Rotunda. There was no safe path to the door, and Sarah screamed, "Mother, come this way. I'll get you out."

"No," Isis yelled, lunging along the back wall in the opposite direction. "I have to destroy the blank."

Smoke and heat scorched Jay's lungs. "Let Sarah help you."

With one last chance to get anyone out alive, he raced Isis to the blank scroll, hoping to haul her and Sarah outside from there. Chunks of stone rained down on the edges of the room. He jumped behind the short table, knocking it over. As the glass shattered, the Q document's matching fragment fluttered toward the door. He grabbed his blank off the floor. Extending it into nearby flames, he flicked it toward Isis. The flames ate it. "It's destroyed. Now let's go."

She may have smiled, but then he realized Isis was alone.

"Sarah? Where are you? Sarah!"

Isis scanned the room, too, then walked with purpose through a wall of fire. Her skirt burst into flames. She kept moving as if nothing happened.

Looking through the flames where Isis was heading, Jay spotted Sarah slumped against the back wall. Isis reached her and pulled her to her feet. In the same instant that Jay ran for the flames, Isis shoved Sarah through them to him, and then she lurched back as though suddenly aware that flames were consuming her. Jay caught Sarah, who was doubled-over and coughing. Blood covered her forehead. The stone walls belched fire. He backpedalled with her toward the door.

"No," she yelled, struggling against him and slipping from his arms.

Grabbing her jacket, he wrenched her back to his chest in a bear hug. Larger hunks of stone were falling. Jay yanked Sarah closer to the door just as a large block landed where they had stood. He marshaled every ounce of strength and propelled them backwards into the courtyard. She grabbed at something as they cleared the doorway. Debris sealed it shut behind them.

Sarah crawled toward the blocked doorway. She looked back at Jay, her faced contorted in pain. Blood and soot streaked her splotchy skin. The heat forced her to retreat. "We have to get her out."

Jay held her tight. Heat seared the exposed flesh of his arms and face. He backed them up, looking for a safe way to re-enter. Fire shot out every opening. "You tried. You did everything you could. She chose to stay. I'm sorry. It's too dangerous." He dragged her further back.

Sarah shook loose. "I found a piece. I see it over there." She shielded her face with her arm and ran for the door before he could stop her. She retrieved something, and scurried back. "It's a fragment of the Q document. Although now, it's two pieces."

"Nice job saving it, but please don't do that again." He covered the cut at her hairline with his palm. "You're bleeding. Put pressure on it."

Tears cut trails in her grimy cheeks. She dropped the Q document's pieces and replaced his hand with hers. "Why didn't she leave? Even after you burned the blank, she refused to save herself."

"She saved you."

"I know." She shook with emotion.

An explosion inside made them back up further. Jay brought the pieces of the Q document Sarah saved with them. He studied the edges. "I think—"

Sarah gasped, staring up. "Oh God, help them. Look."

Jay followed Sarah's gaze to a TV monitor that showed the inferno from the second story. Wall-to-wall flames roiled across the room like waves on an angry sea. The three trapped women's bodies lay on the floor near the room's rear. It made no sense, but the women glowed like heat signatures in infrared. He tried to refocus, thinking his eyes were affected by the heat. He noticed movement on the left.

A pristine white figure entered from the Rotunda. It couldn't be happening—the heat was too intense, the solid flames would combust any living thing. Yet impossibly, the figure was walking through the orange and red flames. The women rose upright and moved to the Stone of the Anointing. The fourth figure walked to the women. It hugged one woman, and then another. The third woman backed away, off the stone. All four merged into the fire.

The screen went dark.

Jay looked at Sarah, she was still staring at the monitor. "What just happened? There's no way, the camera could have even transmitted from in there. Let alone what I saw."

She shook her head. "I don't know. I can't think right now." Sarah shuddered. "She couldn't have survived in there. It was awful. And for what? The blank piece is destroyed. Who will believe us? I hate that she won as much as I hate that she was alive and now is . . . gone again." She closed her eyes.

Jay gave her a brotherly hug. "Your mom left this earth with mine a long time ago, but her love for you lived on. Not even a fire could destroy it."

"That's what makes it so hard." She wiped a cheek, smudging it worse. "Do you think the video was sharp enough to prove that the blank's edge fit perfectly with the Q?"

"I hope not. The match wasn't as good as I'd have liked."

Sarah did a double-take. "What do you mean?"

A voice shouted, "*Dahuf.* Hurry." Ibrahim rushed into the courtyard. Paramedics trailed behind him with stretchers. Police and firemen poured in next, separating Sarah from Jay and ordering them onto stretchers.

From his stretcher, Jay heard Sarah causing a riot, and glimpsed her shoving paramedics around. "I'm not leaving on that thing. Get out of my way." Sarah appeared from behind a phalanx of bodies and edged Jay's paramedic aside. "Give us a minute," she ordered.

The man shrugged, and wisely stepped back.

Sarah stared down at Jay. "What did you do?"

Jay rubbed the stubby hairs on his arm, which had fried into tight little knots. "Lizabeth created a fragment for me to take into the church. It was pretty crude. She didn't have much time." Sarah's eyes nearly burned a hole in him. He quickly explained, "Dad's blank is real. I took it to Lizabeth for safekeeping and brought a fake to the church. The piece of the Q you saved is the matching piece. Without that, Dad's piece might not have mattered. Congratulations, lady. Another Hunt, another hero of the State."

CHAPTER 35

JAY PARKED IN THE shade in front of the low mud and brick building. He grabbed the paper sacks off the passenger seat. It was 9:15, and he was late, but he figured whoever brings donuts is excused.

Doc met him out front of Holy Land Hummer Tours. "Where have you been? Everyone is here, including the news crew. I'll be late for my rounds at the refugee camp." She studied the bags he held behind him. "Those better be donuts."

"They're better than donuts."

Doc rolled her eyes. "Come on. Everyone's out back."

Jay followed her into the building near Qumran and out its back door. Ibrahim and his wife were sitting in the nearest convertible pink Hummer.

Ibrahim honked the horn. "You might be an investor, but you're still late, partner."

"I've been informed. Here, this bag is for the two of you. I've decided this should be a new tradition at Hunt Investment Management."

Jay walked over to Bob Ambrose and Sarah in another

Hummer. "This bag is for you and Bob. Hey sis, maybe I should call you Prin-sis."

She snarled at him and scrounged inside the bag.

Jay gave a large bag to Ibrahim's two-man news crew and ran over to the third Hummer. He grabbed the roll bar and plopped in next to Doc, who had chosen the driver's seat.

Sarah shouted, "What do you call these?"

Jay yelled back, "Home made." He squeezed Doc's hand. "Something I owed Doc. You can't buy them around here."

Doc tore open their bag. She laid on the horn repeatedly. "They're called breakfast burritos. You can't buy this brand anywhere." She kissed Jay. "I knew I could count on you."

From the passenger seat, Jay couldn't honk back or steer. He didn't mind. Something about the look in Doc's eyes reminded him that his best adventures in this desert had started with no destination or plan, just a willing companion and an occasional unexpected breeze. The wind blew across his face. He settled back into his seat. The best adventure was just beginning.

THE END